'A tale brimming with tenderness and romance' *Marie Claire*

'A small-life-big-dreams weepie that'll have you snivelling ecstatically into your cocoa' *Daily Mail*

'This book reduced me to tears many times – and also had me in fits of laughter, all down to the wonderful characters Jojo has created, their secrets, their fragile relationships and brilliantly observed interplay. Spellbinding storytelling. Jojo Moyes is a hugely talented, clever and heartfelt writer and it's just pure pleasure to read her work' Fiona Walker

'An engaging and moving tale of love and loss, bravery and the determination to beat the odds' *Choice*

'A strikingly original tale which captivates from the first page . . . There are all sorts of unusual touches in this magical novel . . . [Moyes] creates a cast of very believable and sympathetic characters and maintains the tension throughout.' *Daily Express*

'Once I had picked it up, I could not put it down . . . I have visited and competed at L'École d'Équitation in Saumur and Jojo captures the atmosphere and environment exactly.' Judy Harvey, FBHS, International Grand Prix rider, British Dressage Trainer, and FEI Judge

'An inspiring love story . . . Billy Elliot in jodhpurs' *Daily Mail*

Also by Jojo Moyes

SHELTERING RAIN

FOREIGN FRUIT

THE PEACOCK EMPORIUM

THE SHIP OF BRIDES

SILVER BAY

NIGHT MUSIC

About the author

Jojo Moyes was born in 1969 and brought up in London. A journalist and writer, she worked for the *Independent* newspaper until 2001. She lives in East Anglia with her husband and three children.

Foreign Fruit won the 2003 RNA Novel of the Year award. *The Ship of Brides* and *Silver Bay* were shortlisted for the inaugural *Good Housekeeping* 2007 Book of the Year award.

Jojo Moyes

THE HORSE
DANCER

HODDER

First published in Great Britain in 2009 by Hodder & Stoughton
An Hachette UK company

First published in paperback in 2010

1

A CIP catalogue record for this title is available
from the British Library

B format paperback ISBN 978 0 340 96160 5
A format paperback ISBN 978 0 340 96165 0

Typeset in Plantin Light by Palimpsest Book Production Limited,
Grangemouth, Stirlingshire

Printed and bound by Clays Ltd, St Ives plc

Hodder & Stoughton policy is to use papers that are natural,
renewable and recyclable products and made from wood
grown in sustainable forests. The logging and manufacturing
processes are expected to conform to the environmental
regulations of the country of origin.

Hodder & Stoughton Ltd
338 Euston Road
London NW1 3BH

www.hodder.co.uk

To C, S, H and L

And to Mecca Harris

Show me your horse and I will tell you what you are

Old English proverb

Prologue

He saw her yellow dress before he saw her, glowing in the fading light; a beacon at the far end of the stables. He stopped for a moment, unsure that he could trust his eyes. Then her pale arm reached up, Gerontius's elegant head dipping over the door to take whatever treat she offered, and he was walking briskly, half running, the metal tips of his boots clicking on the wet cobbles.

'You are here!'

'Henri!'

His arms were around her as she turned; he kissed her, dipped his head to inhale the glorious scent of her hair. The breath that escaped him seemed to come from somewhere in his boots.

'We got here this afternoon,' she said, into his shoulder. 'I've barely had time to change. I must look awful . . . but I was in the audience and glimpsed you through the curtain. I had to come to wish you luck.'

Her words had become jumbled, but he could barely hear her anyway. He was shocked by the girl's sheer presence; the feel of her in his arms after so many months' absence. 'And just look at you!' She took a step back, allowing her gaze to travel from his black peaked cap all the way down his immaculate uniform, then reached up to brush an imaginary fleck from one of his gold epaulettes. He noted, with gratitude, the reluctance with which she withdrew her fingers. There was no awkwardness, he marvelled, even after so many months. No coquettishness. She was utterly guileless; the girl of his imagination made flesh again.

'You look wonderful,' she said.

'I . . . cannot stay,' he said. 'We ride in ten minutes.'

'I know . . . Le Carrousel is so exciting. We've been watching the motorcyclists, and the parade of tanks,' she said. 'But you, Henri, you and the horses are definitely the big draw.' She glanced behind her towards the arena. 'I think the whole of France is here to see you.'

'You . . . get *les billets*?'

They frowned at each other. Language was still a problem, despite their best efforts.

'*Billets*. . .' He shook his head, irritated with himself. 'Ticket. Tickets. Best tickets.'

She beamed, and his brief dissatisfaction evaporated. 'Oh, yes. Edith, her mother and I are in the front row. They simply can't wait to see you ride. I've told them everything about you. We're staying at the Château de Verrières.' Her voice dropped to a whisper, even though no one was near. 'It's very grand. The Wilkinsons have an *awful* lot of money. Much more than we have. It was very kind of them to bring me.'

He watched her talk – distracted by the Cupid's bow of her upper lip. She was here. His hands, in their white kid gloves, cradled her face. 'Florence . . .' He breathed, kissing her again. The scent of the sun infused her skin, even though dusk had fallen. It was intoxicating, as if she had been created to radiate warmth. 'Every day I miss you. Before, there is nothing but Le Cadre Noir. Now . . . nothing is good without you.'

'Henri . . .' She stroked his cheek, her body against his. He felt almost giddy.

'Lachapelle!'

He whipped round. Didier Picart stood at the head of his horse, a groom at his side preparing his saddle. He was pulling on his gloves. 'Perhaps if you think about your riding as much as your English whore we can achieve something, eh?'

Florence did not know enough French to understand but she caught the look that flickered across Picart's face, and Henri saw she had guessed that whatever the other Frenchman had said it was not complimentary.

The familiar anger rose, and he set his jaw against it. He shook his head at Florence, trying to convey to her Picart's stupidity, his irrelevance. Picart had been like this – insulting, provocative – since the trip to England when she and Henri had met. English girls had no class, Picart had exclaimed, in the mess afterwards; Henri knew that it had been aimed directly at him. They did not know how to dress. They ate like pigs at a trough. They would lie down with anyone for a few francs, or the equivalent of a pint of that foul beer.

It had taken him weeks to work out that Picart's bile had little to do with Florence, and everything to do with his fury at having been usurped within Le Cadre Noir, jostled aside by the son of a farmer. Not that that made it easier to hear it.

Picart's voice echoed down the yard: 'I hear there are rooms near the quai Lucien Gautier. A little more fitting than a stableyard, n'est-ce pas?'

Henri's hand tightened around Florence's. He tried to keep his voice calm as he spoke: 'You could be the last man on earth and she would be too good for you, Picart.'

'Don't you know, farmer boy, that any whore will have you if the price is right?' Picart smirked, placed a perfectly polished boot in his stirrup and vaulted on to his horse.

Henri made to step forward, but Florence stopped him. 'Darling . . . look, I'd better get to my seat,' she said, backing away. 'You need to prepare.' She hesitated, then reached up and kissed him again, her slim white hand pulling the back of his neck towards her. He knew what she was trying to do:

tug his thoughts from Picart's poison. And she was right; it was impossible to feel anything but joy when Florence's lips were on his own. She smiled. '*Bonne chance, écuyer.*'

'*Écuyer!*' he repeated, momentarily diverted, touched that in his absence she had discovered the correct word for 'horseman'.

'I'm learning!' She blew a kiss, her eyes filled with mischief, with promise, and then she was gone, his English girl, running back down the long stables, her heels clicking on the cobbles.

Le Carrousel, the annual military festival, traditionally marked the end of a year of training for the young cavalry officers of Saumur. As usual, the July weekend was thick with visitors to the medieval town, keen not just to witness the passing out of the young cavalrymen but the traditional displays of cavalry riding, motorbike acrobatics and the parade of tanks, their great hulls still scarred from the war.

It was 1960. The old guard was teetering in the face of an onslaught of popular culture, of shifting attitudes and Johnny Hallyday, but in Saumur there was little appetite for change. The annual performance of the twenty-two elite French horsemen, some military, some civilian, who comprised Le Cadre Noir, the highlight of Le Carrousel weekend, was always enough to guarantee that the tickets were sold out within days – to the local community, to those who were imbued with a sense of France's heritage, and, on a less cerebral level, to those intrigued by posters all over the Loire region promising 'Majesty, Mystery, Horses that Defy Gravity'.

Le Cadre Noir had been born almost 250 years earlier, after the decimation of the French cavalry in the Napoleonic Wars. In an attempt to rebuild what had once been considered a crack band of horsemen, a school was created in Saumur, a town which had housed an equestrian academy since the 16th century. Here, a corps of instructors had been gathered from the finest riding schools at Versailles, the Tuileries and Saint Germain, to pass on the high traditions of academic riding to a new generation of officers, and had continued to do so ever since.

With the advent of tanks and mechanised warfare, Le Cadre Noir faced questions as to the usefulness of such an arcane organisation. But for decades no government had felt able to disband what had, by then, become part of France's heritage: the horsemen in their black uniforms were iconic, and France, with its traditions of L'Académie Française, *haute cuisine* and *couture*, understood the importance of the tradition. The horsemen themselves, perhaps recognising that the best way to ensure survival was to create a new role, widened their remit: as well as teaching cavalrymen, the school opened its doors to reveal its rarified skills and magnificent horses at public performances in France and abroad.

This was the Le Cadre Noir in which Henri Lachapelle now found himself, and that night's performance was the most symbolically important of the year, in the home of Le Cadre Noir, a chance to demonstrate hard-won skills to friends and family. The air smelt of caramel, wine and firecrackers, and the heat of thousands of gently moving bodies. Around the place du Chardonnet, in the heart of the École de Cavalerie, its elegant, honeyed buildings, the crowds were already swelling. The carnival atmosphere was amplified by the July heat, the still evening, an inflating air of expectation. Children ran to and fro with balloons or sticks of candy floss, their parents lost in crowds that surveyed stalls selling paper windmills and sparkling wine, or merely walking in laughing groups across the great bridge to the pavement cafés of the north side. All the while a low hum of excitement emanated from those who had already taken their seats around the Grand Manège, the vast sand arena of the public performance, and now sat impatiently, fanning themselves and perspiring in the dimming light.

'*Attends!*'

Henri, hearing the cry to attention, checked his saddle and bridle, asked the *dresseur* for the fifteenth time whether his uniform was straight, then rubbed the nose of Gerontius, his horse, admiring the minute ribboned plaits that the groom had sewn across his gleaming neck, muttering words of praise and encouragement into his elegantly trimmed ears. Gerontius was seventeen, elderly in terms of the academy, and would soon be retired. He had been Henri's horse since he had arrived at Le Cadre Noir three years previously, and an instant, passionate bond had formed between them. Here, within the confines of the school's ancient walls, it was not unusual to see young men kissing their horses' noses, muttering endearments they would have been embarrassed to bestow on a woman.

'*Vous êtes prêt?*' Le Grand Dieu, the master horseman, was striding down the centre of the preparatory arena, followed by a coterie of *écuyers*, his gilded uniform and three-cornered cap marking him out as the most senior of the school's practitioners. He stood in front of the young horsemen and their fidgeting horses. 'This, as you know, is the highlight of our year. The ceremony dates back more than a hundred and thirty years, and the traditions of our school from many years before that, back to Xenophon and the age of the Greeks.

'So much in our world today seems to be about the need for change, of throwing out the old ways in pursuit of what is free or easy. Le Cadre Noir believes there is still a place for an élite, for the pursuit of excellence above all else. Tonight you are ambassadors, showing that true grace, true beauty can only be the result of discipline, of patience, of sympathy and self-denial.'

He gazed around him. 'Ours is an art that dies the moment

it is created. Let us make the people of Saumur feel privileged to witness such a spectacle.'

There was a murmur of approval, then the men began to mount their horses, some fiddling with their caps, rubbing at non-existent marks on their boots, little gestures to dispel the anxiety that was creeping in.

'You're ready, Lachapelle? Not too nervous?'

'No, sir.' Henri stood straight, feeling the older man's eyes travel swiftly over his uniform, checking for chinks in perfection. He was conscious that his studied calm was betrayed by the sweat trickling from his temples to his stiff mandarin collar.

'It's no shame to feel a little adrenalin at one's first Carrousel,' he said, stroking Gerontius's neck. 'This old hand will see you through. So, you perform Capriole in the second team performance. Then, riding Phantasme, La Croupade. *D'accord*?'

'Yes, sir.'

He knew the *maîtres écuyers* had been split over whether he should be granted such a visible role in the annual performance, given his history over these past months, the arguments, his perceived and catastrophic lack of discipline . . . His groom had passed on to him the talk in the tack room: that his rebelliousness had nearly cost him his place in Le Cadre Noir altogether.

He had not attempted to defend himself. How could he have explained to them the seismic shift that had taken place within him? How could he tell them that, to a man who had never heard a word of affection, or felt a gentle touch, her voice, her kindness, her breasts, her scent and hair had proven not just a distraction but an obsession far more powerful than an intellectual treatise on the finer points of horsemanship?

Henri Lachapelle's childhood had been a world of chaos and disorder, dominated by his father. Refinement was a two-franc bottle of wine, and any attempt at learning derided. Joining the cavalry had provided him with a lifeline, and his progression through the ranks until he was recommended for one of the rare positions at Le Cadre Noir had seemed the summit of what any man could expect in life. At twenty-five he had believed himself at home for the first time.

He was prodigiously talented. His years on the farm had given him a rare capacity for hard work. He had an aptitude for dealing with difficult horses. There was talk that he might eventually prove a *maître écuyer* – even, in more fanciful moments, another Grand Dieu. He had been sure that the rigour, the discipline, the sheer pleasure and reward of learning would be enough for the rest of his days.

And then Florence Jacobs from Clerkenwell, who hadn't even liked horses but had taken up a free ticket to the French riding-school performance in England, had destroyed it all – his peace of mind, his resolve, his patience. Later in life, with the kind of perspective that comes only with experience, he might have told his younger self that such passion was only to be expected with a first love, that such cataclysmic feelings would ease and perhaps fade. But Henri – a solitary man with few friends who might have offered such sage advice – knew only that, from the moment he had noticed the dark-haired girl who had watched, wide-eyed, from the side of the arena for three nights running, she was all he could think about. He had introduced himself, not even sure why he had sought her out after his performance, and every minute spent without her since felt like an irritation or, worse, an endless, meaningless abyss. And where did that leave everything else?

His concentration disappeared almost overnight. On his return to France he began to question the doctrine, became vexed by the tiny details he considered irrelevant. He accused Devaux, one of the senior *maître écuyers*, of being 'stuck in the past'. It was only when he had missed the third training session in a row, and his groom had warned him he would be let go, that he realised he had to take a firm grip on himself. He studied Xenophon, bent himself to his travails. Kept his nose clean. He had felt reassured by Florence's increasingly frequent letters, her promise that she would be over to see him that summer. And a few months on, perhaps as a reward, he had been given the key role in Le Carrousel: La Croupade – one of the most challenging movements a rider could attempt – displacing Picart and adding insult to whatever that privileged young man had already considered injurious.

The Grand Dieu mounted his horse, a robust Portuguese stallion, and took two elegant steps close to him. 'Don't let me down, Lachapelle. Let us treat this evening as a new start.'

Henri nodded, a sudden attack of nerves silencing him. He mounted, gathered his reins, checked that the black peaked cap was straight on his shorn head. He could hear the murmur of the crowd, the expectant hush as the orchestra played a few exploratory notes, the kind of dense silence that can only come from a thousand people watching intently. He was dimly aware of a murmured 'Good luck' among his fellows, and then he was guiding Gerontius into his place, halfway along the militarily exact line of gleaming, beribboned horses. His mount was eagerly awaiting his first instruction as the heavy red curtain was pulled back, beckoning them into the floodlit arena.

Despite the calm, orderly appearance of its twenty-two horsemen, the graceful nature of their public performances, life at Le Cadre Noir was physically and intellectually testing. Day after day Henri Lachapelle had found himself exhausted, almost reduced to tears of frustration by the endless corrections of the *maîtres écuyers*, his apparent inability to persuade the huge, highly strung horses perform the 'airs above the

ground' to their exacting standards. He had felt, even if he
could not prove, a perceived prejudice against those who had
entered the élite school from the military, as he had, rather
than from the civilian riding competitions, those upper-class
members of French society who had always had the twin
luxuries of fine horses and time with which to build their
skills. In theory, all were equal in Le Cadre Noir, separated
only by their skills on horseback. Henri was conscious that
egalitarianism ran no deeper than their serge uniforms.

Yet slowly, steadily, working from six in the morning until
late into the evening, the farmhand from Tours had built a
reputation for hard work and his skill in communicating with
the most difficult horses. Henri Lachapelle, the *maîtres écuyers*
would observe, from under their black caps, had a 'quiet
seat'. He was *sympathique*. It was the reason that, alongside
his beloved Gerontius, he had been allocated Phantasme,
the explosive young iron grey gelding, who needed only the
slightest excuse for catastrophic behaviour. He had been quietly
anxious about the decision to put Phantasme in such a role
all week. But now, with the eyes of the crowd upon him, the
musical beauty of the strings filling his ears, the even tempo
of Gerontius's paces beneath him, he felt, suddenly, in
Xenophon's words, that he was indeed a 'man on wings'. He
felt Florence's admiring eyes upon him and knew that later
his lips would meet her skin, and rode more deeply, more
elegantly, with a lightness of touch that had the veteran horse
showing off, his neat ears flicking forwards with pleasure. This
is what I am made for, he thought, with gratitude. Everything
I need is here. He saw the flames of the torches flickering on
the walls of the ancient pillars, heard the rhythmic thud of
the horses' hooves as they dovetailed neatly in and out of each
other around him. He cantered in formation around the great
manège, lost in the moment, conscious only of the horse that
moved so beautifully beneath him, flicking out his hooves in

a way that made Henri want to laugh. The old horse was showing off.

'Sit straight, Lachapelle. You're riding like a peasant.'

He blinked, glimpsed Picart as he rode up alongside him, passed him shoulder to shoulder.

'Why do you fidget so? Did your whore give you the itch?' he hissed, under his breath.

Henri made as if to speak, but broke off as Le Grand Dieu shouted, '*Levade!*' and in a row, the riders raised their horses on to their back legs, to a burst of clapping.

As the horses' front feet hit the ground again, Picart turned away. His voice, however, was still clearly audible. 'Does she fuck like a peasant too?'

Henri bit the inside of his lip, forcing himself to keep his cool, not to let his anger travel down the reins to infect his sweet-natured horse. He could hear the announcer explaining the technicalities of the riders' movements, and tried to corral his thoughts, to let the words flow through him. Under his breath, he repeated the words of Xenophon: 'Anger undermines effective communication with your horse.' He would not let Picart destroy this night. '*Mesdames et messieurs*, now in the centre of the arena you will see Monsieur de Cordon performing *levade*. See how the horse balances on his hind legs at an angle of exactly forty-five degrees.' Henri was dimly aware of the black horse rearing somewhere behind him, the sudden breaking-out of applause. He forced himself to focus, to hold Gerontius's attention. But he kept thinking of Florence's face when Picart had yelled his obscenities near her, the anxiety that had passed across her features. What if she knew more French than she had let on?

'And now, you will see Gerontius, one of our older horses, performing *capriole*. This is one of the most demanding moves, for both horse and rider. The horse leaps into the air, kicking out behind him while all four feet are off the ground.'

Henri slowed Gerontius, teaming the resistance of his hands with a swift request from his spurs. He felt the horse begin to rock beneath him, the *terre à terre*, the stationary rocking-horse motion that would build power beneath him. *I will show them*, he thought, and then: *I will show him*.

Everything else disappeared. It was just him and the brave old horse, the growing power beneath him. And then with a shout of '*Derrière!*' he brought his whip hand towards the horse's rear, his spurs to the horse's belly, and Gerontius was leaping upwards, into the air, his back legs shooting out horizontally behind him. Henri was aware of a sudden blinding bank of camera flashes, a great stereophonic *whooo* of delight, applause, and then he was cantering towards the red curtain, taking with him a glimpse of Florence, who had stood to applaud him, her face wreathed in proud smiles.

'*Bon! C'était bon!*' He was already sliding off Gerontius, his hand rubbing the horse's shoulder, the *dresseur* leading him away. He was dimly aware of some exclamations of approval, then a change in tempo of the music in the arena, a glimpse through the red curtain of two other *écuyers* performing their own display on foot, their horses controlled by two long reins.

'Phantasme is very nervous.' The groom had appeared beside him, his thick black brows knotted with concern. He chastised the grey horse, which wheeled around them. 'Watch him, Henri.'

'He will be fine,' Henri said absently, lifting his hat to wipe the sweat from his brow. The groom handed the reins to the waiting horsemen beside him then turned to Henri and carefully removed his cap. This movement was performed bare-headed to prevent the distraction of a sliding cap, but it always made Henri feel strangely vulnerable.

He watched the gunmetal grey horse prance into the arena

in front of him, its neck already dark with sweat, a man at each shoulder.

'Go. Now. Go.' The dresseur brushed the back of his jacket briskly, then shoved him into the arena. Three *écuyers* surrounded the horse, one at each side of his head, another at the rear.

He strode out under the lights, wishing suddenly that, like them, he had the anchoring presence of a horse to hold on to.

'*Bonne chance!*' He heard his groom's voice before it was swallowed by applause.

'*Mesdames et messieurs, voilà La Croupade* which originated in the cavalry of the seventeen hundreds when it was considered a test of a cavalryman's ability to stay in the saddle. Such movements may take four or five years to master. Monsieur Lachapelle will be riding Phantasme without reins or stirrups. This movement, which dates back to Greek times, is even more testing for rider than horse. It is a more elegant version of the rodeo, if you like.'

There was a ripple of laughter. Henri, half blinded by the floodlights, glanced at Phantasme, whose whitened eye was rolling with a mixture of nerves and barely suppressed fury. A naturally acrobatic horse, he disliked being held so firmly at his head, and the noise, sounds and smells of Le Carrousel seemed to have exacerbated his already bad temper.

Henri touched the horse's tense shoulder. 'Sssh,' he murmured. 'It's okay. It's okay.' He glimpsed the quick smiles of Duchamp and Varjus, the two men at Phantasme's head. They were both effective horsemen, quick to respond to a horse's mercurial change in mood.

'Sit deep, eh?' Varjus said, grinning, as he gave him a leg up. '*Un, deux, trois . . . hup.*'

The horse was radiating tension. This is good, Henri told himself, as he straightened in the saddle. The adrenalin will give him greater height. It will look better for the crowd, for Le Grand Dieu. He forced himself to breathe deeply. It was then, as he folded his hands at the small of his back in the traditional passive position that always reminded him uncomfortably of a captive, that Henri looked down to the near side and realised who had been stationed at Phantasme's rear.

'Shall we see what kind of rider you really are, Lachapelle?' Picart said.

He had no time to respond. He lengthened his legs as far as possible, clasped his gloved hands behind him. He heard the announcer say something else, and felt the expectant hush in the arena.

'*Attends.*'

Varjus glanced behind him. The *terre à terre* was building beneath him. '*Un, deux, derrière!*'

He felt the horse building in impulsion, heard the sudden *thwack* as Picart's whip met its quarters. Phantasme bucked, rear end shooting up, and Henri was pitched forward, whiplashed so that he only just managed to maintain the clasp of his hands behind him. The horse steadied, and there was a burst of applause.

'Not bad, Lachapelle,' he heard Varjus mutter, braced against Phantasme's chest.

And then, suddenly, before he had time to prepare, there was another cry of '*Derrière!*' Phantasme's back legs were shooting him up and forward so that this time Henri's arms flew out to the sides as he tried to maintain his balance.

'Not so soon, Picart. You're unseating him.'

Disoriented, Henri heard Varjus's irritated voice, the horse's barely contained squeal as his back braced beneath him. 'Two seconds. Give me two seconds,' he muttered, trying to right himself. But before he could do so he heard another *thwack*. It came down hard from above, and this time the horse's buck was huge; he felt himself pitched forward again, the abrupt, disconcerting distance between his seat and the saddle.

Phantasme threw himself sideways now, furious and the men struggled to hold the horse's head. Varjus hissed something Henri could not hear. They were near the red curtain. He glimpsed Florence in her yellow dress, could see her confusion and concern. And then: '*Enfin! Derrière!*' Before he could reposition himself there was another loud smack behind him. He was thrown forward again, his back twisting, and Phantasme, infuriated by this injudicious use of the whip, leapt forwards and sideways just at the point that Henri finally lost his balance. He was on the horse's plaited poll, he was upside down, reaching for Phantasme's neck as the horse bucked again, before – with an audible *ouf* – he hit the floor.

Henri lay there, dimly aware of the commotion in the arena: Varjus swearing, Picart protesting, the announcer laughing. As he lifted his head from the sand, he could just make out the words: 'And there you go. A very hard movement to sit. Better luck next year, Monsieur Lachapelle, eh? You see, *mesdames et messieurs*, sometimes it takes many years of practice to reach the very high standards of the *maîtres écuyers*.'

He heard the *un, deux, trois* and Varjus was at his side, hissing at him to *remount, remount*. He glanced down, realising that his immaculate black uniform was covered with sand. Then he was up on the horse, hands at his legs, his feet, and they were walking out of the arena to sympathetic applause. It was the most painful sound he had ever heard.

He was numb with shock. Ahead, he was aware of a low argument between Varjus and Picart, but he could barely hear it above the roaring of the blood in his ears.

'What was that?' Varjus was shaking his head. 'Nobody has ever fallen off during La Croupade. You made us look stupid.' It was a moment before Henri grasped that Varjus was addressing Picart.

'It's not my fault if the only thing Lachapelle can ride is an English whore.'

Henri slid off the horse and walked up to Picart, his ears ringing. He was not even aware of the first punch, just of the loud crack as his knuckles met the man's teeth, an almost satisfying give within the sound, a physical knowledge that something had been broken, long before pain raised the possibility that it might have been his hand. Horses shrieked and leapt apart. Men shouted. Picart was splayed on the sand, his hand pressed to his face, eyes wide with shock. Then he scrambled to his feet, launched himself at Henri and head-butted him in the chest, winding him. It was a move that might have felled a bigger man, and Henri was only five feet eight, but he had had the benefit of a childhood in which beatings were common-place, and six years in the National Guard. Within seconds he was atop Picart, his fists flying into the younger man's face, cheeks and chest, with all the rage of the past few months.

His knuckles met something hard and splintered. His left eye closed as a vicious blow met it. There was sand in his mouth. And then hands were dragging him off, batting at him, voices scolding, raised in disbelief.

'Picart! Lachapelle!'

As his vision blurred and righted, as he stood, spitting and swaying, the hands gripping his arms, his ears still filled with the string adagio from beyond the curtain, Le Grand Dieu was standing in front of him, his face bright with rage. *'What. On earth. Is this?'*

Henri shook his head, noting the spray of blood as he did so. 'Sir . . .' He was panting, only now becoming aware of the magnitude of his mistake.

'Le Carrousel!' Le Grand Dieu hissed. 'The epitome of grace and dignity. *Of discipline.* Where is your self-control?

You two have brought shame on us. Get back to the stables. I have a performance to finish.'

He mounted his horse as Picart staggered past, a hand-kerchief pressed to his ashen face. Henri watched him go. Slowly it dawned on him that the arena beyond the curtain was strangely quiet. They had seen, he realised with horror. They knew.

'Two paths.' Le Grand Dieu looked down at him from the Portuguese stallion. 'Two paths, Lachapelle. I told you the last time. It was your choice.'

'I cannot—' he began.

But Le Grand Dieu had already ridden out into the floodlights.

One

'*The horse rearing thus is such a thing of wonder as to fix the eyes of all beholders, young or old.*'

Xenophon, *On Horsemanship*, c. 350 BC

AUGUST

The six forty-seven to Liverpool Street was heaving. It seemed ridiculous that a train should be this busy so early in the morning. Natasha Macauley sat down, already overheated despite the cool of early morning, muttering an apology to a woman who had to move her jacket out of the way. The besuited man who had got on behind her forced himself into a gap between the passengers opposite, and promptly unfolded his newspaper, oblivious to the woman whose paperback he partially obscured.

It was an unusual route for her to take to work: she had spent the night at a hotel in Cambridge after a legal seminar. A satisfying number of business cards from solicitors and barristers lay in her jacket pocket; they had congratulated her on her speech, then suggested future meetings and possible work. But the cheap white wine that had flowed so freely now caused her stomach to gripe and she wished, briefly, that she had found time for breakfast. She did not normally drink, and it was hard to keep track of her consumption at events when her glass was perpetually topped up while she was distracted by conversation.

Natasha clutched her scalding polystyrene cup of coffee and glanced down at her diary, promising herself that at some point today she would carve out a space longer than half an hour in which to clear her head. Her diary would contain an hour in the gym. She would take an hour for lunch. She would, as her mother admonished, *take care of herself*.

But for now it read:

* *9 a.m. LA vs Santos, Court 7*
* *Persey divorce. Child psych evaluation?*
* *Fees! Check with Linda re legal aid situation*
* *Fielding – where is witness statement? MUST FAX TODAY*

Every page, for at least a fortnight ahead, was a relentless, endlessly reworked series of lists. Her colleagues at Davison Briscoe had largely switched to electronic devices – hand-held jotters and BlackBerrys – with which to navigate their lives, but she preferred the simplicity of pen and paper, even though Linda complained that her schedules were unreadable.

Natasha sipped her coffee, noticed the date and winced. She added

* *Flowers/apols re Mum's birthday*

The train rumbled towards London, the flatlands of Cambridgeshire seguing into the grey, industrial outskirts of the city. Natasha stared at her paperwork, struggling to focus. She was facing a woman who seemed to think it was okay to eat a hamburger with extra cheese for breakfast, and a teenager whose blank expression was curiously at odds with the thumping emanating from his earphones. It was going to be an unforgivingly hot day: the heat seeped into the packed carriage, transferred and amplified by the bodies.

She closed her eyes, wishing she could sleep on trains, then opened them at the sound of her mobile phone. She rummaged in her bag, locating it between her makeup and her wallet. A text message flashed up:

Local authority in Watson case rolled over. Not needed in court

9 a.m. Ben

For the past four years Natasha had been Davison Briscoe's sole solicitor advocate, a solicitor-barrister hybrid that had proved useful when it came to her speciality, representing children. They were less fazed to appear in court beside the woman in whose office they had already explained themselves. For her part, Natasha liked being able to build relationships with her clients and still enjoy the more adversarial elements of advocacy.

Thanks. Will be in office in half an hour

she texted back, with a sigh of relief. Then she cursed silently; she needn't have missed breakfast after all.

She was about to put her phone away when it rang again. Ben, her trainee: 'Just wanted to remind you that we – ah – rescheduled that Pakistani girl for ten thirty.'

'The one whose parents are fighting care proceedings?' Beside her, a woman coughed pointedly. Natasha glanced up, saw 'No Mobile Telephones' etched on the window, dipped her head and rifled through her diary. 'We've also got the parents from the child-abduction case in at two. Can you dig out the relevant paperwork?' She murmured.

'Done it. And I got some croissants,' Ben added. 'I'm assuming you won't have had anything.'

She never had. If Davison Briscoe ever abandoned the trainee system she suspected she would starve to death.

'They're almond. Your favourite.'

'Slavish crawling, Ben, will get you a long way.'

Natasha closed the phone, and then her case. She had just pulled the girl's paperwork from her briefcase when her phone rang again.

This time there was audible tutting. She mumbled an apology, without looking anyone in the eye. 'Natasha Macauley.'

'Linda. Just had a call from Michael Harrington. He's agreed to act for you in the Persey divorce.'

'Great.' It was a big-money divorce, with complicated custody issues. She had needed a heavyweight barrister to take the financial side.

'He wants to discuss a few matters with you this afternoon. You free at two?'

She was considering this when she became aware that the woman beside her was muttering, her tone unfriendly.

'I'm pretty sure that's okay.' She remembered her diary was back in her briefcase. 'Oh. No. I've got someone in.'

The woman tapped her on the shoulder. Natasha placed her hand over the receiver. 'I'll be two seconds,' she said, more brusquely than she had intended. 'I know this is a non-mobile carriage and I'm sorry, but I do need to finish this call.'

She stuck the phone between ear and shoulder, struggled to find her diary, then spun round in exasperation when the woman tapped her again.

'I said I'll only—'

'Your coffee is on my jacket.'

She glanced down. Saw the cup balanced precariously on the hem of the cream jacket. 'Ah. Sorry.' She picked it up. 'Linda, can we switch this afternoon around? I must have a gap somewhere.'

'Hah!'

Her secretary's cackle rang in her ears after she had snapped shut her phone. She crossed out the court appearance in her diary, added the meeting and was about to put it back in her bag when something in the newspaper headline opposite caught her eye.

She leant forwards, checking that she had read the name in the first paragraph correctly. She leant so far forwards that the man holding the newspaper lowered it and frowned at her. 'I'm sorry,' she said, still transfixed by the story. 'Could I – could I have a very quick look at your paper?'

He was too taken aback to refuse. She took the newspaper, flipped it over and read the story twice, the colour draining from her face, then handed it back. 'Thank you,' she said weakly. The teenager beside her was smirking, as though he could hardly believe the breach of passenger etiquette that had taken place in front of him.

Sarah cut the second square of sandwiches twice diagonally, then wrapped both sets carefully in greaseproof paper. One she placed in the fridge, the other she tucked carefully into her bag with two apples. She wiped the work surface with a damp cloth, then scanned the little kitchen for crumbs before she turned off the radio. Papa hated crumbs.

Far below, the distant whine of the milk float signalled its departure from the courtyard. The milkman wouldn't deliver up the stairs any more, not since someone had driven off with his float while he was on the fifth floor. He still put out bottles for the old ladies in the sheltered housing opposite, but everyone else had to go to the supermarket, then lug their litre cartons back on overcrowded buses or haul them on foot in bulging shopping bags. If she made it down there, he'd let her buy one; most mornings she made it.

She checked her watch, then the filter paper to see whether the dark brown liquid had drained through. She told Papa every week that the real stuff cost loads more than instant, but he just shrugged and said that some savings were a false economy. She wiped the bottom of the mug, then walked into the narrow hallway and stood outside his room.

'Papa?' He had long since stopped being Grandpapa.

She pushed the door with her shoulder. The little room was glowing with the morning sunlight and for a minute you could pretend outside was somewhere lovely, a beach or a country garden, instead of a tired 1960s estate in East London. On the other side of his bed a small bureau gleamed, his hair and clothes brushes neatly lined up below the photograph of Nana. He had not had a double bed since she'd died; there was more space in his room with a single, he said. She knew he couldn't face the emptiness of a large bed without her grandmother in it.

'Coffee.'

The old man pushed himself up from the pillow and scrabbled on the bedside table for his glasses. 'You're going now? What's the time?'

'Just after six.'

He picked up his watch and squinted at it. He looked curiously vulnerable in his pyjamas, this man who wore his clothes as if they were a uniform. Papa was always properly dressed. 'Will you catch the ten past?'

'If I run. Your sandwiches are in the fridge.'

'Tell the mad cowboy I will pay him this afternoon.'

'I told him yesterday, Papa. He's fine.'

'And get him to put some eggs by. We'll have them tomorrow.'

She made the bus, but only because it was a minute late. Puffing, she hurled herself on board, her bag swinging wildly behind her. She showed her pass, then sat down, nodding to the Indian woman who sat in the same spot opposite every morning, her mop and bucket still in her hand. 'Beautiful,' the woman said, as the bus pulled past the betting shop.

Sarah glanced behind her, at the grimy streets illuminated in the watery morning light. 'Going to be,' she conceded.

'You will be hot in those boots,' the woman said.

Sarah patted her bag. 'Got my school shoes in here,' she

said. They smiled awkwardly at each other, as if, after months of silence, they were embarrassed to have said so much, Sarah settled back in her seat and turned to the window.

The route to Cowboy John's took seventeen minutes at this time of the morning; an hour later, when the roads to the east of the City were clogged with traffic it would take almost three times as long. She was usually there before him, the only person to whom he would give a spare set of keys. Most days, she would be letting out the hens by the time he came sauntering, stiff-legged, up the road. You could usually hear him singing.

Sheba, the Alsatian, barked once as Sarah fiddled with the padlock on the wire gate, then, realising who it was, sat and waited, her tail beating an expectant tattoo. Sarah threw her a treat from her pocket and walked into the little yard, closing the gates with a muted crash behind her.

Once, this part of London had been dotted with stable-yards, tucked at the end of narrow, cobbled streets, behind barn doors, under arches. Horses had pulled the brewery drays, the coal and rag-and-bone carts, and it had not been unusual to see a much-loved family cob or a couple of fine trotters out for a circuit of the park on Saturday afternoon. Cowboy John's was one of the few that remained, taking up some four railway arches, with three or four stables and lock-ups built into each, at the far end of a lane that ended on the high street. There was a walled yard in front of the arches, with a cobbled floor, in which were stacked pallets, chicken coops, bins, a skip or two, and whatever old car Cowboy John was selling, plus a brazier that never went out. Every twenty minutes or so a commuter train would rumble overhead, but neither humans nor animals took any notice. Chickens pecked, a goat took a speculative bite of whatever it was not supposed to eat, and Sheba's amber eyes gazed warily out at the world beyond the gates, ready to snap at anyone who was not on her register.

Twelve horses were resident at the moment, including twin Clydesdales owned by Tony, the retired drayman, the fine-necked, wild-eyed trotters of Maltese Sal and his betting cohorts, and an assortment of scruffy ponies kept by local children. Sarah was never sure how many people knew they were there – the park keeper, who regularly chased them off the common, did and occasionally they received letters addressed to 'The Horse Owners, Sparepenny Lane Arches', threatening court action if they continued to trespass. Cowboy John would laugh and throw them into the brazier. 'Far as I know, horses was here first,' he would drawl.

He claimed to be an original member of the Philadelphia Black Cowboys. They weren't real cowboys – not the cattle-ranching kind, at least. In America, he said, there were city yards like his, bigger ones, where men could keep and race their animals, and young kids came to learn and escape lives that were otherwise ghetto-bound. He had arrived in London in the sixties, following a woman who had turned out to be 'way, way too much trouble'. He had liked the city, but missed his horses so much that he had bought a broken-kneed thoroughbred from Southall market and some near-derelict Victorian stables from the council. As far as anyone could tell, the council had regretted it ever since.

Cowboy John's was an institution now, or a nuisance, depending on where you stood. The officials from the town hall didn't like it, forever issuing warnings about environ-mental health and pest control, even though John told them they could sit out here all night dipped in cheese sauce and they wouldn't see one rodent – he had a posse of mean cats. Property developers didn't like it because they wanted to stick their blocks of flats there and Cowboy John wouldn't sell. But most of the neighbours didn't mind: they stopped by daily to chat to him, or buy whatever fresh produce he had on offer. The local restaurants liked it: sometimes Ranjeet or Neela from the Raj Palace called in if they needed hens or eggs or the odd goat, and then there were a few like Sarah, who was there whenever she didn't have to be at school. With its tidy Victorian stables and teetering stacks of hay and straw, it was a refuge from the relentless noise and chaos of the city streets around it.

'You let that fool goose out yet?'

She was throwing hay to the ponies when Cowboy John arrived. He was wearing his Stetson – in case people didn't get the message – and his hollow cheeks were burnished with the effort of walking and smoking in the already warm sun.

'Nope. It keeps biting my legs.'

'Mine too. I'm going to see if that new restaurant wants it. Man, I've got welts all round my ankles.' They stopped to eye the oversized bird he had bought on a whim at the previous week's market. 'Plum sauce!' he barked, and it hissed in reply.

Sarah couldn't remember a time when she hadn't spent most of her days at Sparepenny Lane. When she was tiny Papa would sit her on Cowboy John's shaggy Shetland ponies, and Nana would tut contentedly, as if Papa's passion for horses was something he shouldn't pass on. When her mother had first left, Papa brought her there so that she couldn't hear Nana crying or, on the few occasions her mother came home, yelling at her, or pleading with her to get straight.

It was here that Papa had taught her to ride, running up and down the back-streets until she had mastered the rising trot. Papa despised the way most of the owners at Cowboy John's kept their horses; being in a city was no reason not to exercise them every day, he said. He never let her eat before her horse had been fed, never let her have a bath before she had polished her boots. And then, after Nana died, Baucher, whom they called Boo, had arrived. They had needed something to focus on, a reason to be out of a home that no longer felt like one. And Papa, who saw dangers for a wide-eyed girl just into her teens, had decided she needed a route out. He began to train the copper-coloured colt and his grand-daughter. He trained her far beyond what the local kids called riding: the vaulting on to a pony's back and haring down the streets until you reached the marshes, the scraping over park benches, fruit crates, any obstacles that offered a thrill. Papa would drill her and drill her about stuff they couldn't even see – the correct angle of her lower leg to within a millimetre, the perfect stillness of her hands – until she wept because sometimes she just wanted to goof around with the others and he wouldn't let her. Not just because he wanted to protect Boo's legs from the tarmac roads, but also because she had to learn, he said, that the only way to achieve something magical was through work and discipline.

He still talked like that, Papa. That was why John and the others called him Captain. It was supposed to be a joke, but she knew they were a bit wary of him too.

'You want tea?' Cowboy John gestured at his kettle.

'No. I've only got half an hour to ride. I have to be at school early today.'

'You still working on yo' tricks?'

'Actually,' she said, with exaggerated politeness, 'this morning we will be working on our half-pass, with a flying change of legs and some *piaffe*. Under the orders of the Captain.' She stroked the horse's gleaming neck.

Cowboy John snorted. 'I got to give it to your old man. Next time the circus comes by they'll be biting his arm off.'

In Natasha's line of work it was hardly unusual to find, within weeks, the child one had just represented up before the court again, recipient of a new ASBO or youth-custody order. Occasionally they might even make the newspaper. But this one surprised her, not just for the severity of his crime but because of who he was. Day after day the children came in and told stories of despair, abuse and neglect. For the most part she could listen without wincing. After ten years she had heard so many that few prompted more in her than a mental checklist: does he meet the criteria? Has she signed the legal-aid papers? How strong is the defence likely to be? Is he a believable witness? Just like the others, Ali Ahmadi should have faded from memory, processed by her staff, another name on the court roster to be swiftly forgotten.

He had come into her office two months earlier, with the wary, hollow-eyed look of distrust and despair that so many wore, feet squashed into cheap, donated trainers, an ill-fitting shirt hanging off his thin frame. He was in need of an emergency injunction to prevent him being sent back to the country he claimed had nearly destroyed him.

'I don't really do immigration,' she had explained, but Ravi, who handled those cases, was off and they were desperate.

'Please,' the foster-mother said, 'I know you, Natasha. You can do this for us.' Two years previously Natasha had represented another of her children.

She had scanned the paperwork, looked up and smiled at him, and after a moment, he had smiled back. Not a confident smile, more appeasement. As if it was expected of him. As she had speed-read the notes, he had started to speak, growing more urgent as the woman translated, his hands illustrating the words she could not understand.

His family had been targeted as political dissidents. His father had disappeared on the way home from work; his mother had been beaten in the street, then disappeared with his sister. Ali's desperation had been such that he had walked to the border in thirteen days. He began to cry silently as he spoke, blinking away the tears with adolescent embarrassment. He would be killed if he returned home. He was fifteen.

It was a fairly unremarkable story, as they went.

Linda had been hovering by the door. 'Can you ring the judge's clerk for me? See if we can get Court four?'

As they left she put her hand on the boy's shoulder – she hadn't realised until then how tall he was. He had seemed to shrink while he told his story, as if parts of him had been hacked away with his history. 'I'll do my best,' she said, 'but I still think you'd be better off with someone else.'

She won him the injunction, and would have thought no more of him, but as she had swept her papers into her brief-case, ready to leave the court, she had noticed he was crying again, in the corner of the courtroom, heaving great silent sobs. A little taken aback, she had averted her eyes as she passed him, but he had broken away from his foster-mother, pulled a chain from his neck and pressed it into her hands. He wouldn't look at her, even as she told him it was unnec-essary. He just stood there, head down, body a question mark, his palms pressed to hers, even though such contact was against the dictates of his religion. She remembered how his hands had enfolded hers in a curiously adult gesture.

The same hands which had, two nights ago, apparently perpetrated a 'prolonged and vicious attack' on an as yet unnamed sales assistant, 26, in her own home.

Her phone sounded again. More tutting, unrestrained this time. With another apology, Natasha stood, gathered her belongings and made her way through the crowded carriage, struggling to stay upright as the train swung suddenly to the left. Tucking her case under her arm, she lurched towards the standing area, and found herself a small space by the window, as close to a mobile-friendly carriage as she could get. She dropped her bags as the caller disconnected, and swore. She had relinquished her seat for nothing. She was about to tuck her phone into her pocket when she saw the text message:

> Hi. Need to pick up some stuff. And talk. Any time next week
> good for you? Mac

Mac. She stared at the little screen and everything around her stilled. *Mac.*

She had no choice.

> No problem

she typed back, and shut her phone.

Once, this corner of the City had been stacked with solicitors' offices, side by side in Dickensian buildings, their gold-painted 'partners' signs promising representation of the business, taxation and matrimonial variety. Most had long moved to new commercial premises, glossy glass buildings on the outskirts of the City, architect-designed spaces that their occupants felt properly reflected their twenty-first-century outlook. So far, Davison Briscoe had resolutely failed to join this trend, and Natasha's cramped, book-stuffed room in the rickety Georgian building that housed her and five other lawyers bore more of a resemblance to an academic's tutoring room than a commercial enterprise.

'Here's the paperwork you asked for.' Ben, a gangly, studious young man whose fair, determinedly smooth cheeks belied his twenty-five years, placed the pink-ribboned file in front of her. 'You haven't touched your croissants,' he said.

'Sorry.' She flicked through the files on her desk. 'Lost my appetite. Ben, do me a favour. Dig out the file for Ali Ahmadi, will you? Emergency judicial review from about two months ago.' Then she glanced at the newspaper she had bought on her way from the station in a vain attempt to persuade herself that what she had read had been a hallucination, perhaps brought on by lack of sleep.

The door opened and Conor entered. He was wearing the blue striped shirt she had bought him for his birthday.

'Morning, Hotshot.' He leant across the desk and kissed her lightly on the lips. 'How'd it go last night?'

'Good,' she said. 'Really good. You were missed.'

'My night for having the boys. Sorry, but you know how it is. Until I get more access I daren't miss an evening.'

'Did you have a nice time?'

'It was wild. Harry Potter DVD, beans on toast. We sure rocked the joint. That enormous hotel bed too big without me?'

She sat back. 'Conor, desperate as I am for your company, I was so shattered by midnight I could have slept on a park bench.'

Ben came in again and, with a nod to Conor, laid the file on her desk. 'Mr Ahmadi,' he said.

Conor peered at it. 'Wasn't that your deportation case from a couple of months ago? Why are you digging him out?'

'Ben, go and get me a fresh coffee, will you? From the shop, not Linda's brown water.'

Conor tossed a bank note at him. 'And me. Double-shot espresso. No milk.'

'You'll kill yourself,' she observed.

'But by God, I'll do it efficiently. Okay,' he said, noting that she was waiting for Ben to leave. 'What's up?'

'This.' She handed him the paper, pointing at the story.

He read it quickly. 'Ah. Your man there,' he said.

'Oh, yes.' She stretched out her arms, letting her face fall briefly on to the desk. Then she reached over and picked at an almond croissant. 'My man there. I'm wondering if I should tell Richard.'

'Our senior partner? Oh, nonononono! No need for a hair shirt, Hotshot.'

'It's a pretty serious crime.'

'And one you could not have predicted. Let it go, Natasha. All part of the job, sweetheart. You know that.'

'I do. It's just that it's . . . so grim. And he was . . .' She shook her head, remembering. 'I don't know. He just didn't seem the type.'

'Didn't seem the type.' Conor actually laughed.

'Well, he didn't.' She took a swig of cold coffee. 'I just don't like having been part of something so awful. I can't help feeling responsible.'

'What? You forced him to attack the girl?'

'You know that's not what I meant. I put up a good case for him to stay in the country. I'm responsible for him being here.'

'Because nobody else could have made that happen, could they?'

'Well . . .'

'Get over yourself, Natasha.' Conor tapped the file. 'If Ravi had been here it would have been him. Let it go. Move on. I'll see you for a quick drink tonight. Are we still on? Fancy the Archery? They've started doing tapas, you know.'

But Natasha had only ever been good at giving advice, not taking it. Later that day she found herself opening Ahmadi's file for a second time, searching for clues, some reason why this boy, who had cried, had held her hands so gently, had been capable of such a random act of violence. It didn't make sense. 'Ben? I need you to find me an atlas.'

'An atlas?'

He had found one within twenty minutes, scuffed and fabric-bound, the spine missing in patches. 'It's probably very much out of date. It has – ah – references to Persia and Bombay,' he said apologetically. 'You might do better looking up whatever you need on the web. I could do it for you.'

'I'm a Luddite, Ben,' she said, flicking through the pages, 'you know that. I need to see it on paper.'

Almost on a whim, she'd decided to look up where the boy had come from; the name of the town had stuck in her mind.

It was then, as she stared at the map, tracing the names of the places with a finger, that she realised none of the care workers, the legal team, his foster-mother had asked Ali Ahmadi the obvious question. But there it was – staring up at her: how could anyone walk nine hundred miles in thirteen days?

That evening Natasha sat in the bar and cursed herself for not being thorough. She told Conor the story, and he laughed, a short, wry laugh, then shrugged. 'You know these kids are desperate,' he said. 'They tell you what they think you want to hear.'

She saw them every day, refugees, 'problem' children, young people who were displaced or neglected, teenagers who had never known a word of praise or a supportive embrace, their faces prematurely hardened, their minds already hard-wired to survival at any cost. She believed she could usually tell the ones who were lying: the girls who claimed their parents were abusive because they no longer wanted to live at home; the asylum-seekers who swore they were eleven or twelve, even when you could make out the thick stubble of adulthood on their cheeks. She was used to seeing the same young offenders, in an endless cycle of misbehaviour and alleged repentance. But she had been *moved* by Ahmadi.

Conor gave her his full attention. 'Okay. Are you sure you got the place right?'

'It's in the statements.' She asked a passing waiter for mineral water.

'And he really couldn't have walked that far?'

'In less than two weeks?' Her voice was sarcastic. She couldn't help it. 'Seventy miles a day. I calculated it.'

'I don't know why you're so upset. You're protected by privilege. You knew nothing of this while you were representing him, so what does it matter? You don't have to say anything. You don't have to *do* anything. Hell, it happens to me all the time. I have to tell half my clients to shut up at first meeting before they tell me something I'm not supposed to hear.'

But if she had checked his story herself, Natasha wanted to say, she might have guessed earlier on that Ahmadi was lying. She might have excused herself from the case – cited 'embarrassment'. That was often enough to get people looking at the facts a little harder. She could have saved that woman, that unknown sales assistant, 26. But she had skimmed the notes. And she had let the boy go, allowed him to disappear between the cracks of London's landscape, assuming that he was one of the good ones who wouldn't reappear in court some day.

If he had lied about how he'd got here, he could have lied about anything.

Conor leant back and took a long sip of his wine. 'Ah, let it go, Natasha. Some desperate kid managed to avoid being sent back to some plague-infested hell-hole. So what? Move on.'

Even when he was dealing with the most high-profile cases, Conor had a deceptively sanguine air, beaming outside court, glad-handing, as if it was of no consequence to him whether he won or not. He patted his pockets. 'Will you get me another? I've got to nip to the cashpoint.'

She checked in her bag for her wallet and found her fingers entangled in something. She pulled it out. It was the little amulet, the roughened silver horse, that Ahmadi had given her on the morning she had won his case. She had resolved to send it to his home – he had too few possessions to give anything away – and had promptly forgotten. Now it was a reminder of how she had failed. Suddenly she remembered the unlikely vision of that morning, an unearthly apparition in urban surroundings.

'Conor – I saw the strangest thing this morning.'

The train had stopped for fifteen minutes in a tunnel outside Liverpool Street station, just long enough for the temperature to rise to a point at which people shifted restlessly in their seats and a low murmur of discontent rippled along the train. Just long enough for Natasha, shielded from telephone calls now, to stare out at the inky nothingness and think about an ex-husband who wasn't yet ex enough.

She had shifted slightly on her feet as, with a harsh squeal of overheated metal, the train edged forward and out into daylight. She wouldn't think about Mac. She wouldn't think about Ali Ahmadi, who had proven so depressingly removed from the person he had presented to her.

And it was at that moment she saw it, so fast, so unlikely, that even as she cricked her neck to look back, she wasn't sure she had registered it correctly. Gone in a flash, swallowed by the blurred streets and backyards, grimy balconies and lead-specked lines of laundry.

But the image had stayed with her all day, long after the train had carried her towards the hazy centre of the City. In a quiet cobbled street squeezed between high-rise blocks, flanked by lorry yards and parked cars a young girl had stood, her arm raised, a long stick in her hand – not in threat but instruction.

Above her, in the middle of the road, perfectly balanced on glossy, muscular haunches, a huge horse reared.

Natasha dropped the silver pendant into her bag, barely suppressing a shiver. 'Did you hear what I just said?'

'Mm?' He was reading the newspaper. He had already lost interest. Move on, he always told her. As if *he* ever could.

She stared at him. 'Nothing,' she said. 'I'll go and get the drinks.'

Two

Boo was not a horse you might usually find in the back-street yards of East London. He was neither a heavy, feather-legged dray nor a ewe-necked thoroughbred pacer, the kind backed rapidly into a sulky so that illegal races could take place on the dual-carriageway, trotting their way into private record books and prompting the transfer of thick wads of illegal betting cash. He was not a well-mannered riding-school hack from Hyde Park or one of the many varieties of short, stout pony, black and white or mulish, which tolerated, with varying degrees of good humour, being ridden down steps, scrambled over beer barrels, or taken into lifts so that, with shrieks of laughter, their owners might canter along the balconies of their blocks of flats.

Boo was a Selle Français, a large-boned thoroughbred, his legs sturdier and his back stronger than that breed might suggest. He was athletic but sure-footed. His short-coupled back made him good at jumping and his sweet, almost dog-like, nature made him tolerant and friendly. He was unfazed by the heaviest traffic, and a fool for company. He was also easily bored, and Papa had hung so many balls from ropes in his stable to entertain him that Cowboy John would mutter that the old man must be trying to get him a place in the basketball leagues.

The other kids at Sarah's school or on the estate got their highs in little paper wraps or plastic bags, skidding stolen cars around shrinking patches of wasteland or spending hours dressing up like celebrities, studying their magazines with far more attentiveness than they ever did their schoolbooks. She didn't care about any of it. From the moment Sarah put on the saddle and breathed in the familiar scent of warm horse and clean leather, she forgot everything else.

Riding Boo lifted her away from everything that was annoying and grubby and depressing. It helped her forget that she was the skinniest girl in her class, and the only one with little justifiable reason to wear a bra, that only she – and Renee, the Turkish girl nobody spoke to – didn't have a mobile phone or a computer. She forgot that it was just her and Papa.

This was what she felt for her horse on their good days: awe at his majesty, the sheer power beneath her, and what he would do for her. He behaved badly only when she failed to ask him properly – her mind still lodged in school, or thirst, or tiredness – and the sweetness that radiated from him when they got it right brought a lump to her throat. Boo was hers, and he was special.

Papa told people who didn't know about horses that he was like a Rolls-Royce after a tractor: everything was finely tuned, responsive, elegant. You communicated quietly, rather than flapping and shouting. You achieved a communion of minds, of wills. She asked Boo: he collected himself, his quarters gathering under him, his great head dropping into his chest, and he gave. His only limits, said Papa, were Sarah's limits. He said Boo had the biggest heart of any horse he had ever known.

It hadn't always been like that: Sarah had two moon-shaped

scars on her arm from where he had bitten her, and when they had broken him there had been days when he would snap off the lunge rein and go tearing across the park, his tail up like a banner, while the mothers shrieked and bolted with their prams and Papa prayed aloud in French that he wouldn't hit a car. Papa told her every time that it was her fault, to the point at which she wanted to scream at him, but now she knew a little more and understood that he had been right.

Horses, perhaps more so than any other creature, were made by man. They might be naturally spooky, or fearful, or bolshy, but their reactions to their world were shaped entirely by what was done to them. A child would give you a second chance because it hoped to be loved. A dog would return to you slavishly, even after you'd beaten it. A horse would never let you – or anyone else – near him again. So Papa never shouted at him. He never lost his temper, or got frustrated, even when it was clear that Boo was being as mischievous or unruly as any teenager.

And now he was eight years old, grown. He was educated enough to have manners, clever enough that his paces floated, elegant enough, if Papa had judged this as correctly as he seemed to judge everything else, to carry Sarah away from this chaotic city and on to her future.

Cowboy John leant on his broom and looked through the gates at the park where the girl was making the horse canter small, steady circles in the corner by the trees, slowing occasionally to praise him or let him stretch out. She wasn't wearing a hat – a rare act of rebellion against her grandfather, who would not allow her so much as sit on that horse without one – and the sun gleamed off her hair as brightly as it did the horse's quarters. He saw the postman cycle past, yelling something to her as he went, and she lifted a hand in greeting, her face still turned to what she was doing.

She was a good kid, not like a lot who came here. They would race their horses on empty streets till their hooves cracked, slinging them back in their stables, sweaty and over-wrought, before they ran home, promising that their mums or dads would be along with the rent money the very next day. They would cheek the adults, spend their feed money on cigarettes, which he confiscated when they were in the yard. 'I couldn't care jack about your lungs. But I ain't about watching my old boys git barbecued,' he would say. This was usually accompanied by a meditative pull on his own cigarette. The last packet he had taken had come from a kid of no more than eight.

He doubted Sarah Lachapelle had smoked a cigarette in her life. The Captain kept her on as tight a rein as he kept that horse: no playing out late, no drinking, no smoking, no hanging about on street corners. The girl never seemed to chafe against it. It was like he'd trained her too.

Not like her mother.

Cowboy John removed his hat and wiped his forehead, already feeling the heat of the day seep through the battered leather into his skin. Maltese Sal had assured him that if he took over the lease the Captain's horse would be safe here, as would that of anyone else who was not in arrears. The place would remain as it had been for forty years, a stables.

'I need a base,' he kept saying to John. 'This is near my home. My horses are comfortable here.' He spoke as if it was already decided. And this ramshackle old yard would be a useful front for whatever you buy and sell, John wanted to answer him, but you didn't say that to a man like Sal. Especially when he was offering the kind of money he was suggesting.

Truth was, Cowboy John was tired. He quite fancied the idea of retiring to the country, swapping his house for a little cottage with a plot of land his horses could graze on. City life was getting uglier and he was getting older, tired of fighting the council, tired of picking up the broken bottles that the drunks and idiots threw over the gates every night for the animals to cut themselves on. He was tired of arguing with kids who didn't want to pay what they owed. Increasingly, he could picture himself sitting on a porch somewhere, looking at a horizon that was a single line of green.

Sal would keep it as a yard. And he was talking a good sum of money, money enough for John to make his dream reality. But still ... Despite the money, despite the lure of peace, of watching his old boys swish their tails in the long grass, part of him was reluctant to let it go to that man. He had a sneaking feeling that Sal's promises carried all the weight of diddly-squat.

'Bon anniversaire!'

Sarah, fiddling to get the key out of the lock, stepped into their flat and heard her grandfather's voice before she saw him. She smiled. *'Merci!'*

She had thought he might have laid the kitchen table with a birthday cake, as he had the previous year, but instead she walked down the hall to find him standing in front of the television. *'Voilà!* Sit, sit,' he instructed, having kissed her on both cheeks. He was wearing his best tie.

She peered at the little kitchen table. 'We're not having tea?'

'Pizza. Afterwards. You choose,' he said, pointing to a menu. Takeaway was a rare treat.

'After what?'

She put down her bag and sat on the sofa, feeling a jolt of excitement. Papa seemed so pleased, a smile twitching at the corners of his mouth. She couldn't remember the last time he had looked like this. Since Nana had died four years ago, he had retreated into himself, emerging only when Boo arrived. She knew he loved her, but his love was not the kind

you saw on television: he didn't tell her he loved her, didn't
ask what was on her mind. He made sure she was fed, washed
and up to date with her homework. He taught her practical
stuff, about money, mending things and horsemanship.
Between them they had long since mastered the washing-
machine, the housekeeping and the cheapest way to do a
weekly shop. If she was sad, he would lay a hand on her
shoulder, perhaps tell her to keep a perspective. If she was
giddy with excitement he would wait until she had calmed
down. If she did wrong, he made his displeasure known
with a certain curtness, a disapproving glance. In short, he
probably treated her a little like he treated a horse.

'First,' he said, 'we are going to watch something.'

She followed his gaze, seeing now the DVD player that
had not been there when she had left that morning. 'You
bought me a DVD player?' She knelt down and ran a finger
across its shiny metallic surface.

'It's not new,' he said apologetically, 'but it is *parfait*. And
it is not stolen. I bought it from the house clearance.'

'We can watch anything?' she exclaimed. She would be
able to rent films like the other girls at school did. She was
always years behind when anyone talked about movies.

'Not just anything. We are going to see *un spectacle*. But
first . . .' He reached behind him to a bottle, opened it with
a flourish and poured. 'Fourteen, eh? Old enough for some
wine.' He nodded as he handed it to her.

She took a sip, trying not to look as unimpressed as she
felt by the sour taste. She would have preferred Diet Coke,
but didn't feel she could spoil the moment by asking.

Apparently satisfied, he adjusted his spectacles, peered at
the remote control and, with a hint of flamboyance that
suggested he had practised this earlier in the day, pressed a
button. The television screen flickered into life and he settled
into the sofa beside her, still upright despite the collapsing

cushions. He took a sip of his wine. She glimpsed his look
of quiet pleasure and leant against him.

The music began, classical music, and a white horse
pranced across the screen.

'Is it . . . ?'

'Le Cadre Noir,' he confirmed. 'Now you will see what we
are aiming for.'

Even those people who knew about horses had rarely heard
of Le Cadre Noir. It was an arcane organisation of élite
French riders that had existed since the 1700s, and still did
in a form recognisable to its originators, an academy at which
debate might revolve around the exact angle of a horse's hind
legs when it performed the thousand-year-old manoeuvres
of *croupade*, or *levade*, and the riders wore an ancient black
uniform. It admitted no more than one or two new members
a year, and aimed not to make money, or to bestow its skills
and knowledge on the masses, but to pursue excellence in
things that most people could not even see. If you knew this
you might question the point of it, yet nobody who saw those
horses moving beneath their sombre riders, lined up in perfect
symmetry or defying gravity with astonishing leaps, could
watch their strange, dancing steps, the muscular acceptance
of their riders' wishes, without being profoundly moved by
their obedience, their beauty, their astonishing agility. And
perhaps, even if you did not particularly like horses – or the
French – you would feel glad that such an organisation still
existed.

Sarah watched the forty-minute display in silence. She was
mesmerised. She wanted to go to Boo and copy what she
had seen. He could do this, she knew it. He was finer, stronger,
than some of the horses she had seen on the screen, but he
had the same power: she had felt it beneath her often enough.
As she watched, her hands and feet twitched, riding the screen

horses, encouraging them into the outlines, the movements that had been performed since ancient Greek times.

Her personal arena might have been a bare-patched, litter-strewn park rather than the vast palace of an historic French town, her outfit jeans and a T-shirt instead of a formal black jacket, gold braid and a peaked cap. But she knew how those men felt: when the camera had lingered on their faces, taut with effort and sympathy, with wanting, she had felt kinship as she never had with the girls at school. All the things Papa had been teaching her began to slot into place. He said they had years of work ahead of them. He said letting her try would be like Cowboy John attempting a marathon, cigarette in hand. And now she saw what he was aiming for, the great goal: *capriole*. The most complex, demanding and beautiful movement a horse could make, taking all four hooves off the ground into a balletic leap, lifting as if it was weightless, kicking out behind in mid-air as if it scorned the laws of gravity. Beautiful. Fearsome. Awe-inspiring.

Sarah had never been able to say what she felt when Papa went on and on about the French school, which was, what chance did they really have? Despite what he said, she had never been able to translate her life at Cowboy John's and their training sessions in the park into the future he had described. Now, as she watched the credits, she realised the DVD had had the opposite effect to the one he had wanted. It had simply confirmed that Papa was indulging a dream. It didn't matter how good her horse was. How could anyone make the most gravity-defying leap of all, from the back-streets of London to the polished glory of Le Cadre Noir?

She felt guilty almost as soon as she had thought it. Her eyes went to him, and she wondered if her thoughts were as transparent as they seemed. He was still staring at the screen. It was then that she saw the tear running down his cheek.

'Papa?' she said. His jaw tightened. He took a moment to

compose himself, and then he said quietly, 'Sarah. This is how you escape.'

Escape what? She had never felt that her life was quite as bad as Papa seemed to think it was.

'This is what I want for you.'

She swallowed.

He held up the DVD case. 'I have a letter from Jacques Varjus, my old friend at Saumur. He tells me they have accepted two women now. For hundreds of years the academy will not take a woman, will not consider it, and now they do it. You don't have to be from the military. You just have to be excellent. This is a chance, Sarah.'

She was a little unnerved by his intensity.

'You have this ability. You need only the discipline. I don't want you to waste your life. I don't want to see you here, hanging around with these *imbéciles*, ending up pushing a pram around this place.' He gestured out of the window towards the car park.

'But I—'

He held up a hand. 'I have nothing to give you except this. My knowledge. My efforts.' He smiled, tried to soften his tone. 'My girl in black, eh? *La fille du Cadre Noir.*'

She nodded mutely. Her grandfather was never emotional, but now he looked vulnerable, regretful, and she was a little frightened. It was the wine, she told herself – he rarely drank. The wine had heightened their emotions. Fiddling with her glass, she tried not to look at his face. 'It was a nice present.'

He dragged himself back to her, seemed to get his emotions under control. '*Non! Un demi cadeau,*' he said. 'You want to know the second part?'

She grinned, relieved. 'Pizza?'

'Pff! Pizza! *Non, non – regards.*' He pulled out an envelope and handed it to her.

'What is it?'

He nodded at it.

She opened it, scanned the contents, and her hands stilled. Four tickets. Two for a coach-and-ferry journey. Two for a performance of Le Cadre Noir.

'From Varjus. *En novembre*. We are taking a holiday.'

They had never been abroad, not even when Nana was alive. 'We're going to France?'

'It's time. Time for you to see, for me to return. My friend Varjus is now the Grand Dieu. You know what that is? The most important, the most experienced horseman in Le Cadre Noir. Non – in France.'

She stared at the leaflet, at the dark-clad riders, the gleaming horses.

Papa seemed filled with new zeal. 'I have filled in the passport forms. All I need is your photograph.'

'But how did you afford it?'

'I sold a few things. *Pas du tout*. You are happy? A good birthday?'

It was then she noticed he wasn't wearing his watch. The Longines had been his wedding present from Nana. So precious that as a child she had not been allowed to touch it. She wanted to ask, but the words had jammed in her throat.

'Sarah?'

She stepped into his embrace, unable to murmur her thanks into his soft, worn jumper because the words wouldn't come.

Three

*'Never deal with him when you are in a fit of passion.
Anger, impatience, fear . . . virtually any human emotion
undermines effective communication with a horse.'*

Xenophon, *On Horsemanship*

In the days when she could think about it rationally, Natasha
would observe, with a kind of dark humour, that her marriage
had begun with her left hand and ended with the right. Odd
that her fingers could precipitate such a disaster, but there
you were.

The irony was that she and Conor had not even kissed
when Mac left. Which was not to say they'd lacked opportunity. As her marriage had begun to deteriorate, and Conor's
joking, attentive lunches had provided welcome relief, he had
made it clear how he felt about her. 'You look hollowed out,
old girl. Terrible,' he would say, with his usual charm. He
would lay a hand on hers, and she would invariably remove
it. 'You need to sort your life out.'

'And end up like you?' The viciousness of his divorce had
become legendary in the office.

'Ah. It's only intense, debilitating pain. You get used to it.'
But his situation meant he understood a little of what she
was going through. Which was more than anyone else did.

In her parents' world, marriages ended through catastrophe,
because of death, disaster or repeated blatant infidelity. They

ended because the bruising had become unbearable, and the collateral damage too great. They didn't die like Natasha's marriage, slowly, from neglect. Frequently, these past months, she had wondered if she was even married. He was hardly ever there, not just emotionally but physically, as he disappeared on increasingly regular foreign assignments. When he was at home their most innocuous communications dissolved into bitter, vengeful exchanges. Both were now so fearful of hurt or further rejection that it was easier not to deal with each other at all.

'There's a gas bill here wants paying,' he would say.

'Are you asking me to do it or telling me that you're going to?'

'I just thought you'd want to take a look.'

'Why? Because you're not really living here? Do you want a discount?'

'Don't be bloody ridiculous.'

'Well, just pay it, then, rather than acting like it's somehow down to me. Oh, and by the way, Katrina rang again. You know, twenty-one-year-old Katrina with the fake boobs. The one who calls you "Mackie." Her voice trembled in a breathy impersonation of the model's.

At this he would invariably slam the door and disappear to a different part of the house.

They had met seven years earlier, on a flight to Barcelona. She had been with friends from law school, celebrating someone's call to the bar. He had been returning after a brief holiday, having accidentally left his camera in his friend's apartment. She should have seen that as a warning, she realised afterwards, emblematic of the chaotic nature of his life, his lack of common sense (hadn't he heard of DHL?). But at the time, she could only think of her good luck at sitting next to the charming, crop-haired man in the khaki jacket, who not only laughed at her jokes but seemed interested, really interested, in what she did.

'So you're going to do what?'

'Act as a solicitor advocate. It's a cross between a solicitor and barrister so I get to represent the people whose cases I deal with. I specialise in children.'

'Child criminals?'

'Mostly kids in care, and I do a bit of divorce too, trying to look out for the child's interests. It's a bit of a growth area because of the Children Act.'

She still tried to work out the best deals for children battered by divorce, still forced local authorities and immigration offices to grant them a temporary home. But for every desperate child, there was a cynical attempt to gain asylum, for every new foster placement, a depressing cycle of abuse and return. She tried not to think about it too often. She was good at it and she told herself that the few lives to which she could make a difference were enough.

Mac had liked her for it. He said she had substance, unlike most of the people he knew through his work. A petulant girlfriend had met him at Barcelona Airport, shooting dark looks as Natasha bade him a polite goodbye. Within six hours he had rung her mobile, having ditched the girlfriend, to ask if he could take her out in London. She shouldn't feel guilty about the girlfriend, he added cheerfully. It wasn't serious. Nothing in Mac's life ever was.

Their wedding had been her responsibility: he would have cohabited indefinitely. She had found, to her slight surprise, that she wanted marriage. She wanted that sense of permanence, the question mark removed from their relationship. There was no proposal, as such. 'If it means so much to you I'll do it,' he said, in bed one afternoon, his legs entwined with hers. 'But you'll have to organise it.' Participant, yet not quite; the story of their married life.

At first she hadn't minded. She understood that she had control-freak tendencies, as Mac jokingly called them. She liked things just so. It was her way of keeping tabs on an otherwise frenetic life, the result of growing up in a crowded, chaotic household. She and Mac understood each other's weaknesses, teased each other about them. But then the baby neither had known they wanted created a division between them that became a chasm.

By the time she miscarried, Natasha had only known for a week that she was pregnant. She had put her missed period down to stress (she was juggling two high-profile cases), and by the time she grasped how late it was, the number of days had been irrefutable. At first Mac had been pretty shocked; and she couldn't be angry with him because she had felt the same. 'What shall we do?' she said to him, stick in hand, praying she wouldn't hate him for his answer.

He had rubbed his hands over his hair. 'Dunno, Tash,' he said. 'I'll go along with whatever you want.' And then, before they'd had a chance to think about what that was, the little bunch of cells, the baby in waiting, had made its own decision and gone.

The grief she felt had shocked her. The relief she had expected failed to materialise.

'Next year,' they agreed, after she had admitted this to him. 'We'll take a couple of good holidays this year. Then we'll try properly.' They were a little giddy with excitement. Mac would get a series of proper assignments, rather than just the odd job. She would get a position in a good chambers that offered proper maternity benefits.

Then she was offered the position at Davison Briscoe, and they had agreed it would be best to wait another year. And then another, after they had bought the house in Islington and Mac had begun to renovate it. That year two things happened: Mac's career took a downturn, and her own went into the stratosphere. For months they barely saw each other. When they did she had to tread carefully, trying not to let her success amplify the lack of his. And then – perhaps by chance rather than anything as definite as trying – she was pregnant again.

Later, much later, he accused her of shutting herself down from him long before she had started the thing with Conor Briscoe. What could she say? She knew this was true, but it had been her right not to talk about it. What was there to say, anyway? Three would-be-babies in four years, none of whom had lived much past the tadpole stage. The doctor had told her she 'qualified' for further investigation, as if she had achieved something. But she hadn't wanted it. She hadn't wanted anyone to touch her, didn't want to have to revisit those bleak hours. Didn't want evidence of what she suspected.

And Mac, whom she'd hoped would break through her anger and tears, whom she'd hoped would hold her, reassure her, simply retreated. It was as if he couldn't cope with her pain, or with the snotty, messy Natasha who didn't get out of bed for a week and wept every time she saw a baby on the television.

By the time she had hauled herself together she felt betrayed. He had not been there when she needed him. It had only occurred to her long afterwards that he, too, might have been suffering. But by then it was too late. At the time she could see only that he chose to travel to another assignment, shouting at her, when she complained, that he couldn't win, that she was always going on at him to do something. Their sex life grew non-existent. She became super-efficient, handling everything with icy resolve, and feeling furious with him when he couldn't.

And all the while the girls kept ringing. Coquettish voices with Slavic accents, insolent teenagers who seemed indignant when he wasn't there. 'They're just work,' he would insist.

'Those portfolios are my bread-and-butter. You know I don't even like doing them.'

Given the lack of intimacy between them, she wasn't sure what to believe. And all the while there was Conor – Conor with the brilliant legal brain, who understood disastrous marriages because of the spectacular collapse of his own. 'A little matter of serial infidelity on my part,' he would say. 'God knows, some women are so unreasonable.' She could see the pain behind the cheery mask, and something in her reached out to it, saw her own life echoed in it.

They had begun to have lunch together, so regularly that it was noticed in the office. Then it was the odd drink after work. What was the harm, when Mac was never around? Sometimes she felt that her flirting with Conor was justified. Mac was probably flirting with someone else right then, in some glamorous location. But when Conor leant across the pub table one night and lightly placed his lips on hers, she withdrew. 'I'm still married, Conor,' she said, wondering even as she spoke why she had included still. And wishing she hadn't wanted so badly to return the kiss.

'Ah. You can't blame a lonely soul for trying,' he said, and took her out to lunch the next day.

It wasn't long before she came to rely on him. She didn't feel guilty; it seemed of no consequence to Mac whether she was nice to him or not. They weren't even arguing any more: their life together had settled into a series of polite enquiries and rebuttals, anger simmering under the surface, from where occasionally, it erupted into something that made him turn away or slam another door.

Their party, long planned, had originally been meant to celebrate Mac finishing the house, to herald their emergence from dust-sheets and plasterboard into something not just beautiful but aspirational. By then she hadn't wanted to throw a party – she felt they had little to celebrate. But to cancel it seemed to make such a definitive statement that she felt she could not.

There were caterers and a four-piece band in the garden. To an outsider it might have seemed she and Mac were a dream couple, with Mac's set, photographers with gazelle-like models and her legal friends mingling, their laughter lifting over the high brick walls. She had realised she should use it as a networking opportunity and, still slightly amazed to be living in a house so large and so smart, knew that the presence of this head of chambers or that QC did her no harm at all. The champagne flowed, the music played, the London sun filtered into the small marquee they had set up at the end of the garden. It was a golden scene.

And she was utterly miserable.

Mac avoided her for most of the day. He was standing in a group of people she didn't know, his back to her, laughing uproariously. All the women he had invited seemed to be six foot tall, she observed bitterly. They wore interesting clothes, apparently thrown together without thought, that made them look sophisticated and sexy. She had not had time to iron the dress she had wanted to wear and the top and skirt she had chosen instead now seemed dowdy, unstylish. Mac had not told her she looked nice. He rarely commented on her appearance now.

She stood at the top of the York stone steps, watching him. Was it too late to save them? Was there anything left to save? As she stood there, he whispered into a tall woman's ear, something that made her narrow her eyes, her smile mischievous. What was he saying? *What was he saying?*

'C'mon,' a voice said beside her. 'You're too transparent. Let's go and get a drink.'

Conor. She let him lead her down the garden, nudging through the groups of people, a smile now fixed on her face.

'You okay?' he said, when they were in the corner of the marquee.

She shook her head mutely.

Conor's eyes lingered on hers. He did not make a joke. 'Margarita,' he said. 'Cure for all known ills.' He got the bartender to make four and, ignoring her protests, forced her to drink two in quick succession,

'Oh, wow,' she said, some minutes later, hanging on to his arm. 'What on earth have you done?'

'Loosened you up a little,' he said. 'You didn't want everyone whispering, "What on earth's wrong with her?" You know what gossips this crowd are.'

'Conor, what have you done?' She giggled. 'I feel about seventy per cent proof.'

'Natasha Margarita,' he said. 'Lovely ring to it. Come on, let's circulate.'

She felt her heels sink into the grass and wasn't sure she had the balance to pull them out again. Conor, seeing her predicament, held out an arm, which she took gratefully. They made their way to some lawyers from a chambers they often used.

'We'll talk to this lot,' Conor murmured. 'Did you know Daniel Hewitson got caught in a brothel last month? Now, whatever you do, don't say, "I hear you were caught in a brothel."' He waited a moment. 'It's all you can think about now, isn't it?'

'Conor!' she murmured, hanging on.

'Better now?'

'Just don't move away from me. I may have to lean on you.'

'Anytime, darling.' With a cheery greeting, Conor thrust them into the group.

Natasha was only dimly aware of the conversation around her. The effects of the margarita seemed to be amplifying as the alcohol flushed through her. She didn't care now – she was just relieved to have Conor beside her. She refused to think about anything other than his presence, made sure she laughed at the right jokes, nodding and smiling at those around her. Her heels sank again and, feeling giddy, she rested against him for support. The garden was so crowded it didn't seem to matter; people at this end were shoulder to shoulder in clusters. When she felt Conor's hand reach behind her back for hers, she took his little finger and held it, trying to convey to him her thanks. He had saved her, stopped her making a fool of herself. It was such an easy step to take, such a natural progression from where they had been, that it was some minutes before she thought that the heat on the back of her neck might not be due entirely to the sun.

She tuned out of the conversation and turned her head, just far enough that she could see Mac standing some twenty feet away. He was staring at her hand. Unbalanced, flushed, she dropped Conor's finger. Afterwards she realised that this was the worst thing she could have done, with its implication of guilt. But the damage had been done.

Mac's expression told her he had gone. Possibly a long time before.

'You should really get a proper haircut one of these days,' Linda said, behind her. In her screensaver, Natasha could just make out the downturn of her secretary's lips. The office tea-towel was slung over Natasha's shoulders, catching little feathers of dark-blonde hair as she worked.

'No time.' Natasha was back to the file in front of her, glasses at the end of her nose, stockinged feet on the desk. 'Got to read through these files. I'm due back in court at two for closing submission.'

'But your highlights have grown out. You need touching up.'

'Can't you do it?'

'I haven't done anyone's highlights for years, and especially not in a lunch hour. You earn enough. You should get a proper job done. One of those celebrity hairdressers.' She picked up a lock of hair and let it fall.

Natasha snorted. 'My worst nightmare.'

'You could make something of yourself if you tried.'

'You sound like my parents. Is there any tea going?'

She speed-read the last page of her notes, then closed the file and reached for the one that sat under it. Her phone beeped. Mac had texted her twice that morning asking when he could come to the house. She had put him off for almost ten days now.

Sorry. Too much on tomorrow. Maybe Thurs. Will let u know

she typed. She had barely put her phone down when it beeped again.

Half an hour. Weds evening.

She didn't want to face him. There was so much going on here. He had stayed away for a year; another day or two wouldn't hurt him. She typed back.

Cannot get away. Judicial review. Sorry.

But today he appeared to have lost patience:

I need my stuff. Next Friday latest. I can pick it up without you being there. Pls advise if locks changed.

She flipped her phone shut, regrouped her thoughts. 'Anyway, Lin,' she said, 'why should I go to a proper hairdresser? Your haircuts are fine.'

'Steady on the praise now, Mrs McCauley.'

'Miss.'

'Oh, yes. I was going to ask you if you wanted to be "Ms" on your correspondence . . . I've got to reorder.'

'Why would I want to be "Ms"?'

Linda shrugged. 'Dunno. You're just that type.'

Natasha ducked forwards, away from the scissors, and spun round in her chair. 'What type?'

Linda was unabashed. 'Independent, wants everyone to know it, and glad to be.' She considered this. '"Ms" is a been-through-the-mill sort of title. Not oh-gosh-I'm-still-hoping-for-the-white-wedding, like "Miss" is.' She placed her hands on either side of Natasha's head and swivelled it so that she faced the front.

'Been through the mill,' Natasha repeated. 'I don't know if you've just insulted me or said something quite nice.'

Ben came in and put another file on the desk. She leant forward to pick it up, prompting a curse from behind her.

'Linda, did that social worker ring back about Ahmadi?' She wasn't sure what she was going to ask but she needed clues: how could she have been so wrong about the boy? Had anyone else worked out that his history couldn't have been as he claimed?

'Ahmadi . . . Is that the kid who was in the paper? The one you represented? I thought I recognised his name.' Linda missed nothing. 'He attacked someone, didn't he? Surprising, really. Didn't seem the type.'

Natasha didn't want to discuss this in front of her trainee. 'They never do. Come on, Linda, you must have finished. I'm due in court in twenty minutes and I haven't had a sandwich yet.'

'How'd you go?'

Conor was waiting for her outside court. She leant forward and kissed him, no longer concerned about the glances of other lawyers. They were an established couple now. Two separated, older, wiser people. Nothing scandalous there. 'Got them. I knew I would. Pennington was woefully underbriefed.'

'That's my girl.' Conor stroked the back of her head. 'Nice hair. Dinner?'

'God, I'd love to, but I've got to sort out a ton of paperwork for tomorrow.' She saw his face cloud and reached for his arm. 'A drink would be good, though. I've hardly seen you all week.'

They walked briskly through the relative peace of Lincoln's Inn and out into the crowded, bustling street. The sun bounced off the pavement as they crossed to the pub, so that Natasha was peeling off her jacket before they got there.

'I can't make this weekend,' Conor said pre-emptively, as they stood at the bar. 'I've got the boys. I thought I should let you know early.'

Conor's two sons were five and seven, apparently far too damaged and vulnerable to be alerted to the existence of Daddy's girlfriend even though he had been divorced from their mother for more than a year. Natasha tried not to look as disappointed as she felt. 'Shame,' she said lightly. 'I'd booked the Wolseley.'

'You're kidding.'

She tried to smile. 'Nope. It's our six-month anniversary, in case you hadn't noticed.'

'And there was me thinking you were a hard-headed unromantic.'

'You don't have the monopoly on nice gestures, you know,' she said coquettishly. 'I guess I'll have to find someone else to take.'

This possibility didn't seem to trouble him. He ordered their drinks, then turned back to her. 'She's going to Dublin for the weekend.' His ex-wife was always 'she'. 'So I've got them from Friday till Monday morning. God only knows what I'm going to do with the pair. They want to go ice skating. *Ice skating*, would you believe? And it's eighty degrees out.'

Natasha sipped her drink, wondering whether it was worth volunteering. If he had to refuse her company a second time there would be a definite atmosphere. Pretending there was no possibility that she might want to accompany him made it safer, easier, for all. 'I'm sure you'll work something out,' she said carefully.

'What about Monday night? I could come straight to yours if you like. Be oiled and ready for you.'

'I guess I'll take what I can get,' she said, keeping any hint of bitterness out of the words. Why wouldn't he introduce her to his sons? Was theirs a transitional relationship, so that it was not worth them getting to know her? Or, worse, did she give off an unmaternal air that made him afraid to introduce them?

Natasha dealt with conflict all day in court, and the past year had left her with little appetite for it in her personal life. 'Monday, then,' she said, smiling.

They finished their wine, discussed work issues, and Conor proffered advice on a judge she had to face the following week. They parted at the pub door, and she returned to her office for another hour. She rang her mother, listened to a litany of her father's health concerns, and tried to imply a social life when her mother asked about it. At nine she locked up, walked out into the late-summer evening and hailed a taxi home.

She watched the London streets fly by, couples strolling lazily out of pubs and restaurants. The world was full of couples when you were alone. Perhaps she should have gone out with Conor, but her work was the only constant in her life. If she let it slide to have dinner with him, her whole life would have been for nothing.

Suddenly she felt overwhelmingly sad and fished in her bag for a tissue, then forced herself to look at one of tomorrow's files. C'mon, Natasha, get a grip, she willed herself, wondering why she felt so unbalanced. The answer wasn't hard to find.

She closed the file, then studied the text messages that had just arrived. She took a deep breath and typed,

Locks unchanged. Come when you like. If late, please leave light on and shut curtains when you go.

Four

'The sweetest of all sounds is praise.'

Xenophon, *On Horsemanship*

When she arrived Ralph was at the gates. She looked at him quizzically, then checked her watch. Twelve years old, he rarely got up before midday. School, Ralph claimed, was an optional extra. He kept largely nocturnal hours. 'Maltese Sal's having a rumble,' he said, gesturing at the truck across the road. Sal was shrugging on his jacket, checking his mobile phone. 'You coming?'

'Where?'

'On the flyover. The one by the football pitches. It's only going to take twenty minutes. Come on – Vicente says we can get a lift on the back of his pick-up.'

He looked at her expectantly, a lit cigarette wedged into the corner of his mouth. 'I helped Sal get the mare ready. She's busting out of her skin.'

She understood now why there were twice as many vehicles as usual outside on Sparepenny Lane. Men were climbing in, slamming doors, their voices low in the still morning. She could hear ignitions starting, smell anticipation in the atmosphere. Sarah glanced again at her watch, unsure.

'Cowboy John's already there,' Ralph said. 'Come on. It'll be a laugh.'

She should have been schooling her horse but Ralph was

standing there, waiting. And she was the only one in the yard who had never seen a race.

'Come on – it'll probably be the last of the summer.'

She hesitated just a moment, then ran after him towards the red pick-up truck, whose engine was already sending purple plumes of exhaust fumes into the still morning air. She hurled her bag into the back, took Ralph's hand and hauled herself up on to the pile of ropes and tarpaulins. Vicente told them to hold on, then pulled out into the quiet street behind four other vehicles, each full of dark-haired men, cigarette smoke trailing out of partially open windows.

'He's got a big bet against the travellers at Picketts Lock,' Ralph shouted, over the noise of the engine. They ducked briefly as a police car went past.

'Which mare?'

'He's racing the grey.'

'The one that kicked the sulky out?'

'He's got a new one and a better set of blinkers. He's got money riding on this, I tell you. *Big* money.' He held his hands six inches apart, a wide grin splitting his face

'Don't tell Papa I came,' she yelled. He took a deep drag, then flicked his cigarette butt into the road. Some things went without saying.

Unlike greyhound racing, or Sunday-league football, sulky racing was an intermittent and unheralded fixture in sporting annals east of the City. There was no stadium, no floodlit track on which the best horses could compete, no regulated bookmaker to offer short odds or shout for punters. Instead, several times a year, the competitors would arrange to meet at some desolate location with a pre-agreed length of smooth Tarmac.

The fact that this 'track' was inevitably a public road was no obstacle to the prospect of a race; pick-up trucks from each side would simply head out shortly after dawn when traffic was low. They would manoeuvre alongside each other until they occupied both lanes of the dual-carriageway, and then, at agreed points, slow to a halt, hazard lights flashing, so that any other vehicles were forced to stop behind them. Before the other drivers even worked out what was happening the rival horses would be on the road, their lightweight two-wheeled sulkies behind them. The race would be run down a mile stretch, accompanied by shouting, sweating, swearing, a blur of legs and whips, the drivers craning forwards as they urged their horses flat out towards some agreed finishing line, perhaps a length of tape held by two youths. Within minutes the tape would have been snapped, the race decided, and the participants would vanish into side-streets to congratulate, argue or hand over winnings. By the time the police arrived there would be little evidence – perhaps the odd pile of horse droppings, a few cigarette ends – to suggest anything had happened there at all.

This, Ralph told her, was Maltese Sal's favoured racetrack. 'New Tarmac, innit?' He slid an appreciative boot over the smooth surface.

They had jumped from the back of the van and now stood below the flyover that led out to the industrial park, watching as money changed hands a few yards away. Tattooed men from mobile homes just visible beneath the pylons sat in the front of gleaming trucks with oversized wheels, mobile phones clamped to their ears, the ever-present cigarettes held between stubby, grimy fingers. They peeled notes from huge wads of cash, spitting into their palms as they shook hands, their cold, glinting eyes betraying the lack of trust and friendship in the gesture. The Maltese side, shorter, sleeker than the travellers, in scruffier vehicles but with immaculate clothes, were on one side of the road, the travellers on the other. Cowboy John leant against a van, puffing meditatively at a roll-up, pointing at the horses and chatting to someone in the passenger seat. A boy Sarah didn't recognise sat bareback on a black horse, legs thrust forward, guiding the animal in and out of the cars on a halter.

A short distance away, Maltese Sal checked the buckles on his horse's harness, chiding it when it fidgeted, a broad smile revealing one gold tooth, a cap rammed on his closely cropped head. He was laughing, berating his opponents' horse, mimicking the unfortunate angle of its legs, the supposed narrowness of its chest.

'They hate him,' Ralph observed, lighting another cigarette. 'He got caught with someone's missus last year. They've made it a seller.'

'A seller?'

Ralph looked at her as if she was stupid. 'If he loses he has to give up the mare.'

'Won't that make him mad?' she said.

Ralph spat on the floor. 'Nah. The Pikeys know all Sal's lot are mob-handed. And they're tooled up, just in case. But I reckon we'll stay on Vicente's truck – case we need to get away in a hurry.' He laughed. He always relished the prospect of trouble.

The men were climbing back into the trucks and Sarah shivered, unsure whether from nerves or excitement. Above them, supported by giant, rough-cast concrete pillars, traffic thundered on the flyover, the beginning of the rush-hour evident in the increasing density of vehicles.

Someone whistled, a dog barked, then Ralph was pulling her to the slip-road. Three trucks reversed, headed back the way they had come, in a pre-agreed formation. They disappeared, ready to join the traffic on the flyover, and then it was just the men standing on the slip-road, and the horses, steam blowing through their nostrils, their hooves picking daintily at the road surface, held firmly at the head by their handlers. Behind the grey mare, Sal crouched in his bright red sulky, legs braced, reins held loosely in one hand, glancing behind him repeatedly, waiting for the signal. His presence was magnetic. Sarah found herself watching him, his wide, confident grin, his eyes, which seemed to know everything. Ralph, beside her, lit another cigarette, muttering under his breath: 'Oh, yes, oh, yes, oh, yes . . .'

All eyes were on the traffic on the flyover now. The men muttered to each other. Still the traffic came.

'I bet Donny's got pulled over. He's got no bloody car tax.' Someone laughed, breaking the tension.

And then there was a shout, and above them, just visible, one of the travellers' pick-ups, its hazard lights flashing through the safety barrier. 'Go!' someone shouted. 'Go!' And, in one fluid movement, the two horses were on the slip-road, sulky wheels almost touching, their two drivers hunched forward, whips held high as they urged them along the emptied stretch of road.

'Go, Sal!' Ralph was yelling, his voice high with excitement. 'Go!' And Sarah felt him grab her sleeve, pulling her towards Vicente's pick-up, which was already revving, preparing to follow the racing horses already almost out of sight.

He shoved her aboard, and then she heard the horns of the stationary vehicles, the screech of rubber, her hands wrapped around the bars on the back windscreen, the wind in her ears.

'He's doing it!' Ralph was yelling! 'He's ahead!' And she saw the grey mare, her unnatural trot too fast, an unearthly pace. She could see the grimace of the traveller, his whip hand raised as he pushed his own horse faster, his expletive as it broke, briefly, into a canter, incurring a roar of protest from the Maltese.

'Go on, Sal! *Muller* him!'

Her heart was in her mouth, her eyes on the brave little

mare whose every sinew strained with the effort of maintaining such a speed at the trot, her little hooves barely
touching the road surface. *Go on*, she willed her, afraid that
she would lose and be handed over to the travellers, lost for
ever in some ragwort-strewn wasteland with the black-and-
white cobs and broken supermarket trolleys. She felt a silent
communion with the little horse, fighting for her own survival
amid the shouting, the sweat and the noise. *Go on*.

And then, with a shout of victory, it was over, the horses
off the flyover as swiftly as they had claimed it, the trucks
peeling away behind them, the cars surging forward in bad-
tempered confusion. And Vicente's truck was swerving left off
the slip-road, Sarah's knees and arms bumping painfully
against the truck's sides as they hit a pothole, her schoolbag
open and her books, pages flapping, flying. She lifted her head
and saw Sal, leaping from the sulky even as the little horse
kept going, his hand high in triumph, a colleague greeting
him with a high-five. She and Ralph were laughing, clutching
each other, infected by the madness and by Sal's victory.

The grey mare would be safe for a few weeks more. Safe
at Cowboy John's.

'I had a nicker on that!' Ralph was yelling, face flushed,
grabbing at her school blazer. 'Come on! Sal said if he won
he'd buy us all breakfast when we get back to the yard.'

Papa was there when she returned after school. He was in
Boo's stable, bending and dipping as he brought a mirrored
shine to the horse's quarters. Sarah could hear his fierce
breathing even before she saw him, and saw the T of sweat
along his carefully pressed shirt before he turned; Papa did
nothing if he couldn't do it properly. It was all those years
of military training.

As she entered the arches, Cowboy John was leaning against
his stable door, drinking a mug of varnish-coloured tea. He

never seemed to put much effort into anything but somehow the yard always got done. 'Circus Girl's here,' he observed, and Ralph, leaning on the rump of a slab-headed black-and-white cob, winked at her.

'Bus was late,' she said, resting her bag on a bale of hay.

'She forgot her tutu,' said Cowboy John.

'You got your maths test back yet?' Papa asked.

'Twelve out of twenty.' Sarah waved the book, hoping he wouldn't see the tyremarks and dirt on the cover. She caught Ralph's eye; he suffered a sudden fit of coughing.

'Did I tell you Maltese Sal bought and sold that black horse today, the one he got from the Italians over at Northolt?'

Her grandfather rested his hand on Boo's chest, and the horse moved backwards obediently. 'The pacer?' he asked. Maltese Sal was forever buying and selling trotting horses.

Cowboy John nodded. 'Man came to pick it up this afternoon.'

'He'll be lucky to get that horse out of a walk,' said Ralph. 'Runs like a bow-legged cowboy in stilettos.'

'Way he sold it, it was Bucephalus.' Cowboy John mimed the shaking of his head. 'Horse came out of its stable like it was ready for the Kentucky Derby.'

'But how—' Sarah began.

'He stuck a marble in its ear,' interrupted Ralph.

Cowboy John hit the boy with his hat. 'You been listening in on me?'

'You've told everyone who came past this morning,' Ralph protested.

'That horse came out shaking his head something wild. Money he got for it, he bought two more. They're coming Saturday. Both for racing.'

Sarah knew Papa disapproved of the old dealers' tricks. He was pretending not to listen.

Ralph removed a piece of gum from his mouth and stuck

it on his stable door. 'Do you remember when you sold that old palomino to the Italian bloke over on the marshes and stuck a piece of ginger in its arse to liven it up?'

Cowboy John's hat shot out again. 'I didn't know how it got in there!' he insisted. 'There was nothing wrong with that horse. Nothing. You kids are slandering me. You're lucky I even let you stay in this yard, the badmouthing I get from you. You should be at school. Why the Sam Hill you never go to school . . .' He stalked off towards the gates, muttering to himself, breaking off to yell at a middle-aged redhead walking past the gates. 'Mrs Parry! Was that you I saw on television last night?' The woman continued walking. He removed his hat and waved it for her attention, as he stood beside the gates. 'It was! I knew it was you!'

She checked her speed, turned her head a little, perplexed. Ralph groaned.

'On *Britain's Next Top Model*! There – see? You're smiling. I knew it was you. You want to buy some eggs? I got some beautiful avocados too. A whole tray of 'em, if you like. No? You come back soon, you hear? When that modelling contract's finished.'

He was grinning when he came back to the railway arch. 'That Mrs Parry from the post office, she is *fiiine*.' He dragged out the word in appreciation. 'If she was twenty years younger . . .'

'. . . she could hand you your Zimmer frame,' said Ralph.

Papa didn't say anything. He was brushing again, hard, brisk strokes: every so often Boo had to brace himself against the pressure.

Cowboy John took another swig of his tea.

Sarah loved afternoons like this, when the horses stood sleepily in the sunshine, and the men traded good-natured insults. Here, Nana didn't feel like a gaping absence. This was where she fitted in.

'Girl, I keep telling your grandpa. This is why he ain't never going to get himself a new girlfriend. Look at that!' She followed his gaze to where Papa's brush swept briskly down Boo's gleaming flank. Cowboy John held out his hands and slid them dreamily to one side, winking at her. 'I tell you, Capitaine, women like a slow hand, *gentle* treatment.'

Papa looked balefully at him, then returned to his task.

'And there was me thinking the French were meant to be great lovers,' said Cowboy John.

Her grandfather shrugged, banging the dust from his brush. 'John, if you cannot yet tell the difference between loving and grooming, it is no wonder your horses look so confused.'

The boys hooted. Sarah smirked, even though she knew she was not meant to grasp the joke, then straightened her face when Papa told her to run for her hat.

The sun was sinking, edging low towards the railway bridge and the flyover beyond. Rush-hour was under way, and around the park queues of traffic waited, the drivers briefly diverted by what they could see on the grass.

Sarah didn't notice them. Papa stood beside her, his arms outstretched, helping to build the contained energy that would propel Boo upwards. 'Sit up straight,' he murmured. 'It's all from the seat, Sarah. Keep your leg on . . . but still, still, ride him from the seat, *comme ça.*'

She was sweating with effort. She could see Papa's whip out of the corner of her left eye – it never touched Boo's fine bay coat – could feel the power building beneath her. She sat as still as she could, her legs resting lightly against his sides, eyes looking straight through his pointed ears. '*Non,*' he said again. 'Forward. Let him go forward. Now try again.'

They had been working on *piaffe* for almost forty minutes, and the sweat had stuck her school shirt to her back, the sun beating down on her hot head. Forwards at a trot, then halt,

then trot again, trying to build up the energy so that he would
trot on the spot, the rhythmic gait that would be the starting
point for the more elaborate moves – which Papa had told
her repeatedly she was not yet good enough to progress to.

Some months ago, when she had begged, he had shown
her from the ground how Boo could be persuaded to *levade*,
balancing on his hind legs, as if rearing, and she was desperate
to try the movements that would bring him off the ground
– the *courbette*, the *capriole* – from atop him. But Papa would
not let her. Groundwork, again and again and again. Certainly
no *levade* in a public park with people watching. What was
she trying to do? Tell Boo he was a circus horse? She knew
he was right but sometimes it was so boring. Like being stuck
in the starting gates for ever.

'Can we break for a bit? I'm so hot.'

'How are you going to achieve if you don't practise? No.
Continue. He's getting it.'

She thrust her lower lip forward in mute protest. There
was no point in arguing with Papa, but she felt as though
they had been doing this same thing for hours. She thought
of the little grey mare that morning. At least she had got to
go somewhere.

'Papa—'

'Concentrate! Stop talking and focus on your horse.'

Two children ran by, one shouting, 'Ride him, cowboy!'
She kept her gaze between Boo's ears. The narrow gap
between them was slick with sweat.

'And forwards. Reward him.' She allowed the horse to move
forwards, then half halted again, attempting to bring him back
with a shifting of weight, the gentlest pressure on the reins.

'*Non!* You are tipping forwards again.'

She collapsed on to the horse's neck, letting out a wail.
'I'm *not!*'

'You are sending him conflicting signals,' said Papa, his

face creased with frustration. 'How can he understand if your legs tell him one thing and your seat the opposite?'

She bit her lip. Why are we doing this? she wanted to shout. I'm never going to be good enough for what you want. This is just stupid.

'Sarah – concentrate.'

'I *am* concentrating. He's too hot and bothered. He's not listening to me any more.'

'He knows you don't listen to me. That is why he doesn't listen to you.'

It was always her. Never the horse.

'You sit there *comme ça*, you are teaching him not to listen.'

She was too hot. 'Fine,' she said, throwing her reins into one hand, and sliding off. 'If I'm so useless, you do it.'

She stood on the hard ground, stunned at her own defiance. She rarely contradicted Papa.

He glared at her, his eyes burning so that, like a disgraced dog, she found hers dropping to her feet.

'*Je m'excuse*,' he said abruptly.

She waited, unsure what he was going to do. But he walked briskly to Boo's side and, with a slight grunt of effort, placed his left foot in the stirrup and sprang upwards, lowering himself gently on to the horse's back. Boo's ears flickered backwards; he was startled by the unfamiliar weight. Papa said nothing to her. He crossed his stirrups over the front of the saddle, so that his legs hung long and loose. Then, his back impossibly straight, his hands apparently doing nothing, he walked Boo once in a large circle, then prompted the horse into action.

Sarah, her hand at her brow, shielding her eyes from the sun, watched as her grandfather, a man she had never seen on a horse, asked, with almost imperceptible movements, for something the horse did not know how to give, and Boo, his mouth white with foam, lifted his legs higher and higher while he moved nowhere. Sarah's breath stilled in her throat. Papa was like the men on the DVD. He did everything while seeming to do nothing. She found that her fists had clenched and thrust them into her pockets. Boo was concentrating so hard now that sweat ran in glossy rivulets down his muscled neck. Still her grandfather appeared to do nothing, while Boo's hooves beat a rhythmic tattoo on the cracked brown earth. Suddenly he switched to the rocking motion, the stationary canter of the *terre à terre*. And finally, out of nowhere, she heard a 'Hup!' and as she stepped back, Boo rose on his back legs, the front pair folded neatly under him, the muscles of his quarters quivering as he struggled to maintain his balance. *Levade*.

Someone shouted, 'Woo-hoo!' from the pavement, and there was a collective murmur of concern from some people behind her. And then he was down. And Papa was swinging his leg over the back of the saddle, the only sign of his exertion the dark shadows on his blue shirt.

He murmured something to the horse, running a hand slowly down his neck, thanking him, then handed her the reins. She wanted to ask how he had done it, why he no longer rode if he could ride like that. But he spoke before she could work out what to say.

'He's trying too hard,' he said dismissively. 'He's too tense. We must take him back a stage so that he worries less about his balance.'

A group of women were sitting on the grass, watching from a safe distance. They were eating ice lollies, their skirts above their knees, revealing sunburnt legs.

'Do it again,' one called.

Sarah was still a little stunned by what she had seen. 'Do you want me to keep trying?' she asked.

Papa ran his hand down Boo's neck. 'No,' he said quietly. Then he rubbed his own face, his hand coming away slick with sweat. 'No. He's tired.' She let out the reins and Boo stretched his neck gratefully.

'Mount up. We'll walk home,' he said.

'There's an ice-cream van over there,' she said hopefully, but he didn't seem to hear her.

'Don't feel too bad,' he said, as he walked. 'Sometimes . . . sometimes I ask too much. He is young . . . you are young . . .' He touched her hand, and Sarah realised that that was as close an admission as she would get that he had been wrong.

They walked once round the perimeter of the park to allow Boo's muscles to stretch and relax, then headed down the footpath to the park gates. Papa was apparently lost in thought, and Sarah didn't know what to say. She kept seeing her grandfather riding. He had looked like someone she had never seen before. Papa had been one of the youngest riders at Le Cadre Noir, she knew. Her nana had told her that only twenty-two were allowed to wear the black uniform with the gold braid that marked them out as masters of their art. Most had already represented their country at international level – in dressage, cross-country or show-jumping – but Papa had done it the hard way: he had risen up through the ranks of cavalry until finally the son of a peasant farmer from Toulon had been accepted, as one of the élite, into the classical school.

When she had first seen him, Nana had told Sarah, gazing at the photograph of them together, she had thought him so handsome on his horse that her heart had stalled and she had thought she might faint. She didn't even like horses, but she had travelled to watch him every day, standing at the front of the public auditorium, lost in contemplation of the man who was himself lost in concentration of something she couldn't understand.

That was what Nana saw, Sarah thought, remembering how he had seemed just to sit there, and Boo had understood, as if by telepathy, what he was being asked for. She had seen magic.

With a nod and a wave to the gateman, who never minded them, they walked up the road towards home, Boo's hooves clattering on the tarmac, his legs moving heavily.

Finally, as they crossed the main road towards the stables, Papa broke the silence. 'John told me he is thinking of selling up.'

He only referred to John by his name, rather than as 'the mad cowboy', if it was serious. 'But where would we put Boo?' she asked.

'He says we don't have to go anywhere else. The yard is to be sold as a going concern.'

Barely a month went by when Cowboy John wasn't offered money to move out of the yard, sometimes vast amounts, sums that made him giggle they were so ridiculous. He had always refused, asked the would-be buyer to explain where he was meant to put his horses, his cats, his hens.

Papa shook his head. 'He says someone close by is interested, and that nothing will change. I don't like it.' He paused to wipe his face, seeming distracted. 'We got the eggs, eh?'

'I told you we did, Papa. They're at the yard.'

'It's this heat,' he said. His collar was dark with sweat. If anything, it was worse than it had been when he was riding. He reached up to the horse's neck as if for support, and ran a hand along his mane, murmuring to him.

When she thought back, she decided she should have noticed then how his mood changed, how he failed to correct Boo when he wouldn't stand quietly at the kerb – he always insisted that a horse stood four-square and quiet when told to halt. Two lorries drove past and the driver of one made a rude gesture. Papa had his back to her so she returned it. Some men liked to believe that girls rode horses for the wrong reasons.

They crossed into the quieter streets, the chestnut trees offering welcome shade. Boo stretched out, pushing at her grandfather's back, as if for attention, but Papa didn't seem to feel it. He rubbed his face again, then his arm. 'Omelette tonight,' he said. '*Omelette aux fines herbes.*'

'I'll do it,' Sarah said. They were crossing the road that led back to the yard, and she held up a hand to thank the driver who had slowed for them. 'We could have a salad too.'

Then Papa let go of the rein he had been holding. 'You take . . . egg,' he said, and screwed up his eyes.

'What?'

But he wasn't listening to her. 'Time to sit . . .'

'Papa?' She glanced at the waiting car. They were still in the middle of the road.

'All gone,' he murmured.

She couldn't work out what he was doing.

'Papa,' she cried, 'we need to get across.'

Boo was fussing, his hooves kicking up sparks on the cobbles, his head jerking back. In front, Sarah's grandfather began to sit down, as if he was folding himself on to a bed, his body angled slightly to one side. The man in the car sounded his horn once, impatiently, then seemed to grasp something was wrong and peered through the windscreen.

Everything slowed down around Sarah. She threw herself off the horse, landing lightly on her feet. 'Papa!' she yelled, pulling at his arm as she hung on to the reins.

His eyes closed, and he seemed to be thinking hard about something going on deep inside his head so that he couldn't hear her, no matter how loudly she shouted. His face had sagged on one side, as if someone was pulling it, and this strange crumpling in a man she had only ever known as held together and contained frightened her.

'Papa! Get up!' The shouting made Boo dance and pull against her.

'He all right?' someone bellowed from across the road.

He wasn't. She could see he wasn't.

Then, as the man climbed out of the car and walked briskly to her grandfather's side, she clung to the wheeling horse and shrieked, her voice shrill with fear: 'John! John! Help me!' The last thing she remembered was Cowboy John, his normal saunter vanished as he took in the sight in front of him, shouting something she couldn't hear as he ran stiffly down the road towards her.

The cleaner moved slowly up the linoleum, the twin brushes of his polisher humming efficiently. Cowboy John sat on the hard plastic seat beside the girl and checked his watch for the forty-seventh time. Almost four hours, they had sat here now. Four hours, and only one nurse stopping by to make sure Sarah was okay.

He should have been back at the yard by now. The animals would be hungry, and he had been forced to lock the gates, so likely tomorrow he'd be getting seven shades of hell from Maltese Sal and the kids about not being able to get in.

But he couldn't leave her. She was just a kid herself, for Chrissakes. She was sitting very still, her hands clasped tightly in her lap, her bleached face a mask of intense concentration, as if she was willing the old man to be well again. 'You okay there?' he asked. 'You want me to get you a coffee?'

The cleaner passed them slowly. He allowed himself a brief glance at Cowboy John's hat, then headed steadily for the cardiac ward.

'Nope,' she said, then added quietly, 'Thank you.'

'He'll be okay,' he said, for the tenth time. 'Your grandpa's tough as old boots. You know that.'

She nodded, but without conviction.

'I bet you someone'll come out any minute now to tell us.'

A slight hesitation. Then she nodded again.

And they waited, ignored by the nurses, who whisked past in plastic aprons, listening to the distant beep and hum of machinery. John fidgeted, wanting an excuse to get up and distract himself. He couldn't get the old man's face out of his mind: the anguished, furious look in his eyes, the jaw still rigid, as he went down, clearly mortified that something like this should overtake him.

'Miss Lachapelle?'

Sarah had been so deep in thought that she jolted when the doctor spoke. 'Yes,' she said. 'Is he okay?'

'Are you . . . family?' The doctor's eyes were on John now.

'As good as,' he said, standing.

The doctor glanced back towards the ward. 'Strictly speaking, I can't discuss this with anybody but—'

'I'm as good as you'll get,' John said slowly. 'The Captain has no other living family, just Sarah here. And I am his oldest friend.'

The doctor sat on a seat beside them. He addressed his words to Sarah. 'Your grandfather has suffered a cerebral haemorrhage. A stroke. Do you know what that is?'

She nodded. 'Sort of.'

'He's stable, but he's a little muddled. He can't talk or do anything for himself.'

'But he'll be okay?'

'He's stable, as I said. The next twenty-four hours are pretty important.'

'Can I see him?'

The doctor looked at John.

'I think we'd both like to know he's okay,' John said firmly.

'He's hooked up to a lot of machinery. You may get a bit of a shock.'

'She's tough. Like her grandpa.'

The doctor checked his watch. 'Okay. Come with me.'

⋆ ⋆ ⋆

Jesus Christ, the old man was in a sorry state. He seemed suddenly thirty years older than he was, tubes up his nose and taped to his skin, his face grey and sagging. John had raised a hand to his mouth involuntarily. Around him machines drew neon lines, calling to each other with soft, irregular beeps.

'What they doing?' he asked, to break the silence.

'Just monitoring his heart rate, blood pressure, that kind of thing.'

'And he's okay?'

The doctor's response was smooth and, John suspected, meaningless. 'Like I said, the next twenty-four hours are pretty crucial. You did well getting help so quickly. It's vital in stroke cases.'

The two men stood in silence as Sarah moved to the edge of the bed and sat on the chair beside it cautiously, as if she was afraid of disturbing him.

'You can talk to him if you want, Sarah,' the doctor said softly. 'Let him know you're here.'

She never cried. Not one tear. Her slim hand reached out to touch his, and held it for a moment. But her jaw was tight. Her grandfather's granddaughter.

'He knows she's here,' John said, and stepped outside the curtain to give her some privacy.

It was dark when they left. John had been outside for a while, pacing the ambulance drop-off point, smoking, ignoring the dark looks of the nurses who walked past. 'Sweetheart,' he told one, 'you should thank me. I'm just keeping you guys in a job.' He needed his smokes. The Captain had always been strong, had given the impression that he'd be there, proud and unbending, solid as a tree long after John had gone elsewhere. Seeing him there, lying helpless in that bed like a baby, nurses wiping him and fixing the drool on his face – well, it made him shudder.

Then he saw her standing by the sliding doors with her hands thrust deep into her pockets, shoulders hunched. She didn't notice him at first.

'Here,' he said, realising she had brought nothing with her. 'Take my jacket. You're cold.'

She shook her head, locked in private misery.

'You'll be no good to the Captain with a chill,' he said. 'Besides, he'll call me all manner of them sorry French swear words if I don't take care of you.'

She looked up at him. 'John, did you know my grandfather could ride – I mean, really ride?'

John was briefly unbalanced. He took a theatrical step backwards. 'Ride? Of course I did. Can't say I agree with all that prancing around but, hell, yes, I knew. Your granddaddy's a horseman.'

She tried to smile, but he could see it was an effort. She accepted the old denim jacket he thrust over her shoulders, and they walked like that, the old black cowboy and the girl, all the way to the bus stop.

Five

'For judging an unbroken colt, the only criterion, obviously, is the body, for no clear signs of temper are yet to be detected'

Xenophon, *On Horsemanship*

The lights were on in the house. She stared as she killed the ignition, trying to remember whether she had left them on that morning. She never left the curtains open: it advertised that no one was in. Except someone was.

'Oh,' she said, as she opened the front door. 'You were supposed to come weeks ago.' She sounded ungracious; she hadn't meant to.

Mac was standing in the hallway, holding an armful of photographic paper. 'Sorry. Work went a bit mental. Things came up. I did leave a message on your phone this afternoon to say I'd be over.'

She rummaged for it in her bag. 'Oh,' she said, still electrified by his presence. 'I didn't get it.'

They stood facing each other. Mac, there, in her house, their house. His hair slightly different, a T-shirt she didn't recognise. He looked better, she saw, with a pang – better for having spent the best part of a year without her.

'I needed some of my equipment,' he said, gesturing behind him, 'except it isn't where I thought it was.'

'I moved it,' she said, thinking as she spoke that this, too, sounded unpleasant, as if she had been determined to remove all trace of him. 'It's upstairs, in the study.'

'Ah. That'd be why I couldn't find it.' He tried to smile.

'I needed to have some of my files down here . . . and . . .' She tailed off. *And it was too painful having all your stuff around. Occasionally, just occasionally I had the urge to smash it with a large hammer.*

She wished she had been prepared for him. She had worked late, drinking too much coffee, even though she knew it would be subtracted in lost hours of sleep later. Her makeup had long rubbed off her face. She suspected she looked pale, worn.

'I'll nip upstairs, then,' he said. 'I won't keep you.'

'No – no! Don't rush. I've got to . . . I need to get some milk anyway. You find what you need.'

I'm sorry, she had said. Mac, I'm so sorry.

For what? His voice had been so calm, so reasonable. You just told me nothing happened. He had looked at her in incomprehension. You really think I'm leaving because of him, don't you?

She was out of the house before she heard his protest. She knew he was being polite. He probably imagined she was late because she had been with Conor. Although he wouldn't say as much. That had never been Mac's style.

She didn't often use this supermarket, which was at the rougher end of the neighbourhood; it was the kind of place where occasionally someone managed to push out a trolley without paying and everyone else in the shop cheered. But she was in her car before she knew what she was doing, had turned off her phone out of fear or bloody-mindedness. She just wanted to get away from that house.

She was standing in the dairy aisle, trying to avoid a mumbling vagrant talking to the frozen yoghurt and her thoughts were humming so hard that she had forgotten why she was there.

Mac, the most unsuitable marriage material her parents
had ever seen, the feckless enigma of a man she had married,
the other battered half of a union that had nearly destroyed
them both, was back in their home.

She had refused to think about him for so long, and he
had made it easy. Sometimes it was as if he had dropped off
the face of the earth. During the last year of their marriage
he had been away so much she had seemed to be single
anyway. When he was there she had found she was so angry
about everything that solitude had seemed easier. Take your
stuff and go, she willed Mac, feeling an uncomfortable echo
of the darker days that had only just receded. I don't want
to deal with any of this. I don't want to feel even the slightest
hint of what I felt last year. Do what you have to do and
leave me in peace.

She was dragged from her thoughts by a commotion in
the next aisle towards the checkout. She walked to the end
of the cereals where she could see what was going on.

An overweight African man had hold of a teenage girl. She
couldn't have been much more than sixteen and was pulling
hard against him, her hair flopping over her face, but he had
her upper arms in a remorseless grip.

'Is everything all right?' Natasha asked, emerging from
behind the porridge oats. She had addressed the girl; the
scene was discomfiting. 'I'm a lawyer,' she explained. It was
then that she spotted the man's security badge.

'There you go. You'll need one of them down the nick,' the
checkout woman said. 'It'll save you a phone call.'

'I wasn't stealing.' The girl shook her arm again. Her face
was pale under the harsh neon lighting, her eyes huge and
wary.

'Hmph. So the fish-fingers just leapt out of the freezer and
landed in your jacket?'

'I just put them there while I went to get some other stuff.

Look, please, let me go. I promise you I wasn't stealing.' She was close to tears. She didn't have the mouthy defiance of the kids Natasha usually saw.

'Walked straight past me, she did,' said the checkout woman, 'like she thought I was stupid.'

'Perhaps she could just pay for them now and go,' Natasha suggested.

'Her?' The big man shrugged. 'She ain't got no money.'

'They never do,' said the woman.

'I must have dropped it.' The girl was peering at the floor. 'I won't come back, okay? Just let me look for my money before someone else finds it.'

'How much are they?' Natasha said, reaching for her purse. 'The fish-fingers?'

The checkout woman raised her eyebrows.

Natasha was tired. She just wanted to go home without the image of a sobbing girl pinned by a security guard on her mind. 'Let's assume this is an honest mistake. I'll pay for them.' The two looked at her as if she was somehow in on the scam until she held out a five-pound note. And then – after an infinitesimal pause – the checkout woman rang up the fish-fingers and handed her the change. 'I don't want to see your thieving little face in here again,' she said, jabbing a nicotine-stained finger. 'Got it?'

The girl didn't answer. She shrugged off the security guard and hurried for the door, the fish-fingers in her hand. It opened automatically, released her, and she was gone, swallowed by the dark.

'Look at that.' The security guard's skin shone under the strip-lighting. 'Never even said thank you.'

'She was thieving, you know. We had her in here last week. Except that time we couldn't prove it.'

'If it makes you feel any better, that's probably the best meal she'll have this week,' Natasha said. She paid for the milk, glanced at the vagrant, who was now arguing with the washing powders, and went out into the night street.

She had walked only a few paces when the girl popped up beside her. If she had been less preoccupied, she might have jumped, would have assumed some dark purpose, but the girl thrust out her hand. 'I found some of it,' she said. 'I think it fell out of my pocket.' On her palm Natasha could just make fifty pence and some coppers. Later she remembered that it was curiously calloused for a girl of her age.

But she didn't want to get any more involved than she already was so she carried on walking. 'Keep your money,' she said. She opened her car door. 'It's fine.'

'I wasn't stealing,' the girl insisted.

Natasha turned. 'You always buy your supper at eleven o'clock at night?'

The girl shrugged. 'I had to visit someone in hospital. I only just got home and there was no food.'

'Where do you live?' The girl was younger than Natasha had originally thought. Perhaps no more than thirteen or fourteen.

'Sandown.'

Natasha glanced at the monolithic, sprawling estate, its tower blocks visible even from this street. It had a reputation throughout the borough. She didn't know why she did it. Perhaps she just hated the look of that place in the dark. Perhaps she wasn't ready to go home to Mac or, worse, to his absence. Around her the city seethed: cars honked in the distance; on the corner two men were having a heated disagreement, their voices lifting in mutual outrage.

I don't think you're as tough as you come across, Conor Deans had said, his voice dropping. *I think there's a whole different Natasha Macauley in there*.

Oh, I'm full of surprises, she had replied. It had sounded, even to her, like a challenge.

The two men were fighting now, rapid, swinging kicks and punches. The energy in the atmosphere transformed, sucked out into a vortex of violence. There were a few yelled expletives, then footsteps as other shadowy men ran towards them. She saw the glint of an iron bar.

'You shouldn't be out by yourself this late at night,' Natasha said, and walked briskly to her car. 'Come on. I'll drop you home.' The girl studied her for a moment, her work suit, her smart shoes, then glanced at the car. Perhaps she reasoned that anyone driving a vehicle as staid and sensible as an old Volvo wasn't likely to abduct her.

'The passenger door lock's broken,' Natasha said, 'if that makes you feel any better . . .'

The girl sighed, as if nothing she could do or say might be of concern to her, and climbed in.

Natasha had started to regret this rash course of action almost before she pulled into the estate car park. Groups of youths hung around in amorphous gatherings, some breaking away to do wheelies on bikes, others throwing down cigarette butts and catcalling insults to each other. They stopped briefly, apparently registering the unfamiliar car as she backed into a parking space.

'You never told me your name,' Natasha said.

She hesitated. 'Jane.'

'Have you lived here long?'

She nodded. 'It's all right,' she said quietly, and made to open the door.

Natasha wanted to go home then, to her secure, friendly living room. To the peace of her comforting house, nice music, a glass of red wine. Her own world. Experience told her she should turn the car around and drive away. Such estates were these youths' domain; some would ever rarely have ventured more than a mile or two outside their confines, and they had a searing, almost feral interest in what went on in their 'manor'. Natasha knew that her car and her suit marked her out as middle class in a world much harder, much tougher than the one several streets away. But then she looked at the pale, thin girl beside her. What kind of person would turf her out without seeing her to the safety of her door?

She tucked her wedding ring surreptitiously into her back pocket, her credit cards with it. If her purse was snatched all they would get was some cash.

'It's okay,' Jane said, watching her. 'I know them.'

'I'll see you in,' Natasha said, in the detached, professional voice she employed with all young clients. Then, when the girl didn't look overjoyed: 'It's fine. I won't say anything about what happened. It's late and I want to make sure you get in safely.'

'Just to the door,' the girl said.

They climbed out of the car, Natasha carrying herself just a little more determinedly upright than usual, her heels clacking officiously on the gum-pocked walkways.

As they approached the stairwell, a boy wheeled past. Natasha tried not to flinch. The girl did not look up. 'That your granddad's new bird, is it, Sarah?' He pulled his hood over his head and wheeled away, laughing, his face shadowed under the guttering street-light.

'Sarah?'

The lifts were out of order so they walked up three flights. The stairwell was depressingly familiar: graffiti-ridden, urine-scented, strewn with abandoned takeaway boxes still emanating the odours of stale fat or fish. Along one corridor music thumped through open windows, and below, a car alarm had gone off. It took Natasha a second to register that it wasn't hers.

'I'm just here,' Sarah said, pointing. 'Thanks for the lift.'

Afterwards, Natasha wasn't sure why she didn't just leave.

Perhaps it was the fake name. Perhaps the girl was just a little too keen to get rid of her. But she kept going, following the girl, who hurried in front. And then they reached the door and she stopped. It was the stunned quality of her stance that made Natasha realise the door was not open to welcome her home. It had been crow-barred. The splintered wood by the lock pointed into a flat in which all the lights blazed.

They stood motionless for a moment. Then Natasha stepped forward and pushed the door wide. 'Hello?' she said. She didn't know what she thought the intruders would do – greet her back? She glanced at Sarah, whose hand had gone to her mouth.

Whoever had been in had long gone. The door opened directly on to a small hallway through which you could see the living room, which was immaculate enough to throw any discrepancy into sharp relief. A gaping absence on a television stand. Kitchen-cupboard doors flung open. Drawers pulled from a little bureau, a frame smashed on the floor. It was this Sarah went to first: she picked it up and tenderly brushed broken glass from the picture. It was a black-and-white photograph of a couple in the 1960s. Suddenly Sarah seemed very young and small.

'I'll ring the police,' Natasha said, pulling her phone from her bag and switching it on. Mac, she saw guiltily, had tried to call.

'There's no point,' Sarah said wearily. 'They never care about anything that happens up here. Mrs O'Brien's flat was done last week and the police said it wasn't even worth them coming up.' She was picking her way around the flat now, disappearing into rooms and coming back.

Natasha went into the hallway and secured the front door with the chain. Below, she could still hear the youths, and tried not to worry about the car. 'What's missing?' she said, following the girl. This was not the chaotic home she had perhaps expected. This was a home with a few decent things, a home in which order mattered.

'The telly,' Sarah said, her bottom lip trembling. 'My DVD. The money for our holiday.' She appeared suddenly to remember something and bolted for one of the rooms. Natasha heard a door being opened, the sound of rummaging. Sarah emerged. 'They didn't get it,' she said, and for a moment there was a tiny smile. 'My papa's pension book.'

'Where are your parents, Sarah?'

'My mum doesn't live here. It's just me and my papa – my granddad,' she said awkwardly.

'Where is he?'

She hesitated. 'In hospital.'

'So who's looking after you?'

She said nothing.

'How long have you been on your own?'

'A couple of weeks.'

Natasha groaned inwardly. There was so much going on in her life, so many things she had to juggle, and she had brought this on herself. She should have walked out of the super-market with the pint of milk she hadn't even needed. She should have stayed at home and fought with her ex-husband.

She dialled her home number.

'Christ, Tash, where the bloody hell are you?' Mac exploded. 'How long does it take you to buy a pint of milk?'

'Mac,' she said carefully, 'I need you to meet me. Bring your tools. And my bag – I need my contacts book.'

It had taken Mac four years to renovate their house. In her parents' eyes, it had been his redeeming feature. He had done the plastering, the carpentry, pretty well everything but the roof and the brickwork. He had even had a hand in the design. He was good with his hands, as deft with power tools as he was with his camera. Natasha hadn't an artistic bone in her body, but he could see things long before they were there: the shape of a room, the composition of a view, or a photograph. It was as if he had a library of beautiful images in his head, just waiting to be translated into reality.

A new lock on a door was no problem, he told her, whistling through his teeth. Natasha had worked out pretty quickly that an emergency locksmith was beyond the girl's means, especially as she was still fretting about the holiday money. Mac had brought an old one with him, and had taken less than forty minutes to get it into place.

'Crista? It's Natasha.' And then, when she was met with blank silence, 'Natasha Macauley.'

'Natasha. Hi. Shouldn't this be the other way around?'

'I know. I've got a bit of an odd situation here. I need to find an emergency placement for a teenage girl.' She outlined the facts.

'We've got nothing,' Crista said. 'Absolutely nothing. We had fourteen UASCs – unaccompanied asylum seeking children – arrive in the borough yesterday morning and all our foster placements are full. I've spent all evening on the phones.'

'I—'

'And before you start with the Emergency Judicial Reviews, you might as well know the only place I'll be able to put her for the best part of tonight is the local police station. You may as well save your time and a judge's and take her straight there. We may be in a better position tomorrow but frankly I doubt it.'

When she went back into the living room, Mac had finished. He had brought an iron strip with him – God only knew where he kept all this stuff – and had screwed it to the door frame. 'Stop anyone getting in again,' he said, as he packed away the last of his tools.

Natasha smiled at him awkwardly, grateful for his practicality, for the fact that he had not issued one resentful word at being dragged out to do DIY in the middle of the night. Now he sat a few feet from Sarah on the sofa. He was examining her framed photographs – the first point of reference for Mac in anybody's home. 'So,' he was saying, 'this is your grandfather?'

'He used to be a captain,' she said. She had a balled-up tissue in her hand and her voice was low.

'That's a fantastic picture,' he said. 'Don't you think, Tash? Look at the muscles on that horse.'

He had a photographer's way of putting people at ease. There was almost nobody with whom he couldn't adopt an immediate and easy intimacy. Natasha tried to look impressed, but all she could think about was that she had to tell Sarah that her next bed would be in a police cell. 'Did you get a bag together?' she asked. 'School uniform?'

Sarah patted the holdall beside her. She seem a little uneasy, and Natasha had to remind herself that the girl did not know the people who had suddenly taken over her life. It was now half past midnight.

'Where are we taking you, then, young lady?' Mac asked, but addressed the question to Natasha.

Natasha took a breath. 'It's a bit difficult tonight. We have to put you in emergency accommodation until we can find somewhere a bit more suitable.'

They both looked at her expectantly.

'I've been on to the people I know and, unfortunately, there isn't much available. It's the time of night . . . and there's been a bit of an influx . . .'

'So, where are we going?' said Mac.

'I'm afraid that tonight we have to take you to the police station. Nothing to do with earlier,' Natasha assured her, as she saw Sarah's face blanch. 'It's just that there are no foster-carers available. Or hostel beds. It's unlikely to be for more than a few hours.'

'The police station?' said Mac, disbelievingly.

'There's nothing.'

'But you must have contacts. You spend your life doing this kind of stuff, forcing authorities to put children up.'

'And sometimes a few end up in police stations. It's only for a while, Mac. Crista says she'll be able to find her somewhere better by the morning. She'll meet us there.'

Sarah was shaking her head. 'I'm not staying in a police cell,' she said.

'Sarah, you can't stay here by yourself.'

'I'm not going.'

'Tash, this is ridiculous. She's fourteen. She can't go to a police cell.'

'It's the only option we have.'

'No, it's not. I told you. I'll be fine here,' Sarah said.

There was a long silence.

Natasha sat down, trying to think. 'Sarah, is there anyone else you know? Any schoolfriends you can stay with? Other relatives?'

'No.'

'Don't you have a number for your mum?'

Her face closed. 'She's dead. It's just me and Papa.'

Natasha turned to Mac, hoping he might understand. 'This isn't that unusual, Mac. It'll just be for one night. But we can't leave her here.'

'Then she can come back to ours.'

She was as nonplussed by his use of the possessive as by the idea behind it.

'I'm not going to dump a fourteen-year-old girl who's just been burgled in a police cell with God knows who,' he added.

'She'll be safe there,' Natasha said. 'It's not like she'll be in a cell with other people. They'll look after her.'

'I don't care,' he said.

'Mac, I can't take her home. It's against every kind of procedure, every kind of advice—'

'Fuck procedure,' he said. 'If procedure says it's right to stick a young girl in a police cell rather than in someone's warm, safe home for a night, then your procedure is fucking worthless.'

Mac rarely swore. It made Natasha realise he was deadly serious. 'Mac, we're not cleared as foster-carers. She'll be deemed vulnerable—'

'I'm CRB-checked. I had all that stuff done when I started teaching at the sixth-form college.'

Teaching?

He turned to Sarah. 'Would you be happier at . . . ours? We can ring your grandpa and let him know.'

She looked at Natasha, then back at him. 'I guess so.'

'Is there any other procedural reason why she can't stay?' He pronounced 'procedural' sarcastically, as if Natasha was searching for reasons to be difficult.

My job, Natasha wanted to say. *If it got round chambers that I was taking in waifs and strays my professional judgement would be called into question. And I don't know this girl. I found her shoplifting in a supermarket, and I'm still not convinced by her explanation.*

She stared at Sarah, trying not to think about Ahmadi, another young person who had seemed desperate, prompting her to go out on a limb. 'Give me five minutes,' she said.

She walked back into the girl's bedroom and rang Crista.

'I'm running late,' Crista said, before Natasha could speak. 'We've got a problem in one of the homes. I've got to pick someone up.'

'It's not that,' Natasha said quickly. 'Crista, I've got a situation here. The girl's refusing to go to a police station. My . . . Mac doesn't like the idea either. He – he's CRB-checked and thinks she should stay at ours instead.'

There was a lengthy silence.

'Crista?'

'Okay . . . Are you family friends of this girl? Do you know her parents? Can we say they asked you to be the foster-carer?'

'Not exactly.'

There was a long silence.

'You know her at all?'

'Met her tonight.'

'And you're . . . happy with this?'

'She seems . . .' Natasha paused, remembering the super-market '. . . a nice kid. Capable. She's just got no one at home and the flat's been burgled. It's . . . difficult.'

She could hear disbelief in Crista's silence. She had known her for almost four years and nothing would have suggested that Natasha might be capable of such a thing.

'Tell you what,' said Crista, eventually. 'Best advice I can give you is that we never had this conversation. There's nothing in the log yet. If you think she's okay, and you think she's safer with you guys, and you'd rather not spend half the night down the nick then frankly I don't need to know she exists until tomorrow. Call me then.'

Natasha flipped the phone shut. The girl's room was neat and orderly, more so than you'd expect from a girl of her age. There were pictures of horses everywhere, large, free-with-this-magazine galloping horses in full colour, small photographs of a girl who might have been her with a brown horse. The backdrops of green meadows and endless beaches were oddly incongruous against the landscape outside the double-glazed window.

She was tired and closed her eyes for a moment, then walked out into the living room. Mac and Sarah stopped talking and looked at her. Sarah's eyes, Natasha noticed, were shadowed blue with exhaustion and shock.

'You're coming to ours, one night,' she said, forcing a smile, 'and tomorrow morning we'll get you sorted out with a social worker.'

She had gone to sleep almost without a murmur. She had been silent during the journey, as if the precariousness of her position had only just dawned on her, and Mac, perhaps guessing this, had gone to some lengths to joke and reassure her. He was barely recognisable as the man she had last spoken to: sweet, considerate, gently spoken. It was painful to see the best of him directed at someone else. Easier when she could remind herself of his deficiencies.

Natasha said almost nothing as she drove, unsettled by the conflicting emotions that the presence of Mac and the girl had brought up in her. The night had become increasingly surreal. He was so familiar and yet, after such a short time, alien. As if he belonged somewhere else.

She had forgotten how nice he could be to young people – because, apart from her sister's children, they had been around so few.

'Is the spare room made up?' Mac asked, as she stood back to let them in.

'There are some boxes on the bed.' His books. Things she had sorted out on the days when she could face such a task. Mac was so absent-minded she had been afraid he would get them mixed up.

'I'll move them.' He gestured to Sarah. 'Why don't you find out if she'd like a drink?'

'Hot chocolate?' Natasha asked. 'Something to eat?' She felt stupid almost as soon as she'd said it, like an elderly aunt who had no idea what the Young People Liked These Days.

Sarah shook her head. She glanced through the open door at the living room. Mac had been sorting out his photographic stuff: boxes of it littered the floor. 'You have a nice house.'

Natasha saw it suddenly through the eyes of a stranger: large, plush, tastefully furnished. It spoke of high earnings, of things carefully chosen. She wondered if the girl could see the gaps, the clues to a man who had recently gone. 'Can I get you anything before you go up? Do you want me to . . . iron your uniform?'

'No, thank you.' She held her case a little closer to her.

'I'll show you upstairs then,' Natasha said. 'There's a bathroom on the landing you can have to yourself.'

'I hope you don't mind,' Mac said, as she came slowly down the stairs. 'I made up the sofa-bed in the study.'

She had half expected it; she could hardly turf him out at this hour of the morning, not after everything he'd done. Still, the prospect of having him sleeping under the same roof was oddly disturbing. 'Glass of wine?' she said. 'I know I need one.'

He let out a long sigh. 'Oh, yes.'

She poured two glasses and handed him one. He sat on the sofa and she kicked off her shoes, then folded her legs under her on the arm chair. It was a quarter to two.

'You'll have to sort everything out tomorrow, Mac,' she said. 'I've got court first thing.'

'Just tell me what to do.'

She observed absently that he couldn't have any work or he wouldn't have offered.

'Write down who I should call, or where I should drop her. I might let her sleep a bit – she's had quite a night.'

'We all have.'

'Nasty shock for her,' he said. 'Would have been hard even for an adult.'

'She handled it pretty well.'

'It was the right thing to do,' he said, waving at the stairs. 'It would have felt . . . wrong to leave her. With all that.'

'Yes.'

They sipped silently.

'So, how are you?' she said eventually, when the weight of not asking became too burdensome.

'Okay. You look well.'

She raised her eyebrows.

'Okay, tired, but good. The hair suits you.'

She fought the urge to touch it. Mac could always do this to her. 'What are you working on?' she asked, to change the subject.

'I'm doing three days' teaching a week, and commercial stuff the rest of the time. Portraiture. A bit of travel stuff. Not much, to be honest.'

'Teaching?' She struggled to keep the incredulity from her voice. 'I thought I'd misheard you.'

'I don't mind it. It pays the bills.'

Natasha digested this. For years he had refused to compromise. When the advertising work had dried up, he had scorned her idea that he teach. He hadn't wanted to be tied down, committed in a way that might stop him doing something more interesting at short notice. Even though it meant that his side of their finances was distinctly feast and famine, usually the latter.

Now he was Mac the Mature, Mac the Motivated. She felt cheated.

'Yup. I got a bit disillusioned with the whole commercial scene. Teaching's not as bad as I thought it would be. They seem to like me.'

Oh, surprise, Natasha thought.

'I'll keep doing it till I work out where I'm going. It doesn't pay brilliantly.'

She stiffened, braced herself as if for impact. 'And . . .'

'And at some point, Tash, we need to think about sorting out the house.'

She knew what he was saying. Permanent financial settlements. 'Meaning?'

'I don't know. But I can't live out of a suitcase for ever. It's been almost a year.'

She stared into her glass for a long time. So, this is it, she was thinking, but when she looked up at him she made sure her face was blank.

'You okay?'

She drank the last of her wine.

'Tash?'

'I can't think about this now,' she said abruptly. 'I'm too tired.'

'Sure. Tomorrow, perhaps.'

'I'm in court first thing. I told you.'

'I know. Just whenever you—'

'You can't just pop back and suddenly expect me to sell my home,' she snapped.

'Our home,' he corrected. 'And you can't pretend that this has come out of the blue.'

'For the last six months I haven't even known what country you were in.'

'You could have rung my sister if you needed to get in touch. But it suited you to sit here and let the dust settle.'

'The dust settle?' she echoed.

He sighed. 'I'm not trying to pick a fight, Tash. I'm just trying to get things straightened out. You're the one who was always on at me to get organised.'

'I'm quite aware of that. But I'm tired. I've got a big day ahead so, if it's okay by you, I'd like to divide up the marital assets some other time.'

'Fine. But I may as well tell you that I need to be in London from now on, with somewhere to stay. And unless you have a really good reason, I'd like to use the spare room until we've sorted things out.'

Natasha sat very still, making sure she had heard him correctly. 'Stay here?'

'Yes.'

'You are kidding?'

He raised a small smile. 'Living with me was that bad, huh?'

'But we're not together any more.'

'Nope. But I own half of this property and I need a roof over my head.'

'Mac, it'll be impossible.'

'I can handle it if you can. It's only for a few weeks, Tash. I'm sorry to play hardball, but if you don't like it you're welcome to rent somewhere yourself. As far as I'm concerned, I've given you the best part of a year with sole access. Now I'm entitled to something.' He shrugged. 'Come on. It's a big house. It'll only be a nightmare if we make it that way.'

He was disconcertingly relaxed. Happy, almost.

She wanted to swear at him.

She wanted to throw something at his head.

She wanted to slam the front door and book into a hotel. But there was a fourteen-year-old stranger in her home for whom she had just agreed to take joint responsibility.

Without another word, she stalked out and up the stairs to the bedroom that no longer felt like hers, wondering how hard it would be for estate agents to sell a house in which the owner's head had actually exploded.

Six

'It is the same with horses and with men: all distempers in the early stage are more easily cured than when they have become chronic and have been wrongly treated.'

Xenophon, *On Horsemanship*

The girl in the photograph was beaming up at her parents, who each held one of her hands as though they were about to lift her off the floor. 'Fostering,' the poster read. 'Make All the Difference.' Not her parents, then. In any case there was no family resemblance. They were probably all models, paid to act a happy family.

Suddenly irritated by the child's smile, Sarah shifted on her seat in the social worker's office, and glanced out of the window from where she could just make out the scrub and trees of the municipal park. She needed to get over to Sparepenny Lane. She knew Cowboy John would take care of Boo that morning if she didn't turn up, but it wasn't the same. He needed to go out. He needed to keep up with his training.

The woman had finished scribbling. 'So, Sarah, we've got most of your details now and we'll set out a care plan for you. We're going to try to find you a temporary home until your grandfather is better. Does that sound okay to you?'

The woman talked to her as if she was about the age as the child in the poster. Every sentence went upwards at the end as if it was a question when it was clear that there had been no questions in what she had said.

'I'm from the Children's Services Reception and Assessment Team,' she had said. 'Let's see if we can sort you out, shall we?'

'How does this work?' Mac said, beside her. 'Are there families who . . . specialise in taking kids for short periods?'

'We have a lot of foster-families on our books. Some young people – our clients – will be with them only for a night. Others might stay several years. In your case, Sarah, we'll hope it's just a short time.'

'Just until your grandfather's better,' Mac said.

'Yes,' the woman said.

There was something not quite definite in the way the woman had answered, Sarah thought.

'But there are lots of young people in similar situations to you, Sarah, families who need a bit of help. You mustn't worry.'

Mac and his wife had talked only to her over breakfast, not to each other. She wondered if they had had an argument, whether it was something to do with her. She couldn't remember Papa and Nana ever arguing. Nana would joke that she could argue with Papa but he would never argue back. When Papa was cross he just went very quiet, his face set in stone. 'It's like arguing with a statue,' she would say conspiratorially, as if it was some big joke between them.

Tears prickled behind her eyes, and she clenched her jaw, willing them away. She was already regretting having gone with Mac and Natasha. Last night she had been afraid, but now she saw that her life was being taken over. By people who didn't understand it.

The woman had looked at a file. 'I see your grandparents have a residency order for you. Do you know where your mother is, Sarah?'

She shook her head.

'Can I ask when you last saw her?'

Sarah glanced sideways at Mac. She and Papa never talked about her mother. It felt strange to air the family laundry in front of strangers. 'She's dead.' She stumbled over the words, quietly furious that she had to give out this information. 'She died a few years ago.'

She saw the sympathy on their faces, but she had never even missed her mother, not like she did Nana. Her mother had never been a warm embrace, a pair of arms to fall into, but a chaotic, unpredictable shadow over her early years. Sarah remembered her as a series of images, of being dragged into different people's houses, left to sleep on sofas, the hum of distant loud music and arguments, an uneasy sense of impermanence. And then, when she had gone to live with Nana and Papa, order, routine. Love.

The woman was scribbling. 'Are you sure there are no friends you can stay with? Any other family?' She sounded hopeful, as if she didn't want to deal with Sarah. But Sarah had to admit that there was not a single person who might want her in their home for weeks on end. She was not popular. Her few friends lived in flats as small as hers; she knew no one well enough to ask, even if she had wanted to.

'I need to go,' she said to Mac quietly.

'I know,' he said. 'Don't worry, the school knows you'll be late. It's more important that we get you sorted out.'

'And where did you say your grandfather is now?' The woman smiled at her.

'He's in St Theresa's. They said they're going to move him, but I don't know when.'

'We can find that out for you. We'll put a contact arrangement in place.'

'Will I be able to see him every day? Like I have been?'

'I'm not sure. It'll depend on where we can place you.'

'What do you mean?' said Mac. 'Won't it be somewhere close to her home?'

The woman sighed. 'I'm afraid the system's under immense pressure. We can't always guarantee that clients will be as close to their home as we would like. But we'll make every effort to ensure that Sarah sees her grandfather regularly until he can come home.'

Sarah could hear huge gaps between the woman's words, holes where there should have been certainty. She had visions of herself being placed with some smiling family miles from Papa. From Boo. How was she supposed to look after him if it took her hours to get anywhere? This wasn't going to work.

'You know what?' she said, glancing at Mac. 'I can look after myself. Actually, if someone could just help me a bit, I'll be fine at home.'

The woman smiled. 'I'm sorry, Sarah, but legally we're not allowed to leave you by yourself.'

'But I can cope. It was getting burgled that was the problem. I need to be near my home.'

'And we'll make every effort to ensure that that happens,' the woman said smoothly. 'And now we'd better get you to school. Your social worker will meet you afterwards and, hopefully, take you to your placement.'

'I can't,' she said abruptly. 'I need to be somewhere after school.'

'If it's an after-school club, we can set that straight with the school. I'm sure they won't mind you missing a session.'

Sarah tried to work out how much to tell them. What would they do if she told them about Boo?

'Right, Sarah. If we can move on to religion, I won't keep you much longer. Can you tell me which of these categories you fall into?'

The woman's voice receded and Sarah found herself staring

at Mac. He was uncomfortable in this place, she could tell. He kept fidgeting as if he would rather have been anywhere else. Well, now he knew how she felt. She hated him suddenly, hated him and his wife for putting her in this mess. If she hadn't been so shocked yesterday she would have patched up the door herself. Cowboy John might have helped. And she'd still be at home, running her life, still seeing Boo twice a day, coping, hanging on for Papa's return.

'Sarah? Church of England? Catholic? Hindu? Muslim? Other?'

'Hindu,' she said mutinously, and then as they looked at her, disbelieving, she said again, 'Hindu.' She almost laughed when she saw the woman writing it down. Perhaps if she made life really difficult for them they'd have to let her go home. 'And I'm a strict vegetarian,' she added. Mac's face told her he was remembering the bacon sandwich he had made for her at breakfast. She dared him to contradict her.

'Ooohh-kaaaay.' The woman carried on writing. 'Nearly done. Mr Macauley, if you need to go now I can take it from here.'

'And I'm claustrophobic. I can't live anywhere where there's a lift.'

This time the woman's expression was sharp. Sarah suspected she was not quite as sympathetic as she had initially appeared. 'Well,' she said crisply, 'I've got to speak to your school and your doctor. No doubt if there are any real requirements or problems they'll confirm them.'

Mac was scribbling. 'You all right?' he asked Sarah quietly.

'Just great,' she said.

He looked troubled. He knew he had ruined her life, she thought. He handed Sarah a piece of paper. 'My numbers,' he said. 'Any problems, you give me a call, okay? I'll help you any way I can. That's okay, right?' he added to the woman.

She smiled at him. Sarah had noticed that loads of women

smiled at Mac. 'Of course. We encourage clients to keep to as much of their normal routine as possible.'

Mac stood to leave and handed her the folder of documents and personal papers he had taken from the flat for her. 'Take care, Sarah,' he said. He lingered, as if he was not quite sure whether he should go. 'I hope you get home soon.'

Sarah kicked at the leg of her chair and said nothing. Doing and saying nothing, she was discovering, was the only power she had left.

'Thank God. I thought we were going to have to call up Mr Snappy Snaps.'

'Sorry. Got caught up in something.' Mac dumped his camera bags on the floor. He kissed Louisa, the art director, whom he recognised, then turned to the girl who was sitting at the mirror, texting furiously, oblivious to the attentions of the makeup artist behind her, twisting her hair on to huge ceramic rollers. 'Hi, I'm Mac,' he said, holding out a hand.

'Oh. Hi,' she said. 'Serena.'

'You should have been here an hour ago.' Maria tapped her watch. Her jeans were positioned so low on her hips that they were almost indecent; above them, two layers of floating dark fabric were tied skilfully to reveal a shapely midriff. Behind her, someone was fiddling with a CD-player.

'Just thought I'd give you extra time to work your magic, sweetheart.' He kissed her cheek, sliding his hand across her bare back. 'I'll set up, shall I? Louisa, do you want to talk me through the brief again?'

Louisa outlined the kind of look and ambience they wanted for the shot of the young actress; the wardrobe girl nodding attentively. Mac nodded too, appearing to give her his full attention, but his mind was in that children's welfare department. He had run down the steps of the dispiriting building forty minutes previously, feeling less relieved than he had expected. Sarah had looked absolutely miserable, shrinking in on herself as they had sat in that office and the extent of her altered situation had dawned on her. He had half considered asking Tash if the girl could stay with them, but even as he had formulated the sentence, while they made breakfast in loaded silence, he could see the absurdity. Tash had made it clear that her job was compromised by Sarah's presence, and she could barely cope with having him in the house. It no longer even felt like his home. How could he impose on her the presence of a stranger?

'Lots of red. Very bold. We want to make a statement with this picture, Mac. She's not just another young starlet but a serious actress of tomorrow, a young Judi Dench, a less political Vanessa Redgrave.'

Mac eyed Serena, who was giggling at a text message, and stifled an internal sigh. He had lost count of the exceptional young starlets he had shot over the past ten years. Barely two had survived the initial burst of publicity to make it to a sitcom.

'Okay. She is ready for you.' Maria appeared in the doorway, a thin makeup brush between her teeth, pinning up the girl's blonde hair with deft fingers. The wardrobe girl was pulling outfits from the long rail, piling them over one arm. 'I'll bring these out,' she said.

'We'll be ten minutes. I'm just going to check the backdrop.' Louisa left them.

Maria walked up to him. 'I was going to ask why you so late,' she said, in her heavy Slavic accent, 'but then I realised I didn't care.'

He hooked a finger in her belt loop and pulled her close to him. Her hair smelt of apples, her skin of makeup and hairspray, the layered unguents of her trade. 'If I told you, you wouldn't believe me.'

She removed the brush. 'You were out picking up women.'

'Fourteen-year-old girls, actually.'

Her mouth was so close now that he could see the tiny freckle to the side of her upper lip. 'This does not surprise me. You are disgusting man.'

'I do my best.'

She kissed him, then pulled away. 'I have another job after this. Soho. You want to meet up?'

'If we can go to yours.'

'You are at your ex-wife's house?'

'It's my house too. I told you.'

'And this woman does not mind you moving back?'

'I can't say we've discussed it in those terms.'

She narrowed her eyes. 'I don't trust her. What woman with any self-respect would take back her ex-husband like this? When my ex-boyfriend in Krakow tried to return to my house I turned my father's gun on him.' She mimed the action.

Mac considered this. 'That's . . . an option, I suppose.'

'I felt not so good about this afterwards. Turns out he was only trying to return my CD-player.' She turned to leave, reaching into the fruit bowl for a stray grape as she headed for the door. 'Is just as well I missed.'

The darned gates were jamming again. Cowboy John was hauling at them, trying to make them line up as he wrestled with the padlock, when he saw a familiar figure running towards him, her bag bumping against her hip.

'I was just about to close up,' he said, unhooking the padlock. 'I was waiting for you all yesterday. I thought something had happened to you. Where have you been, girl?' He coughed, a hoarse, rasping sound.

'They've put me in Holloway.' She dropped her schoolbag on the cobbles and ran past him to Boo's stable.

He pulled the gates shut and followed her, stiff-legged. The chill of autumn was sidling into his bones. 'You went to prison?'

'Not the prison,' she said, wrestling with the bolt on the stable door. 'Social Services. They said I can't stay at home any more with Papa not being there and they made me go to this stupid family. But they live in Holloway. They think I'm with Papa now – it's the only way I could get here.' She threw herself against the horse's neck and he saw a long shudder escape her, as if the pent-up tension of the day had been released.

'Hold on, now. Hold on.' He flicked on the lights. 'You need to rewind. What the Sam Hill is going on?'

She faced him, eyes glittering. 'Our flat got broken into on Tuesday. And this woman who gave me a lift home, this lawyer or something, she made me stay with her because she said it wasn't safe where I was. And then they took me to Social Services and the next thing I'm living in someone else's house and I've got to stay there till Papa is better. This family in Holloway. And I'd never even met them. It took me an hour and a quarter on the bus to get here.'

'What they want to make themselves busy for?'

'I was fine,' she said, 'until the break-in.'

'Your grandpa know about this?'

'I don't know. I can't get there till tomorrow. They don't know about Boo. I can't let them know or they might put him somewhere too.'

Cowboy John shook his head. 'Don't you worry yourself. He ain't going nowhere.'

'I haven't even got the stables money for you. They took Papa's pension books so I've got nothing except my bus and lunch money.'

'Don't you fret.' She was winding herself into a mini-hurricane. 'I'll sort out the rent with your papa when he's up and about. You got money for your horse's food?'

She thrust her hand into her pocket, counted out the cash and handed it over. 'I've got enough for four bales of hay and a couple of sacks of food. But I need you to feed him for me. I don't even know if I can get here to muck him out.'

'Okay, okay. I'll clean his stable for you, or get one of the boys to do it. What about the blacksmith? You know he's coming Tuesday?'

'I know. I've got some savings. I could pay this month out of that. But I can't pay the rent.'

'I told you, I'll strike the rent until the Captain's back in action.'

'I'll pay you back.' She sounded as if she thought he wouldn't believe her. He took a step backwards. 'I know that. You think I'm stupid?' He gestured towards the other ponies. 'I wouldn't let one of these sewer rats miss a day's rent, but you and your papa . . . Now you just calm down, sort your horse out, and we'll take things a day at a time.'

She seemed to relax a little. She took up a brush and started to groom him, sweeping her arm down his flank methodically, rhythmically, like her grandfather did it, as if she took comfort in the simple action.

'Sarah . . . I'd offer you my own place but it's kinda small. And I been on my own a long time. If I had a bigger house, or a woman around . . . I'm not sure it's the kind of set-up they'd want a girl to be.'

She told him it didn't matter.

He stood there for a minute. 'You okay to lock up if I go?' he said. He could tell she didn't want to leave any time soon. He leant on the stable door, tilting his hat back so he could better see her face. 'I tell you what, Sarah. You want me to go visit with your grandpa for you tomorrow so that you can come here instead?'

She straightened. 'Would you? I don't like to leave him alone for two days.'

'No problem. He'd want to know Boo here was still doing his circus thing. But I got to tell him something. And, sweetheart, I have to talk to you about it too.'

She looked wary then, waiting for some further blow. 'I'm thinking of selling up to Maltese Sal.'

Her eyes widened. 'But what—'

'It's okay. Like I'll tell your grandpa, nothing's going to change. I'm going to hang on here till my house is sold. Day to day I'll still be opening up and taking care of business.'

'Where are you going?' She had put her arms around the horse's neck and was hanging on as if he, too, might be spirited off somewhere.

'I'm moving out to the country. Somewhere with a bit of green. I figure my boys deserve it.' He nodded at his horses. He hesitated. Took the cigarette from his lips and spat on the floor. 'Seeing what happened to your grandpa, Sarah, it shook me up. I'm not as young as I was, and if I only have a few years, then I'd like to spend 'em somewhere peaceful.'

She didn't say anything, just looked at him.

'Maltese Sal's promised me nothing's going to change, girl,' he said. 'He knows about the Captain, knows it ain't easy for you right now. He says he'll keep things just as they are.'

She didn't have to say anything. He could see it in her face. Given where she had ended up right now, how the hell could she believe that?

'Thanks for being so prompt, Michael. Mrs Persey will be here soon and I wanted to run through some of the preliminary papers with you.' She paused as Ben came in, bringing a box of tissues and a bottle of chilled white wine. 'We don't normally encourage "crying time",' she said, as the bottle was placed carefully on her desk, 'but when you have a client of this calibre . . .'

'. . . you let her shed a few tears.'

Natasha smiled. 'And soften the pain with a glass of her favourite Chablis.'

'I imagined this end of town would be more about confiscating the odd can of Special Brew.' A renowned divorce lawyer, Michael Harrington's charm and amused manner of speaking belied a razor-sharp mind. Natasha could remember the first time she had watched him in court, when she had been a trainee and he had been opposing counsel. She had wished she had a tape-recorder so that she could emulate the deceptively easy fashion in which he had punctured their own counsel's case.

'Okay.' She glanced at her watch. 'In brief, married twelve years, second wife, some dispute over how soon she and Mr Persey got together after his first wife left. Just over a year ago she discovered him *in flagrante* with the au pair. Fairly standard stuff. We have two problems. First, there is no agreement on the financial settlement, on grounds of inadequate disclosure of assets. Second, she is refusing to comply with the access arrangements on the grounds that he was physically and mentally abusive to her during the term of the marriage, and verbally abusive to the eleven-year-old daughter.'

'Messy.'

'Oh, yes. The papers don't suggest that this was in evidence during the marriage.' Natasha flicked through her brief. 'She claims she went to every length to hide it, as she didn't want to upset his standing in the business community. Now, she says, she has nothing to lose. But he's threatening to withdraw his offered financial settlement because of the lack of access.'

'I need hardly tell you that this will be a very high-profile case, given his reputation. The hearing is booked for the Principal Registry of the Family Division in the Royal Courts of Justice. The dispute-resolution meeting was an absolute disaster. Meanwhile Mrs Persey seems . . . Well, she seems quite keen to publicise her version of events. It's all I can do to stop her going to the newspapers.' She paused, pressed the tips of her fingers together. 'You'll find, Michael, that she isn't the easiest of clients to represent.'

Ben popped his head around the door. 'She's here.'

The briefest glance towards her, and Michael was on his feet, hand outstretched, ready to welcome Mrs Persey into the room.

Natasha had seen many battered women during her time at Davison Briscoe; she had represented children whose mothers swore their man would never touch a soul, even as the stitches healed on their temples, the bruises still purple beneath their eyes. She had seen women so cowed by years of abuse that they could barely speak loudly enough to be heard. She had never met anyone like Georgina Persey.

'He's threatening me again!' She had both her hands on Natasha's arm even before Ben had closed the door behind her, her brightly polished nails digging into Natasha's flesh. 'He rang me last night to tell me that if he doesn't see Lucy he'll arrange for me to have an accident.'

Her hair bounced on her shoulders in long, carefully smoothed waves. Her expensive clothes hung from a body that was rigorously exercised, and trimmed by years of self-denial. But her face, immaculately made-up, seemed fixed in a perpetual grimace of outrage. When she spoke, it was as if all the energy had been vacuumed out of the room.

'Please sit down, Mrs Persey.' Natasha placed her in front of a chair, poured a glass of wine and handed it to her. 'May I introduce Michael Harrington? The QC we spoke about? He will be representing you in court.'

It was as if Mrs Persey hadn't heard. 'I told him I had it on tape. His threats. Everything. I didn't, of course, but I was so afraid. I told him if he did anything to me I'd give the tape to you. And you know what he did? He laughed. I could hear that whore laughing behind him too.' She looked at Michael Harrington beseechingly. 'He stopped my credit cards. Do you know how embarrassing it is to have your card declined in Harvey Nichols? There were people I knew in the queue behind me.'

'We'll do our best to have an interim settlement in place within a matter of days.'.

'I want a non-molestation order. I want him to stay away from the house.'

'Mrs Persey,' Natasha began,' I've explained to you that it's very difficult for us to help you there without any material evidence that you and your daughter are at risk of harm.'

'He's trying to make me crazy, Mr Harrington. He's putting more and more pressure on me so that I look crazy and the judge will take my daughter away from me.' She spoke only to the barrister, now that he was present. She was one of those women for whom others of their sex were irrelevant, thought Natasha.

'Mrs Persey.' Michael Harrington sat down beside her. 'From the paperwork I've seen so far, I have to tell you that we are at far more risk of you losing her because of your non-compliance with the court's decisions than we are for any suggestion of mental instability.'

'I will *never* leave my daughter in his hands,' she said emphatically. As if she was seeing Natasha for the first time, she pulled up a sleeve and held out her bare arm. A long white scar ran towards the elbow. 'This is from when he pushed me down the stairs. You think he wouldn't do that to Lucy? You think I should let my daughter stay in the house with that man?'

Michael was studying his paperwork. Natasha leant forward. 'We said we needed to corroborate your statements about the risk to Lucy. You told me the nanny once saw your husband strike you, yet there's nothing about it in her statements.'

'That was the Guatemalan nanny, not the Pole.'

'Can we get a statement from the Guatemalan?'

'How should I know? She's in Guatemala! She was no good. We had to let her go.' She took a sip of her wine. 'I found her trying on my clothes. As if they'd fit her! She must have been at least a size twelve.'

Michael Harrington placed the lid on his pen. 'Mrs Persey, did anyone else witness any act of violence towards you or your daughter?'

'I told you! He's so clever! He did everything behind closed doors. He said nobody would believe me.' She burst into noisy sobs.

Natasha met Michael's eye and reached for the box of tissues, which she held out to the woman.

'I'm going to the press!' Mrs Persey stared at her, defiantly. 'I'm going to tell the world what he's like, him and his whore.'

'I suggest we hold fire with the media just a little longer,' Michael said diplomatically. 'It won't endear us to the judge, and it's very important that we appear absolutely blameless as far as our own actions go.'

'You think?'

Both lawyers nodded.

'But it's so awful,' she said, weeping noisily into a tissue. 'So awful.'

'Take your time, Mrs Persey,' Michael said, as she sobbed.

Time ticked by. Amazing how relaxed barristers can be when it was costing someone three hundred and fifty pounds an hour, Natasha thought.

'Now perhaps we can begin again. It's very important that we get this right.'

Natasha sent Ben a text message:

Give yourself an early night. We're in for a long one. See you tomorrow.

* * *

Spending time with the seriously rich was a bit like reading interiors magazines, Natasha thought, as she eyed the clothes on her bed. It made you dissatisfied with your lot. As she had watched that woman with her flawless skin, her exquisitely cut cashmere and silk clothes, her tiny designer shoes, Natasha's serviceable wardrobe had seemed suddenly frumpy, her no-bigger-than-average figure lumpen and overweight. Mind you, she thought, folding her jeans, she had survived marital separation better than Georgina Persey. The woman had rattled on for a further hour, not hearing the advice offered to her, contradicting her own statements, in a confusion of fury, bitterness and perhaps genuine anxiety. By the time she had left even Michael Harrington had been shattered.

Now, standing beside her bed, Natasha jumped when she heard the front door open. There was a brief pause, as if he was weighing up what to say, and then she heard him offer, tentatively, 'Hi,' from the hallway.

Her jaw clenched involuntarily – hi honey I'm home, as if they were somehow a happy family again. She waited a moment, then shouted, 'I'm upstairs,' making sure it didn't sound like an invitation.

Maddeningly, he came up anyway. His head appeared in the doorway, and then he was filling it. 'I'm thinking of getting a takeaway. I wondered if you wanted some.'

'No,' she said. 'I – I'm going out.'

'Going away,' he corrected, clearly having noted the suitcase.

'Just for the weekend.' She walked to the chest of drawers and took out two folded tops.

'Anywhere nice?'

'Kent.' She had wondered whether to tell him about the cottage she had rented since he had gone. But she was afraid he might assume she had somewhere else to live, which would add to his sense of entitlement over the house. Conor had warned her not to reveal anything to Mac, no matter how nice he seemed – *It all comes back to bite you in the end.* 'So you can have the house to yourself for the weekend,' she added. She laid the clothes in the case and went into the en-suite to gather up her moisturiser and makeup.

Mac had thrust his hands deep into his jeans. He was looking around him awkwardly, as if the spectre of their time in this room had floated up to haunt him. She had changed nothing in it since he left, she realised. It was one of the reasons, she suspected, that Conor didn't like staying here.

'So,' he said, 'all-night party for me, then.'

She whirled round.

'I'm joking. You forgot your hair brush.'

She hesitated, then took it. She couldn't tell him she had one at the cottage.

Mac rubbed a hand over the back of his head. 'I take it this is with Conor?'

She kept her back to him now, putting things into the case.

'Yes.'

'How is he?'

'Fine.'

'If this is because I'm here, don't worry about it,' he said. 'You just say the word and I can go out for the evening. I don't want to tread on anyone's toes. Don't feel you have to go.'

'I'm not. I mean you're not,' she lied. 'We go away most weekends.'

'I've got places I can go. Just say the word.'

She continued to pack, his presence making her feel increasingly self-conscious and oddly invaded. The bedroom was her sanctuary, the one place she had been able to feel was still hers since his return. Having him there was a grim reminder of the times they had fallen gleefully into bed, the days they had spent watching DVDs and eating burnt toast . . . the nights when she had lain six cold inches away from him, feeling like the loneliest person in the world. Trainers, boots, jeans. Hairbrush. She struggled to order her thoughts.

'Where in Kent are you going?' he asked.

'What is this? *Twenty Questions*?' It had flashed out before she could censor it.

'I'm just being polite, Tash. We're skirting round each other every day. I'm trying to act as if we can at least have a civil conversation.' He continued, his voice even, 'In fact, I'm the one standing here waving my wife—'

'Ex-wife.'

'—almost ex-wife off to a weekend with her lover. I think that's pretty civilised, don't you? Can you not meet me halfway?'

She wanted to tell him she was finding this difficult, far more so than even she had anticipated, but even that small admission felt like giving too much away. 'Just . . .' she said '. . . a little village near the Sussex border.'

He frowned, shifted his feet on the varnished floor. 'Well, I shouldn't be around much longer. The agents rang to tell me they'd finished the details. It goes on the market tomorrow.'

That feeling of being winded again. She stood in the middle of the room, a pair of boots dangling from her hand.

'We did agree, Tash,' he said, catching her expression.

'Don't keep calling me that,' she said irritably. 'I'm Natasha.'

'I'm sorry,' he said. 'If I had enough money not to do this, I wouldn't. I don't like the thought of the house being sold either. Don't forget how much time I spent on it.'

She held the boots to her. Outside someone had started to play music, the beat bouncing relentlessly off the frontages of the terraced houses.

'But perhaps it will be easier in the long run.'

'I doubt it,' she said briskly. 'But if it's got to be done, then let's get it over with.' She zipped the case shut and, with a brief smile that wasn't very much like a smile at all, Natasha walked past her soon-to-be-ex-husband and down the stairs.

Seven

*'Any sudden signal will bewilder a spirited horse, just as a
man is bewildered by any sudden sight or sound or other
experience.'*

Xenophon, *On Horsemanship*

OCTOBER

They had moved him again, and it took Sarah twenty minutes
to locate him. He was in the stroke ward, where he had been
until last week when pneumonia had sent him back to
Intensive Care.

'We did hope he'd be a bit further along by now,' said the
nurse, as she showed Sarah to his curtained area, 'but it's
the dysphagia – the trouble swallowing. Poor old boy, he's
struggling a bit.'

'He's not a boy,' Sarah said curtly. 'He's seventy-four.'

The nurse's stride faltered, as if she was going to say
something but then she simply walked faster so that Sarah
had to skip a little to keep up. She stopped outside a blue
floral curtain and pulled it back to allow Sarah in.

Sarah drew a chair close to the bed. The back had been
raised so that he sat half upright. Sarah ached at the sight of
his greyed chin, resting loosely on his chest. She had never
seen her grandfather with more than overnight stubble, and
this forfeit of his personal care would pain him.

She opened the cabinet beside his bed quietly, trying to

assess whether his belongings had been brought back to this ward with him. Often she had to chase the nurses to find out where they were. Since he had been at the hospital two pairs of pyjamas had disappeared, with the new bar of soap she had brought and a bag of razors. She scanned the shelf, noting with relief his washbag, a small towel, and the picture of him and Nana. She lifted it out and put it on top of the cabinet. If she positioned it carefully he could look at her all day.

She glanced at her watch, trying to work out how much time she had. The Hewitts had strong ideas about routine. They wanted her at their house by four o'clock, even though she had told them where she was going. It was almost two now, and nearly impossible for her to get to Sparepenny Lane in time to take Boo out.

She touched her grandfather's hand. His skin, dry and papery, made something inside her contract. Four weeks in hospital seemed to have sucked the essence out of him, shorn him of his robustness. It was hard to see him as someone who had ridden a rearing horse just weeks ago. The reversal in their positions made her feel giddy, rootless, as if nothing in her world made sense any more.

'Papa?'

He opened an eye and peered vacantly at the blanket. She wondered whether he was working out where he was. Then he lifted his head slowly.

'Papa?'

His expression was blank. She glanced at the array of medicines on the trolley beside him. He would be given antibiotics for some weeks, the nurses had told her, just to be on the safe side. She reached forward and put his glasses on his face. 'I brought you some yoghurt.' Now that they had removed the tube from his throat, she tried most days to bring him something he could swallow easily. She knew he detested the hospital food.

His eyes softened, and she could see that he knew her now. She laid her hand on his. 'The black cherry. The one you like.' His hand clenched under hers. 'Just thought I'd tell you, Boo's starting to get his winter coat already, but he's really well. We did lots of walk to canter yesterday, and he didn't hot up once. I've upped his food a bit, as the nights are colder. I'm giving him an extra scoop of sugar beet – is that okay?'

It was the slightest nod, but it was enough. Things were as they should be now: her seeking his approval.

'I'll be heading over to him when I leave here. I thought I might take him for a walk up to the marshes. I can't go to the park because it's Saturday afternoon. Too many people. But he'll enjoy a nice stretch out.' This was a lie but, these days, Sarah edited everything. It was important that he had only good things to think about while he was here, with nothing else to do.

'And the new family I'm staying with are nice. Lots of food, but not as good as ours. When you get back I'm going to treat us to a great big fish stew with lots of garlic, like you like it.'

His fingers twitched under her hand. This was his bad hand, the one he struggled to lift. She kept talking, as if mundane chat could persuade some normality back to their lives. 'Do you want a drink?' she asked finally. She held up the plastic beaker with his water. A slight inclination of the head. She held it to his lips, and tilted his chin a little with her other hand, so that the water would drip into his mouth. She had lost her squeamishness about doing such tasks for him now. She had found that if she didn't do them, they were unlikely to be done at all.

'*Temps*,' he said.

She looked at him.

'Bread. *Chapeau*.' His eyes closed in irritation.

'You want the nurse?'

A frown.

'Let me set you upright a little more.' She reached behind him for the pillows, trying to prop him so that he was less collapsed. She adjusted the bed with practised hands, then arranged his pyjama jacket around his neck so that he appeared a little more dignified. 'Better?'

He nodded. He looked defeated.

'Okay. Don't get upset, Papa. The doctor said it will come. He said it can be the last thing to come. You remember. And you've not been well so I'm sure all the drugs didn't help. They might have muddled you up.'

Disapproval shrouded his eyes. He didn't like her to patronise him. And then, as she watched, his gaze slid towards the table, towards her bag. 'The yoghurt. You want some of the yoghurt?'

He sighed, relief flooding his features. '*Chapeau*,' he said again.

'Okay,' said Sarah. '*Chapeau*.' She pulled a teaspoon out of her bag and peeled off the lid.

Even with the benefit of a year's distance, it was hard to see the truth of what had prompted the end of their marriage. Perhaps it was impossible to find truth in such situations; perhaps all you could ever expect was two people's truth. Court truth – no absolutes, just points of view, dependent on who could argue them better. Except somehow it had ended long before they ever got the chance to argue it out at all.

In the early days after Mac had left, Natasha had told herself that it had been for the best. Their characters were fundamentally different. Feeling angry all the time had drained her, turned her into someone she didn't like, and it was clear that last year neither had been happy. It was possible that if they had spent more time together they would have grasped this sooner. She told herself so many times.

But she had been unable to sit alone in the London house. It was, after all, he used to joke, 'The House That Mac Built', and he had permeated every inch of it. Every room held an echo of what she had lost: the staircase he had rebuilt, the shelves he had had to put up twice, the spaces where books, CDs, clothes had been. Most of what he had taken with him, he had put into storage, and even that bothered her: the things they had loved, had chosen together, sitting in some impersonal space because he would rather have them locked away than suggest that any part of him still shared her life.

'I'll pick the rest up in a week or two,' he had said, as she stood rooted to the hall floor. She remembered feeling conscious of the cold stone beneath her bare feet. She had nodded, as if somehow agreeing that this was a sensible course of action. And then, as the door had closed behind him, she had allowed herself to slide slowly down the wall and on to the floor. She had sat there for an unknown period of time, made catatonic by the scale of what had happened.

For weeks afterwards, long before her family and friends knew that her marriage was over, at weekends, early in the morning or late at night, in the spaces when it was impossible for her to be in her office and lose herself in work, she had climbed into her car and driven. She drove through city streets, across elevated motorways, under bridges and on to dark, sparsely lit dual-carriageways, pausing only to refill her car with fuel. She drove and listened to the radio, to the talk shows whose callers were supposed to remind her that her life wasn't that bad, but somehow didn't. She listened to the political programmes, the documentaries, the dramas and soaps. She didn't listen to music – the aural equivalent of strolling across a minefield. Just when you thought you were fine some meaningful song would shatter you without warning. We danced to that, had a barbecue to that. She would fiddle with the dial as tears streamed down her cheeks. Better to listen to the news, tut at the headlines, marvel at the rabid views.

Her brain, only half functioning, focused on the twin requirements of listening and driving until one Saturday morning she ended up in Kent. She had felt an unexpected clawing in her stomach and realised, with some surprise, that she hadn't eaten for almost eighteen hours. She had seen a tea-room, the kind of deliberately olde-worlde shop-front place that catered for non-English ideas of England. After she had eaten half a buttered bun (she had struggled to stomach anything for weeks) she paid, and went out to walk in the watery autumn morning along the lanes around the village, relishing the smoky scents, the rotting leaves, the sharp, bitter taste of the sloes in the hedgerows. To her surprise, she had felt a little better.

When she had come across the little house with a to-let sign, halfway down a lane that had seemed to lead only to a farm, she didn't bother to look around it. She rang the agent's number and left a message, saying that if it was still available she would rent it. Money didn't buy you happiness, she reflected afterwards, but it certainly provided you with better places to feel miserable.

Since then Conor had come down with her most weekends when he didn't have his boys. He wasn't practical, as Mac had been, but he was happy to keep her company. He would lie on the sofa reading the papers, build a fire for the sheer pleasure of watching one or help her rustle up a meal. Most of the time, if the weather was good, he sat outside and enjoyed a beer while she clipped and pruned the garden into shape. She knew little about plants, but soon discovered a pleasure in weeding or pottering round a garden centre, far removed from the myriad urban miseries that pervaded her job.

She had rented the cottage for almost a year now, and the work she had put into the garden had paid off this summer: perennials had risen, unchoked, from enriched soil, roses had bloomed, apple trees had borne fruit. The woman at the farm at the bottom of the lane, which had turned out not to be a farm but a stables, had dropped bags of manure at the gateway. 'No, I don't want anything,' she had said. She was a brisk sort. 'I'm deluged with it. The more you pile on your roses the better.'

The Kent house had given her a little peace of mind. It held no history for her and needed constant practical attention. At weekends when she didn't make it down there, she was restless in her home.

And now she had a new reason to avoid being in London.

It had taken Mac almost a year to collect what he had left behind.

'So . . . what are the boys doing this weekend?'

'Not sure. I think *she's* taking them to her mother's.'

'Not sure? Not like you.'

'Yeah. Well. She was so bloody sour when I dropped them I didn't get into the small-talk.' Conor's mouth turned down as he spoke.

Natasha was constantly astonished by the physical signs of resentment that engulfed him when he talked about his ex-wife. 'But you said they liked the skating,' she reminded him.

They were in Conor's midlife-crisis sports car. He glanced into his rear-view mirror, then changed lanes, his own voice lightening. 'Loved it. I was like someone's grandmother, but the pair of them were going backwards on the ice within twenty minutes. D'you have any water? Christ, I'm parched.'

She reached into her bag, and brought out a small bottle and unscrewed the top for him. He lifted it to his lips and drank.

'Did you take them to that restaurant I told you about? The one with the magician?'

'Yes,' he said. 'They loved it. Sorry – meant to mention it.'

'Do you think they'd like to go again?'

'Why not?' He took another long swig. 'I might take them next Sunday. I'm pretty sure I'll have them then.'

Natasha watched him, then took the bottle from him as he handed it to her. She rarely stayed at Conor's apartment – she had never been in such a starkly impersonal home. Apart from two pictures of his boys, a scattering of toys and brightly coloured bedding in the second bedroom, nothing in it suggested it was any more than a hotel suite. Conor lived with the aesthetic of a monk. He had a washing-machine, but his laundry was taken away and delivered back ready to wear, because he disliked seeing clothes hanging around the place. He did not cook – why would he, he said, when the local restaurants did it so much better? The kitchen stood gleaming and unused, cleaned twice a week for no reason.

She suspected some part of him bridled at his new life, that his refusal to put down roots in the executive apartment was his way of saying he didn't intend to stay there for long. He unbent a little in the Kent cottage: when he laid the fire, lit a barbecue, or rearranged a shelf, she glimpsed the uxorious man he might once have been.

'You know . . . I'm not meant to say anything but if the Persey case goes well, Richard might want a word with you.'

'About what?'

'Oh, come on. You're not that naïve.' A small smile played around his lips.

'Making partner?'

'Don't look so surprised. You've been bringing in the business lately, and this Persey case is raising our profile. I know he was concerned about you doing more family law, but he's surprised it's paying off so fast. What have you got coming up next week?'

She tried to calm her mind, which had suddenly spun off in unexpected directions. 'Another meeting with Harrington about Persey. A child abduction. Oh, and an age challenge for a young asylum-seeker. Another of Ravi's.' She remembered she hadn't checked her phone that morning and picked up her bag. 'Kid arrives without papers, says he's fifteen, local authority says he's not.' He was a Section 17: the authorities would be forced to pay for his care. If they could prove he was older, he would be transferred to the National Asylum Support Service. It was always a matter of expense.

'Will you get it?'

'It's going to be tough. The onus is on us to prove he's a child. My only hope is procedural – he was never served with a screening officer's report once the age issue came up. I'll fight them on that.' The paperwork on the child was chaotic, and such cases were getting harder to win: policy pressure from above meant that most were either assessed as adults or simply sent home.

'You sound doubtful. About his age.'

'I don't know what to think. I mean, he's not shaving or anything, but he could be lying. They all seem to claim they're fifteen, these days.'

'That's very cynical, Hotshot. Not like you.'

'Well, it's true. Or there's a lot of very bristly kids around.' She could feel him staring at her.

'You never did say anything about that Iranian kid of yours, did you?' She looked up at him. 'The one you were going on and on about – Mr Mileage – who didn't come from where he'd said he did. Or go where he was meant to go.'

'Ali Ahmadi? No.'

'Not even to the social worker?'

She crossed her arms. 'What would I have said? The whole thing was pointless.'

'Good. You could really have done yourself some damage there. It's not your job to judge people. Your job is just to provide the best representation with the information you've been given.' He glanced at her, perhaps conscious that he might have sounded patronising. 'I just thought you got way too worked up about him. So the boy couldn't have walked as far as he said he had. He wasn't trying to deceive you personally.'

'I know.' She *had* taken it personally – she hated being lied to. It was why she had felt so guilty about Mac for so long.

'You couldn't have known what he was going to do.'

'I *know*,' she said. 'You're right. But . . . it does colour the way I'm viewing all of them. I'm reading the briefs and looking for the holes.'

'But it's not your business to be forensically examining their stories.'

'Maybe not, but it doesn't alter the fact that that kid is now headed for the Crown Court. And it's partly my fault.'

Conor shook his head. 'You're way too hard on yourself. You're not accounting for human nature. Christ, if I looked too hard at the stories of the people I represent I'd have no bloody business whatsoever.'

She unscrewed the lid of the water bottle and drank some. 'Most of the time I can convince myself. I'm doing something good. I think I'm on the better end of the law. That's not to say your end isn't great, but you've never wanted the same things out of it that I have.'

'The money.'

'Yes.' She laughed. 'But the thing with Ahmadi . . . well, I guess it *has* made me cynical, and I never wanted to be that.'

Conor grinned. 'Get over yourself, girl. If you never wanted to be cynical you should have been working in a hospice, not a bloody law firm.'

Conor was not the possessive type; if anything he had been at pains throughout their relationship to make clear that he was unable to give her any great show of commitment. He didn't mess her around: he was there when he said he would be, rang when he'd promised to, but equally he kept the invisible walls around himself. He expressed neither desire nor need. He was affectionate, without suggesting it might mean anything. So she had little reason to believe that her new domestic arrangements might be a problem. Until, as they unpacked his car, she told him.

'He's been there all week?' Conor put down his case.

'Since Tuesday.'

'And you never thought to tell me?'

'I've hardly seen you this week. And it was difficult. I'm not going to rush past you outside court whispering, "Hello, darling, my ex-husband's moved back in."'

'You could have rung.'

'Yes. But I didn't want to. Like I said, it felt awkward.'

'I imagine it would.' He picked up his case, and a bag of shopping, then walked into the house, his back bristling.

'But it's not like that, is it?' she said, catching his tone.

'I don't know, Natasha. How is it?' His voice was excessively calm.

She followed him into the kitchen. She had left some flowers on the sink the previous weekend and they had wilted, brown petals curling over the edge of the vase. 'He's got nowhere to stay, and he does own half the house.'

He turned around to face her. 'I could be terminally ill, bankrupt and lobotomised and you still wouldn't get me within fifty feet of my ex and her house.'

'Well, we haven't been through the whole process you have.'

'You mean you haven't got divorced. Am I missing something here?'

'You know we're going to, Conor. It's just early days.'

'Early days? Or not quite definite?'

He had begun unpacking the shopping with unnecessary vigour. Even though he had his back to her, she could make out the rigidity of his jaw. 'Are you serious?'

'You've just told me your not-quite-ex-husband has moved back in with you. How can I not be serious?'

Natasha stalked past him. 'Jesus Christ, Conor! As if my life weren't bloody complicated enough. You're the last person I'd expect to be playing Mr Possessive.'

'What's that supposed to mean?'

'You won't commit to a holiday and now you're giving me a hard time over how my ex and divide up our assets?'

'It's not the same.'

'No? You won't even introduce me to your kids.'

He threw up his hands. 'I knew it. I knew you'd bring them into it.'

'Well, if you really want to get into this, yes, I will. How do you think it makes me feel that you act like I don't exist? You won't even let me meet you for coffee if they're around.'

'They're still in shock. Their lives have been in complete turmoil. Their mother and I can hardly speak to each other. Introducing them to mummy number two is hardly going to help matters, is it?'

'Why do I have to be mummy number two? Can't I just be your friend?'

'You think kids are stupid? They'll work out what's going on pretty damn quickly.'

She was shouting now: 'Well, so what? If we're together, I'm going to be a fixture in their lives at some point. Or am I the one who's missing something?'

'Of course you're not. And, yes, we're together. But what's the bloody hurry?' Then his voice softened: 'You don't understand kids, Natasha. You can't until you've had some. They . . . they have to come first. They're so sore still. So sad about everything. I have to protect them.'

She stared at him.

'And I couldn't possibly understand that, could I, Conor? What with being *barren* and all . . .'

'Oh, shit. Natasha, don't take it like—'

'Get lost,' she hissed. She ran up the stairs, two at a time, and shut herself into the bathroom.

The horse's nostrils were like saucers, flared so wide that she could see the fleshy pink beyond the black velvet. Its eyes were white, and its ears flicked back and forth, constantly checking the activity behind it, its slender legs mimicking some elaborate two-step. Maltese Sal dismounted from the two-wheeled sulky, stepped up to the animal and ran a hand down its neck, which was mirrored with sweat. 'What do you think, Vicente? Is he going to make me some money?' He began to unhook the sulky from the harness, motioning to his nephew to do the same on the other side.

'He'll cost you some. There's something funny about his gait. I don't like his legs.'

'This horse won fourteen times out of fifteen. His legs are better than yours. This is the equine equivalent of a supermodel.'

'You say so.'

'You can't spot a trotter from a pacer. This horse is good. I can feel it. Ralph? You gonna hose my horse's legs for me?'

Ralph leapt forward to take the horse, which, now freed from the constraints of the little chariot, wheeled balletically around the yard, causing him to grab at its reins.

Sarah ducked in past them, closing the gates behind her.

Cowboy John appeared to be elsewhere, and she always felt a little self-conscious around Maltese Sal's men.

He was always surrounded by them. There was, allegedly, a Mrs Sal, just as most of his men had wives, but Cowboy John had said that, as far as he knew, she never left the damn house. 'I think he kept her in there the last twenty years. She's just good for cooking, cleaning and—' He adjusted his hat. 'Never mind.'

She was conscious of their stares as she made her way up to Boo's stable, and grateful when they were distracted by Ralph's haplessness at hosing the jittery beast's legs.

Sarah always felt sorry for the trotters and pacers: fine-limbed and doe-eyed, they were shipped into the yard, fed up to the gills, driven relentlessly until their legs went, or Sal lost interest, and then just disappeared. Papa disapproved of the way they were forced to pound up and down the roads, the fierce punishments meted out to those who showed fear or disobeyed. There would be silent exchanges of looks when Sal lost his temper and thrashed one. But no one ever said anything to him. He wasn't that kind of person.

Boo whickered softly when she entered the stable, his head already reaching over the stable door, searching for treats. She gave him a mint and held his neck, breathing in his sweet scent, letting him nose her pockets for more treats then set about refreshing his water and tidying the straw bedding.

Despite Cowboy John's help, caring for Boo was becoming increasingly difficult. The Hewitts, whose immaculate home had never housed so much as a goldfish, had become frustrated by her apparent failure to arrive home when they expected her. She had no explanation for them (she had swiftly exhausted late buses, detentions, an emergency visit to her grandfather, and knew she was no longer believed) and would endure yet another exasperated lecture about how important it was that they always knew her whereabouts, about the perils of disappearing for hours at a time. Then – if she suspected they were really monitoring her – she would miss classes the next day. School did not seem to have registered her absences yet, but she knew she was on borrowed time. But what choice did she have? Sometimes it was the only way she could get to the stables to feed him.

She let Boo out of his stable and walked him on a long lead rope up and down Sparepenny Lane, keeping to the kerb to avoid the passing cars and talking softly to him when pent-up energy caused him to skitter sideways or balk at a road sign. It was only to be expected: he was a horse who liked to work, who needed not just the physical challenge but the mental exercise. 'Too smart for his own good,' Cowboy John would say, after Boo had undone the top bolt of his stable for the umpteenth time.

'Too smart for you,' Papa would retort.

'How much brains he need for the Big Top?'

She stood at the top of the lane, quiet now as dusk fell, and tried not to think about how fragile Papa had looked that day. What would it feel like to have the steel core of you reduced to something feeble and dependent? It was hard, seeing him like that, to believe he would return to their flat, to their old life. But she had to believe he would.

She walked the horse up and down once more, apologising to him for her lack of time, as if he might understand. He tossed his head, his pricked ears and easy jog a mute request to go faster, further. When she turned back towards the gates, his head dropped a little, as if in disappointment, and she was suffused with guilt. Maltese Sal and his friends were up the far end of the little yard, smoking and talking over each other. As she pushed the gate open, she could see Ralph hovering at the edge of them. He idolised Maltese Sal; when Sal tossed him a cigarette he would actually colour with pleasure.

It was as she opened her lock-up, where she stored her feed, that her heart sank. There were four flaps of hay – less than half a bale. She had been so busy that week she had forgotten to ask Cowboy John for more. His was locked up.

She reached into her pockets, searching for loose change, with which she could perhaps buy a little more from Ralph. Forty-six pence and her bus pass.

She heard a sound behind her. Sal was opening his own lock-up. He was whistling. Through the doorway, she saw the neatly stacked bales, the bags of expensive horse feed. She had never seen so much good forage in one place. As she stared, he turned abruptly and she blushed to be caught looking.

He peered past her into her lock-up. 'You short, huh?'

At first she didn't answer him. She busied herself opening a hay net.

He sucked his teeth. 'Looks like the cupboard's bare.'

'We're fine,' she said.

Maltese Sal let the door close behind him and took a step towards her. His shirt was immaculate, as if he had been nowhere near a horse, and his gold tooth glinted when he opened his mouth. 'You got enough hay?'

She met his eye, then looked away. 'John was . . . going to lend me some.'

'John's got business to sort out. He isn't back till tomorrow. So, you got a problem.'

'I've got enough.' She began to scoop the four flaps into her arms. She straightened and made to move past him, but he stood in her way, not blocking her, but enough that she had to ask him to move.

'You got a nice horse.'

'I know.'

'You can't feed a horse like that shit off the floor.'

'It's just till tomorrow.'

He took the cigarette from his mouth and pulled a piece of hay from the bundle she was carrying, put the glowing end against it and watched it reduce to a blackened wisp. 'Good for burning. Nothing else. Your grandfather's still sick, huh?'

She nodded. A train rumbled overhead, but she didn't take her eyes off him.

'I don't want you to feed your horse that shit. Here, put it down.' He stuck his cigarette back in his mouth, walked into his lock-up and brought out a bale of hay. It was still slightly green and gave off a soft, meadowy scent. He carried it, effortlessly, swinging it by its twine, into her lock-up and put it in the corner. As she stood against the wall, he went back and got a second. Then he picked up a large bag of premium horse feed and, with a grunt, swung it through her doorway. 'There,' he said. 'That'll keep you going.'

'I can't,' she whispered. 'I haven't got any money.'

He seemed to see right through her. 'You pay me when you got the money, okay? If I'm going to run this place I don't want to see a good horse going down because of a bad diet.' He kicked his heel into the four flaps of hay. 'Stick that on the brazier.'

'But—'

'You take it from John, yes?' His eyes were on her. She nodded reluctantly. 'So take it from me. Now I need to get on.'

He walked away into the yard, a slight swagger in the way he moved.

Sarah watched him as he rejoined the men, then stooped to breathe in the smell of the new bales. It was better quality than she was used to. She suspected that if Papa had been there he would not have allowed her to accept it. But that was the whole point.

She glanced at her watch and flinched. She had fourteen

minutes before she was due back at the Hewitts'. Fourteen minutes to make a fifty-five-minute two-bus journey. She cut the strings on the bale and grabbed an armful, half walking, half running to where her horse stood waiting.

The silence of a London house had a curious poignancy to it, she observed, as she closed the door behind her, her call echoing into nothing. Somehow the quiet that hung over a London street and into a stilled hallway made hers feel far emptier than her place in the country. Or perhaps it was the possibility that, these days, someone else might be in it.

Natasha stepped over the now omnipresent camera-bags and went into the living room. She sighed a little at the sight of the photographic lights stacked in a corner, and checked the answering-machine; the steady red light told her there were no messages.

She sniffed for hints of wine or cigarette smoke, a signal that he might have had people over, but there was nothing. The sofa cushions were indented, telling of a night in front of the television, and she picked up each one in turn, plumping it and replacing it neatly, then felt vaguely irritated that she had done so.

She walked back into the hallway, picked up her bag and went upstairs, the sound of her footfall echoing in a way that made her feel self-conscious, a stranger in her own home.

She and Conor had recovered the weekend after its acrimonious start, but she knew they had been shocked by the ferocity of their argument, by the sudden spectre of feelings both had sought to deny. She was secretly pleased it mattered to him that Mac was there, but simultaneously resentful. He was asking her to grant him a say in her life without offering to make any more space in his own. 'You will meet the kids, Hotshot,' he said, as he had dropped her off, 'I promise. Just give me some more time, yes?' He had not asked to come in.

She dropped her bag on her bed and undid the catch. She would load the washing-machine, then iron her work shirts in front of the television. Later she would sit at her desk and prepare the paperwork for court tomorrow morning, making sure she had everything she needed; a Sunday-night routine that was as familiar to her as her left hand.

Natasha stood still for several minutes, somehow paralysed by this new atmosphere. Despite the lack of his presence, Mac felt omnipresent in the house, as if he had reclaimed it for his own. 'You want to check he's not taking books, pictures, and squirrelling them away,' Conor had said. 'Giving him access to everything is the divorce equivalent of writing a blank cheque.' But she didn't care about the prospect of losing stuff, even if she'd believed Mac capable of taking it. It was his presence, the air around him, that disoriented her.

She realised she was still angry with him; angry that he had not been there when she needed him, angry that he had returned to disrupt her life when she had rebuilt it. Typical Mac, crashing in with no thought of the consequences. She blamed him for the weekend, even while the rational part of her knew it was not his fault. She blamed him for the fact that she had had to leave her home. And to all of this he seemed impervious: he walked in, as he always had, with his charming smile and easy ways, as if nothing could hurt him. As if their marriage had been the smallest blip on his emotional radar.

Almost without knowing what she was doing, Natasha went across the landing to the spare room. She called again, then pushed tentatively at the door, registering Mac's rumpled bed, the piles of unwashed clothes in the corner by the linen basket, the faint sweet smell of dope.

Not so reformed, after all. She hovered in the doorway, then found herself treading quietly through the room and into the en-suite bathroom. His razor stood in a glass, with toothpaste and a brush. The bathmat lay skewed on the tiled floor and she fought the urge to straighten it. But the mess was perversely reassuring: an echo of the man she knew he was. Chaotic. Imperfect. This is why we're divorcing, she reminded herself, and almost felt fondly towards him for that reassurance.

It was as she made to walk out again that she caught sight of the pot on the glass shelf at the end of the bath, packaged in an expensive cream and gold box: a woman's moisturiser. Beside it, a packet of makeup remover pads.

Something in her cooled and solidified. And then, blinking, her feet landing without care or quiet, Natasha turned and walked swiftly out of the spare room.

Eight

'The majesty of men themselves is best discovered in the
graceful handling of such animals.'

Xenophon, *On Horsemanship*

The carpet in the headmaster's room was a deep plush blue,
so luxuriant and soft that almost no pupil who ended up in
there was able to banish the thought of how it might feel to
shed their shoes and socks and sink their bare toes into it.
Perhaps it accounted for how distracted many of Mr Phipps's
errant visitors appeared, rather than reflecting accurately the
level of ADHD in the school.

Sarah was not distracted by the carpet. She was distracted
by the fact that she had not been able to get to the stables
for almost forty-eight hours.

'It's the fourth time you've missed double English in this
half of the term, Sarah. It used to be one of your better
subjects.' Mr Phipps examined the papers in front of him.

She twisted her hands in front of her.

'I know things are a bit difficult for you at home, but your
attendance record was always good. Are you having problems getting to school? Are you foster-family not helping?'

She couldn't tell him the truth – that she had told the
Hewitts she had lost her bus pass, and the money they had
given her for fares had gone towards Boo's bedding.

'They have an obligation, Sarah, to ensure you get to school.

So, if they're not helping you get here for your morning lessons, we need to know about it.'

'They are helping.'

'Then why have you missed the classes?'

'I . . . get confused about the different bus routes. I missed the bus.'

Boo was beginning to react to the loss of his routine. That morning he had almost broken out of his stable, then had spooked at a woman with a baby buggy and careered into the road so that a taxi had blared its horn. Sarah had stood in front of the bonnet, yelling at the driver. When she had got Boo to the park he had bucked, then braced himself against her instructions, setting his mouth against the bit. She had been angry and frustrated with him, and regretted it afterwards when they walked home sweating and miserable.

'The local authority will pay for a minicab. We'll do what it takes, Sarah, if transport really is the problem.' He placed the tips of his fingers together. 'But I don't think that's the whole story. It says here that you've missed geography twice on Thursday afternoons, and PE three times on Friday afternoons. Do you want to tell me how that came about?'

She stared at her feet. Someone with a carpet so rich couldn't possibly understand a life like hers. 'I went to see my granddad,' she muttered.

'He's in hospital still, is he?'

She nodded. Even Papa had been cross with her when she had turned up on Friday. He had looked up at the clock on the wall and muttered: 'Wrong. *Après*.' She hadn't had to struggle to grasp his meaning. He had told her she was not to come at that time again. But he had no idea. He didn't know that she spent half her days running across north-east London, hopping from one foot to the other at bus stops, or jogging down back-streets, trying to get to and from the stables in time to meet everyone else's deadlines.

'Is your grandfather's health improving?' The headmaster's expression had softened.

If she was a different sort of person, Sarah thought, she would have cried – everyone knew Phipps couldn't bear girls to be in tears. 'A bit,' she said.

'It's an unsettling time for you. I do understand that. But you should see school as a constant in your life, something to lean on. If you're struggling, Sarah, you should talk to us. To me or your teachers. Everyone here wants you to succeed.' He leant back in his chair. 'What you can't do is take time off to see your grandfather whenever you want to. You'll be starting to think about exams soon, and this time is crucial in your school career. There are a few subjects you find difficult, aren't there? So you need to keep your attendance up in order that, whatever else is going on in your life, you leave here with a solid education behind you.'

She nodded, not meeting his eye.

'I want to see an improvement, Sarah. A real improvement. Do you think you can do that?'

Cowboy John had been there the last time. He had been to see Papa and the first thing he had said when he stepped through the gates was that he was letting her off the back rent. He would tell Maltese Sal, and she would be square. She just had to start afresh when Sal took over. She could tell from his face that he had thought she'd be relieved. But she had felt the blood drain from her face. She knew what this meant: that he no longer believed Papa would be able to pay him back.

He no longer believed that Papa would come home.

'No more skipping class, Sarah. Right?'

She raised her face. 'Right,' she said, and wondered if Mr Phipps could see straight through her.

*　　*　　*

Natasha jumped when she found him in the kitchen. It was a quarter to seven. When they had lived together he had barely stirred until ten.

'Got a job up in Hertfordshire. Publicity shot. Makeup, hair, the full works. It's going to take me a good hour and a half to get there.' Mac gave off a faint aroma of shampoo and shaving cream, as if he had already showered. She had heard nothing, she thought, as she covered her shock by making breakfast.

'Hope you don't mind. I used the last of the teabags.' He lifted a hand, waving a piece of toast. He was reading her newspaper. 'I'll get some more while I'm out. You still drink coffee, right?'

She closed the cupboard door. 'I guess I'll have to,' she said.

'Oh. And you know I told you I'd be away Thursday for a couple of days? Well, the job fell through so I'll be here after all. Are you okay with that?'

'Fine.' He had spilt some milk on the worktop.

'You want this?' He motioned towards the newspaper. 'Sorry. Didn't mean to muscle in.'

She shook her head. She tried to work out where to sit. Opposite him, and they risked touching feet. On the adjoining side of the table, she might seem to be cosying up to him. Paralysed by these two choices, Natasha remained standing by the kitchen units with her bowl of cereal.

'I'll keep the sports section. You can have the main. Any news from the estate agent? I meant to ask last night.'

'There are two couples coming round at the weekend. Incidentally, I'd appreciate it if you didn't smoke dope in the house.'

'You never used to mind.'

'Actually, I did. I just never said. But that's not the point. If we've got people coming to the view the house, I don't think it's a good idea for it to smell like an Amsterdam café.'

'Noted.'

'And the agent has keys so you won't have to be here.'

He adjusted his chair so he could see her better. '*I* don't have to be here? You're away again?'

'Yes.'

'That's a lot of weekends away. Where are you going this time?'

'Does it matter?'

He held up both palms. 'Just making polite conversation, Tash.'

'I'm going back to Kent.'

'Nice. You must like it. Conor got a place there, has he?'

'Something like that.'

'Doesn't come here much, does he?'

'I wonder why.' She focused on the cereal.

'You surprise me. It's not like he was so worried when we were still together ... Okay ... okay,' he said, as her head shot up. 'I know. Year Zero. We're not supposed to discuss What Went Before.'

Natasha closed her eyes, taking a deep breath. It was too early in the morning for this. 'Of course we can discuss what went before, Mac. I just think life will be easier if we don't make sarcastic comments about whatever went on in our marriage. Or didn't,' she added meaningfully.

'I'm cool with it. I told you that if he wants to come here I can make myself scarce. We can have set nights, if you like. I'll stay away Tuesdays, you stay away Wednesdays, that kind of thing.' He studied something in the newspaper with great concentration, adding: 'We can be modern.'

She reached across for her coffee. 'I assume this will all be sorted out long before we start regularising "date nights".'

Date nights. She felt the existence of the invisible woman keenly – she knew that at the weekends when she was not there, the woman was, even if Natasha no longer crept into the spare bathroom to confirm it. Sometimes she suspected she could detect her scent in the air. Other times it was just Mac's demeanour. He was loose, relaxed – like he used to be after they had spent much of the day in bed. You've been having sex all weekend *in our house*, she would think, then curse herself for it.

The cereal had turned claggy in her mouth. She finished her mouthful and pushed the bowl towards the dishwasher.

'You okay?'

'Fine.'

'Fine again. Not finding this too hard?'

Sometimes she felt he was testing her. As if he wanted her to say she couldn't bear it, and leave. Don't leave, Conor had warned, despite his feelings. The moment she left the house she would lose the moral and legal advantage. If Mac had invested a lot of time and effort in it he might not want to leave as much as he told her he did.

'He's the one who wants to sell it,' she had protested.

'That's what he wants you to think,' he had replied. Conor could see subversive possibilities in almost any kind of behaviour. He viewed Mac's presence as one would that of an occupying enemy. Don't give an inch. Don't retreat. Don't let them know your plans.

'Not finding it hard at all,' she said brightly.

'Great.' His voice softened. 'I did worry a bit about how it would work out before I came back.'

She wasn't sure she believed this. Mac looked as if nothing worried him. That much hadn't changed. 'Well, as I said, don't worry on my account.'

He was staring at her.

'What?' she said.

'Nothing changes, does it, Tash?'

'Meaning what?'

He studied her for a moment, his smile absent. 'You still don't give anything away.'

Their eyes locked. He looked away first and gulped his tea.

'Oh, by the way, I bunged a load of washing in last night and there was some stuff of yours in the basket so I put that in too.'

'What stuff?'

'Ah . . . blue T-shirt. And underwear, mostly.' He finished the tea. 'Lingerie, I should say.' He flicked a page in the newspaper. 'Gone up a notch since we split, I noticed . . .'

Heat flooded Natasha's face.

'It's okay. I put it on a low temperature. I know about these things. I may even have put it on the hand-wash setting.'

'Don't,' she said. 'Don't . . .' She felt horribly exposed. The thought of it.

'Just trying to be helpful.'

'No. No, you're not. You – you're—' She picked up her briefcase and pushed past him towards the door, then spun around. 'Don't touch my underwear, okay? Don't touch my clothes. Don't touch my stuff. It's bad enough you're staying here without rifling through my pants as well.'

'Oh, get over yourself. You think the biggest thrill I could get is going through your laundry? Jesus Christ, I was only trying to help.'

'Well don't, okay?'

He slammed the paper down on the table. 'Don't worry. I won't go anywhere near your pants in future. Hardly ever did anyway, if I remember.'

'Oh, that's nice,' she said. 'That's really, really nice.'

'Sorry. I just—' He let out a long breath.

They stared at the floor, before their eyes lifted, met and locked. He raised his eyebrows. 'I'll do my washing separately in future. Okay?'

'Fine,' she said, and shut the door firmly behind her.

*   *   *

Sarah was bent low over her horse's neck, her toes jammed in the stirrups, the wind whipping tears that tracked horizontally from the corners of her eyes. She was going so fast now that her whole body ached; her hands, braced on his withers as she gripped the reins, her stomach as she fought to maintain her position against the joint forces of wind and gravity, her legs as they struggled to stay against his sides. Her breath came in gasps, her arms pressed against his neck as he flew, the thunder of his hoofbeats filling her ears. She wouldn't stop him. He had needed this for weeks, and here the marshes were wide and flat enough for her to let him go until he was tired.

'Go,' she whispered to him. 'Go on.' The words flew backwards into her throat. Boo would not have heard her even if she had shouted; he was lost in some purely physical world of his own, instinct telling him to relish this freedom, to allow his tight muscles to stretch, his legs to fly across the rough ground, his lungs to tighten with the sheer effort of maintaining such a speed. She understood it. She needed it too.

In the far distance steel pylons stalked the skyline, strung together by cables that traced a delicate progression across the city. Below them, on a thin strip across the marshes, raised on concrete pillars, the traffic moved in a never-ending procession. Several horns sounded at a distance; possibly at her, she could not focus long enough to tell. Boo was moving faster than the cars and lorries caught in the rush-hour traffic, and the thrill this gave her threatened to transmute into fear as she wondered whether she would be able to stop. She had never gone so far with him before, never let him run so fast. He swerved to avoid an old bicycle frame in the long grass, almost unseating her, and as she struggled to maintain her balance, she could feel his great quarters gathering under him as he pushed faster, now blurring her vision, causing her breath to stall in her chest. She lifted her head from his neck, spitting out the fronds of his mane that whipped at her skin, trying to gauge how much distance she had left. She pulled slightly on the reins, recognising that she had little strength left to pull him back, should he fight her. Some distant part of her hardly cared: how much easier it would be for them to keep going. To race up that grassy bank, straight across the motorway, skidding through the cars, his shoes sending up sparks. They would jump the cars, the fences. They would fly under the pylons, past the warehouses and car parks, and keep going until they hit the countryside. Just her and her horse, galloping through the long grass into some uncomplicated future.

But some part of Boo was still owned by Papa. Feeling the increasing tension in the reins, he slowed obediently, his ears flicking back and forth, as if he was trying to check that he had read her message correctly. Sarah allowed herself to sink back into the saddle, her body slowly becoming upright, reinforcing what she was telling him, to slow. To do as she asked. To return to their world.

Some fifty feet from the dual carriageway, Boo slowed to a walk, his frothing sides heaving with the effort of what he had just done, his breath leaving his flared nostrils in short, noisy bursts.

Sarah sat very still, squinting back at the distance she had covered. She was no longer in the wind, but the tears in her eyes kept coming.

Ruth, the social worker, was at the school gates. Sarah had been searching for loose change in her schoolbag when she caught sight of her. She was standing just to the side, her neat little red car parked across the road, as if she did not want to be obtrusive. Every single kid gawped at her as they came out of the gates. Sarah walked up to her reluctantly; Ruth could not have been more conspicuous if she had worn a tabard with 'Social Worker' in neon letters across it. They all had that look, like plain-clothes policemen.

'Sarah?'

Her heart leapt as she grasped the possible significance of the woman's presence. Ruth must have registered it because, as Sarah hurried towards her, she said, 'There's nothing wrong with your grandfather. No need to worry.'

Her chest deflating with relief Sarah followed her reluctantly to the car. She opened the passenger door and climbed in. She had planned to see Papa tonight; half of her wondered whether she could persuade Ruth to give her a lift. It was then that she noticed the two black bags on the back seat. At the mouth of one she could see her tracksuit bottoms. Five weeks and two moves had told her what those bags meant. 'Am I going somewhere?'

'Sarah, I'm afraid the Hewitts have had enough.' She started the car. 'It's not you – they think you're a lovely girl – but taking responsibility for someone who keeps disappearing is too much for them. It's the same story as with the MacIvers. They're frightened something will happen to you.'

'Nothing's going to happen to me,' Sarah said, her voice tinged with scorn.

'The school is equally concerned. They tell me you've been skipping classes. Do you want to tell me what's going on?'

'Nothing's going on.'

'Is there some boy involved? Some man? That's a lot of time you've been disappearing for, Sarah. Don't think we don't notice. Between the Hewitts and the school we've added it up.'

'No. There's no boy. No man.'

'So what is it?'

Sarah scuffed her feet in the footwell. She wished Ruth would just drive somewhere instead of sitting outside the school so that everyone could stare into the car as they filed out of the gates. But she was waiting for her to answer. 'I wanted to see my granddad.'

'But it's not just that, is it? I went to the hospital on Tuesday when the school last rang to tell me you'd disappeared. I went to pick you up but you hadn't been there that day. Where were you?'

Sarah stared at her hands, which were still blistered from the reins. They were going to find out. She knew it. She thought of Boo, of the feeling of him beneath her, the fleeting sense of freedom as they ran towards a different future. She edged her hand into her bag, checking reflexively for the keys to the stableyard.

'You've got to help me, Sarah. I'm running out of options for you. You've been through two foster-families in five weeks. These are good people, nice people. Do you want to end up in care? I can put you in a residential home where they'll make sure you stay in. We can impose a curfew, or get someone to accompany you to school and back every day. Is that what you want, Sarah?'

Sarah reached into her bag and pulled out the piece of paper.

'Anything you need,' he had said, 'anything at all.' 'Mac,' she said, lifting her face to Ruth's. 'I want to go back to Mac's house.'

Ten people. Six lots of viewings. And not a single offer. The estate agent had been apologetic. 'It's interest rates,' he had said. 'It makes people nervous. Takes them twice as long to make an offer.'

'But we need to sell this house.' Natasha had surprised herself. She had not wanted to leave, but that was before Mac had taken up residency.

'Then I can only suggest a price reduction. Everything sells if it's cheap enough. Oh, and if you don't mind me saying, it might help if you could tidy up the spare room a little. It never helps if potential buyers are having to step over men's – ah – underclothes to get to a bathroom.'

Natasha lay in the bath, wondering how much they should drop to achieve a sale. It had to be enough to attract buyers, but too much and she would feel cheated. It was a beautiful house in a nice street. This area of London was on the up – everyone said so – and she needed enough to buy a flat somewhere else.

When she thought about living in a flat again, Natasha couldn't dispel the cloud of gloom that settled over her. You reached your mid-thirties and expected to have laid the foundations of your life. You should have met a partner, settled in the house you loved, made a good career. Perhaps a baby or two. Her resolutely flat stomach was just visible beneath the floating relief map of bubbles. One out of four. Not a great tally, when it came down to it. And since the episode with Ahmadi she wasn't even sure how confident she felt about the career.

'Natasha?'

She sat up in the bath and checked that she had remembered to lock the door. 'I'm here,' she called. *Please don't let him have brought anyone home.*

She heard the dull thud of things being dropped on the floor, his footsteps on the stairs. His equipment was steadily encroaching along the hall – piles of lights, canvas camerabags, foil light enhancers – so that soon she would be forced to play stepping-stones every time she wanted to enter or leave the house.

'I'm in the bath,' she called again. She heard him stop outside the door and felt oddly self-conscious. She could almost see him in his T-shirt and jeans, running a hand over the top of his head.

'I've been to the supermarket,' he said. 'Bought a load of stuff. It's in the kitchen. Teabags and all.'

Great, she thought. You want a medal?

'And I called the estate agent. They said those last people still might offer. It's only two days since they viewed.'

'They won't, Mac. You like somewhere, you offer straight away. You know how it works.'

She could hear him receiving a text message. When he spoke again he sounded distracted, as if he was texting back. He had never been able to do more than one thing at a time. She sank lower into the bath, letting the bubbles rise up to her chin, so that Mac's voice became muffled. 'Anyway, I guess he told you there's someone coming next Wednesday. So you never know.'

They had viewed this place together, Mac coming straight from an assignment so that his camera still hung around his neck. She had told him he looked like a poseur, but he had taken pictures of the rooms, and later they had both been excited by the light, the space. They had put in an offer the following morning.

'And I had another call.' He was tentative this time.

Natasha wiped her eyes. 'What?' She pushed herself upright.

'From Social Services. That girl who spent the night with us.'

'What about her?'

'They've asked if we'd consider fostering her for a few weeks. Apparently her current placement isn't working.' He paused. 'She asked to come to us.'

The girl's wary eyes gazing at her breakfast plate. Her shocked face confronting the devastation of her fifth-floor front room.

'But we don't know her.'

'She's told them we're friends of her family. I didn't like to contradict. But I guess it's irrelevant. I said I didn't think it would be possible.'

Natasha climbed out of the bath. 'Why?'

He didn't answer immediately. She heard him move closer to the door.

'You just seemed . . . reluctant before. I wasn't sure if you'd want someone you didn't know in the house, what with everything. I told them you might have too much work on.'

'We don't know anything about her.'

'True.'

She wrapped herself in a soft white towel and sat on the side of the bath. 'What do you think?' She was facing the door.

'I wouldn't mind, if it helped her out for a few weeks. Just till we sell the house. She seemed an okay kid.'

She could hear it in his voice. He would be as relieved as she would. A different focus. An enforced break in the tension.

She thought back to a stolen packet of fish-fingers. The girl had sworn she would have paid for them. Come on, she told herself. Not all these kids are on the make. She might just need a chance.

'Tash?'

It might be the closest to parenting she was ever going to get.

'I don't see why a couple of weeks would hurt,' she said, 'but you'd have to fit your work around her. I've got a big case coming up and I won't be able to take time off.'

'I think I can manage that.'

'I don't know . . . It's a big responsibility, Mac. You'd have to play an equal part – lay off the dodgy cigarettes, drink less. You couldn't just come and go as you pleased. It would be a big change in lifestyle for you. In fact, I don't know if you—'

'I'll ring them,' he said, his footsteps already headed for the stairs, 'and find out what we do next.'

Nine

*'First, then, it must be realised that spirit in a horse is
exactly what anger is in a man.'*

Xenophon, *On Horsemanship*

She heard Sarah coming down the stairs before she saw her.
Her footfall was deceptively light, almost as if she wanted
not to be heard, but for Natasha, still acutely aware of the
presence of other people in her house, it was enough to make
her break off from her files. She had been working at the
kitchen table (she had lost her study to Mac's sleeping arrangements) and now leant back in her chair to see through the
doorway. 'Are you going out?'

Sarah whipped around in the hallway, almost as if she
hadn't expected to be seen. She was wearing a puffy jacket
and a striped woollen scarf. 'I won't be long,' she said.

'Where are you off to?' Natasha tried to make her question
casual.

'To see a friend.'

Natasha stood. 'Would you like a lift?'

'No . . . thank you.'

'Well, shall I pick you up afterwards, now that it's darker
in the evenings? It's no problem.'

Sarah raised a smile. It wasn't terribly convincing. 'No,
thanks,' she said. 'I can get the bus.' And before Natasha
could say anything else, she was gone. Natasha was left staring

at the front door, her pen still hanging loosely from her fingers.

Sarah had been with them for ten days, and after the initial strangeness of the first two, when she had barely spoken, and hidden in her room if Natasha was at home, the three had fallen into something like a routine. Natasha would make breakfast (she was usually the first up) and Mac would drop Sarah at school, on the advice of the social worker. He was in charge for the first couple of hours after school, and then, depending on how late Natasha stayed at work, either Sarah and Mac, or the three of them would eat together in some facsimile of family life. It was awkward, at first, eating with Mac. Conversation was forced and tentative. But he chatted to Sarah, and if she didn't say much in return, they had at least settled into something that felt a little safer and even, on occasion, companionable. Sarah's life, her small needs, even her recalcitrance, gave their exchanges a focus.

Twice, the school had rung to say she had missed lessons. Sarah insisted she had been confused by her timetable. Or, once, that she had been present and the teacher was mistaken. They had been warned by Ruth, the social worker, that the girl did not always follow the routines set for her. 'We've had some issues about her not being where she should be,' Ruth had said. Natasha had felt they were not getting the full story.

'Surely that's the whole point of being a teenager?' Mac had said cheerfully. 'I was never where I was meant to be.'

'I just don't think you should give her too much freedom,' Ruth continued, directing her comments at Natasha. 'By all accounts her grandfather was quite strict, and she seems to be responding to the lack of that stability by going a bit off the rails. She's missed quite a few classes, and seems pretty unwilling to talk about what she's doing. I'm not suggesting she'll be a problem for you,' she added quickly. 'I'm just telling you that she seems to be a child who thrives better on routine, and if you can negotiate some boundaries with her about when and where she goes out, I think it will work better for everyone.'

They had the advantage, Ruth had said, smiling, that Sarah had asked to be with them. 'We find that young people do much better in their chosen environment. I'm sure that will be the case here.'

Natasha had not had time to feel flattered by this. Now that Sarah had settled in, she seemed to want to spend as little time with her as possible. She was monosyllabic over supper, escaped to her room most of the time she was at home, and was out so often that sometimes it felt as if they were not housing another person at all.

That first dinner Mac had said, 'Okay. We've never had someone your age as a houseguest before. How do you want to play this?' He had been so cheerful, so relaxed.

Natasha had stood at the stove, scraping burnt pizza from the baking tray, trying not to look as if she was eavesdropping.

'I usually visit my friends after school,' she said cautiously.

Mac shrugged. 'Fine. Let's say twice a week to start with. I think you should come straight back on the other days and we'll run through your homework together. Although I can't say I'll have the faintest idea what you should be doing.'

'I'm used to letting myself in and out.'

'And we're not used to having anyone else here so we'll need a little time to adjust, Sarah. I'm sure we can give you some keys of your own soon, but just work with us for now. Okay?'

The girl had shrugged. 'Okay.'

Natasha had thought having her here was simply Mac's smokescreen for their discomfort with each other. But he was throwing himself into Sarah's care. He had stopped smoking, and drank no more than one glass of wine or a beer each night. He had scanned the cookery books so that he could cook when Natasha was not at home. He seemed to know instinctively how to talk to Sarah, what she might like to eat, or watch on television. She occasionally smiled at things he said, had confided a few daily events to him when she came home from school.

Natasha struggled to find the right tone – she sounded frequently, even to her own ears, as if she was addressing a client. 'Do you need anything? What kind of things do you generally have for a school lunch?' It sounded awkward, interrogative, and Sarah wore an expression of wariness during such exchanges, as if that was how she viewed them too.

Sarah had not wanted her to help personalise the guest bedroom. She had smiled politely at Natasha when she showed her the new duvet cover she had bought, the toiletries she had placed in Sarah's bathroom. She had gently refused Natasha's offer to go out at the weekend and buy some posters or pictures to put up. Natasha had snuck into the room one afternoon when the girl was at school, trying to get a grip on who she was, what she might need, but her few belongings had offered little: some cheap, chain-store clothes, no different from those of any other teenage girl she saw around, a photograph of her with two old people, probably her grandparents. Some books on horses and her school uniform. Oddly, despite her neatness, her shoes were often filthy, covered with mud, and her jeans bore dirty marks and a pungent smell that Natasha couldn't identify. When she tried to bring this up one evening, Sarah had coloured and said she and a friend had been walking a dog in the park.

'It's okay. She'll open up, given time,' Mac said, after Sarah had disappeared to her room. 'Think how strange it is for her. Her whole life has been turned upside down in the past couple of months.'

Hers isn't the only one, Natasha wanted to say. But she

took her files and went to work in the kitchen, feeling, as she increasingly did, like an intruder in her own home.

'. . . so I won't be going to Kent this weekend.'

Conor seemed unable to believe what he was hearing. 'You and Mac are fostering a kid?' he repeated.

'Don't say it like that, Conor. We're not fostering her in that sense. She's just someone I met who's staying till her grandfather's on his feet again. It's – it's actually making life easier. Things are less tense all round.'

Conor hadn't seen it in quite the same light. 'Am I missing something here, Hotshot?' he had said, running his fingers along his leather case. 'First he moves back in with you. Now you're fostering a kid together. And you can't come away with me to the cottage because you're playing happy families.'

She had stayed very calm. 'It's her first weekend. The social worker is visiting on Friday evening to make sure she's settled in okay, and I can't just disappear as soon as she's moved in.'

'So you're playing happy families.'

'Conor, it was impossible as things were. I think Mac found it just as hard. Having a third person in the house means we don't have to deal with each other in the same way.'

'It's all very neat, but I'm having trouble seeing it like that. When you have children you—'

'It's not *having* children. This is a girl with her own life, her own interests. She's hardly even there half the time.'

'So what's the point if she's hardly there? You said her being there meant you didn't have to deal with each other.'

God, she hated arguing with a lawyer. 'Don't twist my words. She asked to stay, and both Mac and I saw it as a way of making a difficult domestic situation a little less difficult. And a way of helping a young person who's in a mess.'

'How altruistic of you.'

She walked round her desk to where he was sitting, and perched beside him. She lowered her voice. 'If you met a perfectly nice kid who needed a home for a few weeks – someone whose life you could maybe change for the better – wouldn't you say yes?'

She had him there.

'You're a father. Imagine if it was one of your children. Wouldn't you hope some decent people would take him in?' She tried to get him to meet her eye. 'By the time we've sold the house, she'll be back home and all three of us can go our separate ways. It works for everyone.'

She reached out to take his hand, but he withdrew it, cocked his head to one side. 'Sure. I can see all that. But just explain one thing to me.' He leant forward. 'How did you describe your set-up to the authorities? Surely it must seem strange to them . . . two people who've barely seen each other in a year, who don't even like each other by all accounts, suddenly offering to take on a troubled soul . . .'

She took a deep breath.

'Oh. Oh, I knew it . . .'

'No, Conor, it's—'

'You didn't tell them, did you? They think you're still together. To all intents and purposes, you're just another married couple.' His voice was scathing.

'There was no point in raising it . . . And you know very well that, professionally, I've never changed my name.'

'How convenient.'

'I just never got round to telling everybody,' she protested. 'There's absolutely nothing more to it than that. People know me as Macauley professionally. I couldn't work out what to do.'

'And now Mr and Mrs Macauley are adopting a little girl. Well, that tidies things up nicely for you, doesn't it? A family once again.'

'We're not adopting her. She's a teenager who needs some-where to stay for a few weeks. Come on, Conor. Please don't start looking for things that don't exist.'

But he seemed to see a whole plethora of motives, subterfuge, deception. For days now he had been off with her, had pleaded prior engagements when she asked him out or had avoided her altogether. He'll come round, Natasha told herself. She stared at her mobile phone, which showed, for the fourteenth time that day, that no one except her office had rung. Work, she told herself. Just focus on your work.

The house was silent. For another couple of hours it would be hers again. She dropped her head into her hands and closed her eyes. Then she lifted it and, taking a breath like someone emerging from water, rang her office and spoke into the answerphone.

'Ben,' she said, 'when you get this can you pull together all the expert witness statements in the Nottingham case? I'll need them on my desk when I get in. And let me know imme-diately if you hear back about Court Three. I think the Local Authority in the Thompson case is going to appeal.'

It had happened again. Three fresh bales of hay sat against the wall of her lock-up, giving off a faint sweet scent, an echo of summer meadows. Against them rested an unopened bag of feed. Sarah had paid for none of it. She held the cold padlock, staring at the sight that had greeted her twice in the last couple of weeks, and felt an uneasy mixture of gratitude that Boo would have food, and concern over where it had come from.

Autumn had crept over the stables, bringing with it chilly nights and a seemingly insatiable hunger to the horses. Sarah peered out of the lock-up at the brazier, into which Cowboy John was feeding several manila envelopes, talking to his dog. He had been clearing out the brick shed he called his office, burning several years' worth of unopened official correspondence. She had asked him for hay, but he had told her, apologetically, that he had sold all but what he needed for his own horses to Sal.

She filled a haynet, then trudged up the yard to Boo's stable. She topped up his water buckets and cleared his bedding, breaking off occasionally to stick her chilled fingers inside her horse's blankets, where his coat was soft and warm, pausing to listen to his rhythmic chomping.

She had thought staying with the Macauleys would make things easier, and to some extent they were. The house was nice. It was closer to school, and to the stables. But money was a problem. Without Papa to pay the stable rental she was struggling. Natasha insisted on making her sandwiches, instead of giving her lunch money, and they had replaced her bus pass so she couldn't ask for fares. They gave her pocket money every weekend, which none of the other foster-families had, but it still didn't cover what Boo cost.

She didn't like to think how much she owed now. Even without the hay.

She thought of the jar she had seen in Natasha's room. The woman couldn't have the faintest idea how many pound coins it contained. Passing the doorway, Sarah had been transfixed by it, calculating that there were probably hundreds, all mixed in with silver coins. Natasha Macauley signed cheques without looking at the amounts. She had left a credit-card statement on the kitchen table that showed she had spent almost two thousand pounds the previous month, although Sarah hadn't had the courage to check what she had spent it on. The lawyer seemed to have so much money that she didn't even care about the coins she threw into the jar. She probably just didn't want them weighing down the pockets of her business suits.

Sarah knew what Papa would say about girls who took money that didn't belong to them. But increasingly she found herself answering him back: *So what? You're not here. How else am I supposed to keep our horse until you come home?*

'Sarah.'

She jumped. Cowboy John had disappeared somewhere, and Sheba hadn't barked, as she normally would if someone came in. 'You gave me a fright.' She stepped back against the door to her lock-up, the padlock still in her hand.

Maltese Sal stood behind her, his face indistinct in the evening gloom. 'I was passing and saw the gates open,' he said. 'Just wanted to make sure everything was okay.'

'Everything's fine,' she said, turning and wrestling with the key. 'I was about to go home.'

'You locking up for John?'

'I've always had a set of keys,' she said. 'I help him out if he needs to go early. I . . . I don't mind carrying on when you take over.'

'When I take over?' The gold tooth glinted. 'Sweetheart, I own this place. Have done for over a week now.' He leant against the doorframe. 'But, sure, you can keep your keys. It might be useful.'

Sarah scrabbled on the floor for her schoolbag, grateful that the flickering sodium light on the pavement outside meant Sal couldn't see her blushing.

'Where you going?'

'Home,' she said.

'Your granddaddy's back?'

'No,' she said. 'I'm – I'm staying with someone.'

'It's dark,' he said. 'Not good for a young girl to be out alone at night.'

'I'm okay,' she said, hauling her bag on to her shoulder. 'Really.'

'You want a lift? I got plenty of time.'

Still she couldn't make out his face. He smelt of tobacco, not cigarettes but something rich and sweet. 'I'd better not.'

She made to move past him, but he stood there. She suspected it was a game for him, making people uncomfortable. She wondered if his men were in another part of the yard, laughing at her.

'You got the hay, okay?'

'Thank you. Sorry. I meant to say.' She reached into her pocket, and pulled out the money she had counted that morning. 'This is for the last two lots.' She handed it to him, flinching slightly as her fingers met his hand.

He held it up, scrutinising it under the light. Then he laughed. 'Sweetheart, what's this for?'

'The hay. And the feed. For two weeks.'

'This wouldn't cover two of those bales. That's good stuff in there.'

'Two pounds a bale. That's what I pay John.'

'This is way better than his. Five pounds each, those bales. I told you I'd only feed your horse the best. You owe me three times that amount.'

She stared at him. He did not appear to be joking. 'I haven't got that much,' she whispered. Sheba was whining at her legs.

'That's a problem.' He nodded, as if to himself. 'That is a problem. Because there's the back rental as well.'

'Back rental?'

'According to Cowboy John's books you haven't paid for six weeks.'

'But John said he was letting us off the back rent. Because of my granddad.'

Maltese Sal lit a cigarette. 'His promise, sweetheart. Not mine. Far as I'm concerned, I've taken on a going concern and the books say there's a big black deficit against your name. I'm not a charity. I need the rental.'

'I'll talk to him. I—'

'It's not his place any more, Sarah. It's me you owe the money to.'

Sarah began to calculate six weeks' rent, adding it to the money he said she owed for the food. The figure made her head swim. 'I . . . can't find that sort of money, not straight away.'

'Well . . .' Maltese Sal stepped back so that she could pass. He began to walk towards the gates. 'That's okay for now. I'm not going anywhere, Sarah. You sort it out and see me later.'

She was just coming out of court when Linda came hurrying up the stone steps. Natasha turned from the solicitor she had been chatting to, and Linda thrust a piece of paper into her hand, still puffing. 'You need to ring this woman. She says some girl called Sarah didn't turn up at school again.'

'What?' Her head was still full of court proceedings.

'They rang shortly after ten. I didn't like to interrupt you.' Linda nodded towards the courtroom. Then, when Natasha didn't seem to be getting the message: '*Sarah didn't turn up at school this morning.* They assumed you'd know what this meant. Is she a client? I was trying to think who they were talking about.'

Natasha glanced at her watch. It was a quarter to twelve. 'Did you ring Mac?'

'Mac?' said Linda. 'Your ex Mac? Why would I ring him?'

Natasha began to search for her mobile phone. 'Don't worry. I'll explain some other time.' Finding it, she strode down the corridor, past the lawyers and clients standing in huddles, until she reached a quiet corner.

'Natasha?' He sounded surprised to hear from her. In the background she could hear laughter and music, as if he was at a party.

'The school rang. She's not there again.'

'Who? Sarah?' He broke off, instructed someone to shush. 'But I dropped her off at a quarter to nine.'

'Did you see her go through the school gates?'

A pause. 'Now you mention it, no. She waved me off. Christ, I didn't think we were going to have to hold her hand.'

'They've rung me twice. Legally we're meant to report her as missing after two hours. You'll have to sort this, Mac. I've got less than an hour, then I'm stuck in court all afternoon. I won't be out until four, given the way this morning went.'

'Damn. I'm in the middle of a shoot and then I've got a job in South London.' She could hear him thinking. He always hummed when he was trying to work something out. 'Okay. You ring the school, check she hasn't arrived, and I'll go home, make sure she's not there, and ring you back.'

Sarah wasn't at home or at school, and she wasn't at the hospital either. Mac called as Natasha paced her office, bolting a sandwich, and told her not to ring the social worker until the evening. 'Let's talk to her first,' he said.

'What if something's happened to her? Last time it was just one lesson. This is the best part of a day. Mac – we need to ring her social worker.'

'She's fourteen. She's just kicking up her heels, probably out of her head on cider in some doorway with her mates.'

'Oh, that's reassuring.'

'She'll be back. She won't go far from her grandfather, will she?'

Natasha couldn't share his certainty. That afternoon she struggled to keep her mind on the hearing. When she glanced at Lindsay, her twelve-year-old client, sitting sullenly, flanked by her guardian and social worker, who were overseeing the final hearing for a secure-accommodation application, she saw Sarah's blank little face as she tried to leave the house. Something was going on that they didn't know about, and it made Natasha nervous. She swung between concern that the child was genuinely struggling with something, and a growing, nagging anxiety that she had invited a whole heap of trouble into what had been her safe, orderly existence.

'Your notes,' Ben whispered, as he slid into the seat beside her. 'You left them outside on the chair.'

'Christ. Thanks.'

I should have considered this more carefully, she told herself, as she listened to the lawyer for the local authority. I got so worked up about the prospect of sharing a house with Mac that I didn't think about the possibility that things could get even more complicated.

'Mrs Macauley, have you anything to add?' the judge asked.

She wasn't on top of this. She felt her normal focus dissolving. 'No, your honor. That's all.'

'I thought you were going to bring up the psychiatrist's report,' Ben whispered.

Damn. She stood up abruptly. 'Actually, with apologies, your honour, there is one further item I would like to draw to your attention . . .'

Mac was at the kitchen table when she arrived home. She threw her case down by the fridge and unwound her scarf from her neck. 'Still nothing?' she said.

'Not since you left work, no.'

'It's getting dark. How long do you think we should leave it before we ring someone?' A tight knot of anxiety had settled in her stomach during his first telephone call and had grown into an oversized, weighted ball. She had played through the conversation with the social worker several times. The authorities would think they were stupid or, worse, careless. The one thing they had asked them to do was make sure she went to school. The case workers would talk. They might call into question Natasha's professional ability. And underneath these concerns, the terrifying voice at the back of her head, the voice she attempted to drown with reason, practicality, another phone call to Mac. *What if, this time, something really has happened? I've had no practice at this. Real parents have years in which to get used to this level of anxiety.*

'We'll give her another half an hour,' Mac said. 'That takes it to six o'clock. By then we'll have given her enough chances.'

She sat down opposite him, and accepted the glass of wine he had poured for her. He was not smiling now. His relaxed air of earlier had disappeared, replaced by silence, tension. 'Did you get to your other job okay?' she asked.

He shook his head. 'I thought I should go to the school gates for chucking-out time. Just in case she turned up.' He sighed and sipped his wine. 'Besides, my head wasn't in it. It's fine. They let me reschedule for tomorrow.'

Their eyes met briefly. *As long as she's here by tomorrow.*

'I was useless in court,' she offered. 'Couldn't keep my mind on the job at all. I was surprised at myself.'

'Not like you.'

'No,' she said. She had lost the case. Ben's expression as she left the High Court had told her she was the reason why.

'Kids, eh?' Mac said mirthlessly.

They jumped as they heard the doorbell. 'I'll go,' he said, pushing himself back from the table.

She sat there and sipped her wine, listening to him open the front door. He muttered something she couldn't hear, and then his footsteps were returning down the hallway. Behind him, her face half obscured by her scarf, the chill evening air still radiating from her clothes, stood Sarah.

'Welcome back,' Mac said, turning to her. 'We weren't sure whether you'd booked into another hotel.'

Her eyes were just visible and darted between them as she tried to gauge how much trouble she was in.

'Care to tell us where you've been?' Mac's voice was light, but Natasha could detect frustration in it.

Sarah pulled down the scarf a fraction. 'Went out with a friend.'

'Not this evening,' Mac said. 'I meant all day. When you were supposed to be at school.'

She kicked at something invisible on the floor. 'I wasn't feeling well.'

'So . . .'

'So I went for a walk. To clear my head.'

Natasha could bear it no longer. 'For nine hours? You went for a nine-hour walk to clear your head? Do you have the slightest idea how much trouble you've caused?'

'Natasha—'

'No!' She brushed aside Mac's warning. 'I lost a case today because I was so busy worrying about where you were. The school has been on at us every hour. Mac had to cancel an important job. The least you can do is tell us where you've been.'

The scarf was pulled up again. Sarah stared at the floor.

'You are here as our responsibility, Sarah. That means we're legally responsible for you. We have to make sure you get to school, and that you come home again. As a matter of law. Do you understand?'

She nodded.

'So, where were you?'

There was a long, uncomfortable silence. Finally the girl shrugged.

'Do you want to end up in secure accommodation? Because this is the fourth time you've disappeared in ten days. If you do this again, and the school notifies your social worker first, instead of us, you will end up in secure accommodation. Do you know what that is?' Natasha's voice had lifted now. 'It means you'll be locked up.'

'Tash . . .'

'It won't be up to us, Mac. They'll just decide we're

incapable of taking care of her, and if they think she's at risk of disappearing, they'll apply for court proceedings to put her in secure.'

The girl's eyes were wide over the scarf.

'Is that what you want?'

Sarah shook her head slowly.

'Come on,' said Mac. 'Let's calm down. Sarah, we just want you to stick to the rules, okay? We need to know where you are.'

'I'm fourteen.' Her voice was quiet but defiant.

'And you're in our care,' said Natasha. 'You asked to come here, Sarah. The least you can do is play by our rules.'

'I'm sorry,' she said.

She didn't look sorry, Natasha thought. 'Tomorrow,' she said, 'Mac will be taking you in before registration and handing you over to your teacher. And one of us will be at the school gates when you come out. Until you prove to us that we can trust you to be where you say you are.'

Mac stood up, went to the cupboard and pulled out a bag of dried pasta. 'Okay, we'll leave it there and trust that this won't happen again. Sarah, take your coat off and sit down. You must be hungry. I'll make us some food.'

But Sarah turned on her heel and walked out of the kitchen. They heard her tread heavily up the stairs and the door of her bedroom close emphatically behind her.

There was a short silence.

'That went well.'

Mac sighed. 'Give her a chance. She's having a tough time.' Natasha swallowed some wine, let out a long breath, then looked at him. 'Does this mean it isn't the time to tell you that money has been disappearing from the jar in my room?' She wasn't sure he'd heard her. 'Quite a lot. I just noticed that the level has dipped. And I remember tipping four pound coins into the top of it the other night. Yesterday they were gone.'

He carried on pouring pasta on to the scales.

'Oh . . . no . . .' she said.

'I didn't want to say anything,' he said, 'but I remember dropping a fiver out of my jeans pockets on to the coffee-table the other night, and making a note to myself that I'd pick it up in the morning. When I came down it was gone.' He went to the kitchen door and shut it silently. 'You think it's drugs?' he asked.

'I don't know. I've never suspected her of being high.'

'No . . . she doesn't seem . . .'

'It's not clothes,' she said. It was one of the things Natasha had found almost endearing. Sarah seemed uninterested in fashion and celebrity magazines, spent no more than ten minutes in the bathroom each morning. 'She doesn't have a phone, to my knowledge. And she doesn't smell of cigarettes.'

'Something's up.'

Natasha stared at her wine glass. 'Mac,' she said, 'I have to tell you something. When I first met her, she was being held for shoplifting.'

He stopped what he was doing.

'It was just a packet of fish-fingers. I bumped into her in a supermarket. She swore she was going to pay for it.' *I've been fooled again. I thought I was doing a good thing. Stupid, guilty, middle-class liberal. I'm totally out of my depth.* 'I'm really sorry,' she said. 'I should have told you.'

He shook his head. She realised, with gratitude, that he wasn't going to make a big deal of it. 'Do you think . . .' she said, tentatively '. . . that we have—'

But Mac interrupted her. 'I can't do it tomorrow,' he said, finally tipping the pasta into the boiling water. 'But give me a day or two and I'll follow her. See what she's up to. We'll get to the bottom of this.'

Ten

'*What a spirit and what mettle; how proudly he bears himself – a joy at once, and yet a terror to behold.*'

Xenophon, *On Horsemanship*

For two days Sarah was a model of obedience. She allowed Mac to accompany her to the classroom, albeit bristling with resentment, and was there, scuffing her shoes, at the school gates when he arrived to pick her up. But the beauty of teenagers, thought Mac, was that they always assumed they were cleverer than everyone else. And Sarah was no exception.

On day three, as he dropped her at school, he told her he didn't have time to run inside with her, and would she be okay going in by herself? He saw the brief glint in her eye, quickly suppressed, then he waved, accelerated away as if he was in a hurry and drove around the block. He pulled up by some garages, counted to twenty, then drove round slowly and back on to the high street past the school. Pupils were still streaming in through the gates, bags slung low over their shoulders, shouting at each other or gathered in huddles round mobile phones. And, sure enough, there was Sarah, heading in the opposite direction, half walking, half running up the road towards the bus stop.

Mac prayed she wouldn't turn around, but she was already too focused on where she was going. Damn it, Sarah, he told her silently. Why are you so determined to sabotage your own future? He watched as she leapt on to a bus, registering the number and its destination. The wrong direction for the hospital, he noted. The social worker had taken her to see her grandfather the previous week and had mentioned its location. Mac had promised to take her this weekend, and had written down the address. So where was she headed?

He sat in his car behind the bus, no longer able to see her, but trusting he would catch sight of her when she jumped off again. He allowed two cars to cut in front of him, to make himself less conspicuous, but the rush-hour traffic ensured that cars and bus made little headway.

Please let it be a boy, he willed, fiddling with his radio. If it was, they could invite him round, talk to them both. A boy would be manageable. Timetabled. But not drugs. Please don't let it be drugs.

For twenty minutes the car crept across London and on to the City. He drew fierce protest from white vans, shouting at him for failing to go faster, and rude gestures from smart women who might have known better. When it got bad, he pulled in for a few seconds and let people pass, wondering at the number of tickets he was going to get for repeatedly edging into the bus lane. He had come so far now that he couldn't afford to lose her. It started to rain as he reached the edges of the Square Mile, and he strained to catch sight of her dark uniform among the suited City workers with umbrellas who jumped on and off the bus at each stop. Here, where the population grew denser, it was increasingly hard to tell. Several times he wondered if he had already missed her, if he was on some wild-goose chase, but he stayed where he was.

Finally, where the glass towers of the financial district began to morph into the grimier buildings, residential blocks of flats, he caught sight of her. She skipped off the bus, ran around the rear of it, and leapt on to the island in the middle of the road. Mac held his breath, knowing that if she glanced to the right she would see him. But her attention was on the traffic going the other way. She let go of the railing and ran across. Before Mac realised he was now facing the wrong way, she was off down a side-street.

'Shit,' he said aloud. '*Shit, shit, shit.*' He wrenched the car out from behind the bus, throwing up a hand of apology as the vehicle behind him screeched to a halt, and shot through an amber light on the crossing, so that a woman pedestrian thumped the side of his car in protest. '*Sorry, sorry, sorry,*' he muttered, accelerating as fast as he could towards the roundabout. He skidded around it and back on to the main road facing the opposite way, peering through the windscreen as he tried to spot her. He drove until he saw the little side-street she had disappeared down, then realised, as he began to indicate, that it was one-way. The wrong way.

Mac hesitated for just a moment. Then he accelerated down it, praying he could get to the next street before anyone came the other way. 'I know . . . I know . . .' he shouted at the moped, who careered towards him, its rider shouting obscenities from under his helmet.

And then, at the crossroads, there was nothing. He could see no cars and no people, just a row of lead-stained Victorian buildings, the entrance to a car park, a block of flats. On his left he could make out the high street, a café and an Indian takeaway briefly obscured by a bus. On impulse, he turned right, driving slowly now on the cobbles, glancing down each street he came to in search of a girl in school uniform. Nothing. It was as if she had disappeared into thin air.

Mac pulled on to the lane, and into a parking space. He sat there for a moment, cursing himself. Cursing her. *What the hell am I doing? I'm chasing a schoolgirl I hardly know across London, and for what?* In a few weeks she would be gone anyway. If she wanted to wreck her life with stupid boyfriends or drugs, was that really his problem? Her grandfather would get better, he would straighten her out, and they would all get on with their lives.

His phone was ringing. He reached down into the passenger footwell, discovering that his erratic driving had sent his belongings flying out of his pockets and on to the floor. It took him a couple of minutes to locate it.

'Mac?'

Maria.

'Hey,' he said.

'Don't say it, you wanted to ring me but you're trapped under large piece of furniture.' Her voice was bruised with hurt. He didn't take it personally – she used that tone if her tea was the wrong colour. 'You were going to ring me about lunch.'

'Christ,' he said. 'Sorry, sweetheart. I've got caught up in something. I'm not going to make it.'

'Is job?'

'Not exactly.' He leant back in his seat, ran his hand over his head.

'Is your ex-wife again. You two are making mad, passionate love all night and you no longer have the energy for me.' She started to laugh.

'It's nothing to do with Natasha.'

'In Poland, Natasha is most popular name for prostitute. You know this?'

'I'll tell her. I'm sure she'll be glad to hear it.'

Maria shouted at someone, then returned to the phone. 'Is very sad for you. You won't see me for two weeks.'

'No?' Was that Sarah at the other end of the narrow road? He peered out, but when the girl turned she was pushing a pram.

'Have got major-major job in Caribbean. I told you.'

'You did.'

'For Spanish *Elle*. Guess who is shooting.'

'Maria, you know I don't know one fashion photographer from another.'

'Sevi. Everyone knows Sevi.'

He'd have to ring Tash and tell her he'd lost her. They'd decide whether to call the social worker.

'He did cover shoot for *Marie Claire* this month.'

Perhaps he could ring the school and say she had an appointment. Then he'd force her to tell him where she'd gone.

'*Marie Claire*,' she repeated, for emphasis.

'They must have mislaid my copy at the newsagent this month.'

'You are very sad man. Very many bad jokes.'

'Maria, sweetheart,' he said, 'I have to go. I need to make a call.'

'Are you becoming homosexual?'

'Not today, no, but I'll give it some thought.'

'My sister has married homosexual. Did I tell you this?'

He had stopped listening. A large brown horse was emerging through a pair of wire mesh gates further up the road. It jumped slightly at a dustbin, then skittered sideways as it came down the cobbled road towards him, its hooves clattering on the hard surface. He squinted as it got closer; the inside of his car was steaming up. But there was no doubt about the identity of the rider. He was electrified with shock.

'Maria – got to go. Ring me from wherever and we'll sort something out.' He shoved the phone into his pocket, and then, as the horse was a good twenty feet away, opened his door quietly and climbed out. Sarah's hair was tied back, her slender frame perched lightly on the huge animal, her school sweatshirt clearly visible. It jumped sideways again, but she didn't seem to move. He saw her reach down and stroke its neck, as if reassuring it.

Mac shut his door and moved swiftly to the boot from which he pulled out his Leica, his eyes barely leaving the girl on the horse. He locked the car, and began to walk down the road behind her, watching as she sat quietly, apparently oblivious to the noise and chaos of the city around her. As they turned the corner, he saw she was headed for the park.

He thought for a moment, then reached for his phone and dialled the number, stepping into a doorway so that his voice did not carry on the wind. 'Is that the school office? Hi . . . yes. It's the guardian of Sarah Lachapelle here. I'm ringing to say she's got a doctor's appointment this morning and won't be in. Yes, I'm very sorry . . . I know I should have called earlier . . .'

Until Papa had become ill, almost half of Boo's training had been done from the ground. Papa had long-reined him, standing behind him, encouraging him to understand the various pressures of his hand and rein as instruction; to adjust his balance, to bring his hindquarters further under him, to bend to the left or right. Sarah would be positioned at his head or shoulder, reinforcing whatever her grandfather instructed with gentle pressure or voice, sometimes a faint shiver of a schooling whip. This way, Papa had explained, Boo could learn without having to cope with her loss of balance as well. Papa always made it sound as if she was a liability, that her presence made life harder for Boo. She had long since stopped taking it personally.

He had once owned a horse called Gerontius, who had been long-reined for three years before anyone was allowed to sit on him. It is not a substitute for training, he would tell her. It was the foundation of training. All the 'airs above the ground,' the *sauts d'école*, stemmed from such building blocks. They could not be bypassed.

That was all very well, Sarah thought now, but she needed to ride. She sat, allowing him to stretch out a bit, chiding him with her voice as he startled at street-lamps, traffic cones and drain covers, obstacles he wouldn't have blinked at six weeks ago. She had been forced to stay away for two days: two days in which he might have been fed and watered but would not have stepped outside his stable. For an intelligent, fit horse like Boo, it was tantamount to torture, and she knew she was likely to pay for it.

It had started to rain harder, and Sarah held up an arm, asking the traffic to stop as she crossed the road. Boo had caught sight of the grass now, and she felt his energy build beneath her. The rain would empty the park, allowing her room to work without interruption. But the horse was excited, possibly too much so. After his confinement, his hooves would react to that springy surface as if to an electrical charge.

Listen to me, she told him, with her seat, her legs, her hands. But there was something exhilarating about knowing such power was just waiting to be unleashed.

Levade, a little voice said, inside her head.

Papa had told her she was not to try it, that it was too ambitious a movement. *Levade* asked the horse to shift its weight on to its back legs, keeping at an angle of thirty-five degrees. It was a test of strength and balance, a transition to the greater challenges of classical dressage.

But Papa had done it. She had done it from the ground. She knew Boo was capable of it.

Sarah breathed in the damp air, wiping the moisture from her face. She trotted Boo in small circles, halting, then moving forward, forcing him to concentrate on her, creating an invisible arena between the park bins, the bollards and the long edge of the children's play area. When she was sure he was warmed up, she began to canter, first on one rein, then on the other, trying to hear her grandfather's instruction: sit deep, hands still, legs back a little, more contact on the outside rein. And within minutes she was lost, transported from the endless frustrations of living by someone else's rules, of the money she owed, of the sight of Papa, frustrated and unhappy in a bed that smelt of chemical pine and old people. It was just her and Boo, locked into their paces, working until they steamed under the fine mist of rain. She brought him back to walk, and loosened the reins, allowing him to stretch out. He no longer jumped at the noises of the street, or at the three double-decker buses: hard work had relaxed him, grounded him. Papa would be pleased with him today, she thought, running her hand along his wet neck.

Levade. Would it really be such a sin to test him a little? Would Papa ever have to know? She took a deep breath, and gathered up the reins again, urging him into a slow trot, which she gradually restricted until he was in *piaffe*, lifting his hooves rhythmically on the spot. She straightened her back, trying to remember Papa's instructions. The hind feet must come under the horse's centre of gravity, the hocks almost sinking to the ground. She leant back a little, her legs encouraging him, telling him that his energy must go somewhere, holding him back with the faintest pressure on her reins. She clicked her tongue, a series of instructions, and he tensed, listening to her, his ears flicking. He couldn't do it, she realised. She needed a second person, someone to explain to him from the ground. Then she felt his rear sink beneath her, and for a moment she panicked a little as if it would unbalance them both, but suddenly his front end was rising in front of her and she leant forwards to help him, feeling him quiver as he tried to maintain it. They teetered there, defying gravity, Sarah regarding the park from a new, heightened angle.

And then he was down. Caught off-guard, she collapsed on to his neck and he shot forward, bucking once, twice with exuberance so that she struggled to stay on.

Sarah pushed herself upright and laughed. She felt a great bubble of elation rise inside her, and clapped the horse on the neck, praising him, trying to convey to him a sense of his own magnificence. She reached down and put her arms around his neck. 'Clever, clever horse,' she said again, watching Boo's ears flick, listening to her approval.

'Impressive,' said a voice behind her. Sarah twisted in the saddle. Her stomach lurched.

Mac's jacket was dark with moisture. 'May I?' he said, then strolled forward and stroked Boo's neck. 'He's hot,' he observed, drawing back his hand and rubbing his fingertips together.

She couldn't speak. Her thoughts dissolved, and sick dread flooded her.

'Have you finished? Shall we head back?' Mac gestured towards Sparepenny Lane.

She nodded, her fingers tightening on the reins. Her mind raced. She could go now. She could just urge Boo on, and the two of them could fly across the park towards the marshes. She could go miles before he could catch her. But she had nothing. Nowhere to go.

She walked slowly back to the yard, Boo stretching his neck down, apparently wearied by the intense work, her own posture now defeated. She studied Mac's back as he walked, unable to detect anything from his demeanour.

She halted in front of the gates. Cowboy John appeared from his shed and opened them. 'Taken a shower, Circus Girl? You're drenched.'

He patted the horse as he passed, then caught sight of Mac, hovering beside her. 'Can I help you, young man? You interested in some eggs? Fruit? I got some fine avocados in today. I can do you a whole tray for just three of your English pounds.'

Mac was staring at Cowboy John as if he'd never seen anything like him. It might have been because John was wearing his scruffiest cowboy hat, a red handkerchief and the neon jacket that one of the road fixers had left the previous year. But it was probably the huge joint clamped between his yellowing teeth.

'Avocados?' said Mac, recovering. 'Sounds good.'

'Better than good, my man. These are on the very point of ripeness. Any riper they'd be busting out of their skins and whipping themselves into a guacamole. You want a feel? By God, that's gotta be the best offer you'll get all day.' He gave a dirty chuckle.

Mac walked in through the gates behind her. 'Show me the way,' he said.

Sarah led her horse to his stable. She removed the saddle and bridle, wiped off the raindrops and put them carefully into her lock-up, then began to muck out. At the far end of the yard, she could see Cowboy John presenting Mac with fruit and vegetables. Mac was nodding. He kept glancing around the yard, as if trying to take everything in, apparently asking questions. She could see John pointing out the various horses, his hens, the office. Mac seemed interested in all of it. Eventually, as she filled Boo's bucket with clean water, John and Mac strolled under the railway arch and up to the stable. It was raining even harder now, little rivers of water running down the slope, weaving through the cobbles.

'You done there, Circus Girl?'

She nodded, standing close by the horse.

'I never seen you for two days. You been having trouble getting over here? Old Boo here was threatening to bust out on me again this morning.'

She glanced at Mac, then at the ground. 'Something like that,' she said.

'You seen your grandpa?'

She shook her head. She thought, to her horror, that she might cry.

'We're going over there now,' said Mac.

Her head shot up.

'You want to?' he asked.

'You know this girl?' Cowboy John stepped back theatrically, then gestured towards Mac's cardboard box of fruit. 'You know Sarah? Man, you should have said something. I'd never have sold you that crap if I'd known you was a friend of *Sarah*'s.'

Mac raised an eyebrow.

'I can't sell you those,' John said. 'You come back in my office and I'll give you the good stuff. I just keep that out there for the passers-by. Sarah? You say howdy to your old man for me. Tell him I'll be dropping by Saturday. Give him these.' He threw her a bunch of bananas.

As Mac followed John back to the office, Sarah could just make out a smile playing around his mouth.

Her clothes were still wet when she climbed into the car. He had received a parking ticket, and he was peeling it off the windscreen and leaning inside to throw it into the glove compartment when he noticed she was shivering.

'You need something dry to wear?' he said. 'There's a spare jumper in the back. Put it on over your uniform.'

She did as he asked. He pulled out into the road and began to drive, his brain racing as he tried to work out what to say. When they reached the traffic-lights, he said, 'So that's what it's all about. The absences. The disappearing.' He didn't mention the money.

She gave the smallest nod.

He indicated and turned left. 'Well . . . you're certainly full of surprises.' He felt reassured. She was just a kid with a pony. If a slightly oversized one.

'What was it you were doing? The whole jumping-up-in-the-air thing?'

She muttered something he couldn't hear. '*Levade*,' she repeated, louder.

'Which is?'

'A movement from *haute école*. It's like dressage.'

'Dressage? Is that the thing where they go round in circles?'

She smiled reluctantly. 'Something like that.'

'And the horse is yours?'

'Mine and Papa's.'

'He's pretty smart. I don't know anything about horses, but he looks amazing. How'd you end up with a horse like that?'

She observed him for a moment, as if calculating how much information he could be trusted with. 'Papa bought him from France. He's a Selle Français. They use them in the French riding academy Papa trained at.' She paused. 'He knows everything there is to know about riding.'

'Everything there is to know . . .' Mac murmured. 'Have you been doing that for long?'

'Long as I can remember,' she said. She was swallowed by his jumper. She had brought the sleeves over her hands, and brought her knees up under it. She resembled a very defensive ball of wool. 'We were meant to be going back. To see them. In France. Before he got ill.'

Mac could see her crossing the road between the buses and the lorries, then lost in concentration as she drew hoof-print circles in the grass. What on earth have we ended up with here? he wondered.

'It was going to be a treat,' she ventured. 'For me and him. A holiday. I've never been abroad.'

She fiddled with the sleeves of the jumper. 'I didn't want to miss it. Papa didn't want to miss it.'

'Well . . .' Mac glanced into his rear-view mirror '. . . a lot of people postpone their holidays when someone's ill. I'm sure if you explain what happened to him the travel agent will let you go when he's better.' He watched her bite her nails. 'We'll call them later. I'll help you, if you like.'

She smiled at him again, cautiously. Twice in one day, he thought. Perhaps we can do some good here, after all. He reached forward and set the satellite-navigation system. 'Right. Hospital,' he said. 'Let's turn the heating up. Can't have your grandfather seeing you soaked to the skin.'

Mac knew almost as little about medical matters as he did about horses, but it was clear even to him that, whatever Sarah chose to believe, Mr Lachapelle was not going on holiday – or even coming home – any time soon. He lay partially propped by pillows, his skin the liverish tone of the properly ill, and did not wake when they entered his room. Finally, when Sarah took his hand, he opened his eyes. Mac stood awkwardly near the door, feeling like an intruder.

'Papa,' she said softly.

The old man's eyes were immediately fixed on her, a veil lifting as he registered who was before him. He smiled lopsidedly.

'Sorry I couldn't come the last two days. It was difficult.'

The old man shook his head. He gave her hand a small squeeze. She saw his gaze slide over to Mac. 'This is Mac. He's one of the people looking after me.'

Mac felt himself being scrutinised. Despite the old man's frailty, there was something starkly assessing in his eyes, as if he was strafing him for clues.

'He's . . . very kind, Papa. Him and his wife,' she said,

and Mac saw she had blushed, as if in her determination to reassure the old man she had exposed herself too much.

'Pleased to meet you, Mr Lachapelle.' Mac stepped forward and took the old man's hand. '*Enchanté.*'

Another small smile. A broader one from Sarah. 'You never said you knew French.'

'I'm not sure your grandfather will agree that I do,' he said. He took the chair on the other side of the bed. Sarah busied herself with her grandfather's cabinet, checking his washbag, repositioning the photographs.

Mac, uncomfortable in the silence, spoke again, conscious that his voice was a little too loud. 'I've been watching your granddaughter ride. She's amazingly talented.'

The old man's eyes slid back to Sarah.

'I rode out this morning.'

'Good,' he said slowly, his voice creaking like an underused hinge.

Sarah's smile this time was instantaneous and transformative. 'Good!' she repeated, as if confirming what he had said.

'Good,' the old man said again. The three nodded at each other in satisfaction. Mac guessed that this was a major breakthrough in conversation.

'He tried really hard, Papa. It was raining, and even though you know he can be really bad in the rain, he managed to stay focused. His mouth was super-light, and he was listening, really listening.'

Sarah was riding now, her back straight, her hands in front of her. The old man was drinking in everything she said, as if he would absorb every detail. 'You would have been pleased. Really.'

'I never saw anything like it,' Mac interjected. 'I don't know anything about horses, Mr Lachapelle, but when I saw him doing all that leaping around on his back legs, it took my breath away.'

There was a sudden silence. The old man turned slowly to face his granddaughter. He was no longer smiling.

Mac faltered: 'It looked . . . great . . .' Sarah, he saw, had blushed to the roots of her hair. The old man kept his eyes on her.

'*Levade*,' she whispered, her voice heavy with guilt. 'Sorry.' The old man moved his head from side to side. 'He was just so full of energy. And I needed to give him something new to keep his attention. He needed a challenge . . .'

The more she protested, Mac saw, the more the old man shook his head in mute fury. '*Gourmand*,' he said. '*Non gourmand*. Small. Again.' Mac struggled to make sense of what he was saying until he realised there was no sense. He remembered dimly that stroke patients had trouble finding the right words. 'The. *Avant. Non*. Horse. *Horse*.' Evidently frustrated, he set his jaw and looked away from Sarah.

Mac felt mortified. Sarah was biting her nails. The old man's expression was mutely furious. This was all his fault, he thought. He tried to pretend he wasn't there, but then he lifted his camera, still hanging around his neck, and held it up. 'Er . . . Mr Lachapelle? I took some pictures of Sarah working. Trotting and stuff. I was wondering, would you like to see?' He leant over the bed and flicked through the digital images. Finally alighting on one that was unlikely to raise the old man's ire, he enlarged it. Sarah placed her grandfather's glasses on his face.

He studied it, seeming to disappear from them for a moment. Then he turned to Sarah, closing his eyes as if in great concentration. 'Mouth,' he said finally. His fingers fluttered.

Sarah peered at the picture. 'Yes,' she agreed. 'He was resisting me there. But he only did that at the start, Papa. As soon as I got his hindquarters engaged he lightened up.'

The old man nodded, apparently satisfied, and Mac felt a slow breath easing out of his own chest.

'Have you got any others?' Sarah asked him. 'From later on?'

Mac flicked through, then handed the camera to Sarah. 'Actually I've got to go and make a couple of calls,' he said. 'I'll leave you two alone. Here, Sarah, you can sort through the images like this. Enlarge them with this button so you and your grandfather can see them better. I'll meet you downstairs in half an hour.' He lifted the old man's hand. 'Monsieur Lachapelle, it was a pleasure.'

'Captain,' said Sarah. 'Everyone calls him Captain.'

'Captain,' said Mac, 'I hope to see you again soon. I promise we'll take good care of your granddaughter until you come home.' God only knows when that will be, he thought, as he left the room.

'You're kidding.'

'Nope. You want to see it?' He handed her the print he'd run off once he'd got home, Natasha reached into her bag, pulled out some glasses and peered through them. She hadn't had glasses before, he noted.

'It's not drugs,' he said, when she failed to speak.

She nodded. 'That's true.' She took them off and looked up at him. 'But a *horse*?' She handed back the prints. 'What the hell are we supposed to do with a horse?'

'Far as I can tell we don't have to do anything. She owns it, she looks after it.'

'But . . . all this time? That's where she's been?'

'I haven't confronted her about the money, but I think we can assume that's where it is going.'

'How does a kid like that end up with a horse?'

'She keeps it under a railway arch,' Mac continued. His brain was still spinning with the images of the inner-city yard. 'Turns out it's something to do with the granddad. He's some kind of horse master. And it's not a common-or-garden Thelwell pony,' he said. 'This beast is like something out of a Stubbs painting. It's pretty highly strung. She does all this . . . dressage stuff with it. Leaping around in the air.'

'Oh, God.' Natasha looked into the distance. 'What if it injures her?'

'Far as I could see, she was in pretty perfect control.'

'But we don't know anything about horses. The social worker didn't say anything.'

'The social worker doesn't know. She doesn't want them to know. She thinks if they do it will be taken away from her. Is she right?'

Natasha shrugged. 'I haven't a clue. I don't suppose there's much of a precedent.'

'She made me promise,' Mac said, 'that we wouldn't say anything.'

She was incredulous. 'We can't promise that!'

'Well, I did. And she's promised she won't miss any more school. I thought it was a pretty good deal.'

He had dropped Sarah at school at lunchtime, having hastily scribbled her a note. She had seemed unable to believe he was colluding with her. 'This is the only time,' he had warned, aware that he had already been too soft. 'We'll sort it out when you get home. Okay?'

She had nodded. She hadn't said thank you, Mac noted grumpily, then laughed at himself as he drove off. Thinking like a parent. How often had he heard his friends moaning about the supposed ingratitude of their kids?

Natasha sat down. She had muttered something about a tough case, inter- and intra-familial abuse, as if he would know what she was talking about. He realised, a little guiltily, that for years he had rarely listened to anything she told him about her work.

'Look, this is good news, Tash,' he said. 'It means she's not on drugs. It's not some dodgy bloke. She's just a teenage girl obsessed with horses. We can handle that.'

'You make it sound easy.' Her voice was almost resentful.
'But we've got a problem here, Mac. She can't cope with the
horse by herself. That's why she's bunking off school. You
told me the grandfather had been doing most of it. Who's
going to look after the horse while she's supposedly sticking
to her lessons? Are you going to do it?'

He half laughed. 'I can't. I know nothing about horses.'

'And I know even less. Is there someone who can do it for
her?'

Mac thought back to the old American with his dodgy
cigarettes. 'I think not. Yeah, I see your point,' he agreed.
'That's difficult.'

They sat in silence for some time.

'Okay,' said Natasha. She didn't look him in the eye. 'I've
got an idea.'

Eleven

'Make him familiar with all sorts of sights and all sorts of noises. Whenever the colt is frightened by any of them, he should be taught, not by irritating him but by soothing him, that there is nothing to fear.'

Xenophon, *On Horsemanship*

It should probably have been obvious from the start, Natasha thought afterwards, that the Kent idea would be a disaster. Sarah had fiercely opposed the idea of moving her horse. 'No. He needs to be here, where I can keep an eye on him,' she had said.

'He'll be perfectly safe at Howe Farm. Mrs Carter's an expert horsewoman.'

'She doesn't know him. He'll be surrounded by people who don't know him.'

'I'm sure Mrs Carter knows even more about horses than you do.'

'But she doesn't know about *him*.'

It was odd, Natasha had thought, that this girl who had said virtually nothing for days was now raising her voice so insistently. 'Sarah, you haven't got time to do it all yourself. You've said as much. And if you want us to keep our side of the bargain, and not inform the authorities, you have to accept that we need to find a different way of looking after him, with your papa away. At Howe Farm he'll be cared for all week. Then we can go and see him at weekends, and you can spend all day with him.'

'No.' Sarah's arms were folded, her jaw set. 'I'm not leaving him somewhere I don't know.'

'But you'll *get* to know it. And it's just a short-term measure. It sounds like a more professional set-up than where he's at.'

Sarah virtually spat out her response. 'He's happy where he is.' She glared at Natasha. 'You know nothing about him. He's happy living at Sparepenny Lane.'

Natasha struggled to keep her voice even. 'But it's not working, is it? Until we know when your grandfather's coming home, we can't manage as things are. You can't manage as things are.'

'You're not taking him away from me.'

'Don't be dramatic, Sarah. Nobody's taking him away from you.'

'Think of it as a holiday for him.' Mac was sprawled across the sofa, eating an apple. It was his house too, Natasha had to keep reminding herself. 'He can spend all day cantering around in the fields, or whatever it is horses do. That's got to be better than being stuck under a railway arch, hasn't it?'

With a barrister's assessing eye, she could see that Mac had her there. For a moment, Sarah seemed to weaken.

'I don't suppose he's had much time just pottering in a field, has he?' Mac threw his apple core at the bin. It hit the target with a metallic thud.

'I let him graze on a long rope sometimes,' she said defensively.

'But that's not the same as having the freedom to trot around as he likes, is it?'

'But he's never been in a horsebox.'

'Then he'll learn.'

'And he—'

'Actually, Sarah, much as I hate to lay down the law here,

this isn't really up for discussion,' Natasha said firmly. 'You haven't got the time to look after him and do your studies. Mac and I don't know enough about horses to help you. We're happy to pay for him to be at Howe Farm, and when your grandfather's up and about we'll pay for him to be brought back here, and you can carry on as you did before. Now, if you'll excuse me, I've got to go and do some work.'

She faltered as she left the room. Mac had looked suddenly awkward at the mention of Sarah's grandfather, as if he knew something he wasn't saying. She felt Sarah's mutinous eyes burning into her back long after she had left the room.

The journey was traumatic. They hired a professional horse-moving firm from Newmarket to transport Boo, as Sarah called him, on a Saturday. The enormous lorry had battled to get down Sparepenny Lane, Mac told Natasha afterwards, and the driver had seemed nonplussed at the address of the yard, even more so when he saw what it comprised. 'He was used to racing stables,' Mac said. 'Grand places.'

'I'm not surprised, given what they charged,' Natasha retorted. The horse, already spooked by some microcosmic change in the atmosphere, refused to enter the lorry. Sarah begged and pleaded with him, swore at everyone to keep back and attempted repeatedly to lead him up the ramp and into the plush interior. But Boo stopped, pulled back against her, several times rearing in fright, sending the small crowd of passers-by leaping backwards, as he clattered backwards on to the cobbles. The longer it went on, Mac said, the more people stopped in the street to watch, and the more upset the horse had become, sweating, white-eyed and almost uncontrollable. Boys had wheeled past on scooters; drivers, blocked by the horsebox, blew their horns bad-temperedly;

Cowboy John, smoking in the gateway, tipped back his hat and shook his head, as if everything that happened was a matter for mild disapproval.

Twice Sarah yelled at the observers to go home, to give them some quiet, until the driver and his helper told her they didn't have time to let this go on any longer and, with a mixture of brute force and a long webbed rope, forced the horse inside, from where they could hear him neighing, his hooves crashing against the sides, even as the lorry moved forward slowly and headed for the high street.

Sarah was not allowed to travel with them ('Insurance, mate. Sorry'). When Mac persuaded her, white-faced, into his car, he observed that her palms were bleeding.

She refused to speak to him the whole way down.

All this Mac told Natasha on his mobile phone, during a brief stop on the motorway. She had gone down ahead in her car to prepare the cottage. At least, that was what she had told them she wanted to do. In truth it was to eradicate any signs of Conor and, more importantly, to prepare herself for what felt like an invasion into the one remaining space in her life that was still just hers.

The cottage had only two bedrooms. Sarah would have the spare room and Mac would sleep on the sofa. Even the thought of having them there made her feel hemmed in, trapped. She was afraid that, once Mac left, this house, too, would be polluted by her failed marriage; a space that had been free of him, of memories, would now carry an unwanted echo. How on earth had she ended up here? How had she so comprehensively sacrificed her independence, her peace of mind and possibly her relationship? Conor ignored her pointedly at work, saying he was busy if he made the mistake of picking up his phone to her. She had texted him that morning, infuriated by his cold-shouldering her:

> Just because your wife did you over does not mean I am cut from
> the same cloth.

She had sent it before good sense could persuade her not to.

> I do not deserve this, Conor.

She had flipped her phone shut and sat in the silent kitchen, half waiting for a response. But none had come, and she had felt even worse.

Natasha walked out into the garden, feeling the approach of winter in the hairs that stood up on her arms. She had last mown the lawn two weeks ago, but the increasing chill had slowed its growth and it still looked even and green. She had raked up the leaves, pruned the shrubs she could identify, and planted long rows of bulbs where once there had been scrub. Above the beds stood rows of glowing Chinese lanterns, their dried orange heads glowing in the grey autumnal air. The last of the roses bloomed gamely from spindly bushes. Where once this had been a place of neglect and wilderness, there was now beauty of sorts.

She took a deep breath and hugged herself, telling herself she had really had no choice but to do what she had done. With luck, Mac would never need to come here again. She would ferry Sarah down at weekends – although, from the sound of it, the girl would want to spend all her time with her horse – and Conor need never know that Mac had been here. Perhaps one day Conor and Sarah might get on. He understood kids, after all. He knew how to talk to them. Unlike her.

Natasha walked slowly round the borders, watching her shoes darken with moisture, wishing she didn't feel quite so unbalanced by Sarah's presence in her life. Every conversation they had seemed skewed, as if she could never strike the right tone. Mac, meanwhile, treated the girl with the casual ease of an older brother. When they shared some in-joke at the kitchen table, or when they discussed her grandfather, Natasha felt excluded.

Sarah, she thought, did not like her. She treated every casual enquiry as if it was an inquisition, and seemed to regard Natasha with barely veiled suspicion. When Mac had told her on the phone that Sarah was refusing to talk to him in the car, she had felt almost joyous. It's not just me! she wanted to shout. She can be cranky with you too!

If Natasha forced herself to be honest, she knew Sarah was aware that she didn't trust her. Yes, the money had probably gone towards the horse. Yes, there were no signs of drug or alcohol use. But the girl seemed somehow too contained, as if there were still things they had not been told.

She couldn't say any of this to Mac. How could she when she had kept the existence of the Kent house from him for weeks? And his answer to everything was simply that Sarah had been through so much that she was bound to be guarded. His tone implied that Natasha was at fault for her failure to understand.

Fantastic, Natasha wanted to say. I've ended up housing my ex-husband, a teenage girl who doesn't like me and paying for a bloody horse. How much more understanding do you want me to be?

He called her again at a quarter to one. 'Can you come down to the stables and meet us?' he asked. 'You know this woman, right?'

'I've just put lunch on the table,' she said, eyeing the fresh rolls, the pan of soup on the stove.

'You want to tell the horse that? He's just shot out of the

lorry and nearly killed someone,' Mac said. 'Oh, Christ! Sarah's shouting at the woman. Better go.'

Natasha grabbed her coat and ran down the lane. When she arrived, Mac was trying to mollify Mrs Carter whose mouth had set in a grim line of disapproval.

'She's been a bit worked up,' Mac was saying. 'She was worried about him. She didn't mean what she said.'

'Anyone who keeps a horse here,' Mrs Carter said, 'has to abide by my rules.'

'I don't want to keep him here,' Sarah interjected, from behind the stable door. Every now and then a horse's head appeared beside her, then disappeared restlessly into the gloom.

From inside the stable, Natasha could hear the sounds of splintering boards.

'If he goes through that wall,' Mrs Carter said to her, 'I'm afraid you'll have to pay for it.'

'It's because you frightened him.'

'Sarah, please,' Mac said. 'Of course we'll pay for any damage.'

We? thought Natasha.

Two men were waiting by the horsebox. 'Is someone going to settle up?' one asked. 'We need to get going.'

Natasha walked over to them, fishing in her jacket for her wallet. 'Bit of a handful,' one observed.

'I'm afraid I don't know much about horses,' she said.

'I wasn't talking about the horse,' he replied.

She turned as Sarah let herself out of the stable. The argument between the girl and Mrs Carter seemed to be escalating.

'I've had horses for forty years' young lady, and I'm not having that kind of behaviour in my yard. I'll not stand for someone like you being so rude.'

'You didn't give him a chance,' Sarah was shouting. 'He's never been out of his yard before. He was frightened.'

'That horse needed to come out of the box before he hurt himself.'

'You should have left it to me.'

'Sarah,' Mac shushed her again, 'come on. Let's all calm down. We'll pay for any damage,' he said again.

'I don't want that woman having anything to do with him,' she appealed to Mac.

Mrs Carter turned to Natasha. 'You said he was well behaved. You said the girl was well behaved.'

Sarah opened her mouth, but it was Mac who spoke up. 'He was very quiet in his other stable,' he said. 'I saw him. He was cool.'

'Cool?' Mrs Carter repeated.

'He's fine around people who know how to treat horses.' Sarah kicked at the ground.

'Young lady, I'll have you know I—'

'One week,' Natasha interrupted. 'Please just look after him for a week. If you really think he's unmanageable I'll arrange to have him taken back.' She looked at Sarah. 'And then we'll all have to think again.'

The lorry was pulling away down the drive. Natasha thought of the soup, congealing in its pan in her kitchen. 'Please, Mrs Carter, Sarah's obviously overwrought, as is the horse. And we can't take him away today. Logistically it would be impossible.'

Mrs Carter sighed. She glared at Sarah, who was stretching over the stable door, still trying to pacify her horse. 'I can't guarantee daily turnout.'

'That's fine,' said Natasha. She had no idea what the woman was talking about.

'And she'll have to keep him in the block round the corner, away from the others.' She turned on her heel and stomped towards her office.

'Great. That's settled,' Mac said. He grinned, as if this had been a foregone conclusion. 'I'm starving. Come on, Sarah. Let's leave him to calm down and get some lunch. You can come straight back to see him afterwards.'

Sarah ate her soup in record time and spent the afternoon at the stables. Mac suggested they should leave her to it. She was a nice kid, his reasoning went. Mrs Carter would probably see as much if they were left to their own devices. They both loved horses. Surely they'd find common ground pretty quickly.

Natasha wished she felt as confident as he did.

After she'd left, they sat in the kitchen with Mac pushed back his chair. She could see him studying the picture of her parents that had previously hung in the office of their London house, the bits of crockery she had brought down with her.

'This isn't Conor's place, is it?' he said, as she cleared the plates.

She saw it through his eyes: a feminine space. Not that she chose things that were frilly or flowery but there was care in the way the objects were placed, a gentleness of tone and arrangement that betrayed the sex of its inhabitant. 'I haven't bought it, if that's what you're asking. I just rent it.'

'I'm not asking anything. Just . . .' he swivelled in his chair, taking in the living room through the doorway '. . . a bit surprised.'

She didn't know what to say so she said nothing.

'And this is where you come every weekend.'

'Most weekends.' She was suddenly self-conscious, as if she might drop the dishes.

'I never saw you as the country type.'

'And I never saw myself as the divorced type. But, hey, stuff happens.'

'Between you and Sarah, you're full of surprises.'

'Well, you turning up on my doorstep wasn't exactly sign-posted.' She ran the water into the sink, grateful for something to do. It felt so strange, having him here, as if he'd turned into someone she didn't know. It was hard to believe sometimes that they had ever been together. He seemed so altered, so removed, and she was conscious that little in her own life had moved on.

'Thanks,' he said, into the silence.

She was primed for the sarcastic payoff.

'For what?'

'Letting us come down here. I can see it's not easy for you.'

There was no hint of sarcasm in his voice. His brown eyes were sincere. It scared the hell out of her. 'It's nothing.'

'In that case, is this the right time to tell you I've had a pad in Notting Hill all along?' He was laughing even before she spun round. 'Joking!' he said. 'Tash, I'm joking!'

'Hilarious,' she said dismissively, then wondered why she was smiling.

'She'll calm down eventually, you know,' he said, after a pause.

She stilled. So he had seen it too.

He came to stand beside her at the sink. She kept her eyes on the washing-up. 'I think . . . nothing much else matters to her apart from her Papa and that horse. Given everything that's happened, she's probably terrified she'll lose him too. And it's making her overreact. She's not hard to read.' He handed her a stray spoon.

To you, maybe, she thought. But she couldn't admit it aloud.

'I blew up some prints,' he said, as he sat down again. 'They're in my car. If I make the tea, will you take a look at them?'

There was nothing else for her to do. She tried not to flinch at the sight of him rummaging around for mugs and teaspoons. With him making tea in Conor's place, she felt as if she was being unfaithful. She was grimly conscious of the irony.

They sat down in the living room, Mac on the chair Conor usually favoured, herself on the sofa opposite. Mac was sorting through a clear folder of photographs. 'This place, where she keeps him, it's like something out of the Victorian age – except for the car and stuff. This old guy,' he pointed at an ageing black man in a battered cowboy hat, 'told me there's a few of these little yards still dotted around the East End. There used to be more, but developers have bulldozed them.'

Natasha looked at the cramped yard, the glowing brazier and loose chickens, trying to reconcile it with its location. It was like a cross between Steptoe and Son and something hidden, magical, a remnant of a long-gone way of life. There were hens, goats, oversized horses and skinny kids. Against a towering heap of pallets, a gleaming, streamlined train passed overhead, its occupants oblivious to the tableau beneath them. This was Sarah's provenance. This was her world. Where did a place like this fit into the modern day? How did a girl like Sarah fit in at all?

'What do you think?'

When she looked up from the prints, Mac's gaze was on her. He really did want to know.

'I've not seen anything like them, that's for sure.' Her eye was caught by another image, a horse rearing, a slight but familiar figure clinging to its back. A break in the clouds had illuminated the horse's head in sunlight, an ethereal juxta-position against the grimy street behind. She realised, with a jolt, that she had seen it before. Once, from a moving train.

'But do you like them?' Mac's voice had lifted. 'Because I was thinking of doing a photographic project. I was going to show the curator at that gallery near Waterloo – you remember? The one where I held that show three, four years ago? I told him about them and he's asked me to show him.' He leant forwards, adjusting his broad hands around the one she was holding. 'I thought I might crop this one, just here. What do you think?'

He had shot this set on film, not digital, he continued. He had used his old Leica, and these were about a tenth of the images on the contact sheets. It had been impossible to take a bad photograph in that place. Everywhere he looked there had been a framed shot for the taking. It would be a lost world, this yard, before long. The cowboy had told him. John knew of maybe five left of an original thirty. Mac might even go and check out the others Perhaps he could make it a series. He was voluble, enthusiastic: She had not heard him talk like this about his work for years.

Eventually he tailed off. 'I'm boring you,' he said, smiled apologetically and collected up the work.

'No,' she said, handing him the prints from her lap. 'Really. They're wonderful. I think they . . . they're the best thing I've seen you do.'

His head shot up.

'Really,' she said. 'They're beautiful. Not that I know anything about photography.'

He grinned. 'You are the woman, after all . . .'

'. . . who once shot a whole roll with the lens cap on. I know.' They laughed awkwardly. In the ensuing silence, she tapped out a tattoo on her knee.

'Anyway,' he said, standing up, 'we've given her an hour and a half. We'd better go and see what trouble National Velvet's causing down the road.'

She straightened the magazines on the table, feeling, peculiarly, as if she'd lost something. She couldn't look at him. 'Yes. Yes, I suppose we'd better.'

*   *   *

They walked back down the lane towards Howe Farm, muffled against the cold air, Natasha self-conscious and out of place in her blue wool coat. As they walked their elbows bumped and she moved away.

She had heard couples describe their exes as their best friends. How could that be? How could you segue so easily from passion – whether love or hatred – to the kind of easy familiarity where you might link arms? She could remember moments when she had hated Mac so much she had wanted to kill him, times she had wanted him so much she had thought she would die from it. How could all that energy be converted into something as neutral, as *beige*, as friendship? How could he have divorced himself from that without a visible scar? She knew the end of their marriage still lay too close to her surface, revealed itself in her gestures, her un-natural responses to him, her ever-present flashes of anger. Yet he sailed on, oblivious, a ship on perennially calm waters. Natasha thrust her chin down behind her scarf and walked a little faster, as if she was impatient to get there, hoping her confusion didn't show on her face.

It was a long way from the cramped urban yard of Mac's photographs. Around a picturesque red-brick courtyard, middle-aged women and teenage girls, slim thighs clad in rainbow-hued jodhpurs, chatted over a tinny transistor radio as they groomed horses and swept stables, brief snatches of their conversation carrying towards her.

'He never tracks up properly on sand. It's like he locks up behind.'

'I was doing a three-loop serpentine with a change of legs in the middle . . .'

'Jennifer had him on barley straw until he started coughing. It's costing her a fortune in shavings . . .'

Horses stood patiently beside mounting blocks, or thrust noses curiously over their doors, engaged in silent communion with each other. It was a closed world, its language and customs alien, its inhabitants bonded by a passion she couldn't begin to understand. Mac was observing it all with interest, his hands restless against his sides, as if they were lost without a camera to hold.

Sarah's horse was not in his stable. The door was wide open. Mrs Carter came out of her office. 'I said she could use the school for half an hour, against my better judgement. I thought she should let the animal rest, but she said he'd settle quicker if he was working.' Her opinion was clear in the set of her jaw. 'Can't tell her much, can you?'

'Her grandfather's pretty knowledgeable. He teaches her most things.'

'Didn't teach her much in the way of manners.' She sniffed. 'I'd better go up and take a look. Make sure she's not messing up the arena.'

Natasha caught Mac's eye, and realised, dangerously, that she wanted to giggle.

They followed Mrs Carter's slightly arthritic limp, trying not to step on her Jack Russell, and turned to where Sarah was standing in the middle of a sand school. The horse was on two long reins, trotting around her, changing direction and back again to some unseen instruction, now slowing until it appeared to be trotting on the spot. She stood close by his quarters, almost pressed against him. Surely the one place you were not meant to stand was directly behind a horse.

Natasha thrust her hands deep into her pockets, watching in silence. The horse was trotting so slowly now that he appeared to be floating, his knees lifting, a gentle bounce to his gait. She could see the animal's intense concentration, mirroring the girl's. His flanks were quivering; his head dipped as he lifted and lowered his hooves in time to some unheard beat. And then he was off again, cantering in a small circle around the girl as she murmured again.

'It's like ballet for horses,' Mac said, beside her. He had his camera to his face, and was shooting off a reel of film. 'I've seen her do this up-and-down thing before. Can't remember the name of it.'

'*Piaffe*,' Mrs Carter said. She was standing beside the gate, watching intently. She had become rather quiet.

'She's good, isn't she?' he said, lowering his camera.

'It's a talented horse,' Mrs Carter conceded.

'She wants to do . . . dressage with him. Something like that. Kind of ballet movements. Air something.'

'Airs above the ground?'

'I think that's what she said.'

Mrs Carter shook her head. 'I don't think you can have got that right. She wouldn't be doing airs above the ground. Not at her age. That's the preserve of the European academies.'

Mac thought for a moment. 'She definitely said dressage.'

'Well, she needs to work on her basic tests to start, prelim, novice, elementary . . . If she's good she can work up to medium in time, with proper instruction, but she won't get anywhere if she's not competing him.'

She sounded so certain that Natasha felt a pang of sympathy for Sarah. She wasn't sure what she was seeing, but the girl was so lost in concentration, so focused on the horse's movements. There was no sign here of the resentful teenager, just a kind of calm competence, love of what she was doing, a silent, willing reciprocation from the animal alongside her. This is it, she thought. Your great passion.

'You haven't seen her ride yet,' Mac was saying, as if in Sarah's defence. 'She's fantastic.'

'Anyone can look good on a halfway decent horse.'

'But she just sits there. Even when he does this rearing thing . . .' He mimicked the action of a horse coming on to its hind legs.

Mrs Carter's eyes widened. 'No horse should be encouraged

to rear,' she said firmly. 'If it falls over backwards it could injure or even kill itself. And its rider.'

Mac made as if to speak, then let out a long sigh and closed his mouth.

They had finished. Sarah turned now, and began to walk Boo towards the gate. His head was low, and he appeared relaxed. He nudged her back with his nose as she approached them. 'He likes it in here,' she said, apparently forgetting herself for a moment. 'His whole action changed. He thinks it's springy.' She was grinning. 'He's never been in an arena before.'

'No? But where do you work him at home?' Mrs Carter opened the gate to allow her out. Natasha took several nervous steps back.

'In the park, mainly. There isn't really anywhere else.'

'A park?'

'I've marked off an area next to the playground.'

'You can't work in a park. In the summer the ground's too hard, and in the winter you'll damage his tendons if it gets muddy. You'll wreck his legs if you're not careful.' Mrs Carter's voice held a hint of scolding, and Natasha saw Sarah bristle.

'I'm not stupid,' she retorted. 'I only work him when the ground's good.'

The brief exultant open smile was gone. This is how it goes, with children, Natasha thought. One hard word at the wrong time, and they feel squashed. She guessed that Sarah would not smile again at Mrs Carter.

'Well, put him in the stable now. The one behind the others. As we discussed.'

Sarah stopped. 'But he'll get lonely up there by himself. He's used to being with other horses.'

'He'll hear them,' Mrs Carter said firmly. 'He's too big for that stable. And, besides, I have to get Brian to fix the holes he kicked in the wall.'

'Do as Mrs Carter says,' Mac urged. 'C'mon. He seems

happy now.' The look Sarah gave him was of resentful compliance. Natasha couldn't work out why it made her feel so odd, until she realised what else she had seen in Sarah's face. Trust. The girl walked the horse into the new stable.

'Right. I need you to fill in some forms,' Mrs Carter said, steering them towards the office. 'I'd like a cheque for the deposit, too, and the repairs, if you wouldn't mind.' She was picking up speed, her dog trotting behind her. She placed a hand on Mac's arm – all women did that, given the chance. 'You know, he's not a bad horse. The best thing you could do for him, Mr Macauley,' she said quietly, 'is find him a new home. Somewhere he can fulfil his potential.'

There was a brief silence.

'I think,' Mac said, 'I'd rather make sure that happened to his owner.'

When they got back to the cottage Sarah disappeared to her room. Natasha spent some time searching for clean towels and tidying the linen cupboard. It was only when she went back downstairs that she thought to check her phone, which had been on the table.

There was a missed call from Conor, and a text message from the estate agent:

Mr and Mrs Freeman hv offered on yr hs. Pls call ASAP

Mac was outside, collecting logs from the woodpile. She watched him bending and stooping easily as he threw the dry logs to one side, then stepped into the kitchen to make the call. It was, the agent advised, a 'sensible' offer, only a couple of thousand below their asking price. The buyers were chain free and in a position to move quickly. 'I'd recommend your acceptance, given the state of the market,' he said.

'I'll talk to my— I'll get back to you. Thank you,' she said, and rang off.

'I'm surprised you don't have muscles like Schwarzenegger, lugging these about.' Mac staggered through the doorway, somehow too large for the little house, bearing a full log basket. He dropped it with a crash beside the fireplace, sending showers of wood splinters and dust across the floor.

'That's because I usually bring in two or three logs at a time, not the whole basket.'

He dusted off his hands on his jeans. 'Shall I build it up, then? Nice to get a fire blazing. You can feel the temperature really dropping out here.' He shook himself theatrically, bits of bark spraying from his jacket. The cold had turned the tips of his ears pink.

She wondered at how relaxed he was, building a fire in what must surely feel like another man's house. He arranged the logs on top of the kindling, then crouched, lighting the newspaper underneath, blowing until he was sure that the first licking flames had taken hold.

'We've had an offer on the house,' she said, and held out her phone. 'Two thousand less than we were asking but they're chain free. The agents think we should go ahead.'

He held her eye a fraction longer, then turned back to the fire. 'Sounds good to me,' he said, placing another log in the grate. 'If you're happy.'

In a film, she thought afterwards, that would have been the point at which she said something. The point at which the whole thing really did become irretrievable, when feelings, actions, took on a momentum of their own. But no matter how hard she thought, she couldn't work out what she wanted to say.

'We'll have to tell Sarah,' she said, 'in case . . . in case things move quickly and we have to find her somewhere else to stay.'

'Let's cross that bridge when we come to it.' He didn't look up from the fire.

'I'll go and ring them, then,' she said, and walked back to the kitchen, her socked feet cold on the hard floor.

Mac had asked if he could cook. He pulled from the boot of his car a box of ingredients, covered them with a tea-towel, and announced that they were not to look until it was ready. Natasha, a little disarmed by her ex-husband's acquisition of culinary skills, found she felt less thrilled by the prospect of this uncharacteristic treat than unbalanced again. Why did he have to turn into Mr Perfect almost as soon as they had split up? He looked better, behaved better, had committed to a grown-up job. He had lost none of his charm. Her life, in comparison, had stalled. It had been as much as she could manage just to keep going. She was oddly reassured when the food arrived on the table.

'It's . . . ah . . . Mexican,' he said, the faintest hint of apology in his voice. Natasha and Sarah regarded the brown gravelly mound in the blue bowl, the tacos still in their packet. Strips of an unrecognisable substance lay in a slimy film of oil, interlaid with something red. Their eyes met briefly across the table and they broke into spontaneous giggles.

'Okay . . . so I still haven't quite mastered the timing,' Mac said. 'Sorry. The beef might be a bit overdone.'

'What's that?' Sarah prodded at the sludgy mound. It looked, Natasha thought, trying to keep a straight face, like something her horse might have left behind.

'That's refried beans,' Mac said. 'Haven't you had refried beans before?'

She shook her head, mildly suspicious, as if this might be some practical joke.

'It tastes better than it looks. Honest.'

He waited, watching them.

'Oh, okay,' he said. 'Let's get a takeaway.'

'There are no takeaways, Mac,' Natasha said. 'It's the country. Look,' she broke open the packet of tacos, 'if we smother it all in sour cream and cheese it'll taste fine. That's all Mexican food's about anyway, right?'

After supper Sarah disappeared for a bath, then emerged to say that, if it was okay by them, she'd go to bed. She clutched a battered paperback under her arm.

'It's only nine thirty!' Mac exclaimed. He and Natasha had moved to the little front room where his feet rested on the log basket. 'What kind of teenager are you?'

'A tired one, I should imagine,' Natasha said. 'You've had quite a day.'

'What's the book?'

Sarah pulled it out from under her arm. It was covered in red paper, held together with sticky tape. 'It's my granddad's,' she said, and then, when they looked expectant, 'It's Xenophon.'

'You read classics?' Natasha couldn't hide her surprise.

'It's about horsemanship. Papa used to read it so I thought it might help . . .'

'The Greeks can teach you about riding?'

She handed it to Mac, who examined the cover. 'Nothing very much changes,' she said. 'You know the white horses of Vienna?'

Even Natasha knew of the gleaming white stallions. She had assumed they were just a decorative tourist attraction, like Beefeaters.

'Their riders still work from the Treatise of La Guérinière and that was written in 1735. *Capriole, croupade, curvets* . . . The airs, the movements, that is, haven't changed since they were performed in front of the Sun King.'

'A lot of the principles of law date back that far,' said Natasha. 'I'm impressed that you're interested in classical texts. Have you read *The Iliad*? I've got a copy upstairs. You might enjoy—'

But Sarah was already shaking her head. 'It's just . . . it's just about teaching Boo. While Papa isn't here.'

'Tell me something, Sarah.' Mac reached for a taco and put it into his mouth. 'What's it all about?'

'What?'

'This fine-tuning stuff. All this making sure your feet are in exactly the right place. That your horse moves his legs exactly this way or that. That his head is exactly *here*. I mean, I can see the point of jumping things or racing. But I watched you in the park, going over and over the same things, again and again. What's the point of *that*?'

She was startled, Natasha thought, as if the question had been heretical.

'What's the *point* of it?' Sarah said.

'Of doing those little movements so obsessively. I can see it looks lovely, but I don't get what you're pursuing. Half the time I can't even see what you're aiming for.'

She had washed her hair and, damp, it still held the tiny, regular furrows of the comb's teeth. She looked at him steadily. 'Why do you keep taking pictures?'

He grinned, enjoying this. 'Because there's always a better one to take.'

She shrugged. 'And I could always do it better. *We* could always do it better. It's about trying to achieve the perfect communication. And a little movement of your finger on a rein or a tiny adjustment of weight might do that. It's different every time because he might be in a mood or I might be tired, or the ground might be softer. It's not just technical – it's about two minds, two hearts . . . trying to find a balance. It's about what passes between you.'

Mac raised an eyebrow at Natasha. 'I think we get that,' he said.

'But when Boo gets it,' Sarah continued, 'when we get it right together, there's just no feeling like it.' Her eyes drifted sideways, her hands closing unconsciously on imaginary reins in front of her. 'A horse can do beautiful things, incredible things, if you can work out how to ask him properly. It's about trying to unlock that, unlocking his ability . . . and then getting him to do it. And, more than that, getting him to do it because *he* wants to. Because doing it makes him the best he can be.'

There was a short silence. She was a little awkward now, as if she had revealed too much.

'Anyway,' she said, 'he'd rather be at home.'

'Well, you'll have him back soon,' Mac said cheerfully, 'after his little holiday. And we'll be just a bad memory. Something for you to tell your friends about.'

'I don't think,' Sarah continued, as if she hadn't heard, 'he'll be very happy when I'm not here in the week.'

Natasha felt impatience swelling within, sharpening her tone. 'But we've been through this. Even if he's in London you wouldn't be able to see him. At least here you can be sure someone's taking care of him. Come on, Sarah . . .' She hadn't meant to sound irritated, but she was exhausted.

Sarah made as if to leave the room, but turned back. 'Are you selling your house?' she said, from the doorway. 'I heard you talking when I was in the bath,' she added.

It was too small a house for secrets. Natasha looked at Mac, who blew out a long breath. 'Yes,' he said. 'Yes, we are.'

'Where are you moving?'

He threw the box of matches towards the ceiling and caught it. 'Well, I'm probably moving to somewhere in Islington, and I'm not sure where Natasha's going, but you needn't worry. It isn't going to happen for a while, long after you're back with your grandfather.'

She dawdled in the doorway. 'You're not together any more, are you?' It was an observation more than a question.

'Nope,' said Mac. 'We're just staying together for the sake of the children. That's you, by the way.' He hurled the book at Sarah and she caught it. 'Look, don't worry about us,' he said, catching her discomfort. 'We're good friends, and we're happy to stay together until everything's sorted out. Aren't we, Tash?'

'Yes.' It came out as a croak. Sarah was watching her and she felt that the girl could see through her, sense her discomfort.

'I'll sort out my own breakfast,' Sarah said, tucking the book under her arm. 'I'd like to go down the lane as early as I can, if that's okay.' And then she was gone, creaking up the narrow stairway to bed.

The first night Mac and Natasha had spent in their London house they had slept on a mattress on a dusty floor. Somewhere in the move from her flat the bolts that fitted the two parts of their divan bed together had disappeared and, exhausted after a day's unpacking, they had laid the mattress in front of the heater in the living room and covered themselves with a duvet. She remembered it now, lying in his arms beneath the bare windows that looked out on to the darkened street, a distant plane crossing the night sky. They had been surrounded by teetering cardboard boxes that would stay unsorted for months, someone else's wallpaper, the strange feeling of sleeping in a house that they owned but was not yet theirs. The two of them, camping in that space, had somehow added to the sense of otherness, of unreality. She had lain there, her heart beating too fast, not even picturing where they would be, what this house would become, but relishing one small, perfect moment, a convergence of happiness and possibility that she suspected she knew even then could not last.

Feeling his arm resting across her body, the vast space of

the old house around them, she had been filled with the sense that they could do anything. As if this was simply the starting point for something as endless as that sky. And she had turned to gaze at him, this beautiful, besotted man, running her fingers lightly over his sleeping face, dropping kisses on his skin until he woke slowly and, with a sleepy murmur of surprise and pleasure, pulled her against him.

Natasha poured herself a large glass of wine. She stared at the television, unsure what she was watching. She felt strangely exposed and realised, with horror, that her eyes were pricking with tears. She turned a little away from Mac, blinking furiously, and took a long swig from her glass.

'Hey,' said Mac, softly.

She couldn't turn round. She'd never been able to weep discreetly. By now her nose would be glowing like a beacon. She heard him get up and walk across the little room to close the door. Then sat down and turned off the television. She cursed him silently.

'You okay?'

'Fine,' she said briskly.

'You don't look it.'

'Well, I am.' She lifted her glass again.

'Has she upset you?'

She pushed herself upright. 'No . . .' This wasn't going to be enough. 'I guess I find the whole horse thing a little exhausting. Actually, just having a teenager around is pretty exhausting.'

He nodded.

'It's not been . . . straightforward, has it?'

He grinned at her.

Don't be nice, she thought. Don't do this. She bit her lip.

'Is it . . . the house?'

She forced her face into an expression of blank nonchalance. 'Oh . . . I suppose it was always going to be a little strange.'

'I don't feel too great either,' he said. 'I love that house.'

They sat in silence, staring into the fire. Outside, the cottage was enveloped by the black night of deep country, muffling sound and light.

'All that work, though,' she said. 'All those years of planning and decorating and imagining. It's just . . . hard, knowing it's all going to disappear. I can't help thinking about what it was like when we first got there, when it was a wreck but with all that potential.'

'I've still got the pictures,' he admitted. 'A print of you knocking through that back wall, all covered in dust, with your sledgehammer . . .'

'It just seems weird, the idea of someone else being in there. They won't know about any of it – about the reclaimed wood banisters or why we put that round window in the bathroom . . .'

Mac seemed suddenly lost for words.

'All that work. And then nothing. We just move on.' She was aware that the wine was prompting her to say too much and was somehow unable to stop herself. 'It feels . . . like leaving a piece of yourself behind.'

He met her eyes, and she had to look away. On the grate, a log shifted, sending a burst of sparks up the chimney.

'I don't think,' she said, almost to herself, 'that I could put that much work in somewhere else.'

Upstairs she heard Sarah opening and closing a drawer against the dull crackle of the fire.

'I'm sorry, Tash.' He hesitated, then reached across and took her hand. She stared at their fingers, intertwined. The strange, yet familiar feel of his skin on hers knocked her breath from her chest.

She pulled away, her cheeks colouring. 'This is why I don't drink very often,' she said, and stood up. 'It's been a long day. And I suppose everyone feels like this when they sell somewhere that they've spent a long time in. But it's just a house, right?'

Mac, face revealed nothing of what he was thinking. 'Sure,' he said. 'It's just a house.'

Twelve

'The gods have bestowed on man, indeed, the gift of teaching
man his duty by means of speech and reasoning, but the
horse, it is obvious, is not open to instruction by speech and
reasoning.'

Xenophon, On Horsemanship

Despite her exhaustion, Natasha slept fitfully. The silence of
the countryside seemed oppressive, the proximity of Mac
and Sarah too great in the confines of the cottage. Downstairs, she could hear the creak of the sofa when he shifted,
the diplomatic pad of bare feet to the bathroom as Sarah
crept to the loo in the small hours. She thought she could
even hear them breathing, and wondered if that meant Mac
could hear every move she made too. She slept, and woke
from brief, fitful dreams of arguments with him, or hallucin-
atory imaginings that strangers invaded her home, until finally,
as the blue light and Arctic orange sun rose above the distant
trees, she stopped trying to force her eyes shut. A kind of
peace descended, as if her mind had been persuaded by
physical circumstance to be still. She lay there, staring at the
lightening ceiling, until she pulled on a dressing-gown and
climbed out of bed.

She wouldn't think about Mac. Allowing herself to get
upset about the house was foolish. Dwelling on the touch of
a hand was the road to madness. She had been drunk and

had let down her guard. God only knew what Conor would have said if he had seen her.

She checked the time – a quarter past six – then listened for the dull roar that would tell her the central-heating timer had kicked in. She gazed at her closed bedroom door, as if she could see through it to where Sarah lay sleeping on the other side of the landing.

I've been selfish, she thought. She isn't stupid, and she can sense my discomfort. How must it feel to have lost so much, to be so dependent on strangers? Money, her age, her background gave Natasha choices that Sarah might never have. For the next few weeks, she resolved, she would be friendlier, disguise her inbuilt reserve and distrust. She would make this short stay useful. A small act, but a worthy one. If she focused more on Sarah, she might be less diverted by Mac's presence. She might be able to prevent herself ending up in the situation she had last night.

Coffee, she decided. She would make coffee and enjoy an hour's peace.

She opened her bedroom door as silently as she could and stepped out. The spare-room door was ajar, and Natasha stared at it for a moment before, on a whim, stepping forward and pushing gently against it. This was what mothers did, she told herself. All over the world mothers were pushing bedroom doors to gaze at their sleeping children. She might feel a little of what they felt. Just a little. It was somehow easier to feel something, to try to feel something, when the girl was asleep.

She was interrupted by the shrill ring of the telephone and pulled back her hand. Calls at this time of the morning only ever meant bad news. *Not mum and Dad*, she begged some unseen deity. *Or my sisters, Please.*

But the voice at the other end of the phone was not a family one. 'Mrs Macauley?'

'Yes?'

Mac was waking. She watched him unwind himself from the sofa.

'It's Mrs Carter here from the stables. I'm sorry to ring so early, but we've got a problem. Your horse appears to have escaped.'

'How the hell did it get out?' Mac sat, rubbing at his eyes. He was wearing an old T-shirt she recognised, worn soft over the years.

'She said they sometimes work out how to shift the bolts. Something to do with banging into the door and making it jump. I wasn't really listening.'

Oh, God, she was thinking. What are we going to tell Sarah? She's going to be hysterical. And she'll blame us for forcing her to bring him here.

'What do we do?'

'Mrs Carter's husband is out on a quad bike, scouring the local fields. She's going out in her four-by-four. She asked if we could grab a head-collar and get the car out. She's afraid he might make it up towards the dual-carriageway. He could have been out all night.'

Natasa hugged herself, shivering. 'Mac, we're going to have to wake her and tell her.'

Mac rubbed his face. His expression told her he was dreading that course of action as much as she was. 'Don't,' he said, pulling on a sweater. 'Let's try and find him first. No point panicking her if he's only in one of the nearby fields. She was so exhausted last night that hopefully we can find him before she wakes up.'

There was a light frost on the ground, and as they drove up the lane, the tyres crunched on the silvered tarmac. They went slowly, with the windows open, straining for sight or sound of a large brown horse. Every moving shadow in a

distant copse, every mark on the icy ground suggested some
recent presence. Natasha tried to form a mental map of the
surrounding lanes, tried to second-guess the intentions of an
animal she had never so much as petted.

'This is hopeless,' Mac said, not for the first time. 'You
can hardly see over the hedges, and the noise of the engine's
going to disguise anything we might hear. Let's get out.'

They parked the car at the top of the village. There was a
place just by the church, Natasha remembered, where they'd
be able to see most of the valley. Conor's binoculars remained
in her pocket; she wasn't sure that she could distinguish
Sarah's big brown horse from any other that might be in a
field.

It was light now, but the air was still chilled from the night
and she was cold. She had grabbed a coat but the T-shirt she
wore underneath was no protection against the near zero
temperature.

Mac was standing on a vault, staring across the graveyard,
squinting against the low sun. As she gave him the binoculars,
he caught her hugging herself. 'You okay?'

'Bit cold. I guess we came out in a hurry.' What if Sarah's
woken? she thought suddenly. What if she's already discovered
he's gone?

'Here.' He took off his scarf and handed it down to her.

'But then you'll be cold.'

'I don't feel it. You know that.'

She took it and put it on. It still carried the warmth of his
skin, was so suffused with the scent of him that she felt briefly
giddy and covered it up by walking away from him towards
a stile. She knew his scent so well, the faint citrus herbiness.
His clean maleness. What kind of masochism was this? She
whipped the scarf off again and, sure he wasn't watching,
stuffed it into her pocket, pulling her collar up.

'I can't see him,' Mac said, lowering the binoculars. 'This

is hopeless. He could be anywhere. He could be behind a tall hedge. In a forest. He could be halfway to London – we simply don't know how long he's been gone.'

'It's our fault, isn't it?' Natasha folded her arms across herself.

'We were just trying to help.'

'Yup. We've really managed that so far.' She kicked at the ground, watching the crystals of frost disappear on her shoes.

He stepped down nimbly, laid a hand on her upper arm. 'Don't beat yourself up. We're just trying to do what's best.'

They glanced at each other, his words echoing around them.

'We should go back.' He walked past her towards the car. 'Perhaps Mrs Carter has already found him.'

She suspected neither of them believed it. Something told her that where Sarah was concerned there were no uncomplicated happy endings.

They made the short drive back in silence. If Mac noticed she was no longer wearing his scarf he said nothing. The house was still, shrouded in darkness, and they let themselves in quietly, glad of its warmth.

'I'll put the kettle on.' Natasha peeled off her coat and stood next to the range, resting her pink fingers on its hot surface.

'What are we going to tell her?'

'The truth. I mean, hell, Mac, perhaps she left the bolt undone. It may even be her fault.'

'She seemed pretty rigorous to me. Oh, Christ.' He ran a hand over his unshaven chin. 'This is going to be messy.'

Natasha pulled out two mugs and began to make coffee, dimly aware through the doorway of Mac pacing the room. He was at the windows, pulling the curtains back, and she was vaguely aware of the room flooding with grey light, illuminating

the evening detritus, vinegared wine glasses and a grate full
of ash.

Coffee, she thought. Then she would ring Mrs Carter. And
wake Sarah.

'Tash.'

Her jaw tightened reflexively. When was he going to stop
calling her that?

'Tash.'

'What?'

'You'd better come over here.'

'Why?'

'Look out of the window. The side one.'

She padded over to him, handed him a mug and peered
out at her garden. Before her, what had once been a neat,
rectangular lawn was now a morass of mud and churned turf.
The Chinese lanterns had disappeared and the stems of the
last foolhardy blooms had been broken, trodden into the damp
earth. Towards the boundary with the open field, her carefully
erected willow fencing had been felled and now lay in a broken
heap against the apple tree. Her pots were smashed on the
patio flagstones. It was a battleground, a crime scene. It was
as if her beautiful, carefully tended garden had been bulldozed.

Natasha tried to take in the extent of the devastation, her
breath stalling, as her disbelieving gaze moved closer to the
misted window.

Just visible to the left of the patio, a short distance away
on a garden bench, lay Sarah's sleeping form. She was
wrapped in her winter coat and covered with the muddied
remains of what had once been Natasha's best winter duvet.

A few feet away from her trailing hand, oversized in the
little garden, determinedly seeking out the few remaining apples
that hung from the bare branches, small clouds of steam
emanating gently from his nostrils, stood a large brown horse.

Thirteen

*'To turn a horse you must first look in the direction you
want to go.'*

Xenophon, *On Horsemanship*

Sarah sat on the top deck of the bus and counted out the
money in her pocket for the fourth time. Enough for two
weeks' rent, five bales of hay and one bag of feed; enough
to fill her lock-up for another fortnight. Not nearly enough
to stave off Maltese Sal. It was a quarter past three. He rarely
got to the yard before four thirty. She would leave what she
had with Cowboy John, or under the office door with a note,
and with luck she would be gone before she had to have
another conversation with him about it. Both times since she
had returned Sal had mentioned the arrears. Both times she
had promised to find the money, with no clear idea of how
she would do it.

She was just relieved to be back. Boo had been returned
to Sparepenny Lane less than a week after he had been taken
away. Mac and Natasha hadn't had much choice about it:
the woman at the stables had gone mad, saying she'd spent
two hours driving around in the dark looking for him, accusing
Sarah of being irresponsible and idiotic and saying didn't she
know there were yew bushes and privet and half a dozen
other things that could have poisoned him in that garden?
Even Mac hadn't stuck up for her. He and Natasha had acted

like she was some kind of criminal, just for mucking up a bit of grass. And she hadn't seen Mac grim before. Not angry, exactly, just that disappointed look people gave you before they let out a deep sigh.

He had worn that disappointed look as he walked her and Boo back to the stables. His hands shoved deep in his pockets, he had told her that Natasha's little garden had been precious to her, that just because Natasha didn't show much emotion it didn't mean she didn't feel it. Everyone had something they were passionate about, that they would wish to protect; surely she should know that better than most.

She had felt bad when she saw Natasha crying in the hallway. She hadn't realised how clumsy Boo would be in the garden, only that it was a place where he could be safely enclosed. Close to her. Mac didn't say much more, but the gaps in what he did say made her uncomfortable. He ended by suggesting that perhaps it would be wise if she and Natasha gave each other some space.

Nobody allowed her to say what she wanted: that they couldn't blame her for everything. She had told them both, loads of times, that she couldn't be separated from Boo. They had to understand she couldn't have left him in a strange place, calling across the black fields for what he knew. The real joke was, she had stayed so close to the house so they wouldn't worry about her.

The bad atmosphere had lingered for a few days after they had returned to London. She could tell that Natasha was still wound up about it. Sometimes she heard her and Mac talking in low voices, closing the doors quietly when they started as if she couldn't tell they were talking about her. Mac would always come out afterwards and be all forced and jolly when he saw her, calling her 'Circus Girl', like Cowboy John, and making out like it was all okay. She had been afraid, for a bit, that they would tell her to leave. But things settled back into a routine of sorts. She got up early now and did stables before school. For a few days Mac had even been up in time to give her a lift. Those mornings he had taken pictures of the yard, of Boo and Cowboy John, but then he'd got a load of teaching work and didn't come at all.

The previous evening he had called her into the kitchen (Natasha was at work; she was pretty much always at work) and handed her an envelope. 'John told me how much you need,' he had said, handing it over. 'We'll pay for Boo's keep for now, but you have to do the work. And if we find you've missed any school, or not been where you should be, we'll send him somewhere else. Is that a fair deal?'

She had nodded, feeling the notes through the thin white envelope. It was all she could do not to snatch it. When she looked up, he was watching her. 'So . . . do you think this might stop . . . some of the loose change in the house going missing?'

She had blushed then. 'I guess so,' she mumbled.

She couldn't tell him about the money she owed Sal, not while they were both still pissed off with her. Not while Mac had virtually accused her of stealing.

She tried to look on the bright side. They weren't so bad. Her horse was with her. Life was as it should be. Or as close as it could get to it, without Papa being home. And yet sometimes, while she sat on the bus in the morning, she remembered how Boo had looked in that soft sand arena, how he had seemed like he was almost floating, his pleasure at being somewhere where he had the chance to be as good as he could be. She remembered her horse, far from the smoke and the noise and the rumbling trains, galloping round and round the soft green paddock, his fine head raised, as if he were drinking in the far, far horizons, his tail held high like a banner.

* * *

'So, how's it going?'

Ruth Taylor accepted the mug of tea, leaning back a little in the plush beige sofa. It was not the kind of living room she tended to see in her everyday work, she thought, noting the artwork on the walls, the burnished expanse of antique oak floorboards. And it was nice to get a cup of tea and not have to worry about where the mug had been.

'Everything all right?' She pulled Sarah Lachapelle's file from her bag, seeing wistfully that she had four more visits that afternoon. No plush beige sofas in that lot. Two check-ups on young asylum-seekers in a grotty B and B on Fernley Road, a boy who swore his stepdad was beating him up and a crack-addicted teenage mother in Sandown.

The couple looked at each other. A definite unspoken something passed between them before the man spoke. 'Fine,' he said. 'All fine.'

'She's settled in okay? It's been – what – four weeks now?'

'Four weeks three days,' said the woman. Mrs Macauley had arrived just after Ruth and was now perched on her chair, her briefcase by her feet, checking her watch surreptitiously as if she was waiting for permission to rush off again.

'And school? Any problems with attendance?'

Another exchange of a glance. 'We had a few problems at the start,' Mr Macauley said, 'but I think we've ironed them out. We seem to have . . . reached an understanding.'

'You've given her some boundaries, as we suggested.'

'Yes,' he said. 'I think we all understand each other a little better.'

Oh, but he was cute. Just her type, all messed-up hair and twinkly eyes. *Mustn't*, Ruth scolded herself. Mustn't think like that about clients. Especially not those whose wives were sitting next to them.

'She's in good health,' he continued. 'Eats well. Does her

homework. She has . . . her own interests.' He turned to his wife. 'Don't know what else to say, really.'

'Sarah's doing fine,' she said crisply.

'Don't worry. I'm not here to judge you, or mark you on your parenting skills.' She smiled at them. 'This is an informal placement – kinship care, as we call it – so we don't get too involved. I've already spoken to Sarah, who says she's happy here. But I just thought that, given her recent history, it would be a good idea for me to stop by to check how it was going.'

'Like I said,' said Mr Macauley, 'it's fine, really. We've not heard from the school that there are any problems. She doesn't keep us awake with loud music. Only six or seven boyfriends. Not too many class-A drugs. Joke,' he added, as his wife glared at him.

Ruth glanced down at her file. 'Do we have an update on her grandfather? I'm sorry, I know I should have rung myself, but we've been a bit up against it in the department.'

'He's improving slowly,' Mr Macauley said, 'although I can't say I'm an expert on these things.'

Ruth wished she wasn't wearing the brown skirt. It made her legs look stumpy. 'Oh, yes. I remember now. Stroke, wasn't it? Hmm. Not recovering quite as fast as they'd like. Are you . . . happy with her continuing to stay? I know we originally thought this would only be a couple of weeks . . .'

They exchanged another look.

'Strictly speaking, once you've gone beyond six weeks, we should undertake a review, perhaps consider a special guardianship order, which would give you some parental responsibility.'

'There is one possible complication,' Mrs Macauley said. 'We'll be selling this house fairly soon. In fact, we've accepted an offer on it.'

'And will there be room for Sarah in your new home?'

They didn't look at each other this time. The man spoke first. 'I'm not sure yet.'

'You want her to become a looked-after child? To transfer responsibility back to us?' Please don't say yes, Ruth willed them silently. I've got a backlog of care requests as long as your arm. And, believe me, not many homes for those kids that look like this.

'We're trying to work it out. It's just we haven't yet decided where we're – ah – going, have we, Tash? But she's definitely okay here for the next few weeks.'

A few weeks. Anything could happen in a few weeks. Ruth relaxed a little. 'Let's hope she's back with her grandfather before long.' She smiled, looking around her at the living room. 'It's a lovely house. I'm sure you'll be sorry to leave it.'

Neither spoke. She placed her hands on her files and leant forward. 'And how are you both doing? If you're not used to living with young people they can be surprisingly hard work.' She addressed her comments to Mrs Macauley, who had spoken least.

'It's fine,' Mr Macauley said.

'Mrs Macauley?'

The woman thought before she spoke. Ruth noted from the document in front of her that she was a lawyer. No surprise there. 'It's been – more tiring than I'd expected,' she said carefully. 'Then again, I don't really know what I thought it would be like.'

'Any particular problems?'

She considered this. 'No,' she said finally. 'I think . . . it's largely . . . a different way of seeing things.'

'Teenagers are a different kettle of fish.'

Mr Macauley grinned. 'You can say that again.'

'They bring their own challenges. But the school says she's a lot more settled.'

'She's a nice kid,' he continued. 'She's got drive.'

'Perhaps if you ever considered fostering again, you'd be happier with younger children. Do you think you might consider becoming registered foster-parents?' No point emphasising the financial benefits, Ruth thought. These two didn't look as though money was a problem. 'There's a huge shortage in this area,' she added. 'Lots of children in need.'

'I do know that,' Mrs Macauley said, her voice low.

As Ruth watched, her husband nudged his wife's hand with the back of his own. A gentle gesture. Supportive. Curiously, she blushed. 'We'll give it some thought,' he said. 'At the moment we're just taking each day as it comes.'

There was a message under her lock-up door. She kicked it open, picked up the piece of paper and opened it, noting the unfamiliar scrawl.

Howdy, Circus Girl, Sorry I couldn't tell you in person but I got to go back to the States. My sister Arlene got sick, and being as how there's no one else in our family (fool woman done frightened off three husbands), I got to see she's okay.

Maltese Sal has keys and he's gonna feed my animals, but you keep an eye out for me, OK?

Tell Captain I'm real sorry not to get up there this weekend, but I'll be back in a week or two. Gonna bring him some Jimmy Beam too, if I can get it past those Nazi nurses.

CJ

She folded the note neatly and put it into her pocket, feeling oddly shaken by the prospect of John's absence. She had known he had a sister in America – he made constant jokes about how ugly she was – but the few times he had disappeared to see her, Papa had always been left in charge. Now, without his presence or John's, the yard felt rootless. It wouldn't be long, she told herself. Everything would be sorted out soon.

It began to drizzle, and the cobbles were faintly tacky where someone had not swept up the wisps of hay and spilt feed. She put her coat on the peg, and changed into Papa's old overcoat, the one he used to protect his clothes. Knowing, instinctively, that activity would ease her anxiety she checked Sheba's water bowl, then set about the horses, straightening skewed rugs, making sure the stable doors were firmly shut. She mucked out Boo, replaced his hay and water, checked his feet, shooed away the chickens and a new, unidentified goat, then stopped for a brief chat with Ranjeet, from the Raj Palace, who had come to purchase some eggs. Finally she returned to the lock-up to change back into her school shoes.

It was as she was about to close her padlock that she remembered the money in the envelope. She reached into her pocket – and jumped as a hand landed softly on the back of her neck. She spun round, ready to strike out.

'What's the matter? You think I'm a crazy man come to get you?' Maltese Sal was highly amused, the gold tooth in the corner of his mouth just visible in the gloom of the lock-up as he wagged a finger in front of her.

She shivered, her hand creeping to her neck.

'You leaving me a love letter, Circus Girl?'

He took the envelope from her, his other hand holding a lit cigarette, his feet planted firmly apart, as if emphasising his ownership of the place. The scent of aftershave and tobacco smoke now overshadowed the subtle sweet scents of hay and forage. 'You know you can always tell me in person.'

'Money,' she said, embarrassed by the way her voice cracked as she spoke. 'It's your money.'

'Ah . . .' He took it from her, his fingers brushing against hers.

'I've got to go,' she said, picking up her bag, but he held up his palm.

He peeled open the envelope and peered inside. Then he frowned and held it out to her. 'And this is?'

'My rent money. Two weeks. And for the hay and feed.'

Outside it was raining harder. Sheba slunk in behind them, her shaggy coat glistening with jewelled drops. Under the railway arches, one of the horses called, his hooves scuffing on the concrete floor.

'And?' He looked at her expectantly. He was smiling, but it wasn't a real smile.

She swallowed. 'I haven't got it.'

'The arrears?'

'Not yet.'

Maltese Sal hissed through his teeth and shook his head. 'You know, you're lucky I held that stable for you. Two weeks ago you come and get the horse, take him away and never even give me notice. You think that's good manners?'

'It wasn't my—'

'I kept that stable open for you, Sarah, even though I could have let it to twenty other people. Then you just turn up back here with him like nothing's happened. Not even a thank-you.'

'But, like I said, it wasn't my fault. It was—'

'Sweetheart, I don't give a monkey's whose fault it was. All I'm thinking now is, how do I know you're not going to disappear again? With all that money you still owe me? You got keys. You and your horse could be planning to go halfway to Timbuktu tomorrow for all I know.' He had moved a step closer to her, his shirt collar level with her eyes.

She found she couldn't swallow without making a really obvious noise. 'I won't,' she said quietly. 'I always pay my debts. Papa always pays his debts. John knows that.' We never had any debts before this happened, she thought.

'But John ain't here. Your papa ain't here. And this is my yard now, not theirs.'

She couldn't answer him.

A train rumbled over the arches, the lights from the carriages briefly illuminating the little yard, a thousand people passing overhead on their way to their homes, their safe, comforting lives. Sal cocked his head as if considering something. Then he took another step towards her. He was closer now, too close. Her breath stalled in her chest.

His voice lowered: 'Your papa's sick, Sarah.'

'I know that,' she whispered.

'Your papa's real sick, from what John says. So you need to tell me something. How are you going to pay me back what you owe me?' His voice was soft, musical, as though he was singing, as though it would disguise the menace beneath. He was so close now that she could feel the warmth of his breath on her face, could smell the musky scent of his aftershave, his leather jacket, underlaid by something male and unknown.

She tried to keep her eyes down. She had heard dark rumours about Maltese Sal. You didn't mess with him. He had spent time in prison, had bad friends and an interest in things you shouldn't ask questions about.

'So?'

'I told you—'

'You told me nothing. Like I said, I thought you'd upped and gone. Now I got to know I'm going to get paid.' His eyes burnt into her. 'We got to work something out, Sarah.'

She blinked at him, trying not to let her breath tremble.

'We got to work out some way of you returning my investment.'

Don't you understand, she wanted to say to him, that that's all I want too? This debt hung over her, twisted her gut into a knot of anxiety whenever she totted it up. It coloured every trip she made to see her horse so that there was increasingly little comfort in simply being with him. Yet there was no one she could safely confide in about it. No one but Maltese Sal who could lift that burden.

'I could muck out for you,' she blurted.

'I got boys to do that, Sarah.'

'Then I could look after the yard at weekends,' she whispered.

'But I don't need you to,' he said. 'You selling eggs, going up and down with a broom, holds no value for me. You understand that? The concept of value?'

Sarah nodded.

'I'm a businessman. That said, I've tried to accommodate your special circumstances. I've tried to be understanding. Anyone else, Sarah . . .' He shook his head. 'I'd have lost patience long ago.'

He glanced behind him, out through the archway, to where the rain was now running down the cobbles and towards the gates, gleaming under the sodium lights. For a moment, she thought he was going to leave. That that was it. But he turned back to her.

He took another silent step forward so that she was backed against her door. Then he raised a hand, and gently picked a hayseed from her hair, holding it in front of her before flicking it away with strong, calloused fingers.

She kept her eyes straight ahead, trying not to flinch. Maltese Sal smiled, a long, slow smile, his eyes telling her that it was okay, he understood. Then, as she tried to smile back, he placed that hand on her right breast, running his thumb slowly across the nipple. This was done so lightly, and with such casual certainty, that it took her two seconds to register what he was doing.

'Doesn't have to be about money, Sarah,' he said softly. Then, with a quick smile, he removed his hand before she had a chance to lift her own in protest.

Her skin burnt with its imprint. Her cheeks flamed. Air locked in her throat.

'You're growing up fast, sweetheart,' he said, pocketing the envelope and shaking his fingers, as if he'd just touched something hot. 'Always a way through for a pretty girl. You just let Sal know.'

And he was gone, whistling, through the wire gates as she stood, frozen, her bag dangling limply from her hand.

'I'm out this evening.' They had finally closed the front door on Ruth. As she departed, she had given Mac one of those smiles – the slightly too wide ones that women always gave him – and, despite herself, it had irritated Natasha. She thanked God she had arranged to meet her sister.

'Okay. I promised I'd take Sarah to the hospital after school anyway. But I'll be out tomorrow, if that's okay?' He didn't volunteer where.

'Okay.' Natasha stepped forward, but he didn't move out of the way. 'I've got a meeting, Mac, and I'm late already,' she said. He was wearing the jeans she had once loved, she noticed, a deep indigo, soft and buttery, faded where he always insisted on carrying too much in the pockets, despite her entreaties. She remembered resting against him during a weekend away several years previously, the wind stinging her ears, her hands thrust deep in those rear pockets.

'I bought you something,' he said. He reached behind him, and held out a large bag of mixed bulbs. 'I know it's only a start, but . . . you were so sad.'

She took them from him. The mesh bag left little bits of soil on her hands.

'I'll help you, if you like, next weekend. I can fix the fencing, at least.'

She swallowed. 'It'll all grow back. Eventually.' She lifted her eyes to his and smiled. 'But thank you.'

She had a sudden vision of Mac, laughing and chatting, his tool-belt hanging from his waist, herself tenderly replacing the lost plants. Is this wise? she wanted to ask. Haven't our paths wound too closely already?

They stood in the hallway, each lost in thought. When Mac spoke, it was clear that their minds had headed in different directions. 'We haven't really talked about this, Tash, but what do we do if the old boy doesn't get better?' He leant against the front door, blocking her way out. 'He's not good, you know. I can't see him bouncing back quickly.'

Natasha took a deep breath. 'Then she has to become someone else's problem.'

'Someone else's *problem*?'

'Okay. Someone else's responsibility.'

'But what do we do about the horse?'

She pictured the animal, treading carelessly over her patio, a path of strewn debris in its wake. That day, it had stopped being a thing of grace and beauty to her.

'Mac, the day we leave here we stop being a family. We stop being able to offer her a home, horse or not. Your job won't allow for full-time guardianship and you know mine certainly won't. We're struggling through every day as it is.'

'So we let her down.'

'It's the system that lets her down. It doesn't have the flexibility or resources to deal with someone like her.' Seeing his expression, she tried to soften her voice. 'Look, they might be able to find the horse a temporary place at a sanctuary or something until a new home can be found for her, perhaps in the countryside, if she's that desperate to keep it. It might work out better for her.'

'I don't imagine that's very likely.'

'Well, I can ask around. See what the options are. Without giving anything away.'

He still didn't move from the door. Natasha's watch told her she'd be late for her meeting.

'Do you want her to go?'

'I never said that.'

'But . . . you don't seem to like her.'

'Of course I like her.'

'You never say anything nice about her.'

She rifled through her bag to hide the colour that had risen in her cheeks. 'What am I supposed to do? Don't make me out to be the bad guy here, Mac. She was a stranger. I've offered her my home – and, might I add, misled Social Services in the process about our relationship. I've paid out hundreds of pounds to move her horse to Kent and back. I've sacrificed my beloved garden—'

'That's not what I'm saying.'

'Then what are you saying? That we should be bonding over makeup tips? I've tried, okay? I've tried to take her shopping. I've offered to do up her room. I've tried to make conversation. Have you ever considered the possibility that she just doesn't like me?'

'She's a *kid*.'

'What? So she's incapable of disliking someone?'

'No. I just mean it's an adult's job to overcome it.'

'Oh. So now you're the expert on child-rearing.'

'No. Just someone with a bit of humanity.'

They stared at each other.

She placed the bulbs on the hall table and picked up her document case, her cheeks scarlet. 'It must be nice being you, Mac. Everyone loves you. Hell, that bloody social worker was nearly sitting on your lap. And, for whatever reason, you have the same effect on Sarah, and that's great for both of you.' She grabbed her phone. 'But don't attack me for not having the same effect, okay? I'm doing my best. I'm giving up my home. I'm sacrificing my relationship simply by having you two here every day, by playing happy bloody families. I'm just struggling through, day to day. I'm doing my bloody best.'

'Tash—'

'And STOP calling me TASH.'

She pushed past him, wrenched open the front door and was off down the steps, still hearing his voice above the thumping of her heart and wondering why tears had sprung to her eyes.

'Okay. You're clinically insane.' Jo peeled off her rubber gloves and walked to the kitchen table where Natasha was nursing a glass of wine. 'Mac? Your ex-husband Mac?'

'But that's the point, isn't it? He's not properly ex yet so he does have a claim on the house.'

'Then you should move out. This is insane. Look at you. You're a wreck.'

Dottie, Jo's youngest, walked into the kitchen chewing a dog's rubber bone. 'No, sweetie. You'll get worms.' She removed it from the child's mouth, which she plugged with a piece of dried apricot even before Dottie had a chance to protest. 'Do Mum and Dad know?'

'Of course they don't. It's only going to last for a few weeks.'

'You've got to get out. Go to a hotel. You were a mess when you were living with him. This isn't going to help you move on, is it? For Chrissakes, Tash, you only really started to get your life together in the summer. BED, you two!' she yelled, at the distant sound of fighting from the front room. 'I really should get this one down too. Are you okay for a minute if I plonk her in now? It's a quarter to eight.'

'Fine,' said Natasha. She was secretly relieved when the adorable Dottie, with her plump, jam-smeared face and talcum smell, was removed from the room. The older children had somehow lost enough of their babyness to seem like people. Dottie was an acute, piercing reminder of something that should have been hers. An absence to which she was still not quite reconciled.

'Say night-night to Aunty Tash.'

Natasha steeled herself for the kiss, forcing herself to look casual.

'No,' said the child, burrowing her head in Jo's legs.

'Dottie, that's not nice – you say night-night to—'

'It's fine. Really.' Natasha waved her away. 'She's tired.' She knew her sister would see this brisk response as yet another sign of her defective maternal gene.

'Give me five minutes to read her a story.'

Jo had put on weight, Natasha thought, watching her hoist the child on to her hip with the fluid ease of long practice. She moaned constantly about having no time, about how children had ruined her figure, all the while dunking another digestive into an ever-present mug of tea. 'Blood sugar,' she would explain. 'Stops me shouting so much at tea-time.'

For a long time, Natasha had avoided her sister's house. During her own miscarriages – only one of which her family knew about – she had found Jo's noisy home, with its finger paintings, chipped plaster and plastic toys, too strong a reminder of the babies she had lost. She had hated herself for not being stoic enough to overcome her envy of those three children, but it had been easier to pretend she was just too busy. Her family had called her driven, a workaholic, ever since she had applied to law school. She was the academic one, the achiever. When she explained that she was just too weighed down by work to attend family lunch, that she had this or that case to prepare for, she knew she would be missed with an indulgent comment, perhaps a certain wistfulness on her mother's part at her apparent failure to devote her energies to the more important things in life.

They had not dared mention her personal life since Mac had left. 'At least you've got your work,' they would say, on the few occasions that she did make it, comforting themselves with their belief that that was all she had ever really wanted anyway.

Jo was back some ten minutes later, chucking the apricot at the sink, then scraping her hair back into a ponytail. 'Desperate to get to the hairdresser,' she said. 'I had an appointment last week but Theo got the lurgy. I had to pay fifty per cent anyway – bloody cheek!'

She sat down, took a long, appreciative sip of white wine. 'Uh. Thanks for that. Bloody gorgeous. Right. I'm going to let the others stay up or I'll never get to talk to you.'

'And are you all right?' Natasha asked, suspecting her sister often thought her self-obsessed. Single, childless women of a certain age were. She heard it all the time. 'And David?'

'Nothing that two weeks in the Seychelles and some plastic surgery wouldn't fix. Oh, and sex. Can't remember what *that* was like.' She snorted. 'Anyway. You. You never bloody tell me anything. Spill.'

Her life had become this peculiar intense little bubble, Natasha realised. Here was normality. Her own life wasn't normal in the slightest. 'I only thought he'd be there for a couple of weeks,' she said. 'It wasn't worth telling.'

'I mean it, Tash. Move out. I'd offer you a room here but we'd drive you nuts in five minutes.' She had another swig of wine. 'You've got the money. Go and book yourself into a lovely spa hotel. Get a massage and a manicure every night after work. Take the cost off his share of the house. He's the one driving you out. The nerve of him.'

'I can't.' Natasha doodled with one of the children's crayons.

'You can. God – I'd jump at the chance. What heaven!'

'No, I can't.' She sighed, braced herself. 'Because I've sort of taken on responsibility for someone. A girl.'

Afterwards, Natasha felt vaguely regretful that she had seen so little of her sister in the last couple of years because, against all expectations, Jo's reaction to this news had been magnificent. She had got Natasha to repeat the story twice, and then, as Natasha explained, voice faltering with awkwardness, she had risen from her chair, walked around the table and hugged her younger sister very tightly, leaving floury marks on her dark suit. 'God, Tash. That's wonderful. What an utterly fantastic thing to do. I wish more people were like you. I think it's brilliant.' Jo sat down, her eyes shining. 'What's she like?'

'That's the thing. It's not how I thought it would be. She and I . . . we just don't seem to gel.'

'She's a teenager.'

'Yes. But she gets on with Mac.'

'Saddam Hussein would have got on with Mac. He's ninety-seven per cent flirt.'

'I have tried, Jo. We just seem to rub each other up the wrong way. It's not gone how I expected . . .'

Jo leant towards the door, perhaps checking that her children were not within earshot. 'I'll be honest with you. The moment Katrin was thirteen she turned into an utter cow. It was as if my sweet baby disappeared and this hormonal monster replaced her. She looks at me with such . . . disgust, like I'm physically repulsive. Everything I say gets on her nerves.'

'Katrin?'

'You've hardly seen her lately. Swears like a trooper. Answers back. Steals odd bits of money, although David pretends not to notice. Fibs about anything. She's a fully fledged member of the precocious-bitch club. I can say that because I'm her mother and I adore her. If it wasn't for the fact that I know the old Katrin's still in there, and have faith she'll re-emerge some day, I'd have chucked her out months ago.'

Natasha had never heard her sister talk in such unsentimental terms about her children. It made her wonder how much of motherhood she had chosen to block out, preferring instead to picture the hazy, rose-tinted version that she felt she'd been denied. It made her wonder if she'd been too hard on Sarah.

'It's not you. And it sounds like she's gone through all sorts. Just . . . be there for her.'

'I'm not like you. I can't do that stuff.'

'Bullshit. You're brilliant, all that work you do with disadvantaged children.'

'But they're clients. It's different. I'm struggling . . . And there's something else. I got turned over by a boy I represented. He made out he'd undergone this terrible journey, and later I found out he'd lied. Now I've lost faith in my ability to see whether I'm being taken for a ride.'

'You think she's taking you for a ride?'

'I don't feel I'm getting the full story.'

Jo shook her head. 'She's fourteen. There'll be all sorts of stories you're not getting, unrequited love, or bullying, or weight problems, or some little cow at school that won't be her friend any more. They don't tell us this stuff. They're frightened of being judged, or told off.' She laughed. 'Or, worse, that we'll charge in and try to sort it out.'

Natasha stared at her sister. How did she know all this?

'Look, I doubt she's deceiving you in any meaningful way. There's probably a frightened little soul in there who might be quite glad to open up to someone. Take her out for a meal, just you and her. No, not a meal.' She chewed at a fingernail. 'Too much pressure. Go and do something together. Something you like. Nothing too intense. You may find she relaxes a little.' She patted Natasha's arm. 'Go on. At the very least it'll take your mind off that git being in your house. And remember you're doing something wonderful just by having her in your home.'

'It's a small thing.'

'Doesn't make it any less wonderful. Right. Now let me get those two terrors up to bed.'

And Mac? she wanted to ask. How do I feel better about Mac? But her sister had disappeared.

The old man took the fork from Sarah with his better hand and put the slices of mango into his mouth slowly, with silent, intense satisfaction. Mac had bought a ready-prepared pack from the supermarket on the way over, and Sarah was spearing each small piece, then handing him the white plastic fork, allowing him the dignity of feeding himself.

Mac waited until they had finished, the Captain carefully wiping his mouth with a paper napkin, before he pulled out the folder. 'I've got something for you, Captain,' he said.

The old man turned his head towards him. He seemed perkier today, Mac thought, his responses more alert, his language a little less confused. He had demanded water twice, quite clearly, and said, '*Chérie*,' when he had seen Sarah.

He pulled a chair to the other side of the bed, and opened it so that the contents were clearly visible. 'We've decided to decorate your room.'

Before the Captain could look bemused, he pulled out the first print, a black-and-white A4-sized blow-up of Sarah and her horse performing the stationary trot she called *piaffe* at the park. The old man peered at it, then turned towards his granddaughter. 'Good,' he said to Sarah.

'He did well that day,' she said. 'He was really listening to me. Really trying. Every movement . . .'

'Little act of beautiful,' he said carefully. Apparently overcome by this sudden rush of language, she crept on to the bed and slid over beside him. Her head lay against his pyjama-clad shoulder.

Mac, trying not to look, took out another. 'I think this one was . . .'

'Shoulder-in,' she said.

'*Je ne peux pas voir*,' the old man said. He waited patiently while Sarah placed his glasses on his face, then gestured to Mac to move the print closer. Mac held up another beside it. The Captain nodded his approval.

'These are all for your room,' Mac said, and reached into his pocket for the Blu-Tack. He began to stick the pictures carefully around the bed, slowly obscuring the blank, pale green walls, which had been enlivened only by a 1980s watercolour print and a notice entreating visitors 'Please wash your hands'. A couple more he affixed to the end of the Captain's bed.

He watched carefully, gazing at each in turn as if he was drinking in every last detail. He would stare at them all day, Mac guessed.

When he had told Sarah what he was going to do, during the drive over here, she had examined the pictures in stunned silence. 'That okay?' Mac had said, worried by her lack of response. 'I didn't include any of the ones of you doing things you're not meant to do, the going-up-on-his-back-legs and stuff.'

She smiled at him, but it was a sad smile. 'Thank you,' she said. Her voice suggested she had not seen many unexpected acts of generosity, had expected even fewer.

'And I've saved the best until last.' Mac unwrapped the one he'd had framed. Even Sarah had not seen it. It was not expensive, just a lightweight wood frame and cardboard mount, but behind the polished glass, the photograph of the girl, her cheek pressed to that of her horse, was bright and clearly defined enough for the old man to make out every detail. It captured her vulnerability, the strangeness of a face that hadn't quite decided whether it was going to be beautiful, pressed in a kind of ethereal communion to the Stubbsian finesse of the horse's bone structure. The monochrome, the high resolution, gave the two faces dignity, mystery, which would have been absent in colour. It was one of his best works, Mac knew. He had known it almost as soon as he had taken it. When he had seen the finished print, his heart had skipped a beat.

'Baucher,' the Captain said, still staring at the picture. 'Sarah.' He pronounced it 'Sara'.

'I love that picture,' Mac said. 'It was just before we left the yard one morning last week. She didn't even know I was taking it. I love the way the light from Sarah's face moves on to the horse's. The way their eyes are both half closed, like they're somewhere else in their heads.'

The man at the gallery had thought so too. He wanted to show the work, he had told Mac. He loved it. A part of London that was disappearing, he said. Echoes of the Dublin horse children. But better. He had suggested a price for each work that made Mac's eyes widen.

'They may appear in an exhibition in the spring, if that's okay with you, but these copies are yours. I thought it would be nice for you to have something to look at . . .'

There was a long silence. Mac wasn't someone to whom uncertainty came often but now he felt its chill. It's too much, he thought. I'm simply reminding him of what he has lost. He's afraid I'm exploiting her. Who was he, anyway, to come in here like Lord Bountiful, taking over the old man's space, deciding what he should spend his days looking at? Was plastering his walls with these pictures – a world he could not enjoy – rubbing his nose in his immobility?

Mac took a pace towards the wall. 'I mean, if it's too much I can—'

The old man was gesturing to him, beckoning him closer. As Mac stooped, he took Mac's hand between his own and pressed it. His eyes were moist. '*Merci*,' he whispered huskily. '*Merci, Monsieur*.'

Mac swallowed hard. 'It's nothing,' he said, forcing a casual smile. 'I'll do you some more next week.'

It was only then that he noticed Sarah. Unusually, she had barely spoken all evening. She was still leaning against her grandfather, her hand wrapped tightly around his arm, as if she did not want to leave him again. Her eyes were tight shut and her face was tilted away. A solitary tear trickled down her cheek, illuminated by the strip lighting. She was a startling picture of misery.

She was such a self-contained girl, so practical, so obsessed with her horse, that sometimes Mac forgot how lost she must feel. How much she must miss the grandfather she had spent her childhood with. He felt awkward again and shoved the Blu-Tack back into his bag.

'Anyway,' he said, I'll meet you downstairs, Sarah, if that's okay. Fifteen minutes?'

He placed the framed picture on the bed and left the room, haunted by his last image of the old man, perplexed, his trembling hand lifting towards his granddaughter's hair, her face buried in his shoulder as she tried to hide her tears.

Fourteen

'I am far from saying that because an animal fails to perform all these parts to perfection, he must straightway be rejected, since many a horse will fall short at first, not from inability, but from want of experience.'

Xenophon, *On Horsemanship*

A few years previously, when Mac and Natasha had first moved into their street, the neighbourhood had been described, optimistically, as 'up and coming'. If that was so, she had thought at the time, it was some way from arriving. The street was characterised by a shabby uniformity. Three-quarters of the houses had not seen fresh paint in five, perhaps ten years. Outside, on a road with no yellow lines, defunct cars without wheels stood on bricks, while dented hatchbacks ferried young families to and from their chores.

The houses, their stucco Victorian frontages cracked and peeling, stood back from small front gardens, with perhaps an errant privet hedge, a motorbike covered with a tarpaulin or a few dustbins with ill-matched, collapsing lids. She often paused to chat to her neighbours, Mr Tomkins, the elderly West Indian painter, Mavis and her cats, the housing-association family with eight gap-toothed children. They had been companionable, commented on the weather, enquired what Mac was doing to the house now, whether she knew about the plans to introduce residents' parking, that a Buddhist

centre had moved into the high street. As far as any road in
the capital had a sense of community, this one did.

Now Mr Tomkins was gone, Mavis was long buried, and
the housing association had sold off its interests, its tenants
shipped to God only knew where. Now nearly all the houses
were painted porcelain white, their cracks carefully filled, their
front doors tasteful colours from Farrow and Ball. Topiary
yew or bay trees flanked the front steps, and half of the little
gardens had become smartly cobbled driveways, or were
hemmed in by unfriendly glossy ironwork. Outside stood oversized 4×4s, glossy Mercedes estates. Stressed professionals
nodded a brief greeting to each other as they hurried to and
from the station, the size of their mortgages guaranteeing that
there was little time for more.

It was an affluent street, throwing its remaining few long-
term inhabitants into sharp relief, their peeling windows and
net curtains like remnants of a former age.

Financially Natasha knew she had benefited from this
process of gentrification, but in her gut she felt a deep unease
at the polarisation of her world. It was now a street that
mirrored its neighbours, little oases of aspirational middle-
classness, ringed by estates that conspired to look darker,
harder and more threatening, populated by people with fewer
and fewer chances to escape.

The two worlds never collided now, unless it was through
the criminal (the latest stolen car or burglary, a purse snatched
at the mini-mart), the commercial (everyone had a cleaner,
or a childminder, of course) or the structurally formalised
(Natasha, representing a twelve-year-old whose alcoholic
parents refused to take him home).

Natasha thought of this now as she drove into the Sandown
estate, past the burnt-out cars and flickering street-lights.
Sarah sat silently beside her, clutching her keys. She had not
spoken since they left her grandfather's ward, and Natasha,

still shocked by what she had seen, had not attempted to make her. Nothing had confirmed the magnitude, the fool-hardiness of what they had taken on, more than the sight of the old man, his frail neck supported by pillows, his face sagging slightly on one side.

'He's getting there,' the stroke nurse had said cheerfully. 'We've come a long way, haven't we, Henry?'

'Henri,' Sarah had growled. 'It's pronounced Henri. He's French.'

The nurse had raised her eyebrows at Natasha as she walked out.

'How – how long do you think he'll have to be here?' Natasha had hurried after the woman while Sarah greeted her grandfather.

The nurse had looked at her as if she was a little back-ward. 'He's had a stroke,' she explained. 'It's a how-long-is-a-piece-of-string question.'

'But you must be able to give me some idea. Days? Weeks? Months? We're . . . looking after his granddaughter so it would be good to have some idea.'

The nurse glanced back. Sarah was tidying her grand-father's bedclothes, talking to him while he watched her steadily. 'You really need to speak to his consultant, but I can tell you it's definitely not days,' she said. 'And I wouldn't put money on weeks either. He suffered a severe stroke, and he still requires a lot of rehabilitation.'

'Is it something . . . a young person could manage? His care?'

The nurse pulled a face. 'Someone of her age? No. We wouldn't recommend it. It's way too much responsibility for a child. At the moment Mr Lachapelle still has hemiparesis – that's weakness – down one side. He needs help washing, getting on and off the lavatory. We've had a few problems with bedsores and his language isn't a hundred per cent. He's having physiotherapy twice a day. He can feed himself now, though.'

'Will he stay here?'

'We're a long-term unit. I don't think it would be appropriate to put him in a care home yet, not while he's still improving.' She checked her watch. 'I'm sorry, I have to go. But he is progressing. I think the pictures helped, funnily enough. Gave him something to focus on. We all like them.'

Natasha look back at the little side-room, at Mac's work all over the walls. This other Mac again, charming the nurses, helping the sick, even in his absence.

They pulled into the sprawling estate and drove to the Helmsley House car park. It had started to rain, and a few of the youths Natasha had seen the first time she had met Sarah were sheltering under hoodies, flicking matches at each other. They watched her get out of the battered Volvo, but were distracted when someone's phone rang.

'What is it you wanted to pick up again?' Natasha walked behind Sarah up the dank stairwell. The rain hissed around them, pouring through broken guttering, swirling into drains blocked by crisps packets and chewing-gum.

'Just a few books,' she said, and added something else that Natasha could not hear.

They walked along the balcony, unlocked the door and closed it swiftly behind them, Natasha grateful for the solid protection of Mac's iron brace on the frame. Inside, the flat was cold. Sarah had last been here several weeks previously, with Ruth the social worker, and they had turned off the heating and collected more of Sarah's things. She disappeared into her bedroom now, while Natasha stood in the front room. It was tidy, but bore the chilled, neglected air of a long-empty home. All the photographs had been removed, either to Sarah's room at their house or to the hospital ward, and the walls were blank and unfriendly.

She heard the sound of drawers being opened and closed, and the zip of a holdall. Sarah would not be returning to this home, she was sure. Even if the old man recovered he couldn't manage those stairs. The thought hung heavily on her. Did Sarah realise this? She was an intelligent girl. What did she think would happen to her?

She caught sight of a photograph that had not been moved – on the hall wall, of Sarah, three or four years old, being held by a grey-haired woman with a smile that matched Sarah's. She was like any other child: safe, anchored in the embrace of her family, her clear eyes untainted by fear or uncertainty. Within a matter of years she had become dependent on the kindness of strangers.

Natasha's head sank into her hands. This was the down-side of parenting, the utter, utter responsibility for someone else's happiness.

'I tell you what, let's go out to eat,' Natasha said, as they climbed back into the car, brushing raindrops from their sleeves. 'How d'you fancy a pizza?'

Sarah looked sideways at her and Natasha realised, with shame, that she was surprised by this casual invitation. She had seemed withdrawn the past few days, even by her self-contained standards. She had asked to eat alone in her room twice, and barely communicated, even with Mac, who had previously made her laugh.

Natasha thought back to what her sister had said. It was her responsibility to do something, at least to try. 'Go on. I don't fancy cooking, and it's been a long evening. I know a nice place at the far end of the high street.' She tried to sound cheerful, relaxed. God, it would have been so nice if Sarah could show some enthusiasm, even pleasure. How often had she gone out in her old life, for goodness' sake? 'The pizzas are pretty good,' she said.

Sarah clutched her holdall on her lap. 'Okay,' she said.

The restaurant was only half full, and they were shown to a table near the window. Natasha ordered garlic bread and two colas, while Sarah gazed out at the busy, darkened street, the holdall tucked neatly under her chair. She chose a ham and pineapple pizza from the menu, then barely touched it, picking at the slices so slowly that Natasha wondered whether she was developing an eating disorder.

'So,' she said, when the silence between them became uncomfortable, 'have you always been interested in horses?'

Sarah nodded, pushing a piece of mozzarella across her plate.

'Through your grandfather?'

'Yes.'

Sarah's eyebrows rose just enough to tell Natasha how stupid she thought the question.

'Which part of France did he come from?'

'Toulon, originally, and then he lived at Saumur. At the academy.'

Natasha persisted: 'How did he end up living here?'

'He fell in love with my grandmother. She was English. That was why he stopped riding.'

'Wow.' Natasha pictured the French countryside, the move to an estate like Sandown. 'And what did he do when he got here?'

'He worked on the railways.'

'That must have been hard for him. To leave the horses. France. His whole life.'

'He loved her.'

To Natasha's ears, that had sounded almost like a rebuke. Were things really so simple? If you loved someone that much, should your environment become unimportant, the sacrifices you made disappear into your past? It was clear that horses were the old man's passion, a passion that had not been extinguished despite his self-imposed exile. But how had he come to terms with what he had lost?

She remembered the picture of Sarah's grandmother, a woman used to being loved. Her face bore nothing but content, despite the loss of Sarah's mother. Natasha thought of the petty squabbles, the relentless accumulation of toxic ill-feeling that had led to the end of her own marriage. Was her generation simply deficient in being able to maintain love on such an epic scale?

'How did you meet Mac?'

Natasha's fork halted by her mouth. She put it down on her plate. 'It was on an aeroplane.'

'Did you like him straight away?'

Natasha thought for a moment. 'Yes,' she said. 'He . . . he's an easy person to like.'

She seemed to accept this.

He's charmed you too, Natasha thought, a little wistfully.

'Did you leave him or did he leave you?'

Natasha took a sip of her cola. 'Well, it wasn't quite as straightforward as that . . .'

'So he left you.'

'If you're asking me who left the house, yes, he did. But at that point we would both have agreed we needed a breather from each other.'

'Do you want to get back together?'

Natasha felt colour rise to her cheeks. 'It's not really an issue. Why do you ask?'

Sarah pulled a tiny piece of crust from her pizza and placed it in her mouth. She chewed, swallowed, then said, 'My nana once told me she hoped Papa would die first. Not because she didn't love him but because she was worried about how he'd cope without her. She thought she'd manage better than he would.'

'But you and he coped together.'

'He's not as happy as he was when she was alive. My nana could always make him laugh.' She thought about it. 'I can't make him laugh. Especially there. He hates it.'

'The stroke ward?'

Sarah nodded.

'It must be hard for him,' Natasha replied carefully.

'It's worse for him than if he'd died.'

Natasha's knife and fork stilled in her hands. Sarah's words probably contained some truth, no matter how unpalatable. For someone whose whole life had been spent outdoors in the pursuit of physicality, of agility, to be trapped in an existence like that, fed, changed like a baby, it must be near-unendurable.

She tried to keep her voice level. 'He'll get better,' she said softly. 'The nurse did say he was progressing.'

Perhaps Sarah hadn't heard this, or perhaps it contradicted what she suspected to be true, but she closed her knife and fork on her plate, signifying that she had finished, despite the physical evidence to the contrary. 'Do you think he'll be home in time for Christmas?' she asked.

Natasha lifted her napkin, stalling for time, but even that short hesitation must have spoken volumes. 'It's impossible for me to say. I'm not an expert.'

Sarah chewed her lip, fixed her eyes on something in the street.

'I'm sorry, Sarah,' Natasha said. She was so pale. She might even have lost weight. Natasha wondered whether to reach out a hand. 'I know this must be very hard for you.'

'I need some money,'

'Sorry?'

'I need to buy Papa some things. Christmas presents. New pyjamas and stuff,' Sarah said matter-of-factly.

Knocked off kilter by the change of subject, Natasha put another piece of pizza into her mouth and chewed.

'What does he need?' she asked, when she'd swallowed. 'I can pop into the shops tomorrow on my way to work, if you like.'

'I can do it, if you give me the money.'

'You won't have time, Sarah. All your time is taken up with Boo and your schoolwork.'

'I can go out at lunchtime.'

'That doesn't make sense. You're not meant to leave the school grounds then. I can't see when else you'd be able to do it.'

'This is because I took the change from your bottle, isn't it?'

'No. I just don't want you missing any more—'

'I'm sorry, okay? I'm sorry about that. It was when I couldn't tell you about Boo. I'll pay it back.'

'That's really not necessary.'

'Then let me buy some things for Papa. I need to be the one who chooses them,' she insisted. 'I know what he likes.' Her voice rose against the clatter of the restaurant cutlery. 'They keep nicking his toiletries, and his clothes, and I can't buy anything myself because Social Services took his savings books. I wouldn't ask unless I really had to.'

Natasha wiped her mouth with the napkin. 'Then let's go together on Saturday morning. We'll get whatever you think he needs and I'll drop you at the stables afterwards.'

Sarah's eyes betrayed her feelings about this idea.

Why did she want to go by herself? Natasha wondered. Was it that she didn't want pyjamas, and that the money was for something else? Or was it simply that being with Natasha for another outing was too much? She felt exhausted. Sarah was staring out of the window, as unknowable and unreachable as she had been at the start.

'Do you want anything else? Some ice-cream?'

Sarah shook her head. She didn't even look at her.

'I'll settle the bill,' Natasha said wearily, 'and then we'd better go. I didn't tell Mac we were going out.'

She didn't trust her. Sarah cursed herself for having taken the money from Natasha's change jar. If she'd left it alone, she could have helped herself to some now when it really mattered.

She placed her foot on her holdall, reassuring herself that it was still there. Social Services had taken Papa's pension and savings books, to ensure the rent got paid, but they hadn't known about his Premium Bonds. If she could cash them in, and avoid Maltese Sal for a bit longer, she might still be able to pay him off. She saw him again, felt his hand on her breast, heard his words in her ear, and shivered.

She needed that money. She thought of the other things she had picked up: an old glass ornament, which she had wrapped carefully in a jumper, and which she thought she might be able to sell to the man in the house-clearance shop. Her CDs, which someone might buy at school. Something. *Anything.*

'Goodness,' Natasha said. 'It's a quarter past ten. I had no idea it was so late.' She pulled out her wallet to pay the bill. She put a card into the hand-held machine and was chatting to the waiter as she punched in the number.

2340.

Easy to remember.

She closed her eyes, wincing at what Papa would say if he knew she had even thought in the way she had. Nothing could excuse stealing, he would tell her, when one of the boys downstairs was carted off in a police car for the fourth time that week. You stole something, you gained nothing. You were actually diminished by the act. Papa did not even believe in credit. He had never, he said, owned anything he couldn't pay for.

But as she walked back to the car, following the crisp click-clack of Natasha's high heels along the wet pavement, those four digits beat a rhythmic tattoo, imprinting themselves on a dark corner of her mind.

He had promised to drop her home, and now asked her to wait on the steps for two minutes while he ran in and picked up his car keys. Sarah's light was on, he noted. Natasha's car was absent. She had said she might be working late, but he was surprised that she had left Sarah alone for so long. As he stood on the step, fumbling for his key, Maria was suddenly behind him. She pressed against him, her long, sinuous form snaking around his. 'Let's go in.'

'No.'

'You owe me. That was the worst film I have ever seen. You owe me an hour and a half of my life back.'

'Granted. But not here.'

She pulled a comedy frown. 'But I miss you. It has been more than a week! I will show you my white bits,' she offered, pulling out the waistband of her low-cut jeans to reveal the tanned abdomen beneath. 'They are very, very small,' she added breathily. 'You will have to look *very* closely.'

Maria was beautiful, and uncomplicated, and she wanted him. He suspected she didn't love him, or even need him, and he couldn't help but like her for it. He needed this robustness, wanted to know that, no matter what he did, he wasn't going to hurt her.

'Sweetheart, I can't,' he said.

'You bring me here at weekends. Why not now?'

He glanced down the road. 'Because my ex will be back soon and it's not fair.'

She pulled away from him. 'It's not fair on me. Grrr! Why you letting your life be dictated by this miserable woman? You told me she has boyfriend, yes?'

'Yes.'

'She has sex with him?'

'I don't know,' he muttered uncomfortably. 'I guess so.'

'Of course she does.' She laid a hand on his chest. 'Lots of sex with this horrible old man. Two horrible dreary people together. So how you know she's not with him now?'

He tried to remember what Natasha had said that morning, whether she would be out this evening. He had been trying to catch a cricket score and hadn't been paying attention. 'I don't.'

She grinned. 'Having disgusting sex with him. Horrible, dreary-person sex. But laughing at the thought of her ex-husband, who does not dare have sex with his beautiful girlfriend in his own house in case the thought of this upsets her.' She smiled sweetly at him, revelling in his discomfort.

'You are a very bad woman.'

'Oh, I can be much worse.'

'I don't doubt it.'

'Then come. You sneak me into your room. We have quickie and then I go. It will be like we are teenagers again. Well, like you are teenager. For me it's not such a leap.' She wrapped her arms around his waist, fed her hands into his back pockets, pulling him towards her.

He glanced at his watch. He couldn't guarantee that Sarah would be asleep. 'Tell you what, let's go to yours.'

'My two cousins are staying at my flat. And my uncle Luca. Is like Piccadilly Circus. With *bigos*.'

'*Bigos?*'

'Is . . . stewed cabbage.'

'Well, that's a turn-on.'

'Mac . . .' Her voice dropped to a husky murmur. 'Mac . . . I like your house.' She twirled her fingers in his hair. 'I like your room. I like your bed . . .'

He tried to stay resolute. 'I'm sure I could get to like *bigos*.'

She narrowed her eyes, smiled that catlike smile. 'You know what this word means? In translation?'

'I haven't got my English–Polish dictionary on me.'

'*Trouble,*' she whispered, her lips grazing his ear. 'Is word for *trouble.*'

Sarah would probably be asleep. Even if she wasn't, was that really so bad? She tended to stay in her room most evenings anyway.

They had let her have the small portable television as she didn't want to watch what anyone else wanted. Or perhaps she just hadn't wanted to be with them.

Maria pulled back a little. She looked down, then lifted her eyes to his. 'You can't say you haven't missed me,' she observed.

Natasha was probably at Conor's house, he rationalised, as he propelled Maria, giggling, through the front door. And Maria was a woman with a very short attention span. An old phrase jumped into his consciousness, even as he forced away the voice that warned him against what he was doing. It concerned gift horses and mouths.

'The lights are on. Mac must be home already,' Natasha said, as if she couldn't think of anything else to talk about. Her mouth had compressed into a thin line, Sarah saw. She pulled her key from the ignition and retrieved her bag from the footwell behind her, leaving a faint trail of expensive scent. 'Do you need a hand with that bag?'

As if she were a child. 'No,' said Sarah. 'Thank you.' She couldn't let go of the holdall. Some parts of this evening it had seemed that holding on to it was the only thing that had kept her upright.

'You'll have to get the bus in tomorrow,' Natasha continued, as she locked the car behind them. 'Mac texted me earlier to say he's got some job on early, and I'm afraid I have to be in a meeting. Will that be okay?'

'Yes.'

'And we'll make sure your grandfather gets some nice new things. I'm happy to pay for them, Sarah.' She opened the front door and turned to face her as she closed it behind them.

She was wearing her sympathetic face, the one she probably used on her clients. It was warm in the house, and Sarah peeled off her coat.

'It's not a matter of trust, Sarah. Really. If I didn't trust you I wouldn't have you in my home. I just think it would be better if we did it together on Saturday afternoon. I'll get my paperwork done in the morning and I can pick you straight up from the stables. We'll go to any shop you want. We could get a cab to Selfridges, if you like. How does that sound?'

Sarah shrugged. Even without looking at Natasha she could tell she was exasperated.

'Look, it's late. You'd better go up and we'll talk again in the morning.'

They turned when they heard clattering in the kitchen. Natasha took off her scarf as she headed towards the door. 'Mac? I was just telling Sarah about—'

She stopped dead as a tall blonde woman dressed only in a man's T-shirt and knickers stepped into the hallway, carrying two glasses of wine. She had the kind of hair you see in shampoo adverts, impossibly fine and glossy, and endless lightly tanned legs. Her toenails were little seashells of rosy polish. 'You must be Natasha.' She smiled, balanced the glasses clumsily in one hand and held out the other. 'I am Maria.' The smile was wide but not friendly. It had something of a smirk in it. Sarah stood behind Natasha, fascinated, as the hand dangled, outstretched, in the air.

Natasha seemed to have lost the ability to speak.

'Mac has told me so much about you,' the tall woman

said, taking back her hand with no apparent offence. 'I was going to make tea, but you don't have any soya milk, do you? Dairy is *so* bad for the skin.' Her eyes lingered on Natasha's complexion a moment too long. 'Do excuse me. I must get back upstairs. Someone is waiting . . .' Grinning, she moved past Natasha, her braless breasts buoyant under the T-shirt, a faint musky scent trailing in the air as she passed.

Natasha didn't move.

Sarah watched the scene, her mouth slightly open. Natasha was quite pale, and her knuckles had whitened on the handle of her briefcase. She looked like Sarah felt when she was going to cry and didn't want to.

After a few moments, Sarah took a tentative step forward. 'Do you want me to make a cup of tea?' Someone had to do something. It was awful to see anybody going through that. '*I* like normal milk,' she added feebly.

But it was as if Natasha had forgotten she was there. She looked up, her eyes widening, and forced her face into a smile. 'That's . . . very sweet. But no thank you, Sarah.' She didn't seem to know what to do.

Sarah hugged her bag. She wanted to hide in her room, but if she went upstairs she might look as if she was taking sides, and she wasn't sure how she felt about what had just happened.

'You know . . .' Natasha raised a hand to her cheek. Colour had returned to her face, and she was quite pink now. 'You know . . . I think I might . . .'

They heard a door open and laughter. Then Mac was scrambling down the stairs, his hands on the banisters. He was wearing jeans and his top half was bare. 'Tash.' He halted halfway down. 'I'm sorry. I thought you were . . . I thought Sarah was . . .'

Natasha stared at him. She looked, Sarah thought, suddenly

very tired. 'Classy, Mac,' she said, in a small voice. She stood there a little longer, nodded, as if confirming something to herself, then turning on her heel, walked out of the house, shutting the door firmly behind her.

Fifteen

'For what a horse does under constraint . . . he does without understanding. Under such treatment horse and man alike will do much more that is ugly than graceful.'

Xenophon, *On Horsemanship*

Sarah lay in her bed, her knees pulled up to her chest and her arms wrapped around them. The goosedown duvet rested lightly on her curled form, creating a soft nest, a cocoon she pretended she need never leave. The Egyptian cotton sheets still held the delicious linen-spray smell that the cleaner used when ironing; it contained lavender and rosemary. The curtains, a heavy grey silk lined with voile, let in a soft light that buffered her from too abrupt an awakening. But as the room, with its antique chest of drawers and huge Venetian mirror, its little glass chandelier, lightened, she felt herself grow darker.

She stared at the wall, concentrating on her breathing. If you didn't think about it, your breath just travelled in and out of your body regardless. Didn't matter what you did, running, riding, sleeping, it just went in and out, doing its job, keeping you alive. As soon as you thought too hard about it, it became a passive thing. Waiting for you to fill your lungs. Stalling when you thought bad thoughts, when you felt your stomach tighten with fear.

There was no avoiding him now. He would be there on

Friday; he always was. He would be there at the weekend. He would not be fobbed off with what she had scraped together so far. She closed her eyes, forcing the thoughts away, breathing in and breathing out again.

Papa would probably be awake now; he had always been an early riser. Was he staring at the wall? Waiting until daylight revealed the images of the horse, the granddaughter he loved? Was he picturing himself on lost horses he had known, locked in silent concentration as they danced their way across some vast arena? Or was he drugged into a half-sleep, dribbling, being sponged brusquely by agency nurses who talked to him as if he was not only too old to understand but stupid? Sarah hugged her knees tighter, a shudder escaping her.

The previous evening, Papa had held her hand in his trembling fingers. His skin had felt papery, his old scent now replaced by something sharp and disinfectant. He was no longer himself. Every time she saw him, no matter what they said about recovery, he was a little more distant, a little more despairing, as if the bits of him that made him Papa, the Captain, Nana's adored husband, were being expelled with each breath. Sometimes it seemed she knew exactly how he felt.

Two miles away, Natasha woke to the sound of her neighbour's bath running and mused sleepily on the selfishness of people who thought it acceptable to turn their television up to full volume even at a quarter past six in the morning. Why did anyone need to listen to the television while they were in the bath? Was there nowhere they could simply sit in silence?

A news break. Half past six. She could even make out the time through the paper-thin walls. She pushed herself upright, felt the first warning shots of a weighty headache and, for a moment, struggled to work out where she was, a nagging sensation of some half-remembered event already hinting at a greater problem. A cloud was creeping overhead towards her. And there it was: an unfamiliar bedcover. Her handbag, slung over the back of a chair. Patterned beige carpet. A near-empty bottle of red wine.

The previous night flooded back to her and she lay on the hotel pillows, closing her eyes. The way that woman had looked at her, as if she was an irrelevance. The laughter in her eyes that hinted at secrets exposed, a past derided. How could he have done that? She wiped her eyes. Then, why would he not? What had this been for, after all, if not their final separation? What could she expect of him? So many images: Mac, when they had been together, surrounded by women who seemed to regard her as something less than an obstacle. The look of him: a man who turned women's heads, always one step higher than her on the ladder of human attraction, and the women knew it. They had let her know it too. At first she hadn't thought it mattered, when he had shone the full beam of that charm only on her, when she had felt adored, needed, wanted. She had told him jokingly, at parties, to 'go off and flirt', watching as his eye met hers later, telling her they were nothing compared to her.

And then, with each miscarriage, her confidence in her own femininity had shrunk. She would find herself silently assessing other women's fertility, comparing herself unfavourably. To her eyes, they looked fecund, ripe. Young. She had begun to feel old, dried up inside. And there he stood, charming them, perhaps already planning some new relationship with a younger, more beautiful partner. One who would give him children. How could he be expected to hang around now? He got angry when she said as much. In the end it had been easier to say nothing. Conor had been the first man to make her feel that Mac had been the lucky one.

Mac was not hers. It was entirely possible he never had been. It had simply been disguised again by their having lived together, the artificial closeness forced upon them by circumstance.

Natasha got heavily out of bed, walked into the bathroom and turned on the taps. Then she went into the bedroom and turned on the television. Very loudly.

Sarah's mastery of the near-silent footfall would have put an Indian tracker to shame. These last weeks it had not been uncommon for her to appear unheralded behind him on the stairs or beside him in the kitchen. It was as if she had decided to be as unobtrusive a presence as possible, to take up no space, disturb the house with no sound. Normally the faint creaking of a teenage girl making her way downstairs would not have roused him. But Mac had been awake for hours.

The previous evening Maria had left shortly before eleven, a good half an hour after Natasha had driven off. There had been little point in following her: he had had no idea where she was going or what he would say to her if he found her.

Maria had snorted scornfully when he came back upstairs, sat heavily on the bed and declined the glass he held towards him. 'She is pissed off about the wine? I will buy her a new bottle. Is only supermarket wine anyway.' She took a sip. 'In Poland is very rude to be so inhospitable.'

He knew that Maria knew it wasn't about the wine and, just for a moment, he felt intense dislike for her. It had been deliberate cruelty, and she had enjoyed it.

'I think you'd better go,' he had said.

'Why you care anyway?' she exclaimed, pulling on her jeans, wiggling ostentatiously. 'You not even see her for a year. You getting divorced in weeks. You told me this.'

He couldn't answer her. Because he didn't want to hurt Natasha's feelings? Because when he had first moved back in he had thought, in some stupid, optimistic way, that they might somehow end up as friends? That once they had made their way past the mess and trauma of divorce, that funny, sarcastic, brilliant woman might still be in his life? Or because the sight of her face, pale with shock and hurt, the reproach behind the glittering fury in her eyes, would haunt him through the small hours?

He rose, splashed his face with cold water, pulled on his jeans and padded downstairs. Sarah was in the kitchen, her school uniform neatly pressed, making a sandwich. 'Sorry,' he said blearily. 'I should have made your lunch.' He rubbed at the bristles on his chin, wondering if he had time to shave.

'Natasha usually does it,' she said.

'I know. I guess I wasn't thinking straight last night. You off to the stables?' He glanced at the clock. 'You'll be cutting it fine.'

'I'll be okay.'

'I'd give you a lift but I've got—'

'I don't need a lift,' she interrupted.

'You want an apple for Boo?' He reached into the fruit bowl and threw one at her, expecting her hand to shoot out and catch it. It had become something of a routine for them. But she stepped aside, letting it thump on to the limestone floor.

He picked it up and studied the stiff, slim back, the self-consciously erect posture. 'Are you angry with me?'

'Not my business,' she said, packing the sandwiches neatly into her schoolbag.

Mac picked up the kettle and filled it. 'I'm sorry about last night.'

'I don't think it's me you should say sorry to.' She was pulling on her coat.

'I didn't know she was coming back,' he said.

'But it's still her house.'

'*Our* house.'

'Whatever.' She shrugged. 'Like I said. It's not my business.'

He made himself a coffee, astonished at how bad a fourteen-year-old girl could make a grown man feel. He had known Natasha would be angry. He hadn't expected this.

'Can I have some money?' She was standing behind him, ready to leave.

'Sure,' he said, glad to do something, anything, that might lift the atmosphere of opprobrium. 'How much do you need?' He began to rifle through his pockets.

'Fifty?' she ventured.

He sorted through the money in his hand. 'Here,' he said, holding out a silver coin.

'Fifty pence?'

'You wanted fifty pounds? Very funny. Look, I've got a job this morning. I'll get some money out of the machine this afternoon. You can have a tenner. Treat yourself. Go for a burger with your mates later.'

She didn't seem as pleased as he had hoped she might. But it would be better if he didn't have to worry about what he was going to do for supper this evening and if Sarah was safely out of the way.

He needed to speak to Natasha. But he didn't know what the hell he would say when he did.

Each legal brief received by a barrister – other than those concerning government business – was tied with a pink ribbon. This anachronism was not just a matter of tidiness, or some arcane method of filing. The ribbon had a purpose; it symbolised the barrister's ability to detach him or herself emotionally from the case. The barrister was instructed specifically for their independence, their objectivity. When the ribbon was retied, the brief was returned. The barrister left behind the facts of the case.

That said, some cases, Natasha thought, as she sat opposite Michael Harrington, were easier to be objective about than others. They had met at his office to discuss the Persey divorce case, which was about to begin. 'You look tired, Natasha,' he said, and called for his pupil. 'I hope the details of this brief aren't keeping you awake.'

'Not at all.'

'I think we should have a con with Mrs Persey tomorrow morning. I see we're also awaiting statements from the forensic accountants. Can you bring them to that meeting? I'd also like to finalise which witnesses each of us will take.'

He was staring at her, and she wasn't sure how long she had been peering down at the papers.

'Natasha? Are you okay?'

'Fine.'

'Can you be there?'

She glanced at her diary; one day was already hideously tight. 'I'll make time.'

'Good. Right. That's probably it for today.' He stood, and she gathered her things together. 'No, no. I didn't mean you to go immediately. Do you have a few minutes? Time for a quick drink?'

She thought back to the previous evening. 'Tea will do me,' she said, and sat down again. 'Thank you.'

'Good.'

His pupil had stuck her head around the door.

'Beth, can you make us two cups of tea, please? Sugar? No sugar in either. Thank you.'

Abruptly, he changed the conversation. He talked about his adult children, his rediscovered passion for yachting. They discussed a lawyer they both knew who had recently been involved in a legal-aid scandal. 'Actually,' he went on, 'I've been meaning to talk to you for a while. We've been attempting to restructure things here, change the balance of our chambers. And we're likely to have a vacancy.'

She waited.

'I've been watching your career with interest. I liked your work in Richmond versus Turner, and the case you did with the abduction triplets. A lot of the instructing solicitors I speak to mention your name and they have only good things to say.'

'Thank you.'

'If a vacancy were to arise here, might you be interested?'

Natasha was taken aback. When she had been in training, Harrington Levinson had been held up as the epitome of a modern, progressive chambers with a fearsome reputation. Now Michael Harrington, the founder, was actively seeking her out. 'I'm very flattered,' she said. His pupil came in with the tea. They waited until she had closed the door behind her. 'I should tell you that there is a possibility I'll be made a partner at my current firm.'

'I'm not sure that's the best move for you. You know that many solicitor advocates are now choosing to move into full-time advocacy?' he said. 'The stepping-stones are in place. And we would be happy to have you as a probationary tenant. You could be at the bar in less than two years.'

She tried to digest what he was saying, its implications. She would leave the day-to-day chaos of her solicitor's job behind, and adopt the more distant stance of a barrister. There would be none of the daily involvement with her clients' lives that took place now. Since Ali Ahmadi, she had no longer known if that mattered. 'Michael, this is a big move, obviously,' she said, thinking of Conor. 'I'll need to consider it carefully.'

He scribbled on a piece of paper and handed it to her. 'My numbers. Don't try to reach me through the clerks – they guard me like mastiffs – but do speak to me. Any questions you want to ask about our set-up – money, pupillages, offices, anything.'

'Would you want references?'

'I know everything about you that I need to know.' He smiled. 'Where are you off to next? Another con?'

She stared at the pink ribbon, forcing herself to remember what it was supposed to symbolise. 'Something like that,' she said finally, and put her cup and saucer on the desk. 'I'll ring you, Michael. Thank you. I'll consider your offer very carefully.'

There had been little to mark it out from the other modern, flat-fronted houses, in an ugly maroon brick, the doorbells at the entrance the only clue that these little dwellings were subdivided into even smaller flats. But on the pavement, still blowing forlornly in the wind, the crumpled dirty length of incident tape under the privet hedge told its own story. Its contrasting colours offered a clue to the gravity of what had gone on behind that door.

She stood on the pavement, looking up at the blank, net-curtained windows. Where would Sales Assistant, 26, be now? Was she there, peering out from behind the curtains, or still in hospital? Was she too afraid to return home? Had she wondered about the trail of events that might have led the young man to her?

What had made Ali Ahmadi pick this particular address? How had his epic journey from the other side of the world ended with six short steps up to this particular front door? How had one small omission on her part, on someone else's part, led to such a cataclysmic event?

An old lady passed her, pushing a tartan shopping trolley. Natasha, stepping aside, attempted to raise a small smile, but the woman merely glanced at her with rheumy eyes and continued on her solitary, determined route.

Natasha felt a lump in her throat. Perhaps she was not there for clues. Perhaps it was to offer a mute apology. I should have checked him out, she told the woman silently. If

I'd checked the name of the town, the distance he claimed to have walked, I might have saved you. In doing nothing to save him, I could have saved you.

She was interrupted by her phone.

'You haven't forgotten your four-fifteen? I thought you'd be back by now.' It was Ben.

'Postpone it,' she said. She stood by the car, gazing two girls who pushed buggies past on the other side of the road. Both were talking into mobile phones, apparently oblivious to the babies and each other.

'What?'

'Cancel it. I'm not coming in for the rest of the day.'

There was a lengthy silence.

'What do I tell Linda? Are you okay?'

'Yes. No, actually, I don't feel great. I'm going home. Say I'm very sorry. Reschedule for later in the week. It's Stephen Hart. He'll understand.'

It was after she'd disconnected that she remembered going home was no longer an option.

Jessica Arnold had had twenty-three boyfriends, fourteen from her year, four from the year above, and the rest out of school, from the Sandown and surrounding estates. Her current boyfriends were older men, who waited outside the school gates in low, souped-up cars that roared off down the road, pulsing with loud music, the instant she climbed in. She had slept with most of them – this was not an idle boast, as was much of what was said of who had 'experience' in their year – but detailed in scrawled messages in the toilets, and the empty pill packets, which had been known to drop from her satchel, and in the faces of the men in the cars. They were not the kind of men to be satisfied with a long-drawn-out kiss on a park bench. Jessica wore the purple marks on her neck like a badge of pride. She had to behave like that, as if it was of her choosing, as if it was what she had wanted, or she would simply be a slag.

If Jessica was at one end of the spectrum of year ten's sexual activity, Sarah was lurking at the other, with Debbie Dermott, who wore thick glasses and braces, and Saleema, who had to wear a burkha whenever she was outside school and never spoke to boys, let alone kissed them. It wasn't that Sarah was ugly, just not very interested in them.

The boys she knew would not want to hear about Boo and his steady progression from the moves of *basse école* to the more complicated demands of *haute école*. They would not want to come to the yard with her and share a bus ride home. They would make stupid remarks about the yard smelling, shout and worry the horses, and smoke near the straw. They wouldn't understand her life.

She had never told Papa but sometimes, in the few aching moments late at night when she did feel overwhelmed and her body was filled with a sense of loss for something she didn't understand, she pictured herself at Le Cadre Noir. She would be the finest rider they had ever seen. There would be a handsome young captain in his black uniform with the gold epaulettes. He would be a brilliant horseman, and would understand everything she wanted. He wouldn't drive multi-stickered uninsured cars around the estate, boast of the number of ASBOs or TWOCs he had notched up, and offer slobbery kisses that tasted of kebab and chilli sauce. It was a chaste, horse-driven romance, with huge gaps in knowledge at its heart, gaps that Jessica's satchel and the graffiti only hinted at.

This was what she had always assumed was her future; she had known it as clearly as she had known Boo's. But she had seven pounds fifteen pence from the sale of her CDs and ornaments, Mac's ten pounds, and a Premium Bond certificate that would take at least three weeks to redeem, and only then with her grandfather's signature.

That knowledge gap looked as if it would close sooner than she had thought.

'I need to talk to you.'

'You got my money?'

'That's what I wanted to talk to you about.'

'So talk.'

She nodded across the yard to where his men were standing. 'Not with them here.'

He was packing away his grooming brushes, each one gleaming, immaculate, as if it had never seen the dust on a horse. He shoved the last one into place and now looked up at her, registering. 'What do you want, Circus Girl?'

She lowered her voice, twisted the strap of her schoolbag around her left wrist. 'I wanted to know,' she said, quietly, 'how much . . . how much you would let me off . . . if . . .'

He didn't answer at first. He didn't smile. He didn't show surprise, pleasure. He didn't, as she had half hoped, burst into noisy laughter and tell her he was only joking and what kind of man did she think he was?

He nodded a little, as if confirming something to himself, then looked at her and turned on his heel. He walked over to his men, who were standing around the brazier, the cold air clouding their breath so that you couldn't tell what was smoke and what was simply the cold air. He was gesturing at them, muttering something she couldn't hear. They shrugged, patted pockets for keys and cigarettes, flicked waste paper into the fire. Ralph looked at her from across the yard as if he was reassessing her. Perhaps it was just jealousy that she had Sal's attention, but she suspected she was someone else in his eyes now. Not the granddaughter of the Captain, a mate with whom to share the odd adventure, just someone to be traded, of no value. He did not look at her as he left.

She walked up to Boo's stable and let herself in, fiddling with his rug, laying her head against his warm skin to glean some comfort from it. His great head swung round to investigate her, to work out what she was doing, and she stroked his face, her fingers tracing the bones beneath the soft skin.

She could see Sal through the doorway, walking jauntily, a cigarette held lightly between thumb and finger. He saluted, shouted something in Maltese as the men disappeared through the gates. Then as the last car pulled away, he wedged them shut, pulling the heavy chain through in a loop. It was dark now, and Sheba paced restlessly at their base, perhaps waiting for Cowboy John to return.

And then he was walking up to Boo's stable, whistling like someone who hadn't a care in the world.

'So,' she said, trying to sound tough, when he stood at the door. She tried to mimic the girls from Sandown, the ones she heard screeching at the boys on bikes. Hard. Nonchalant. As if nothing could hurt them. 'How would this work?'

He acted as if he hadn't heard her. He took a deep drag of his cigarette, then walked into the stable and shut the door. Boo had lost interest in her and gone back to his hay, chewing steadily behind her. Only the sodium light from outside the yard crept in now. It was hard to see his face, although she saw that the light illuminated her, turning her body a ghostly orange.

'Take off your top.'

He said it so casually; as if he'd asked her to lock the gates. 'What?'

'Take off your top. I want to have a look at you.' He took another drag of his cigarette, his eyes not leaving hers.

She stared at him. Not *now*, she thought. I'm not ready for this *now*. I just wanted to work out what you were suggesting. 'But—'

'If you don't want to sort this out . . .' He made as if to turn away, his face closing. 'You're just playing kids' games. You let me think I could take you seriously.'

He took his cigarette from his lips with two fingers and flicked it out on to the concrete. It glowed briefly before it was extinguished by the wet. Then she saw the cold, hard set of his face and her mind raced.

Almost before she knew what she was doing, she pulled her top over her head. She had been wearing a sweatshirt. Without its fleecy lining she felt the cold air licking at her, the draught through the door penetrating with icy fingers what had been warm and protected.

He turned. She couldn't see his eyes, but she felt them on her, extracting every last bit of what he would decide was her value. It was, apparently, not hers to define. She felt invaded by his gaze, as if he could see past her bare skin to the raw flesh underneath. *It will soon be over*, she told herself, forcing herself to stand straight, almost defiant in her posture. *And then I will owe him nothing. It will all be okay.*

'And your brassière.'

He spoke slowly, but it was a command. The voice of someone who only ever got what he wanted.

She checked she had heard correctly. 'But what do you want—?' she protested. 'You haven't said—'

'You're telling me what to do now? Dictating terms?' His voice hardened.

She was shivering, goosebumps rising on her arms.

She closed her eyes. Her heart thumped so loudly she could barely hear him.

'Take it off.'

She swallowed hard, then reached behind her, her jaw clenched to to stop her teeth chattering, out of fear or cold, she wasn't sure. Without opening her eyes, she removed her bra. It was a cheap, flimsy thing, slightly too big. Papa had been buying socks at the same time, and she had been so embarrassed at the prospect of him noticing her purchase in the department store that she had run out without trying it on. He took it from her now, dropped it to the ground at one side of her. She was naked from the waist up. She felt the cold air on her skin, her nipples tightening in protest. She heard his sharp intake of breath, the footsteps bringing him closer, and realised she had toppled into an abyss. One she hadn't even known was there.

She couldn't open her eyes, couldn't breathe. She stood there, a thing, a nothing, extracting herself from her body so that this was not her, Sarah, standing bare in the stable, with Sal's new horse whinnying in the next arch and the dog barking outside and the sound of someone talking on the street. This was not her, with this man's hot, dry hand now sliding across her cold skin, his warm breath near her face, his foul, alien words murmured into her ear. A strange, alien scent in her nostrils, his sharp belt pressed painfully against her hip as he pushed her back against the chilled stone wall. The real world receded until it was just him and those words and his insistent, relentless touch that was not hers to stop. It was not her. Not her. What had happened to Sarah anyway? This was no longer her life, her family, her future. She had no say in any of it. So what difference did it make to have this man now claiming possession of her, inch by kneading, explorative, hot-breathed inch? She was hypnotised, absent, a nothing.

It was not her, after all, whose hand he now enclosed and pulled from her trembling side towards him, as her clenched teeth choked back her fear. *It is just one small thing,* she repeated, her voice repetitive in her head. *One small thing, and then it will all be over.* She heard a zipping sound, his laboured breathing, now growing in intensity, rasping. She heard the words and thought – dully – *do I?*, and felt against her fingertips rough denim, then something soft and warm, yet unyielding. Something that instinct told her she should not be touching.

And she could not help herself. She snatched back her hand as his own strong fingers clamped around hers, propelling them back on to warm flesh, insisting, not even persuading. *Telling*. But it had unleashed something in her, released her. A shout escaped her, and she was pushing him, hitting him, yelling at him – '*Get off! Get off me!*' as Boo flinched and jumped sideways, his hooves crashing against the stable wall. And then, snatching up her bag, she was out of his grasp, away, out of the dank lock-up, running for the gates, and then, wrenching them open, the pavement, towards the bright lights of the rush-hour high street even as she pulled her sweatshirt on over her head.

'I wondered if you'd be here.' Conor was standing in front of her, holding a pint. 'Richard wanted to talk to you this afternoon. I had to make excuses for you.' When she didn't speak, he added, 'And Linda's worried about you.'

She leant back in the booth. 'Linda is far too interested in everybody's lives. You can see for yourself – I'm fine.'

Conor's eyes travelled across the empty glasses in front of her. He removed his coat and slid into the booth opposite. It was the end of the working day and the pub was filling up. He took a sip of his beer. 'I rang your home. But your – your young houseguest had just got in and said she didn't know where you were.'

She took another sip of her drink. If you drank enough white wine it tasted like acidic grape juice. 'I'm not staying there.'

He stared at her. 'Okay, Natasha. What's going on?'

'Oh, you're interested now?'

'Look, I can see that something is going on with you. You haven't missed an appointment in five years, and suddenly you're taking the afternoon off for no obvious reason whatsoever.' He didn't add, 'And you're drunk.' He didn't have to.

'Brilliant, Holmes.' Her voice was low and measured. She

realised she actually loved Chardonnay, as unfashionable as it might be. Why had she not discovered this sooner? 'I went to look at the home of the woman Ali Ahmadi attacked.'

'Why the hell did you do that?'

'I don't know.'

'I thought you'd left all that stuff behind. Why the hell are you still worrying about it?'

She blinked. 'Because it still troubles me. I keep thinking about her. I keep thinking about *him*.' A pair of slim brown hands held in supplication. Around a woman's neck.

'This is ridiculous, Natasha. You're not . . . you're not behaving rationally.'

'Ah. That will be because I'm drunk.'

'Okay. I'll put you in a cab home. Come on, Hotshot.' He took her hand, but she pulled it away.

'I'm not going home.'

'Why?'

'Because I'm staying in a hotel.'

He regarded her as one might an unexploded bomb. 'You're staying in a hotel.'

'The Holiday Inn.'

'Can I ask why?'

No, she wanted to yell. No, because you bailed out of my life long ago, at the first sign of trouble. No, because you've ignored me and made me feel like crap for weeks. No, because you've behaved like my happiness was none of your concern. 'It was simpler.'

She heard the question in his silence. She could just make him out on the other side of her table. Why didn't he go? 'It was easier, okay? You were right. It got too complicated at home. I made a mistake even thinking I could cope with it. Happy now?'

He said nothing. She swallowed hard and tried to concentrate on the glasses in front of her, but they kept swimming up to meet her. She frowned at them until they fell obediently into some kind of order.

Finally she gave up and looked at him. His eyes were kind, his expression sorrowful.

'Oh, Hotshot. I'm sorry.' He got up and walked round to her side of the table, sat down beside her and sighed. 'I'm sorry,' he said again.

'Don't worry. It was a ridiculous thing to attempt. I must have been mad.'

'Well, yes, there is that.' He put his arm around her shoulders, and pulled her to him. She leant against him a little reluctantly, unbending in his arms. 'I'm sorry,' he murmured into her hair. 'I'm a jealous fool. I never wanted to see you unhappy.'

'Liar.'

'Okay. I didn't want to see you happy with him. But I never wanted . . . this.'

'I'm fine.'

'Obviously. And I'm not. And it's all my own fault.' He stooped, held her face and tilted it towards his. 'Come to mine.'

'What?'

'You heard me.'

She shifted out of his embrace. 'Conor,' she said, 'I don't know. My life is a mess. I've got myself into a complete hole and I don't know how I'm going to dig my way out of it.'

'I know how.' He pushed her hair out of her eyes. 'Come to mine.'

'I told you, I've got—'

'To stay.' He paused. 'To live, if you like.'

She didn't move, unsure she had heard him correctly.

'Let Mac clear the whole thing up,' he continued. 'He's got you into this mess. And you come . . . come and live with me.'

'You don't have to do this.'

'I know I don't. But, believe me, I've thought of nothing else this past couple of weeks. Imagining the two of you eating dinner together, chatting away, doing . . .' he rubbed his face '. . . God knows what. Don't tell me if you have, by the way, because I don't want to know. But it got me thinking. Let's just get on with it.'

'"Get on with it,"' she repeated. 'You old romantic.'

He had said it. He had offered her the thing she had wanted for months, even if she hadn't been able to admit it to herself. Perhaps it was the shock of the previous evening, or the last weeks, but she didn't know how to respond. 'It's a big move, Conor. We're both . . .'

'. . . a mess. Matching messes.'

'You make it sound so inviting.'

'I mean it, Natasha.' He hesitated. 'I love you.'

She emptied her glass. 'I don't know. This is a little out of the blue.'

'You'd rather stay at the Holiday Inn. I knew you always had a thing for that roundabout.' He was speaking a little too fast now, his laughter brittle.

She felt a sudden tenderness and reached for his hand. 'I'll come tonight,' she said. She leant against him, letting herself be enfolded. She closed her eyes as he rested his chin on her shoulder, oblivious to the glances of those at the next table. 'But let's just take things one step at a time.'

Sixteen

*'When he finds himself in close proximity to the foe, he must
keep his horse well in hand. This . . . will enable him to do
the greatest mischief to the enemy, and to receive least
damage at his hands.'*

Xenophon, *On Horsemanship*

Fifteen times he'd tried to call her between Monday night
and this morning, and every time he had gone straight to the
answering service. Her office claimed she was 'in court'. That
they no longer asked who was calling made him suspect she
had briefed them not to put him through. He had stopped
leaving messages now, just her name, his name. He had long
since forgotten what he had wanted to say.

He poured himself another coffee, cursing Natasha's jug,
which always seemed to spill no matter how carefully you
directed it. He remembered suddenly the beautiful Italian
coffee-maker they had received as a wedding present, a
gleaming Gaggia, which sat in some storage unit in west
London. It seemed stupid now that he had been so determined to take what he considered he was owed, even when
it meant that nobody got to use it. He would give her the
coffee-maker, he vowed. He hadn't used it in a year. He
couldn't possibly miss it. He had made several such vows in
the past few days.

Upstairs Sarah was asleep. She had gone straight to her

room when she came in on Monday evening, refused food and drink and didn't want to talk. She had been so evasive, avoiding eye contact, hiding in her room, that he had suspected he was still being punished. Odd, really, that she was suddenly so loyal to Natasha. He had wanted to knock on her door, to put her straight, remind her that *actually*, strictly speaking, it had been Natasha who had been unfaithful first. But as he considered it he realised how ridiculous it would be to harangue a fourteen-year-old girl to justify his own actions.

Yesterday she had pleaded illness, had spent the day locked in her room. She was peaky, a translucent pallor to her skin. She hadn't had to try very hard to persuade him to let her have the day off.

At twenty past six, some thirty-six hours after Natasha had left, he heard a key in the front door. She shut it quietly, slipped her shoes off on the doormat and walked down the hall in her stockinged feet. She was wearing the suit she had disappeared in, but with a T-shirt underneath. His T-shirt, probably, Mac thought.

They stared at each other.

'I've got a big case on,' she said. 'I've just come to change my clothes and pick up my phone charger.' Her face was pale, free of makeup, her hair still slightly matted from sleep. She looked exhausted.

'I tried to ring you. Loads of times.'

She waved her phone. 'Dead. As I said, I need my charger.' She started up the stairs.

'Natasha, please, hang on for five minutes. We really need to talk.'

'I haven't time today. I've got to be in my office within the hour.'

'But we do need to talk. Are you coming back this evening?'

She stopped halfway up. 'I'll be late. And when I do get back I'll be working on my papers.'

'Are you still angry with me? About Maria?'

She shook her head unconvincingly.

He took the stairs two at a time, pushing past her so that he stood above her, looking down. 'Oh, come on,' he said. 'It's not like you haven't got a boyfriend. Christ.'

'And it's not like I ever got him to come here and humiliate you,' she shot back. 'Look, I don't want to do this now—'

'No. You never do. But seeing as we are, how did Maria being here humiliate you? You and I aren't together. You've always been perfectly open about having a boyfriend. All that happened was you actually met her. Look, I'm not saying it wasn't a bit undiplomatic but it was a genuine mistake. I thought you were out. I'd never have invited her in if I'd known . . .'

She didn't seem to want to look at him.

'Tash?'

When she finally did, her eyes were cold. She seemed oddly defeated. 'I can't do this, Mac. Okay? You win. Have the house until it's sold. Have whoever you want here. I don't care any more.'

'You don't care about what?'

'I just think it'd be better for everyone if we ended this charade now.'

Mac spread his arms across the stairs so that she couldn't pass him. 'Whoa, whoa, whoa. What? You're just leaving? And how's that going to work? What are we doing about Sarah? You know I can't take care of her by myself.'

'I'm going as soon as we can sort out her next placement. She would have had to leave within a matter of weeks anyway. We'll just bring the date forward.'

'You can't hang on just a bit longer? A couple of weeks?'

She spoke the words as if she had rehearsed them: 'You know as well as I do that her grandfather isn't getting better. She needs to go to a stable family who can look after her properly. Somewhere she's not being used as some kind of buffer between two grown people who are apparently incapable of dealing with each other in an adult manner.'

'That's how you see this?'

'Are you going to tell me it was any different?' She forced her way up another step so that he had to move back if they were not to stand touching each other. Apparently realising her advantage, she went up another.

'And the horse?'

'Believe it or not, Mac, the horse is not top of my list of priorities right now.'

'So you can just walk away from her?'

'Don't you dare,' Natasha said. 'Don't you *dare* use her. This is about you and me. No matter how we behaved in front of her or anyone else, this was never going to end in happy families, Mac, and you know it.' Her knuckles were white where she gripped the banister. 'I've thought about nothing else for the last thirty-six hours. We should never have offered her a home when it wasn't a proper home in the first place. We've been unfair to her to pretend otherwise.'

'That's what you think.'

'No, that's what I know. It's time for us to be honest – with her and with ourselves. Now, please excuse me but I really need to get changed.' She pushed past him and made her way up the rest of the stairs.

'Tash.'

She ignored him.

'*Tash* – don't end it like this.' He reached out to her. 'Come on, I made a mistake.'

She turned to him, her expression mixture of emotions – anger, resentment, sorrow. 'How are we meant to end it, then, Mac?'

'I don't know. I just hate this. I hate you . . . being like this. I just thought we . . .'

'What? That we were all going to wave goodbye to each other fondly and sail off into the sunset?'

'I don't—'

'Divorce is never tidy, Mac. You know what? Sometimes people aren't going to like you. Sometimes that famous Mac charm just isn't going to work. And—'

'Tash—'

She let out a long, shuddering sigh. 'And I – I can't be around you any more.'

Outside a car pulled up, its stereo inappropriately loud for the early hour. They stood inches apart on the stairs, neither able to move. Mac knew he should walk down, but he couldn't lift his feet. He could smell a trace of perfume, a scent he no longer recognised as hers. He could see her hand, still clutching the banister for support she couldn't do without.

'You know what's worst about all this?' He waited for the next verbal blow. 'You know what I really can't stand?'

He couldn't speak.

'This is like . . . It feels like it did before you went in the first place.' Her voice cracked. Then she walked heavily to her room.

Upstairs, Sarah shrank back from the banister and ran into her room. Her ears rang with Natasha's words. It was all falling apart. Natasha was going, and she would have to leave too. *We should never have offered her a home.* She hadn't been able to make out everything they were saying, but she had heard that much. She stared at her reflection in the mirror. She was wearing her biggest, thickest jumper, woollen tights under her jeans. Now, however, she felt frozen. Would she be met at school by Ruth, black bags of her stuff on the back seat, and ferried somewhere else? They hadn't even had the guts to talk to her about it.

Sarah sat on the floor by the bed and rammed her fists

into her eyes to stop herself crying. All of the previous day and last night she had felt Sal's hands on her skin, heard his disgusting words in her ears. She had scrubbed herself with Natasha's expensive creams and potions, trying to obliterate his smell, the invisible trail left by his mouth. She had shuddered at the thought of who might come across her bra, still in Boo's stable. For some reason the thought of it lying in the straw upset her more than anything else.

In the next room she could hear Natasha opening and closing drawers, the soft click of her built-in wardrobes.

She would have to tell Papa. She would miss school this morning, and after she had been to the yard, she would tell him she needed him to come home – that he *had* to come home. She would look after him, no matter what they said. It was the only way. If Sal knew Papa was back, he would leave her alone.

Natasha knocked on her door. 'Sarah?'

She scrambled on to her bed, forced her features to reveal nothing. 'Hi,' she said.

Natasha's face was blotchy, the skin white with lack of sleep. 'Just to say I'm a little busy at the moment, and I may be a bit late tonight, but perhaps we could have a chat later?'

She nodded. *A chat. Just a few words while I chuck you back on the rubbish dump.*

Natasha was looking at her carefully. 'Everything okay?'

'Fine,' Sarah said.

'Good. Well, as I said, this evening, all three of us. And ring me if you have any problems. You have my mobile number.'

As she left, Sarah heard something collide with the front door. Ten minutes later when she crept downstairs she found Mac's shoe.

Sal's four-wheel drive sat outside the yard, a gleaming, squat affront, a sight to make her stomach clench and her arms cross defensively in front of her. She took a deep breath, pulled her coat tightly around her neck, then let herself in through the wire gates.

He was at the far end of the yard, talking to Ralph and a couple of his cronies, and they were warming their hands on the brazier, drinking coffee from polystyrene cups. Ralph caught sight of her and busied himself stroking one of Sal's horses. She hoped this didn't mean he hadn't fed Boo for her yesterday. She hadn't come, reasoning that it might be better to let Sal cool down for twenty-four hours.

That hadn't been the sole reasoning, but perhaps she needn't have worried; Sal didn't look up at her, although he must have heard her push back the gates. She prayed he had either failed to notice it was her or perhaps decided it would be better for them to pretend that the other evening hadn't happened. Perhaps he was even embarrassed, although some deeper part of her suspected that Sal had never been embarrassed about anything.

She let herself into her lock-up and swapped her school shoes for her riding boots, acutely conscious of the murmured conversation at the other side of the yard. *Please don't come in here.* She fumbled with the buttons of her coat to change and be out of there before he could enter. She made up Boo's morning feed in a bucket, filled a haynet and, hoisting it over her shoulder, walked briskly to the stable, head down, determined not to meet anyone's eye.

It took her a moment to realise that his door was open. She dropped the haynet.

Boo was not there. His stable door swung open, his straw bedding still scattered with droppings. She glanced down the yard. Why had he been moved to another stable?

She walked down, checking the others. Various heads poked out, skewbald, piebald, chestnut. No Boo. Something clawed at the base of her throat, and panic rose in her chest. She half walked, half ran to where the men were standing, anxiety overriding any feelings she had about speaking to Sal. 'Where's Boo?' She tried to keep her voice calm.

'Boo who?' Sal didn't even turn around.

'Boo-hoo,' muttered one of his men, and laughed unpleasantly.

'Where is he? Have you moved him?'

'Is there a cat trapped somewhere? I can hear a bad noise.' Sal cupped his ear. 'Like a mewing sound.'

She walked around the men so that he was forced to look at her. Her breathing was rapid, the panic spreading like the cold sweat that had broken across her skin. 'Where is he? Where have you put him? Sal, this isn't funny.'

'Do you see me laughing?'

She grasped his coat sleeve. He shook her off. 'Where is my horse?' she demanded.

'Your horse?'

'Yes, my horse.'

'I sold *my* horse, if that's what you mean.'

She shook her head slightly, frowned.

'I sold my horse. You don't have a horse.'

'What are you talking about?'

He reached into his pocket, pulled out a little leatherbound book, opened it and held out the pages for her to see. 'Eight weeks' rent, you owed me. Eight weeks. Plus hay and feed. The terms of your contract say that if you don't pay for eight weeks your horse becomes mine. I sold him to pay your bill.'

The sounds of the street outside were replaced by the ringing in her ears. The ground dipped dangerously in front of her, a deck in high seas. She was waiting for the punchline, waiting for him to deny what his face told her he would not.

'I sold your horse, Sarah, if you really don't get it.'

'You – you can't sell him! You had no right! What contract? What are you talking about?'

He cocked his head to one side. 'Everyone has a copy of the terms and conditions. Yours are in your lock-up. Perhaps you didn't notice them. I'm acting within my legal rights as the owner of the yard.' His eyes were the cold black of fetid, brackish water. They looked through her as if she was nothing. She glanced at Ralph, who was kicking a loose cobble. It was the truth. She could see it in the discomfort on his face.

She turned back to Sal, her mind racing. 'Look,' she said, 'I'm sorry about the money. I'm sorry about everything. I'll find it. I'll find it tomorrow. Just let me have him back. I'll do – I'll do anything.' She didn't care if they heard her now. She would do what Sal wanted. She would steal from the Macauleys. Anything.

'Do you not understand?' Sal's tone had become rough, unpleasant. 'I sold him, Sarah. Even if I was inclined to get him back, I couldn't.'

'Who? Who did you sell him to? Where is he?' She had both hands on him now, gripping him tightly.

He wrested her away from him. 'Not my problem. I suggest you meet your financial commitments next time.' He reached into his jacket. 'Oh, yes. He didn't make such a good price. Bad temperament. Like his owner.' He turned to his men, waiting for the inevitable laugh. 'Here's what you made once your debt was paid.' As she stood there, disbelieving, he peeled off five twenty-pound notes and handed them to her. 'So now we're square, Circus Girl. Find yourself another trick pony.'

She could see from the faint smiles on the men's faces that they knew what she knew: that he would never tell her to whom he had sold Boo. She had crossed him and he had exacted his revenge.

Her legs were weak. She stumbled back into the lock-up, and sat down on a bale of hay. She stared at her hands, which were trembling, and a low moan escaped her. In the corner of the lock-up, behind the door, a white sheet of typewritten paper, with the supposed terms and conditions, glowed ominously in the dim light. He would have put it there yesterday.

She dropped her head on to her knees and hugged them, imagining her horse, frightened, loaded into a lorry, fed into some underpass, eyes wide, head lifted in fear. A million miles away already. Her teeth were chattering. She lifted her head, and through the gap in the door saw the men talking, breaking off to laugh at something. 'Boo-hoo,' one wailed mockingly. Someone threw down a cigarette and ground it under the heel of his boot. Ralph's gaze flickered towards the lock-up, perhaps seeing her curled up there, in the shadows. Then he, too, turned away.

'Nice work,' Harrington said, as they left Court Four. 'You did a great job taking that witness apart. A light touch. We've made a good start.'

Natasha handed her papers to Ben and removed her wig. She was still warm with adrenalin and it had begun to itch. She pulled the two grips from her hair and tucked them into her pocket. 'Tomorrow won't be so straightforward,' she said.

Ben wrestled with the files, then handed her one. 'These are the other accountant's reports we were waiting for. I don't think there's much that's new in there, but you never know.'

'I'll go over them this evening.'

Conor appeared in the corridor. He winked at her, and she waited until Ben was deep in conversation with Harrington before she went to meet him. 'How'd it go?' he said, kissing her cheek.

'Oh, not bad. Harrington pretty much decimated their financial claims.'

'That's what he's paid for. You want to go back to the office first?'

She looked at Ben. 'No, I've got all the papers I need downstairs. Let's go.'

He took her arm, an unusually possessive gesture. 'You still good for this evening?'

She had a sudden image of Mac on the stairs. *You've got a boyfriend,* he had said. *Why should Maria bother you?* 'I can't stay,' she said. She shrugged on her coat. 'I've told Sarah we'll have a talk about her future. But a long soak in your bath and a glass of wine before I have to do it will suit me just fine.'

He stopped. 'Well, you can have the wine, but you may have to hold on the bath.'

She was perplexed.

'I've invited the boys over. I thought you should meet them.'

'Tonight?' She couldn't hide her dismay.

'We've waited long enough. I've cleared it with their mother. I thought you'd be pleased.'

'But . . .' she sighed '. . . I'm right in the middle of a big trial, Conor. I'd rather have met them when I'm a little less . . . distracted.'

He was dismissive. 'You don't have to do anything, Hotshot, just smile, be your usual lovely self. It'll be enough that you're there. Hell, have your bath. We'll just goof around in the living room. We'll let you be furniture.'

She raised a small smile.

'We'll give you a bit of leeway before we force you on to your hands and knees to play horsey.' The word caught at her, but he was grinning to himself, apparently locked in some anticipatory vision of the four of them in his front room. She thought of Sarah, the conversation she had have to have with her and what it would mean for her. But Conor was steering her towards the door. 'And I'm cooking, you lucky, lucky thing. How'd you fancy fish-fingers on white bread with tomato ketchup?'

*   *   *

She couldn't see the words on the front of the bus. She had sat in the shelter for almost an hour now, staring as the red buses trundled along, with a hiss of brakes disgorging one load of passengers on to the pavement and swallowing the next, their brake lights bright in the dark city night. She saw nothing. Her eyes blurred with tears, her fingers and toes numb with cold. She felt paralysed, unable to decide which bus to take, even if she had been able to make out where they were going.

Everything was lost. Papá was not coming back. Boo was gone. She had no home, no family. She sat on the cold plastic ledge, hugged her coat around her and ignored the incurious stares of those who came, waited, then went to continue their own lives.

He said her name twice before she heard it. She had been so locked into her pain, so numb.

'Sarah?'

Ralph was standing in front of her, a cigarette wedged into the corner of his mouth.

'You all right?'

She couldn't speak. She wondered that he would even ask.

He huddled into a corner so that he was hidden by the shelter and the bodies of the people queuing. 'I'm sorry, right? It weren't nothing to do with me.'

Still she couldn't speak. She wasn't sure if she would ever open her mouth again.

'He done it yesterday. He said you owed him a load of money, Sarah. I did try, but you know what he's like . . . Whatever you done you wound him up something major.'

They shipped horses abroad, she had heard, crammed into lorries, deprived of food and water. Some were so weak they were only held upright by the pressure of the others around them. A solitary tear slid down her cheek.

'Anyway.' He spat noisily on the pavement, attracting a

ferocious scowl from a Nigerian woman. 'If I tell you something you mustn't tell him I told you, all right?'

She looked up slowly.

'Cos if you knew anything, he'd know it come from me,
right? So I'm still not going to talk to you in the yard or on
the street or nothing. I'll act like I don't know you, right?'

She nodded. Something was igniting inside her.

He glanced at her, then behind him, and took a long drag
on his cigarette. When he exhaled, it was hard to tell whether
it was smoke or the hot cloud of his breath. 'He's down at
Stepney. Behind the car site. The Pikeys have got him. Sal's
going to race the grey mare against him the day after
tomorrow, him and the bay trotter.'

'But Boo can't pull a sulky. He's never been driven in his
life.'

Ralph looked awkward. 'He has now. Sal put him in his
two-wheeler and drove him down there before breakfast.' He
shrugged. 'He were quite good. Not fast, like the grey mare,
but he never kicked it out or nothing.'

All that long-reining, Sarah thought absently. He would
have obeyed everything Sal told him. 'Where are they racing?'

'Usual place. The flyover. Be about six thirty.'

'What can I do?' she asked. 'How can I get him back?'

'Nothing to do with me, Sezza. I've said too much already.'

He made to leave, but she grabbed his wrist. 'Ralph. Please.
Help me.' Her mind was racing. 'Please.'

He shook his head.

'I can't do this by myself,' she said. But she was still thinking.
She sat, her other hand clenching in her pocket, while Ralph
sucked his cigarette and pretended she wasn't touching him.

'I've got to go, mate,' he said finally. 'Places to be.'

'Look,' she said, 'meet me somewhere. Not near the race
– nowhere Sal could see you. Meet me at the back of the
furniture factory. With Boo's saddle and bridle.' She reached

into her pocket, pulled out the yard keys and pressed them on him. 'Here. You can get them long before Sal's even there.'

'What use are they?'

'To ride him with.'

'What? You're just going to go along and tack him up, are you? Ride away? Please, mister, can I have my horsy back?'

'Just meet me, Ralph.'

'Nah. What's in it for me? If Sal finds out I've had anything to do with you he'll batter me.'

She didn't let go of his wrist, but dropped her voice so that the other passengers wouldn't hear. 'A gold credit card.'

He laughed. 'As if.'

'And the pin number. I promise you, Ralph, I can get it for you. Someone with big money. You can get out loads of cash before they stop it. Maybe even thousands.'

He scanned her face, then removed his arm from her grip. 'You'd better not be mucking me about.'

'You have to promise me you'll be there,' she said. 'No tack, no deal.'

He glanced behind him again, then spat on his palm and held it towards her. 'Friday morning by the furniture factory. If you're not there by seven I'm outers.'

Liam poked the pasta with his fork and wrinkled his nose. 'It looks like bogeys,' he said.

'It does not look like bogeys,' Conor said equably. 'And, Joseph, don't kick the table leg like that, sweetheart. You're going to knock everyone's drinks over.'

'And it tastes like bogeys,' Liam insisted. He shot a glance at Natasha.

'It's just pesto sauce. Your mother says you eat it all the time.'

'I don't like *this* pesto sauce,' Joseph said, pushing his plate away vigorously. It was only Natasha's intervention that stopped his glass of juice spilling over her own pasta.

The boys had not wanted to eat Daddy's fish-fingers. They wanted to go to the pizza restaurant. They had been there for almost three-quarters of an hour and she and Conor had hardly exchanged a word except to order their drinks.

'Joseph, can you sit up, please? I know you don't sit like that at home.'

'But this isn't home.'

'This is a restaurant,' Conor said, 'so it's even more important that you sit up properly.'

'But I don't like these chairs. They make my bottom all slidy.'

Natasha watched Conor prop his younger son upright on the chair beside him for the fourteenth time, and wondered at the expression of resigned patience he wore. Eating dinner with his sons had been like herding fish while negotiating with the potentates of two warring Balkan factions. Every time one thing was established, another war began, whether over garlic bread or napkins or a seat that was apparently too slidy for a small person's bottom. All of this had been directed at their father. They had neither acknowledged her nor sought to bring her into their conversations.

Had the mother briefed them? Had she primed them to collect information on Daddy's girlfriend? Had Natasha been deemed a hate figure long before she had even met them?

She felt Liam's eyes on her and forced a smile, trying not to think about the time she could have spent preparing tomorrow's papers. 'So,' she said, wiping her mouth with her napkin. 'Do you like *Thomas the Tank Engine*? My nephew loves him.'

'No,' Liam said scornfully. 'That's for babies.'

'But you can get really super train sets, grown-up ones, with *Thomas* characters. I've seen them.'

They looked blankly at her.

'What do you like, then?' she said, gamely. 'What are your hobbies?'

'You like riding your bikes, don't you, boys?' Conor interjected. 'And playing computer games.'

'Joseph broke my PlayStation,' Liam said, 'and Mummy says we don't have enough money to get it fixed.'

'I never broke it,' Joseph protested, adding darkly, under his breath, 'Poo-head.'

'Mummy says we have no money. No money for fun things at all.'

'Well, that's not true,' said Conor. 'Your mother gets an awful lot of money from me. And if you're missing out on things, you should tell me. You know I'll always do what I can.'

'Mummy says you give us the briar minimum.'

'I want a Nintendo,' Liam said. 'Everyone at school has one.'

'I'm sure that's not true.' Conor's voice was becoming strained.

'It is.'

'My nieces and nephews aren't allowed computer games,' Natasha ventured. 'They still have lots of fun.'

'Well they're stupid.'

She took a deep breath and forked up some pasta.

'C'mon, boys. Let's tell Natasha some of the fun things we do. Sometimes we take our bikes to Richmond Park, don't we? We like riding our bikes.'

'No,' said Joseph. 'You shouted at me that I wasn't going fast enough.'

'I didn't shout at you, Joe. I just wanted you to be where I could see you.'

'But your wheels are really big and mine are small.'

'And we like ice-skating,' Conor continued.

'You said it was a rip-off,' Liam said.

'I do think it was a little pricy, yes.' Conor cast a look in her direction. 'But we still had a good time, didn't we?'

'You and Mummy are always going on about money,' Joseph said mournfully.

Natasha had lost what little remained of her appetite. She folded her napkin and placed it beside her plate. 'Boys,' she said, reaching for her jacket, 'it's been lovely to meet you but I'm afraid I've got to go.'

'Already?' Conor laid a hand on her arm.

'It's nearly eight, and you know I've got a big day ahead.'

'I thought,' he said, 'that you might just put us first for tonight. Given the occasion and all.'

'Conor . . .'

'I'll be taking them home in half an hour. It's not much longer, for Christ's sake.'

'Look,' she lowered her voice, 'put yourself in Sarah's shoes. She's a kid, and she's about to be moved on to her fourth home in a matter of months. I'll be here with you to see your boys for ever after.' She reached out surreptitiously to touch his hand, conscious of the boys' eyes on her. 'It might even be best if we keep this first meeting short. I'll get to know your boys, Conor, but I have to sort out this mess first. I took her on. I can't just walk away.'

'Sure.' His tone was clipped. He went back to his food as she wrestled her bag from the back of her chair, then added casually, 'Will Mac be there?'

'I have no idea,' she said.

'No,' he said. 'Of course not.'

For a long time before he had become a photographer, Mac had used a strategy in life that if it didn't presage his career perhaps suggested some aptitude for it. When situations became uncomfortable or overly emotional, when he didn't want to have to deal with what was happening in front of him, he would turn down the sound in his mind and view the tableau from a distance, as if he was posing a picture. Raw emotion was filtered by this lens, reduced to a beautiful composition, an extraordinary meeting of light and line. At twenty-three, he had eyed his father's body in his coffin like this; the familiar face too still and cold, as if it had long been left behind. He had framed it, observing with a distant eye the way death had relaxed the muscles and wiped away long-held tensions, along with a lifetime of expression, from the features. He remembered watching Natasha lying in bed after the second miscarriage, curled up under the duvet, her position an unconscious foetal reminder of what she had lost. She had already turned away from him, closed herself off. He had, felt her emptiness echo in himself, until it was almost unbearable, and had focused instead on the way the light played on the folds of the bedcover, the delicate strands of her hair, the haziness of early morning.

And he did it now, watching the two females seated in front of him, the older perched neatly on the sofa in her work suit explaining to the younger why she herself would be leaving the house tomorrow morning and would not return, and why the girl would ultimately move to another, more appropriate home.

Sarah did not shout, beg or plead, as he had dreaded. She just watched Natasha talk and nodded, asking no questions. Perhaps she had anticipated this from the moment she had arrived. Perhaps he had been fooling himself with hopes of how they could make it work.

But it was Natasha who drew his eye. Now, against the pale sofa cushions, her back straight and poised, it was as if a storm had passed over her, leaving skies that, if not blue, were calm; skies under which you could see an awful long way from where you were standing. She's let go, he observed.

Whatever I did the other night, I set her free. This thought
came with unexpected pain, and he realised that he, standing
back, was the most emotional of the three: only he was blinking
back tears. 'We'll work something out, Sarah,' he found himself
saying, as the room became silent. 'I'll pay your horse's rent,
if I have to. We won't just let you fall.'

Finally Natasha rose. 'Right,' she said, looking him full in
the face for the first time. 'We're straight. Everyone knows
what's going on. Are you two okay if I go and pack?' A
shorter-than-average thirty-five-year-old woman, with little
makeup and hair that hadn't been brushed since that morning.
Not a model or stylist, not a vision of classical beauty. Mac
watched her go. Sarah fixed her gaze diplomatically on
Natasha's handbag.

'You okay?' he said to her. Upstairs they could hear
Natasha's heels as she went to and from the airing cupboard.

'Fine,' Sarah said calmly. 'Actually, I'm a bit hungry.'

He smacked the side of his head, forcing a smile. 'Supper.
I knew I'd forgotten something. I'll go and make it. You coming
through?'

'I'll be along in a minute,' she said.

It was as if she had guessed he needed a moment alone.
Or, at least, that was what he thought at the time. Later he
discovered it had been something quite different.

Seventeen

'In moments of danger the master gives his own life into the keeping of his horse.'

Xenophon, *On Horsemanship*

Sarah stood behind the parked Transit van, a hundred yards from the intersection of the two flyovers, oblivious to the small clouds of breath that evaporated into the damp air in front of her. She had been there for the past half an hour, long enough for her toes to lose all feeling in the chilly morning and her jacket to dampen under the persistent drizzle. She stood, beneath the sodium lighting, on this desolate stretch of road where the marshes segued into the city, under the web of pylons tracing the inevitable march towards urbanisation.

She had almost lost hope when she saw the first trucks arriving. Now she shifted, trying to ease the weight of her rucksack on her shoulders, her eyes never straying from them as they disgorged their passengers on to the slip-road. Even from here she could see Maltese Sal's men, clapping their hands in the cold, laughing and exchanging cigarettes, the onlookers who climbed out behind. It was a big race, the biggest she had seen. The side-road under the flyover was filling quickly with a line of vehicles, a small crowd spilling out, the atmosphere upbeat, expectant, despite the early hour, the bleakness of the setting. The end of the race was here, at the beginning of her own. Looking at all these men, the vehicles, she found she was shivering. She reached down, placing her fingers around the reassuring edges of the plastic card in her pocket.

It was twenty-five to seven.

She clenched her toes experimentally in her boots, wondering if it was possible to run on feet she could no longer feel. The men stood in small huddles, some raising brightly coloured umbrellas, chatting as if they were meeting for nothing more than an early-morning catch-up. She had asked Ralph three times if he knew for sure, and each time he had sworn he did. But could she trust him? Could his friendship with her override his worship of Maltese Sal? Was this a trap? She kept thinking of how he had turned away from her in the yard. Ralph lived by his own rules: singular, self-serving. Unreliable. But she had to trust him: she had no other option.

Her stomach rumbled. It was almost twenty to seven. They should have been here long before now. There must have been a change of plan. It was a different race. Boo wasn't coming, she thought, and her heart sank. She couldn't think what she would do if he didn't; she had no back-up plan. Everything was burnt, ruined, from the moment she had left the Macauleys' house. She thought briefly of Mac and Natasha, who would probably have woken up. How soon would they guess what she had done?

A car drove past at a crawl, its driver eyeing her curiously through the slow-moving windscreen wipers, and she pretended to rummage for something in her pocket, trying to look like a normal person, on her way to a normal day.

It was nineteen minutes to seven.

She heard a familiar voice, carrying towards her on the wind. 'Those marshes over there got more green than you boys got. Put yo' money where yo' mouth is.' Cowboy John was sauntering down the centre of the line of vans, his battered

hat shiny with rain, his hand outstretched as he greeted
the others. From here she could just see the glow of his lit
cigarette.

'You come here straight from the airport? Jet-lag's affected
your judgement, Cowboy.'

'You fo'get worrying about my judgement. Worry about
that horse's legs. I seen three-legged dogs with a better turn
of speed than yo' horse.' There was laughter. 'They started
yet? Sal texted me. Told me you guys were starting six thirty.
I should be in bed but my system's all shook up from the
time change.'

'Started back by the Old Axe. They should be along any
time now.'

Her head jolted upwards at the honk of a horn, a yelled
exclamation.

As if on cue there was a silencing of traffic, no cars, no
dull roar of vehicles overhead. There was a vacuum in the
atmosphere; the men stilled, as they waited to confirm what
they were seeing, then jogged forward, up the wet slip-road,
for a better view. And first a small dot, then a distinct outline
– there he was, trotting flat out down the flyover above them,
pinned between the poles of a light blue sulky, his head lifted
with anxiety as a grey-haired, thick-necked man pulled hard
on the reins from the seat of the sulky behind him. Maltese
Sal's grey mare, a short distance away, trotted smartly alongside as Sal leant across to shout an insult as he passed.

She couldn't take her eyes off her horse, his huge, muscular
body trapped between the twin poles, his feet a blur on the
hard road as he passed her. He was wearing blinkers, which
made him seem blind, vulnerable, as if he was some kind of
hostage. They were off the dual carriageway on the exit slip,
briefly obscured by the intersection, then coming back round
in a fluid loop towards the small crowd, as the flyover traffic
surged forward above them. The men on the ground moved

down the slip-road to meet them, and Sarah stepped back behind the white van, holding her breath. She watched the two horses coming back down the side-road, pulling up beneath the huge concrete pillars and there were cheers, exclamations, the sound of slamming car doors, a voice raised in protest. Boo wheeled, unsure whether he should be stopping, and his head was pulled back roughly, causing him almost to drop backwards on to his haunches.

She heard Cowboy John's voice. 'What the Sam Hill is *he* doin' here?'

What if she failed? What if this all went wrong? She felt her breath rise up to her throat and stall, then leave her tight lungs in a long shudder. *Think. Assess.* She had spent her sleepless hours reading Xenophon's advice to cavalrymen, and a sentence floated back to her now: 'To be appraised of the enemy's position in advance, and at as great a distance off as possible, cannot fail to be useful.'

She shifted her position behind the white van, her eyes fixed upon her horse. *I'm here, Boo,* she told him, and readied herself for action.

Mac heard Natasha's shower kick in, glanced at the clock and winced at its confirmation of this unearthly hour. He lay back for a moment, dimly aware that there was something he needed to do. Then the significance of the morning bumped its way into his consciousness. She was leaving. This was it. The whole thing was ending.

He sat upright. Across the hallway, the shower ran, the faint whine of the extractor fan a distant, hesitant descant. She would aim to leave with as little fuss as possible.

'I'll come and sort out the house in time for the move,' she had told him, after Sarah had gone to bed the previous evening. 'Removals. Surveys. Whatever. And I can talk to the social worker, if you'd prefer not to do it yourself. But I won't be staying here from now on.' She had barely looked at him as she spoke, busying herself with odd books from the shelves.

'You don't have to do this, Tash,' he said quietly.

But she had brushed aside his words. 'I've got a big case, Mac. Biggest of my career so far. I need to focus.' There had been no rancour, no anger. It was the Natasha he had hated: that closed-off, unreachable version of his wife. The one whose cool, *faux*-pleasant demeanour spoke of all the things he had apparently done wrong in his marriage.

He heard the doorbell, shrill and invasive. Postman? At this hour? Natasha wouldn't hear it over the sound of running water. Sighing, he pulled on a T-shirt and headed down the stairs.

Conor was on the front step. Mac took in the smart suit, the neatly shaven chin, and recognised, not for the first time, how much he disliked the man.

'Mac,' Conor said evenly.

'Conor.' He wasn't going to make this easy. He stood, waiting.

'I've come to collect Natasha.'

To collect her. As if she was something he had loaned. Mac hesitated, then stood back to allow him into the hall, feeling bitter resentment at every step he took over the threshold. Conor walked in as if he had some claim to the house, turned left into the living room and sat on the sofa with the relaxed confidence borne of familiarity, then flicked open his newspaper.

Mac bit his lip. 'Excuse me if I don't stay and chat,' he said. 'I'll just tell my wife you're here.'

He walked up the stairs, feeling a burning anger at what was happening. The man seated on the sofa Mac had chosen, paid for, was waiting to take his wife away. But even as he acknowledged this caveman growl of protest, some other part of him answered with an image of Maria, barely dressed, clutching two glasses of wine. Her sneaking delight in Natasha's pain.

The shower had stopped. He knocked on the bedroom door, and waited. When there was no response, he knocked again, then opened it tentatively. 'Tash?'

He saw her reflection before he saw her. She was standing in front of the mirror, a towel wrapped around her middle, water still running in droplets over her bare shoulders from her wet hair. She flinched as he entered, and her hand shot unconsciously to her throat. That defensive gesture was a further rebuke.

'I did knock.'

There were half-packed bags all around the room. Inches from a clean getaway, he thought.

'Sorry. In my own world. It's this case . . .'

'Conor's here.'

Her eyes widened. 'I wasn't expecting him.'

'Well, he's downstairs, waiting to collect you.' It came out a little sarcastically.

'Oh,' she said. She took her dressing-gown off the bed and pulled it around her. Bending, she started to towel her hair. 'Tell him . . .' she began. 'Actually, don't worry.'

He ran his hand along the rim of an open suitcase. He didn't recognise many of the clothes that were folded in it. 'So this is it,' he said. 'You just go.'

'Yup. Like you did,' she said briskly, straightening to brush her hair. 'Is Sarah up?'

'Haven't checked.'

'With everything that went on last night, I forgot to mention – she had a form that needed signing. For some school trip.'

'I'll do it.'

She laid her suit on the bed and held first one shirt, then another against the dark blue jacket. When they had been married, she would always ask him what he thought of the match and, more often than not, go with something else. For the first few years it had been a joke between them.

He folded his arms. 'So . . . where should I forward your post?'

'You don't need to. I'll be back every few days. Just call me if there's anything we need to discuss. What do you want to do about the social workers? Do you want me to ring them when I'm out of court this afternoon?'

'No,' he said. 'I'll talk to Sarah first. Work out when would be . . .' He could not say 'best.' Nothing was going to be best for her. 'Tash . . .'

She had her back to him. 'What?'

'I hate this,' he said. 'I know things have got a bit complicated, but I don't see why it all has to end this way.'

'We've had this conversation, Mac.'

'No, we haven't. We've lived here together for the best part of two months and we haven't had any real conversation at all. We haven't talked about what happened between us, or what the hell went—'

He turned abruptly. Conor was in the doorway. 'I thought you might need a hand with your bags.'

He had aftershave on, Mac noticed. Who the hell wore aftershave at this time of the morning?

'Is it this lot on the bed here, Natasha?'

She was about to answer but Mac interrupted: 'If you don't mind,' he said, stepping in front of Conor, 'I'd prefer you to wait downstairs.'

There was a brief, loaded silence.

'I came to get Natasha's bags.'

'You're walking into my bedroom,' Mac said slowly, 'and I'm asking you not to.'

'I don't think, strictly speaking—'

Mac turned on him. 'Listen, mate,' he said, hearing the barely controlled antagonism in his voice, 'I own this house, half of it. I'm asking you nicely to get out of my bedroom – our bedroom – and wait downstairs so I can finish having a private conversation with the woman who, theoretically at least, still happens to be my wife. *If* that's all right with you?'

Natasha had stopped brushing her hair. She glanced between the two men, then nodded discreetly at Conor.

'I'll put the seats down in the car,' Conor said, and walked out, his car keys jangling ostentatiously in his hand.

The room was very quiet now. In the bathroom, the extractor fan clicked off.

Mac felt his heart-rate gradually subside. 'Well, that's it, then.' He tried to smile, but it came out lopsided. He felt foolish.

Her expression was unreadable. 'Yes,' she said, her jaw tight. She began to busy herself again. 'I've got to get on, Mac, if you don't mind. But do ring me tonight when you and Sarah have worked out the time frame for everything.' She picked up her suit and disappeared into the bathroom.

There had been two trotters in this race, Sal's mare and Boo. Boo had not been expected to win, Ralph had told her; there was heavy money against him, despite his good looks, and sure enough he had come last.

From her vantage-point behind the van, she watched the jockey leap down from the sulky, grab at a rein and kick him hard in the haunch. Boo skittered sideways, his head arched backwards in pain. A moan of protest escaped her, and her feet carried her towards him almost without her realising it. Then she caught herself, ducked down, closed her eyes tightly and forced herself to focus, not to act rashly. A hundred yards away, one of Sal's men was holding the sweating mare by one rein, his hands cupped around the flame of his lighter as he attempted to put it to his cigarette.

'I swear, Sal, that's some strange vitamins you been feeding that horse,' he said, as he tucked the lighter back into his pocket.

'It wasn't my horse breaking up there.'

'Spooked by the wind. On that side we took the full force of it.'

'Like I told you up there, Terry boy, this race is *over*.'

Boo was dancing now, unhappy at the weight of the sulky, afraid of another thumping boot, and the man tied him roughly to the wing mirror of his truck, growling at him, his hand raised as if in threat as he walked away. She fired invisible bullets into the back of that fat head, mentally kicked him as he had kicked Boo. She thought she had never been so filled with rage. Forcing herself to breathe, she caught sight of Cowboy John, a short distance away, in urgent conversation with Sal. He was looking at Boo, his hat dripping with rain and shaking his head. Sal shrugged, lit another cigarette. John placed a hand on his shoulder, trying to steer him away from the crowd, but just as he turned, Sal was called back to the ring of men where the money was being counted.

She was calm now. She watched with the forensic attention of a hunter, with the strategic calculation of Xenophon, all the while edging forward, camouflaged by the parked cars, the vast, rough-cast pillars of the intersecting flyovers. She was a matter of feet from Boo now, close enough to see the sweat on his neck, his rain-darkened skin, close enough to assess how many straps bound him to the little two-wheeler. *Don't call to me*, she warned him. The men were arguing beside the grey mare, Sal claiming noisily that he was the winner, claiming Boo as his, another man disputing this. Sal's horse had broken from the trot, two, three times, he protested. He should be disqualified. There was a murmur of dissent, an equal one of agreement.

'We got to get off now,' someone was shouting, in an Irish brogue. 'Get on home. The rozzers will be up here.'

She had slipped to the far side of Boo and saw the horse craning his neck to gauge who this was, trapped by his harness, his blinkers. 'Ssssh,' she told him, running a hand down his heaving flank, and watched his ears flick back and forth in recognition. She glanced at the men, and slipped the poles through the harness, her fingers nimble on the buckles.

Their voices were silenced briefly, and she ducked backwards, behind the pillar, heart beating erratically. And then they lifted again, this time in definite argument. She peeped out, saw money being divided, disputed, slapped into palms, and knew that this was her best chance: they would not look away while money was being counted.

She had but seconds left. Her fingers were trembling as she fumbled with the straps, adrenalin pumping blood into her ears, drowning the sound of the traffic above them. *I'm going to get you out of here, Boo.* Three straps. Two straps. Just one. She was murmuring it under her breath. *Come on.*

It was as she wrestled with the last strap, her fingers slipping on the wet leather, that she heard it, the exclamation she had dreaded. 'Oi! You!'

The big man, the one with the neck wider than his head, was walking towards her. His stride was long, bristling with menace. 'Oi! What do you think you're doing?'

Boo danced sideways now, infected by her anxiety, and she hissed at him to stand. '*Come on,*' she muttered at the buckle, as the other men glanced behind them, determining that something was wrong here, that the girl was not one of them. Then she saw John's confusion, Sal's face, his sudden, shocked recognition. *Come on.*

The man broke into a run. The last buckle would not give. She wrenched at it, her breath coming in short audible bursts. And then, as the man was just feet away, the poles of the sulky dropped with a clang to the ground. Boo was released. Grabbing a strand of his mane she unclipped the rope from his bit, and vaulted on to his back, fear lifting her feet. 'Go!' she yelled, clamping her legs to his sides, and the great horse leapt forward along the side-road, as if this was the moment he had waited for, his muscles gathering beneath her with such power that she had to entwine her fingers in his mane to stop herself being left behind.

Chaos broke out. She heard shouts, the sound of revving engines as she dropped low on his neck, her voice lifting in panic. 'Go on!' she yelled, and hauled clumsily on the right rein, the too-long driving reins, already tangling down by his legs. She pointed him towards the slipway, the small road that led upwards on to the flyover, and then in three, four strides she was on top, hearing the screech of tyres, the horns as she flew across two lanes of dual-carriageway.

And she was galloping along the flyover, high above the city, racing between the cars, barely aware of the drivers who swerved to avoid her. She could see nothing but the distant marshes ahead, hear nothing but the rushing of her blood, knew nothing but that they would surely be behind her. She knew where to go: she had rehearsed this moment for much of the night, going over and over her escape route. And there it was, already coming up to meet her. She could see the exit left, clogged with stationary vehicles, a few hundred yards in front of her, knew that once she reached it, headed left towards the industrial estate, they would not be able to reach her.

It was then that the little blue hatchback pulled sharply on to the hard shoulder, its driver having decided too late to change lanes, oblivious to the galloping horse behind him. She gasped, trying to check Boo's speed, seeing that, with the car there, the queues in the two lanes, she was blocked. She looked right across the dual-carriageway. She could not jump the dividing barrier without heading straight into oncoming traffic. There was no way out. She glanced under her arm, and behind her she saw Sal's red four-by-four, its horn blaring as it fought through the cars. If she stayed on the flyover he would catch her. She swallowed, tasting the metallic bile of fear.

She eyed the car, still flying towards it, urging it to move out of the way. She had little choice. *Forgive me, Papa,* she said silently and, grabbing a handful of his mane, pushed Boo on, aiming for the vehicle's bonnet.

Boo, confused at what was being asked of him, hesitated, heard the answering squeeze of her legs, her words of encouragement, and suddenly he was in the air, his huge muscular back stretching beneath her as he leapt over the car. And she was Xenophon, hearing the sounds of battle below her, her whole body, her whole self, trusting to the courage of the animal beneath her. She was all-mighty, protected, gifted. She was rage and glory, asking for nothing but survival. The world stilled. A silent shout escaped her. Her eyes were closed, then open, seeing nothing except the sky, the swerving cars across her path, and then, with a grunt of impact, they were down, him stumbling on the slippery surface, and she was half falling from his neck, hanging off him, grabbing frantically at too-long reins, mane, anything, to stay on.

He was galloping along the road, his legs a pumping blur and, with a roar of effort, she reached up with her left arm, grabbed at the harness and hauled herself back across him. And they were away, finally swerving off down the side-street that led to the canal as the sound of the blocked traffic, the disbelieving horns, gradually faded behind them.

'Who's your first witness?'

Natasha fired off another text message to Ben, asking him to check again that he had the correct papers for the morning, and that he would indeed be waiting outside the court in thirty minutes. She was in a coffee shop with Conor.

'The child psychologist. One of ours. We're going to frighten the husband with the suggestion that we might be able to stand up the abuse allegations, while Harrington and the solicitor work on Mrs P behind the scenes, trying to get her to agree to access in return for a better financial deal.'

I'm not a complete imbecile Ben replied.

I'll be the judge of that she responded.

'The wife will get what she wants,' Conor said bitterly. 'She'll never have to lift a finger again and a perfectly good father will get his name slung through the mud. I never thought you'd play dirty.'

She nudged him. 'It's the only way I'll be able to keep the child with its mother. Come on, Conor, it's divorce. You'd do exactly the same if you were me.' She squinted across the room at the wall-mounted mirror. 'Is my hair all right? Harrington reckons there'll be press outside for this one.'

'It's fine.'

She couldn't afford to get any of this wrong. It was vital not only to win the case but to use it as a showcase for Michael Harrington. His offer hung in her consciousness, ever present, a little gift to herself in moments when she felt overwhelmed by the mess that was the rest of her life. Would it be so bad to cross the divide? Surely it would be better to move away from all that day-to-day contact with clients. She thought of Ali Ahmadi. If she moved to Harrington Levinson she would be unlikely to make a mistake like that again.

She had not mentioned the offer to Conor. She didn't like to admit to herself why that might be.

He touched her foot with his. 'I've not got much on this morning so after I've dropped you I'll take your stuff home for you.'

He had surprised her. 'Are you sure?'

'Yeah. I never said I'd unpack it, mind. Don't expect me to morph into house-husband mode just yet.'

'Thanks, Conor.'

'No problem, Hotshot. As I said, I've nothing much on for an hour or so.'

'I meant for having me to stay.'

He studied his shoes, then looked up at her a little strangely. 'Why are you saying that? You're not a guest.' He frowned. 'Are you telling me this is just temporary? That I'm a stopgap?'

'Don't be silly. But I don't know how long I should stay, to be honest. I haven't had a chance to get my head round any of it. I just don't know if I should go straight—'

'—from the frying pan into the fire.'

'I didn't say that. But you did make the point that we were both a mess, as you so delightfully put it.'

'Matching messes. Counsel, please get your facts straight.'

Natasha realised she was at the head of the queue for coffee. 'Oh. Sorry. Decaf skinny latte, please.'

'Otherwise known as a Why Bother,' said Conor. The girl at the counter smiled wanly at him, as if she'd heard the witticism only several hundred times a day. 'I'll have a double-shot *macchiato*.'

'Let me get this case out of the way, Conor. I can't think about anything else right now.'

She waited for him to say something, and when he didn't, she reached into her bag. determinedly cheerful. 'I'll get these,' she said. 'Least I can do, seeing as you missed breakfast for me. Do you fancy a muffin?' Then she looked into her purse.

She couldn't see him. She skidded into the yard of the furniture factory and around the corner to where the delivery vans shielded the car park from public view, her breath coming in short bursts, the rain running down her face so that she had to keep wiping her eyes to see clearly. She slid off. Boo was sweating, shaken by the last two day's events, chilled by the now heavy downpour, and she had to pull on the reins to get him to walk forward behind her.

'Ralph?' she called.

There was no reply. Around her the blank windows of the office block looked down with disinterest, her voice muffled by the hiss of the water The shutters of the furniture factory were still down. There would be no one at work for another half an hour.

She stepped forward, peering behind a parked van. 'Ralph?' Nothing.

She wiped the rain from her face, her confidence waning, the adrenalin of the last half-hour seeping away. Just a girl standing in a car park, waiting for trouble.

He wouldn't come. Of course he wouldn't. She had been naïve to think he would. In fact, he might have told Sal where she was due to meet him. She stilled for a minute, observing that if Sal's men came behind her she would have boxed herself into a cul-de-sac.

She forced down rising panic, tried to think strategically. Could she do this without a saddle? Could she do it in this stupid blinkered bridle? The answer was straightforward: she had little choice. She couldn't risk waiting here for whoever might be about to find her. She gathered her reins in her left hand, preparing to vault back on to Boo's back.

'You don't have to shout, Circus Girl.' Ralph stepped out from a doorway and sauntered towards her, pulling his hood over his head. 'Bloody hell,' he observed, looking at the horse.

She ran towards him, tugging the reluctant Boo behind her. 'Did you bring it?' she demanded.

He held out his hand. 'Plastic first.'

'I'm hardly going to stiff you, Ralph.' She reached into her pocket, pulled out a wad of notes.

'Where's the card?'

'Couldn't get it, but here's twenty pounds.'

'Get lost. You think I'm a mug?'

'Fifty.'

'I could sell the saddle for more than that. One fifty.'

'A hundred. That's everything I've got.'

He held out his palm. She counted the money into it. Sal's money. She was glad to get rid of it.

'Where's the saddle?'

He pointed towards the doorway, busy recounting the notes. She asked him to hold Boo while she put it on, her breathing still rapid as she drew up the girth. Then she took off the blinkered bridle, hurled it over the wall into the wasteland beyond, and put on Boo's own.

'I tell you what, girl.' Ralph stuffed the cash into his jeans pocket. 'You've got some bollocks.'

She placed her foot in the stirrup and sprang on to her horse's back. Boo walked backwards, eager now to be off again.

'Where you going to take him? Sal'll be after you, you know. No point trying around Stepney or any of the Whitechapel yards. I'm guessing you could try south of the river.'

'Not round here. Listen, Ralph, I need you to do one more thing for me.'

'Oh, no.' He shook his head. 'You got plenty out of me, Circus Girl.'

'Go to St Theresa's. Tell my granddad . . . tell him Boo and I have gone on our holidays. He'll know where I mean. Tell him I'll ring him.'

'Why should I do anything else for you? Man, you got me up at a quarter past six this morning. That's virtually illegal.'

'Please, Ralph. It's really important.'

He patted his pocket and sauntered off down the road. 'I might,' he said, his oversized trainers loose on his twelve-year-old feet, 'but I'm a busy man . . .'

*   *   *

'I can't talk now, Natasha. I'm about to leave the house.' Mac dropped his photographic bag on the hall floor.

'My credit card, Mac, is it on the coffee-table where I left my bag last night?'

Mac bit back his response: she had left home and could hardly expect him to go chasing around after her loose bits of handbag stuffing. He peered around the doorway. 'Nope,' he said. 'Nothing on it.'

There was a brief silence. He could hear chatter in the background, the clinking of cups. 'Bugger,' she said.

He lifted an eyebrow. Natasha rarely swore. 'What's the problem?'

'Is she there?'

'No. I looked in. She must have left before us.'

'She's taken my credit card.'

'What?'

'You heard me.'

He lifted his eyes to the ceiling. 'You're on her case again. You've probably put it down somewhere.'

'No, Mac. I've just opened my purse to find one of my credit cards missing.'

'And you're sure it's her?'

'Well, it's hardly going to be you, is it? I'm telling you, Mac, she's taken my bloody card.'

'But she won't know the pin number.'

She heard a muffled conversation, then Natasha returned to the phone. 'Damn. I've got to get to the court. I can't possibly be late. Mac, can you—'

'I'll pick her up from school later. I'll talk to her.'

'I don't know whether to stop it.'

'Don't stop it now. She's hardly going to spend it in the canteen. Let me talk to her first. I'm sure there'll be an innocent explanation.'

'Innocent explanation? For stealing my card?'

'Look, we don't know for sure that she has. Let's just talk to her, shall we? Didn't you say she wanted to buy some stuff for the old man?'

There was a long pause.

'Yes, she did, but that doesn't make stealing acceptable.'

He began to protest again, but she interrupted: 'You know what, Mac? These kids may have had tough lives but they're not always the victims.'

He hung up and stood in the hallway. He had felt irritated by Natasha's comments at first, had forced himself to bite back his instinctive response. He didn't remember her being so cynical about her clients. He didn't like her for it.

He was about to pick up his camera bag when he remembered Sarah's odd composure the previous evening, the way she had elected to stay in the living room while he had gone off to make supper. He had believed she was being diplomatic. He still believed that.

He stood for a moment more, then walked slowly back up the stairs and opened the door to Sarah's room.

It was impossible to enter the room of a teenage girl without feeling like some kind of seedy interloper. Mac found he had self-consciously thrust his hands into his pockets, fearful of touching anything. He wasn't sure what he was looking for, just knew he wanted reassurance that things were as they should be. Perhaps that he knew this girl after all. He opened the wardrobe, and sighed with relief. There were her clothes, her jeans, her shoes. Her bed was neatly made. He was about to leave the room when he turned back.

The framed picture of her grandfather was gone. As was the Greek book on horsemanship she had been reading. He stared at the empty spot on the bedside table where both had stood, then walked into the bathroom. No toothbrush. No hairbrush. No soap. And, there hanging over the back of the radiator, was her school uniform. The only set she had.

Mac ran back downstairs and snatched up the phone. 'Tash?' he said, then swore under his breath. 'Yes, I know she's in court. Can you get hold of her for me? It's urgent. Tell her . . . tell her we've got a problem.'

Eighteen

'I think that if I become a horseman, I shall be a man on wings.'

Xenophon, *On Horsemanship*

It had stopped raining. Sarah trotted briskly along the endless grass verges towards the Royal Docks, towards City Airport, watching Boo's coat lift in colour as it dried. He had calmed, reassured by the familiar feel of her on his back, her voice, but her heart still thumped uncomfortably in her chest and her neck ached from glancing behind her so frequently.

The spaces were greater here, the sky a flattened grey infinity above, unbroken by looming buildings. She and Boo could move faster, but they were exposed, and awareness of their visibility caused her to keep going, to stay on the verges where she could easily break away and change course if she had to. She checked for traffic then crossed a tarmac road, Boo's hooves echoing across the empty space. When she hit the grass she began to canter again, leaping the drainage ditches.

The grey cloud was lifting, and suddenly, in front of her, she could see the airport. She had considered the London bridges, but suspected they would be too busy – a girl on a horse would attract attention – so she had headed east, out through the endless, Soviet-style estates of Newham and Beckton, crossing into the flatlands of north Woolwich, letting the shining towers of Canary Wharf recede behind her.

Rush-hour was tailing off now, and the endless stream of
vehicles, the relentless automotive push towards the City was
less evident. The occasional car still passed her, flying perhaps
on some short-cut towards the Blackwall Tunnel, or the Isle
of Dogs, but paid her little attention, a man eating a sandwich, or boy-racer lost in thumping music. She had her
windcheater on, the hood up so that her face was obscured.
This was not an area one would stop in unless it was necessary; with its warehouses and blocks of cheap hotels,
marooned between surging carriageways, it was the kind of
place one only ever travelled through, populated by travelling
middle-ranking executives and salesmen.

Boo was tiring; she slowed to a walk to allow him to catch
his breath, checking the road signs. A grimy pub stood solitary
in a wasteland of grey grass with a few tired houses nearby.
A short way beyond them stood banks of newly built apart-
ments (they were never 'flats', the new ones), the dull sheen
of the Thames, illuminated in mercurial strips where the sun
broke through the clouds, and then, down a poorly asphalted
road, flanked by concrete buildings, the ferry terminal. She
slowed, glanced behind her, and pointed her horse towards it.

'Mr Elsworth, would you please tell the court your full name?'

'I am Peter Graham Elsworth.'

'Thank you. And can you tell the court your profession?'

'I run a psychotherapy and counselling practice that
specialises in treating children, especially those who have
suffered some form of trauma.'

'You have been in practice for more than thirty years and
are considered one of the foremost experts in this field, are
you not?'

Elsworth straightened slightly. 'I have published peer-
reviewed papers in several academic journals, yes.'

Natasha looked down at her notes. Behind her, Mrs Persey

was anxiously tapping a daintily clad foot, letting out barely audible sighs of annoyance and frustration.

'Mr Elsworth, would you say that children tend to process trauma in the same way?'

'No. They process it in as many varying ways as an adult might.'

'So there is no standard response to a traumatic event.'

'That is correct.'

'Is it fair, then, to say that some children may react openly to a traumatic event – for example, crying, confiding in friends or adults – while others, who have endured equally upsetting experiences, may outwardly reveal little?'

Elsworth thought for a moment. 'It would depend on the child's development and their relationship with the people around them – as well as the nature of the traumatic event, of course.'

'If they felt, for example, that revealing something bad had happened to them would upset a parent, might they choose to keep it to themselves?' Her wig, still unfamiliar to her, was beginning to itch. She fought the urge to scratch the back of her head.

'That has certainly been my experience.'

Mr Persey was staring at her. A tall, broad man with fleshy cheeks and a skin tone that spoke of three good holidays a year, he had a fixed, piercing gaze that in other circumstances, would have made Natasha feel quite uneasy. It was not hard to see why Mrs Persey was as fluttery and hysterical as she was.

'Is it also your experience that in a case where parents were involved, parents, say, who were in conflict, a child might hide evidence of trauma if they felt it would prompt further conflict in the relationship?'

'It is a well-known psychological phenomenon. The child tries to protect the parent if it believes that speaking out might cause that parent further problems.'

'Even if that parent might have been the perpetrator?'

'Objection.' Mr Persey's barrister was on his feet. 'Your honour, we have already established that there is no evidence Mr Persey was ever abusive to his child, and to continue with this line of questioning, and with such emotive language, is deeply misleading.'

Natasha turned to the judge. 'Your honour, I am simply seeking to establish that, in such cases, the absence of obvious material or physical evidence, or even verbal testimony from the child, does not mean that no such trauma has taken place.'

Mr Persey's barrister, a heavyweight called Simpson with a whining tone snorted audibly. 'One might as well argue that a woman claiming an abusive relationship should be absolved of the need to show bruises. Except in this case even the child herself is not claiming abuse took place.' He was the kind of barrister who considered it beneath him to go up against a solicitor advocate; there was still a surprising amount of prejudice against lawyers like her.

'Your honour, if you let me continue I will seek to show that children are an exceptional case precisely for this reason. They are far more likely to conceal trauma in an effort to protect those around them.'

The judge did not look up. 'Continue, Mrs Macauley.'

She had bent over her papers again when Ben thrust a note over the bench and into her hand. *Call Mac urgent*, it said. Caught off-guard, she turned to him. 'What does he want?' she whispered.

'Don't know. He just said it was extremely important that you call him.'

She couldn't possibly do it now.

'Mrs Macauley? Would you care to proceed?'

'Yes, your honour.' She motioned Ben away surreptitiously. 'Mr Elsworth, would it . . . would it then be conceivable, in your opinion, that a child who was fearful of one parent could or would conceal any problems in the relationship from the other parent?'

'Your honour—'

'I'll allow it, Mr Simpson. Mrs Macauley, make sure you keep to the point.'

Elsworth glanced at the judge. 'It's dependent on their age and circumstances obviously, but, yes, it is conceivable.'

'Age and circumstances. What do you mean by that?'

'Well, among the young clients I have seen it is often the case that the younger the child the less effective they are at concealing any traumatic event. It tends to reveal itself – even if they are unable to articulate their distress – in other behaviours: bedwetting, obsessive-compulsive disorders, even uncharacteristic aggression.'

'And at what age would you say a child is capable of hiding their distress . . . effectively? So that perhaps he or she does not display any of the characteristics you have just described?'

'It depends on the child, but I have seen children as young as seven and eight who were surprisingly effective at hiding things that had happened to them.'

'Deeply traumatic events?'

'In some cases, yes.'

'So for this to be achieved by a ten-year-old might not be out of the question.'

'Certainly not, no.'

'Mr Elsworth, have you heard of parental alienation syndrome?'

'I have.'

'This is . . . I quote, "a disturbance in which children are obsessively preoccupied with deprecation and/or criticism of a parent. In other words, denigration that is unjustified and or exaggerated". Would that be a fair definition in your view?'

'I am not an expert but, yes, that sounds like a fair definition.'

'Mr Elsworth, you are, as you say, a peer-reviewed academic whose work has appeared in leading psychological journals for many years. Do you believe in the clinical existence of parental alienation syndrome?'

'I don't. But I'm not sure that's an appropriate—'

'Okay, I'll put this another way. Can you tell me how many children you have treated?'

'In general? In my practice? Over the years, well, it would run into thousands. More than two thousand, perhaps.'

'And has any of your young clients ever displayed what you understand as parental alienation syndrome?'

'I have treated many children who have been persuaded to think ill of one parent, even many who have developed animosity to a parent that lasted several years. I have treated many children deeply damaged by their parents' divorce. But I cannot say I believe such psychological states to be evidence of a syndrome. I think that would be overstating the case.'

She let that one sink in for a bit. 'Mr Elsworth, do you know anything about the level of false reporting of physical or sexual abuse of children during divorce or custody cases?'

'I understand there are a number of recent papers on this phenomenon, yes.'

'Peer-reviewed papers? From respected academics? Can you give us an idea as to the latest conclusions about how many such claims turn out to be false?'

'I believe the latest paper, in 2005, showed that there is very little false reporting in such cases. I think a cross-section of studies taken that year showed that the rate of false allegations in a custody context was between one and seven point six per cent.'

'Between one and seven point six per cent.' Natasha nodded, as if confirming this to herself. 'So, more than ninety per cent would be valid allegations of abuse. Would that echo your own experience in practice?'

He paused. 'In my experience, Mrs Macauley, the abuse of children tends to be significantly under-reported, both during and outside divorce and custody matters.'

She caught Michael Harrington's grin of satisfaction. It was all she could do to suppress a smile. 'No further questions, your honour.'

Headed from north to south, the Woolwich ferry was empty. A line of benches stood forlorn and empty on the *Ernest Bevin*, their besuited occupants having departed some minutes earlier on the other side for the Docklands Light Railway. As it docked, she hesitated, then led Boo down the long ramp and on to the traffic deck, positioning him well away from the cockpit. Boo gazed around him and shifted a little on the oily surface as the engines began to vibrate, but was apparently unperturbed by this strange transport. There were no lorries, no cars aboard, just her, Boo, and this empty deck. She glanced behind her again, willing the ferry to move off, praying she wouldn't catch sight of that pick-up truck. She knew, rationally, that there was little chance they could have followed her, but fear had embedded itself in her very bones. She saw that truck everywhere, spectral, coming around corners, parked in front of her. An ever-present threat.

As she stood, Boo's reins taut in her hand, the conductor emerged from the cockpit. A tall, slightly stooping man with a salt-and-pepper beard, he stood very still for a moment, as if to confirm what he was seeing, then walked slowly towards her. Sarah's grip on Boo's reins tightened, and she braced herself for argument. But as he drew closer the man was smiling. 'That's got to be the first horse I've seen on here in thirty years,' he said. He stood still, a few feet from Boo, shaking his head. 'My dad worked on the ferry back in the thirties and forties. He could still remember when nearly all the traffic on here was horse-drawn. Can I pat him?'

Almost weak with relief, Sarah nodded mutely.

'Lovely boy, ain't he?' The man drew his hand along Boo's neck. 'Beautiful animal. Horses up the top, men down the front there, it used to be.' He pointed. 'Course, that was before this series of ferries.' He pointed at the huge yellow and white bridge that braced the vessel. 'He all right, is he? Well behaved?'

'Yes,' Sarah muttered. 'He is.'

'What's his name?'

She hesitated. 'Baucher,' she said, and added, not quite sure why she did so, 'He's named after a famous French rider.'

'Grand name, eh?' The man rubbed Boo's forehead. 'Grand name for a grand old boy. I've got a postcard in there of the old carriage horses on board. From years ago. Hold up and I'll show you once we're moving.'

'How much?' she blurted. 'For him, I mean. How much do we have to pay?'

He looked surprised. 'You don't need to pay nothing on here, sweetheart. Oh, no. Ain't no one paid to cross on this ferry since 1889.' He chuckled. 'About back when I started . . .' He walked stiffly back to his cockpit and disappeared.

The ferry vibrated, then moved off smoothly from the north side of the Thames and out into the murky, swirling water. She stood alone on the open deck beside her horse and gazed down the desolate stretch of river at the hovering cranes, the gleaming hoods of the Thames Barrier and the blue and silver sheds of the Tate sugar refinery, breathing in the damp air.

She was hungry. It hadn't occurred to her for the last twelve hours that her stomach could feel anything except knotted anxiety. She pulled her rucksack from her back, opened it and found a biscuit. She broke off a little and gave it to Boo, whose velvety lips pushed insistently at her coat until she gave in and handed him more.

She stood, with her horse, in the middle of a river, some

strange hinterland, a dreamscape, from which she had not yet quite awoken. But perhaps not so strange; just another horse in a line that stretched back more than a century. And as the distance from the shore grew, her breathing steadied, her mind cleared, as if she was emerging from some great shadow. The pick-up truck was on the north shore, with all the mess and anxiety and fear that had suffocated her for months. It was all quite simple now. She found she was smiling, exercising muscles that seemed to have atrophied during the past few weeks.

'Here,' she said, granting Boo another piece of biscuit. 'Time for us to go.'

Ben handed her another note: *He's rung Linda four times.*

Natasha glanced at it while she fixed her wig, trying to force the hair grip through the mesh. Solicitor advocates had only recently been allowed the privilege of a wig; she had been against it but the partners in her practice had urged her to wear one. Her opponents would take her more seriously, they said. She suspected it was simply that they wanted the chance to up the charges to clients and the wig made that possible.

'Call him back,' she whispered, handing him her switched-off mobile phone. 'His number's in the directory. Tell him I can't talk to him until we're in recess.'

'She said he sounded frantic. Something to do with ... Sarah going.'

Across the room Simpson was attempting to pick apart Elsworth's testimony. He'd have a job with that one, Natasha thought. He was one of the best in his field – and the rates he charged for expert-witness testimony were testament to it.

'Tell him we'll sort out her leaving date after he's spoken to her about my card. And tell him I can't answer any more calls so there's no point in ringing me again.'

She began taking notes, trying to collect her thoughts.

'You got him, right?' From across the bench Mrs Persey's thin fingers wrapped themselves around her wrist. 'Everything you said proves she was abused by him.' Her eyes were large, the strain evident despite the carefully applied makeup.

Natasha caught sight of the judge, who was watching their exchange, his expression unamused. 'We'll discuss it outside. But, yes, it went well,' she whispered, and leant forwards to focus on Simpson.

Within minutes Ben was back. *Not going, gone* the note said. *Disappeared.*

She scribbled, *??? Where?*

He doesn't know. Is this someone in your family?

Natasha's head sank into her hands.

'Mrs Macauley,' came the voice from the front, 'are you all right?'

She straightened her wig.

'I'm fine, your honour.'

'Do you need to take a short recess?'

She thought quickly. 'If your honour would allow it, a pressing matter has come up unexpectedly that I should deal with.'

The judge turned to Simpson, who was staring at her with barely disguised fury, as if she had planned it. 'Very well. We will adjourn for ten minutes.'

He picked up the phone before it had even had time to ring.

'She's gone,' he said. 'Cleared out, with half her stuff.'

'Have you rung the school?'

'I played for time. Rang in saying she was sick. I thought if she turned out to be there, I could say I'd made a mistake.'

'But she's not there.'

'She's gone, Tash. Photos, toothbrush, the lot.'

'She's probably at the stables. Or with her grandfather.'

'I rang the hospital. He's had no visitors today. They're certain of it. I'm on my way to the stables now.'

'She won't leave the horse,' she said confidently. 'Think about it, Mac. She wouldn't leave the horse, and she wouldn't go very far from her grandfather. He matters more to her than anyone.'

'I hope you're right. I don't like this.' Mac, unusually, sounded jumpy.

She thought suddenly of Sarah, silent and strangely accepting, the previous evening. She had known something was not right. But she had been so grateful to the girl for accepting the forthcoming upheaval without making a scene that she had not thought to question it. 'I've got to go back into court. Ring me when you get to the stables. She's got my card, remember? Like you said, she's probably just gone to buy her grandfather some new bloody pyjamas at my expense.'

The cowboy was leaning against the rusting car, talking to one of the young boys, as Mac wrestled with the gate, trying to ignore the Alsatian, which issued a warning growl as he entered. He glanced to the railway arch; the horse's stable was open. Clearly no one was in there.

'Ah . . . Mr . . . ah . . . John? Mac – you remember me? Sarah's friend.'

The cowboy stuck his roll-up into his mouth and shook Mac's hand. He pursed his lips. 'Oh, I remember you, all right,' he said.

'I'm looking for Sarah.'

'You and everyone else,' the old man said, 'from here to Tilbury Docks. I'm damned if I know what the hell's been going on here while I been gone.'

The boy glanced from John to Mac and back again. 'Like I said, John, I've hardly been here.'

'Fat lot of good you are.'

'I don't get involved with nothing. You know that.'

'Has she been here?' Mac said.

'I only seen her for a split second. She never even told me what was going on. It's a mess, that's for sure.' Cowboy John shook his head mournfully.

'Hold on – you *have* seen her? Today?'

'Oh, I seen her. I seen her seven o'clock this morning. Last I seen her she was taking off over the flyover like that damn circus horse had wings. How she never got herself killed is between her and the Almighty.'

'She's been out riding?'

'Riding?' Cowboy John regarded him as if he was stupid. 'You don't know?'

'Know what?'

'I been out looking for her all morning. She's gone. She's took that horse before anyone worked out what she was doin' and she's gone.'

'Gone where?'

'Well, if I knew that she'd be standin' here now!' Cowboy John sucked his teeth, irritated.

The boy lit a cigarette, his face bent low over the flame of his lighter.

Mac went to Sarah's lock-up. 'You got a key for this?'

'I don't own this place no more. I gave—'

'I got one,' the boy said. 'She gave it to me so I could feed her horse when she weren't here,' he explained.

'And you are . . .'

'Dean.'

'Ralph,' said Cowboy John, shoving the boy with long brown fingers. 'His name is Ralph.'

The boy fiddled in his pocket, withdrawing an oversized bunch of keys. He went through them carefully, finally pulling out one that he used on the padlock. Mac pushed open the door. The lock-up was deserted. There was no saddle on the rack, no bridle, only a webbing headcollar and some brushes in a box. 'John? Are you saying you think she's taken off with the horse?'

Cowboy John raised his eyes to heaven, and nudged Ralph beside him. 'Quick, ain't he?' he said. 'Yes, she's taken the darn horse, and she's left me a big ole pile of doo-doo in its place. I got some people who are very, very unhappy. I got a feeling all sorts has been going on here that I don't know about.' He eyed Ralph balefully. 'But, for starters, I got to work out how to tell Le Capitaine in the hospital there I ain't got the slightest idea where his precious little girl is.'

Mac closed his eyes for the longest time. He let out a long sigh. 'That makes two of us,' he said.

The sun was at its highest point, which, given the time of year, wasn't very high at all. It had travelled round so that it faced her, causing her to squint under her hat, and she made a few mental calculations, trying to work out how far she could get before dark. Before Boo became too tired to go on.

An endurance horse could do fifty, maybe sixty miles in a day. She had read about it. Such animals had to be brought up to this standard slowly, their muscles hardened by relentless slow work, their backs and quarters strengthened by regular riding up and downhill. Their shoes had to be checked and their legs protected.

Boo had enjoyed none of these precautions. Sarah talked to him now as they headed through the suburbs at a brisk trot, following the signs for Dartford. She could feel the spring in his paces slackening, read the hope in his ears, his steadied gait, that she might ask him to slow. Not yet, she told him silently, with a faint squeeze of her legs, a gentle urging of her seat. Not yet.

It was busier here, and the sight of a girl on a horse drew curious glances, the odd shout from passing van drivers or children gathered outside the lunchtime queue for the chip shop. But she kept her head down, her only communion with her horse. She could usually get past them before they realised what they had seen.

She found a quiet street before she dared to use a cash machine. She dismounted, walked Boo across the pavement, pulled Natasha's card out of her pocket and typed in the number she knew by heart. It was burnt darkly on her conscience. The machine hummed and considered her request for what seemed an interminable time. Her heart began to thump. They might know by now. Natasha would have discovered what she had done, the extent of her betrayal. She had wanted to leave them a note, to explain, but she couldn't find the words, her head still muddied by fear, shock and loss. And she couldn't risk anyone knowing where she was going.

Finally the message flashed up on the screen. How much money would she like? £10, £20, £50, £100, £250? After the weeks spent scrimping, worrying about individual pounds, the figures were dizzying. She didn't want to steal, yet she knew that, once the Macauleys had worked out she had taken it, the card would be stopped. There would be no more money.

This might be her only chance.

Sarah took a deep breath and placed her fingers on the keypad.

He was waiting outside the courtroom when Natasha emerged at midday. He had his back to her and spun round when he heard her voice. 'Any news?'

'She's taken the horse.'

He watched Natasha register this in stages: first, a kind of blank inability to digest what he had said, then the same disbelief he himself had felt. A kind of embarrassed half-laugh at the ridiculousness of the idea.

'What do you mean she's taken the horse?'

'I mean she's run away with the horse.'

'But where could she go with a *horse*?'

Her eyes left his face and focused behind him on Cowboy John, sauntering along the corridor, humming as he came. It had taken him a while to get up the stairs. 'I don't know why you couldn't have used a phone,' he wheezed, clamping a hand on Mac's shoulder. He smelt of old leather and wet dog.

Mac stepped back, propelling the old man forwards. 'Natasha, this is . . . Cowboy John. He runs the stables where Sarah keeps her horse.'

'Used to run. Hell! If I'd kept a hold of things we'd never've been in this mess.' Cowboy John took her hand briefly, then bent low over his knees, hawking into a handkerchief.

Natasha winced, her hand still in mid-air. A small group of people were watching them surreptitiously. Along the corridor a thin, expensively dressed blonde woman had been shocked into silence.

'So what do we do?'

'Findin' her would be a start. I say we split up and start askin' around. Girl on a horse like that gotta attract some attention.'

'But you said you'd been looking for her this morning and didn't hear anything. John saw her near the marshes,' Mac explained.

John touched the brim of his hat, his rheumy eyes looking off into the distance. 'She knew where she was headed, that's all I'll say. Had a rucksack on her back, and she was hitting some speed.'

'She'd planned it. We should call the police, Tash.'

John shook his head vehemently. 'You don't want to go involvin' busybodies. That's what got her into this mess in the first place. Besides – the police? Nonononono. That girl ain't done nothin' wrong. She's made a mess, yes, but she ain't done nothing' actually wrong . . .'

Mac caught Natasha's eye. Neither of them spoke. He waited, wrong-footed by her reticence. Then he reminded her, 'You were the one who said we had a legal duty to report her missing.'

Natasha peered down the corridor and blinked hard.

'Tash?'

What she said next made him dip his head, as if unsure he had heard her correctly.

'Look, I don't want to report her yet. She turned up the last time, didn't she?' Natasha turned back to John. 'You know her. Where might she have gone?'

'Only place that girl would ever go is to see her grandpa.'

'Then let's go there,' Mac said. 'We'll talk to the old man. See if he has any ideas. Tash?' She just stared at him. 'What?'

'I can't go, Mac. I'm in the middle of a case.'

'Tash, Sarah is *missing*.'

'I'm well aware of that, but she's done this before. And I can't just drop everything every time she decides to take off for a few hours.'

'I gotta tell you, I don't think she's aimin' to come back any time soon.' Cowboy John removed his hat and scratched the top of his head.

'I can't leave this case.' She gestured down the corridor at the thin blonde woman, who was now wrapped in a cashmere shawl, like an accident victim. 'This is the biggest case of my career. You know that.' She couldn't hold his gaze and coloured slightly. His stomach constricted with anger.

'I can't just drop everything, Mac.'

'Then I'm sorry to have troubled you,' he said tightly. 'I'll ring you at Conor's when she turns up, shall I?'

'Mac!' she protested, but he had already turned away. Somehow almost nothing she had done had disappointed him as much as this.

'*Mac!*'

He could hear Cowboy John shuffling and wheezing behind him. 'Aw, hell, you really gonna make me do all them stairs again?'

'The broader the chest so much the handsomer and stronger is it . . . the neck would then protect the rider and the eye see what lies before the feet.'

She couldn't remember Papa holding her – not like Nana held her, as if it was as natural to her as breathing. When she came in from school, she would walk up to Nana's chair and Nana would gather her up, pulling her into her nylon house-coat, that warm, sweet, powdery scent filling Sarah's nostrils, that eiderdown bosom to be leant against, an unending source of love and security. When she wished Sarah goodnight she would hold her longer than she needed to, scolding herself.

After Nana died Sarah, overwhelmed by sadness, would sometimes lean against Papa and he would put an arm around her to pat her shoulder. But it was not an action that came naturally to him, and she always had the feeling that he was a little relieved when she pulled herself together. Sarah had felt the lack of human contact like an ache, long before she understood what it was she was missing.

Her grandfather had been sitting at the kitchen table, perhaps a year or so ago. She had walked in, back early from the stables, and asked him what he was reading. The book was familiar to her, so familiar that she had never been curious about it. And her grandfather, placing it carefully on the laminate tabletop, had begun to tell her about a man with the skill of a poet, the battlefield mastery of a general, one of the first to advocate a partnership with the horse that was not based on cruelty or force. He read her a few passages. The words, if it were not for the arcane tone of their translation, could have come from any modern-day manual on horsemanship: '*Whenever, therefore, you induce him to carry himself in the attitudes he naturally assumes, when he is most anxious to display his beauty, you make him look as though he takes pleasure in being ridden, and give him a noble, fierce, and attractive appearance.'*

She had edged a little closer to him on the seat.

'This is why I always tell you you must never lose your temper with a horse. You must treat him with kindness, with respect. It's all here. He is the father of horsemanship.' He tapped his book.

'He must have really loved horses,' Sarah had said.

'No.' Papa had shaken his head emphatically.

'But he said—'

'It is not about love,' he said. 'There is not one mention of love in this whole book. He is not sentimental. All that he does, all the *douceur* he shows, it is because he understands that this is how you get the best out of the animal. This is how man and horse excel together. Not all this kissing-kissing.' He had made a face and Sarah had laughed. 'Not all this emotion. He knows that the best way for the horse and the man is simply to understand each other, to respect each other.'

'I don't get it.'

'A horse does not want to be a lapdog, *chérie*. It does not want to be dressed up in ribbons, sung to, like these silly girls at the stables. A horse is *dangereux*, powerful. But it can be willing. You give a horse a reason to perform for you, to protect you, by understanding the things it wants to do itself, and there you achieve something beautiful.'

He had watched her, trying to ensure she understood. But she had felt disappointed. She had wanted to believe Boo loved her. She wanted him to follow her around the yard not because she might have food but because he needed to be with her. She did not want to think of him as the means to an end.

He patted her hand. 'What Xenophon is asking is better. He is asking for respect, for the best of care, for consistency, fairness, kindness. Would the horse be happier if he spoke of love? *Non.*'

She had been so determined not to agree with him.

'Surely you can see that there is love in what he does,' he had said, his eyes wrinkling at the corners. 'There is love in what he does, what he . . . proposes. Just because he does not speak of it, it does not mean it is not there in every word. It is there, Sarah. In. Every. Little. Act.' He had banged the table.

She could see it now, even if she hadn't then. It was as close as he had ever come to telling her how much he loved her.

They had rested a little way outside Sittingbourne, Sarah allowing Boo to graze the lush edges of the fields on a long rein, finally hungry enough herself to eat one of the rolls she had packed. She sat in a quiet lane on a plastic bag, protecting herself from the wet grass, and watched her horse's head lift as he was distracted from eating by a distant crow or, on one occasion, a deer beside a copse.

Sarah had ridden fast in open country, galloping down the edges of ploughed fields, following bridle paths when she could, staying on verges to protect Boo's legs. All the while she kept the motorway on her right, the distant hum of its traffic within earshot, knowing she could not get lost while it was close. Boo had been energised by the green. He had bucked several times when she first let him go down a long, flat stretch, his great head tossing with excitement, his tail lifting. She had found herself laughing, urging him on, even as she knew she should be conserving his energy for the hours ahead.

When had he ever been free like this? When had his eyes

been filled only with distant green horizons, his hooves cushioned by soft ground? When had she been free? For a few glorious miles she allowed herself to forget what she was leaving and focus only on the sheer pleasure of being welded to this magnificent animal, sharing in his pleasure at his surroundings, feeling the joy of a superior power that was willing to accede to her. They flew down the edges of the fields, leaping small hedges and ditches filled with brackish water. Boo, infected by her mood, went faster, refusing to steady when he crossed small lanes, instead leaping them, his ears pricked, his long legs eating up the ground beneath them.

I think that if I become a horseman, I shall be a man on wings.

She was on wings, like Xenophon. She urged him faster, gulping, laughing, tears gathering at the corners of her eyes and streaming, horizontally, along her face. He took the bit, stretched out and ran, as horses have run since the beginning of time, for fear, for pleasure, for the glory of doing what they did. She let him. It didn't matter where he was headed. Her heart was elastic, bursting. This was what Papa had meant, not the endless time spent perfecting one movement of his legs, not the circles, the *passage*, the careful weighing up of what could be achieved. One sentence of Papa's kept running through her mind, rhythmic, in time with the muted thud of his hooves hitting the ground.

'This is how you escape,' Papa had told her.

This is how you escape.

'Second visitor this afternoon. He *will* be pleased.' The nurse had just closed the door behind her as they arrived at the Captain's room. She hesitated. 'I have to tell you, he's not done too well the last couple of days. We've got the consultant coming up this afternoon, but we suspect he's suffered another stroke. You may find him a little hard to understand.'

Mac saw the dismay on John's face. He had already insisted

on a lengthy cigarette break outside in the car park so that
he could face the ordeal ahead.

'Second visitor?' Mac said. 'Has his granddaughter been in?'

'Granddaughter?' she said brightly. 'No ... a boy. He
seemed to know him. Nice kid.'

Cowboy John seemed hardly to register this. He gave a
little shake of his head, as if pulling himself together, and
they entered the room.

The Captain's head lolled back on the pillow, his mouth
slightly open. In a matter of days he appeared to have aged
another ten years.

They placed themselves on each side of him, lowering
themselves on to chairs carefully so that they wouldn't wake
him. Mac drummed his fingers on his knees, wondering if
they should be there at all. John glanced at the old man, then
stared fixedly at one of the pictures of Sarah and Boo, the
tired strings of well-used Christmas decorations that hung
on the walls around him. 'I like them pictures,' he said.
'They're good for him to see.'

They sat there for some time, neither willing to wake the
old man and impart the catastrophic news that they had both
failed him in the worst way imaginable. The Captain's breaths
were shallow, as if each one was an effort, an afterthought
by a body too tired to do much more than exist. His left
hand, once strong, was an atrophied claw on his chest, barely
covered by the sheet. His cheeks were cadaverous, the skin
dry and translucent, the mauve veins painfully visible. A transparent cup, half full of milky tea, sat on the table beside him,
a rigid spout emerging upright from its lid.

Mac broke the silence. 'We can't tell him, John,' he whispered.

'It ain't your right *not* to tell him. She's the man's closest
kin. She gone missin', he got a right to help us find her.'

How would he be able to do that? Mac wanted to ask.

How can this knowledge do anything other than destroy him?
He rested his elbows on his knees and dropped his head. He
would rather have been anywhere than here. He wanted to
be out combing the streets, talking to people. He would rather
have been in a police station, confessing his failure as a would-
be parent, canvassing Sarah's friends. A girl and a horse
couldn't just vanish into thin air. Someone must have seen
her.

'Hey . . . hey, Capitaine . . .'

Mac looked up. Cowboy John was smiling. 'How you doin',
you lazy son of a gun? Bored of yo' lie-in yet?'

The Captain moved his head slowly towards him. It seemed
to require an inordinate effort.

'You want anything?' John leant forward. 'A drink of water?
Somethin' stronger? I got some Jimmy Beam in my pocket.'
He grinned.

The Captain blinked. He might have been signalling amuse-
ment. Or he might just have been blinking.

'I heard you not feelin' so good.'

The old man gazed at him steadily.

Mac could see that even John was faltering: he turned to
Mac, then back to the old man.

'Capitaine, I – I got somethin' to tell you.' He swallowed.
'I got to tell you that your Sarah has done somethin' a little
crazy.'

Still the old man stared at him, his pale blue eyes unblinking
now.

'She's took off with that horse of yours. And – and it may
well be that I'm goin' to head off from here and she'll be
back at the yard waitin' for us. But I got to tell you, I think
she's . . .' He took a deep breath. 'I think she's taken him and
gone somewhere.' Behind him, Sarah grinned in black and
white, leaning forward against her horse's neck, a stray lock
of hair blown over her mouth.

'We didn't want to worry you,' Mac began. 'And I have to tell you she's been fine with us. Really. She's been happy – as happy as she could be without you – and certainly never given us any real cause for worry. But this morning I went into her room and that book of yours is gone and a ruck-sack, and when I looked into the bathroom –'

'Mac—' John interrupted.

'– her toothbrush was gone. And it may well be as John says that she's there, laughing at us, now but I wondered if there was anywhere you knew that she might be, whether—'

'Mac, shut the hell up.'

He stopped.

John nodded towards the old man. 'He's tryin' to speak,' he said, and bent low, closer, removing his hat so that he could get his ear close to the old man's mouth. His eyes met Mac's. 'No?' he said, puzzled.

Mac leant forward in his place, straining against the hum of machinery, the chatter of nurses outside the room, to hear the breathy whisper. He sat up. '"I know,"' he repeated.

The old man, he realised, was utterly unperturbed by this disclosure. There was no trace of anxiety on his features. Mac's eyes met John's. 'He says he *knows*.'

Nineteen

'A disobedient horse is not only useless, but he often plays the part of a very traitor.'

Xenophon, *On Horsemanship*

The rain had set in around mid-afternoon. At first it was a few, tentative drops but their weight – and the fast approaching slice of black sky that scudded towards her – warned of what they heralded. It was as if daylight ended within minutes, no gradual creeping into evening, no gentle grading of sunset, just light one moment and then, seemingly minutes later, black, with heavy, drenching rain.

The driver swerved to a halt in front of her. She pulled Boo back, afraid, but the man stuck his head out of the window: 'You idiot! You should be wearing a reflective strip,' he yelled. 'I could have hit you both.'

Her voice, when it emerged, was croaky, hijacked by fear. 'I'm sorry,' she said. 'I – I left it behind.'

'Then get on to the main road,' he said, brake lights winking, 'where you can bloody well be seen.'

It was dark now. The rain came down steadily for almost an hour and Boo, his earlier fizz dissipated with the extra miles, walked and trotted sluggishly, his head as low as she would allow, mane plastered to his neck. Sarah tried to encourage him but she ached too. The rucksack full of items she had believed invaluable had dragged on her shoulders for the past ten miles, and her seat bones were sore so that she shifted periodically, trying in vain to find a way of staying comfortable. Her saddle darkened with water and, despite the waterproof jacket, her jeans were soaked. She knew that if she had to ride much further the rough, wet fabric would chafe her chilled skin. Still, she could see the sodium lights of the town. They would rest soon, she told him.

When she reached the dual-carriageway, the traffic was deafening. She kept to the verge, ignoring the flashing of car headlights, the mind-numbing roar, picking her way past the lorries that lined up on the specially widened hard shoulder, all stationary along the last part of the fast road. She passed cabs where pulled curtains hinted at sleeping drivers, others in which small televisions cast moving shadows around chintzy, domesticated interiors strung with tinsel. She saw Czech lorries, Polish lorries, photographs of families and posters of naked women, handmade signs warning that 'This lorry is regularly checked' and that 'Illegal immigrants will be prosecuted'. One or two drivers caught sight of her as she passed; one shouted something she couldn't hear.

Boo was too tired to be disturbed by any of it. He had started to feel uneven, his legs struggling under the distance. And then there it was, the huge sign arching over the main road. She sat a little straighter, gathered up her reins. As they came over the brow of the hill she saw the ferries, their windows glowing, sitting in the harbour, the elegant twist of the flyovers that guided the traffic towards them.

Two more miles. She felt a germ of something like excitement inside her. She ran her hand down her exhausted horse's neck, pleading with him to go a little further. 'You can do this,' she murmured. 'Just get us there. And I promise I'll never leave you again.'

★   ★   ★

'Could you state your name to the court, please?'

'Constance Devlin.'

'And please state your profession.'

'I am a teacher at Norbridge School. I am head of year four, and have held that position for the last eleven years.' She paused to drink some water, glancing up at the skylight on which rain pattered.

'Miss Devlin, how long have you known Lucy Persey?'

'Well, it's a small school. I've known her since she started in Reception and I taught her all last year. I also do private tuition in languages, and Lucy has had extra lessons for almost two years.'

'Could you speak up a little?' the judge said. 'I'm finding it difficult to hear you.'

The woman flushed. Natasha smiled at her, trying to reassure her. Outside the courtroom, Constance Devlin had been an unusually nervous witness. She was not happy about being dragged into this, she had told Natasha several times. It really was not her job. She had never even been in a courtroom. And she was quite sure the school was not happy for her to be involved in a divorce case either. Natasha had got her measure immediately: spinsterish, truly comfortable only in her own sphere, a world of nice young girls, the cloistered, rarified atmosphere of an exclusive school. She would be devoted to her job, and reduced to tears by the wrong brand of digestives in the staffroom. 'I would really rather you ask me as few questions as possible.' Her shaking hands had belied the careful and determined tone with which she spoke.

'Would you say you know your pupils well, Miss Devlin?' Natasha made her voice as gentle as possible.

'Yes. Probably better than most teachers.' She looked at the judge, twisting a handkerchief nervously between plump fingers. 'We have very small classes. It's a rather . . . good little school.'

'And in the time you have known her, how have you found Lucy Persey?'

Constance Devlin paused. 'Well, she's never been what you'd call one of the more forthcoming pupils. Even in Reception she was a little shy. But she was always a happy little thing. She's bright. She has a good grasp of figures, and her literacy age is well above average.' She smiled a little, thinking of the child. Then the smile faded. 'Although last year . . . she slipped back a bit.'

'Slipped back a bit?'

'Her marks dropped. She's struggled at school.'

'Has her personality changed at all?'

'She has – in my opinion – become increasingly withdrawn.'

Ben entered the court and sat quietly behind her. She half expected another note, but instead he handed her a folder of school reports, and her mind drifted. Mac would be at the hospital now. If he had found Sarah there, would he call her to let her know?

'It says here, Miss Devlin, that Lucy has missed a lot of school.'

'There have been quite a few occasions, yes.'

'An average of fifteen days each school term. With her parents' knowledge?'

'I . . . assumed so. We tend to deal with Mrs Persey.'

'You tend to deal with Mrs Persey.' Natasha let that one hang. Along the bench, she could see Mr Persey whispering urgently to his brief. 'And what reasons did Mrs Persey give for her daughter's absences on those days?'

'It wasn't anything very specific. She would say Lucy wasn't feeling up to it. Sometimes a headache. A couple of times she didn't give any reason.'

'And did the school have any thoughts about these absences?'

'We were a little concerned about the number. And . . . the change in Lucy's behaviour.'

'That she had become withdrawn and had fallen behind in her work?'

'Yes.'

'Miss Devlin, how long have you been a teacher?'

The older woman was breathing more evenly, her voice lifting a little. 'Twenty-four years.' She glanced around the court as she spoke.

Natasha smiled encouragingly. 'In your experience, if there is a change in a child's character and academic performance, teamed with increasing absences, what would you conclude?'

'Objection.' Simpson was on his feet. 'You're asking the witness to extrapolate.'

'I believe Miss Devlin's experience in this field is valid, your honour.'

'Rephrase your question, Mrs Macauley.'

'Miss Devlin, in your experience would such behavioural changes suggest problems at home?'

'Objection, your honour.'

'Sit down, Mr Simpson. I'd like a different wording, Mrs Macauley.'

'In cases where there are problems at home, Miss Devlin, what would you say are the most common behavioural changes that become evident at school?'

'Well . . .' Miss Devlin looked awkwardly at Mr Persey '. . . I would say poor performance . . . perhaps either withdrawn or disruptive behaviour. It can swing between the two.'

'And, during your teaching career, have you taught many children with known problems at home?'

'Oh, yes,' she said, a little wearily. 'I'm afraid that being at a private school does not insulate children from family disruption.'

'Miss Devlin, if there had been something seriously wrong at home, if, say, Lucy had suffered something even greater than the trauma of divorce, do you think you could tell?'

There was a long silence, so long that the judge stopped what he was doing and tapped his pen expectantly. Natasha, waiting for the woman to gather her thoughts, scribbled a note to Ben: *Has Mac rung?*

He shook his head.

'Miss Devlin?' the judge interjected. 'Did you hear the question?'

'I did,' she said, her voice quiet and precise. 'I heard it and the answer is that I don't know.'

Bugger, Natasha thought.

Miss Devlin placed her hands on the wood in front of her. 'I only know that when a child goes quiet they are suffering. Everything about Lucy – her silence, her lack of enjoyment in things that once made her happy, her withdrawal from her friends – tells me she is suffering.' She took a deep breath. 'But I don't know exactly what children like Lucy are suffering because they don't trust us enough to tell us. They don't tell teachers, and they don't tell parents because they can't trust them not to get cross when they say something they don't want to hear. So, no, Mrs Macauley, they don't tell us because half the time nobody listens to them anyway.'

The court was very still. Miss Devlin was talking directly to the parents now, her face flushed, her voice growing in volume and urgency. 'I have seen this week after week, year after year, you see. I have watched these children's worlds fall apart, their lives as they know them dissolved, without any say-so from them. They have no power over where they live, who they spend their time with, who their new mummy and daddy are – goodness, sometimes even what their new last name is – and we, the teachers, the supposed role models, are expected to tell them it's okay, it's how life goes, that they just have to get on with it. Oh, and make sure they don't drop behind with their schoolwork.'

'Miss Devlin—' the judge began.

It was as if a dam had broken: 'But it's not. It's a betrayal. It's a betrayal and we all stay silent about it because . . . well, because life is hard, and sometimes these children have to learn that, don't they? It's just *life*. But if you could see it from where I am, these lost children, these *lost* children, wandering around, lonelier than you could believe . . . all that potential wasted . . . Well, frankly it makes no difference to me whether that child was hit or not.' She wiped her face with a plump palm.

'Oh, yes, I know what you're asking me, Miss Macauley. Yes, that's what I said – that to me it makes no difference. And the fact that I'm standing here, being asked to pinpoint exactly which little bit of that child is hurting and who is to blame, in order to work out who gets to win most in this hideous marital farrago, frankly makes me complicit.'

Mrs Persey was sitting in frozen silence: her husband, along the bench, was muttering furiously to his barrister: 'I am not listening to this! The woman is clearly hysterical.'

'Miss Devlin—' Natasha got no further because the woman held up a hand.

'No,' she said firmly. 'You asked me to be part of this, so I'm going to tell you. Oh, yes, they'll survive.' She nodded sarcastically.

'As you no doubt tell yourselves, they'll grow up a little faster, end up a little wiser. But you know what else? They'll stop trusting. They'll become a little more cynical. They'll spend their lives waiting for everything to fall apart all over again.

'Because it is a rare person, a *rare* person, who can contain their own pain and still give a child the support and understanding it needs. In my experience, most parents haven't got the time or the energy to make sure it happens. Perhaps they're just too selfish. But what do I know? I'm not a parent. I'm not even married. I'm just one of those unfortunate people who gets paid to pick up the pieces.'

She stopped. The courtroom was in total silence, waiting. The clerk, who had been typing at some speed, paused expectantly. But Miss Devlin took a deep breath. When she had apparently composed herself, she turned to the judge. 'Please may I have your permission to leave? I'd very much like to go now.'

The judge appeared utterly taken aback. He glanced at Natasha. She nodded mutely, and was dimly aware of Simpson doing the same.

Miss Devlin gathered up her bag and walked determinedly towards the door. As she passed the bench where the Perseys sat, she stopped. Her ears were pink and her voice quavered as she spoke: 'It will be surprisingly easy for Lucy to head down the wrong path,' she said quietly. 'All you have to do is stop listening.'

Natasha stood very still, watching the short, neatly clad figure disappear through the heavy wooden door. She heard the murmur of dissatisfaction to her right. She saw this scene suddenly as if through someone else's eyes, framed it as Mac might: the parents, for once, more furious with a common enemy than with each other; her junior, grinning with private delight at this unexpected turn of events; the judge, whispering to the clerk. Then she began to unpin her wig. 'Your honour,' she said, 'I'd like to seek an adjournment.'

'You want a what?'

She stood at the foot-passenger ticket office, her jacket dripping on to the floor of the oversized Portakabin. She had removed her hat, but the sight of a girl in boots and wet jeans still drew attention. She could feel the eyes of the other foot passengers burning into her. 'A ticket,' she said quietly. 'For a person and a horse.'

'Are you having a laugh?' The fat man looked past her at

the people in the queue, searching for affirmation. Do you see what we've got here? his expression said.

'I know you take horses. They cross the Channel all the time.' She held up Boo's passport. 'My horse even comes from France.'

'And how do you think he got here?'

'On a boat.'

'Did he row it?'

There was a smattering of laughter behind her.

'A ferry. I know they cross all the time. Look, I've got the money. And we both have passports. I just need to . . .'

He was gesturing to someone seated a short distance away behind the big sheet of glass. A colleague, in the same liveried blazer, got up and approached the window. She took in Sarah's bedraggled appearance, the passport in her hand. 'You can't take a horse on with the foot passengers,' the woman said, when the man had explained.

'I know that.' Anxiety hardened Sarah's voice. 'I'm not stupid. I just want to know how I can get a passage for him.'

'He has to be on a transporter. You need to go via a specialist company. He's got to have veterinary papers. There are Defra rules about transporting livestock.'

'He's not livestock. He's a Selle Français.'

'I don't care if he's a Pekinese. But there are strict controls about how animals cross the Channel and unless you can convince me that two of those legs are fake, that includes him.'

'Can you help me? Can you tell me where I can find a company like that? It's really urgent.'

The damp, brightly lit room was closing in on her. She had tied Boo to the white railing outside and, through the window, she could see him standing obediently, even as a small group gathered around him, children reaching from their parents' arms to touch him.

'I need to cross tonight,' she said, and her voice broke.

'There's no way you'll be doing that, not without papers. We can't just put a horse on a passenger ferry.'

Someone was tutting. She felt suddenly exhausted, tears of frustration pricking her eyes. There was no point. She could hear it in their voices. She turned wordlessly and walked towards the door.

'What did she think it is here? Ride On Ride Off?' She could hear them laughing as she went outside, the cold breeze buffeting her sideways on.

She untied Boo. A transporter? Papers? How was she supposed to have known all this? She gazed across at the ferry. The ramp was down, and vehicles were slowly bridging the gap between land and ship, guided into their narrow queues by men in neon tabards. There was no chance she could get him past them. No chance at all. A great suppressed sob worked its way up through her chest. How could she have been so stupid?

A man approached her. He looked Boo up and down with the kind of benign assessing gaze that spoke of someone who knew horses. 'Are you on some kind of sponsored ride?' he said.

'No. Yes,' she said, wiping her eyes. 'Yes. I'm on a sponsored ride. I need to get to France.'

'I heard what you said in there. You'll be wanting lairage,' he said.

'Lairage?'

'It's like a hotel for horses. There's a place about four miles down the road. They'll be able to sort you out. Here.' He scribbled a name on a business card and handed it to her. 'Go back to the roundabout, take the third exit and you'll find it three or four miles down. Bit basic, but it's clean and it won't cost you too much. Looks like your horse could do with a rest, anyway.'

She stared at the card. 'Willett's Farm', he had written. 'Thank you,' she called, but he had already gone, and her voice was carried away on the sea breeze.

Natasha sat back in her chair, passing the silver horse from hand to hand. It had tarnished a little, and she rubbed it, watching the smudge of grey discolour her fingers.

Richard, the senior partner, was in conversation with a client. His booming voice and the ramshackle acoustics of the old building meant the sound carried up the corridor as if he was next door. He was laughing now, a hearty, explosive sound. She wondered, briefly, what Linda had heard of her own telephone conversations over the past years: booked MOTs, missed smear tests, the spluttering objections of her failing marriage. She had never considered how audible her words might have been.

It was a quarter to four.

The files in front of her were neatly stacked and labelled. She placed the little horse carefully on top. Sarah, in her way, was no different from Ali Ahmadi. She had seen an opportunity and taken it; the route of all children whose early years had forced them to rely only upon themselves. Her behaviour, although unpredictable, was not inexplicable.

And although Natasha was angry, she knew she couldn't blame the girl. She blamed herself, for thinking she could absorb Sarah into her life with no cost, no ripples to upset her carefully organised existence. And, as with Ali Ahmadi, she had been repaid in spades.

It had taken her almost forty minutes to persuade Mrs Persey that Richard was the right person to take over her case.

'But I want you,' she had protested. 'You know what my husband's like. You said you'd be there.'

'We instructed Michael Harrington for a reason. He's the

finest, toughest advocate in this field. Believe me, Mrs Persey, my absence won't disadvantage you in the slightest. With luck, I'll be back within a day or two, and in the meantime Richard is fully briefed and ready for you.'

She had been forced to offer a concession in payment, for the 'inconvenience'. It would, Richard said tersely, have to come from her own fee. Natasha suspected Mrs Persey wouldn't notice whether or not it appeared on her final bill – and would certainly notice the amount a lot less than Natasha – but she was the kind of woman who needed to feel she had gained something from any exchange. If that was what it took to retain the client, Richard said, then that was what had to be done. His little hmph of displeasure when she had uttered the words 'family emergency' had given her sudden sympathy for her colleagues with children.

'Natasha? Is this some sort of joke?' Conor entered her room without knocking. She had half expected him.

'No, it's not,' she said, standing and ferreting in a drawer for her keys. 'Yes, I'm handing over the Persey case and, yes, everyone can manage quite well without me for a couple of days. With luck, I might even be back by tomorrow.'

'You can't just drop the bloody case. This is a huge deal, Natasha. It's in the papers.'

'Richard will take it while I'm gone. She's got Harrington for the financial deal, and after today I'd be very surprised if they don't agree the custody issues. Our mousy Miss Devlin may have done us a favour.'

Conor stood at the other side of her desk, his hands resting on it. 'Mrs Persey wants *you*. You can't babysit her through the lead-up and leave her bang in the middle of it.'

'I've already discussed it with her. I'm not down to take any more witnesses. I can leave the rest to Harrington.'

He began to shake his head, but she blustered on: 'Conor, neither of them really cares about Lucy's welfare – this case is about money and score-settling. That's all most divorces are about, as you well know.'

'But where are you going?' said Conor.

'I'm not sure.'

'You're not *sure?*'

Linda had walked in with a mug of tea, Ben tailing her. 'This is interesting,' she murmured.

'Family emergency,' Natasha said, closing her briefcase.

Conor stared at her. 'The girl. I thought you were putting her back in the care of Social Services. She was meant to be someone else's job now.'

Her eyes told him to be quiet. She could see Ben and Linda's curiosity.

'Let Mac deal with it.'

'I can't.'

'Mac?' Linda repeated, no longer even pretending not to listen. 'Your ex Mac? What's he got to do with anything?'

Natasha ignored her. 'Mac doesn't know where to start,' she said. 'He can't do this by himself.'

'Oh, yes. And we always have to drop everything for Mac, after all.'

'It's not like that.'

'Then let the police deal with it. It's theft.'

Linda put the tea down the table. 'Is this anything I can help with?' she asked.

Natasha said nothing.

Conor's jaw was set. 'Natasha, I have to tell you, if you walk out on this case at this point, you're effectively committing career suicide as far as this firm goes.'

'I have no choice.'

'Don't be so dramatic.'

'"Career suicide"? Who's the one being dramatic?'

'Natasha. It's the *Persey divorce.* You have instructed Michael Harrington. The outcome of this case might decide whether or not you make partner. It may make the reputation of this firm. You cannot just drop everything to chase after some dodgy kid who probably tricked you into looking after her in the first place.'

Natasha stood up and went to the window. 'Lin, Ben, can we have a minute, please?' She waited until they had gone. She had a strong suspicion that they were outside the door, and lowered her voice. 'Conor, I—'

'Didn't you catch her stealing? And you've never been sure about her. Not from day one.'

'You don't know the full story, Conor.'

'I wonder why that is.'

'Okay. What would you do, then, if it was one of your kids?'

'But she's *not* one of *your* kids. That's the whole bloody point.'

'I have a legal responsibility for her. She's a fourteen-year-old girl.'

'A girl who this morning you were cursing for stealing your credit card.'

'Her being a thief doesn't absolve me of responsibility.'

'But is a little thief worth ruining your career for? Jesus, Natasha, just a few weeks ago you were worried that that kid with the mileage problem was going to ruin your career. Now you're about to throw it up for a scumbag you're not even representing.'

She heard his words as one of those children might hear them, *scumbag*, *thief*, writing them off. She reached for her coat.

'Look,' he said, 'I'm sorry. I didn't mean that. I'm just trying to protect you.'

'This isn't about trying to protect me, is it, Conor? This isn't about trying to protect my career.'

'What's that supposed to mean?'

'This is about Mac. You can't bear the fact that I took her

on with him and now that her disappearance means I have to deal with him.'

'Oh, get over yourself.'

'So what is it?'

'I'm a partner in this firm, Natasha. If you disappear halfway through this case, we don't just lose money, our reputation takes a massive kicking. And how hard do you think it'll be for us to pick up a decent bloody silk for the next big case if they think they're going to be left in the lurch halfway through?'

'Who needs to know? I may even be back by tomorrow. And I'll explain it to Harrington. He'll understand.'

'It's more than I bloody can. You're going to throw away *everything* –' there was a horrible emphasis on the word '– on a kid you don't even like and an ex-husband who made your life a misery. Well, good luck,' he said. His voice was icy. 'I hope it was all worth it.'

The building had never been among the most solidly built. But this time the crash of the door against its frame was enough to knock several books off the shelves.

Boo heard the sound before she did. He had been so tired over the last half-mile that she had almost wept with guilt at every step. He dragged each hoof, his head hanging low, begging her with every reluctant muscle to let him stop. But she had had no choice: aching, her bones deadened by tiredness, she had urged him onward. Finally, when she had seen the sign that told her Willett's Farm was a half-mile up on the right, she had dismounted and walked, to allow him even that slight respite, tears of exhaustion mingling with the rain that ran down her face.

And then they had heard it, carried towards then on the blustery wind: a distant crash, a grunt and a squeal, men's voices raised, then gone as the gust briefly changed direction.

The effect on Boo was electric. His head shot up, his exhaustion forgotten, and he stopped, his whole body tuning to this unexpected sound. Horses are cynical creatures, Papa had once told her. They will always expect the worst. Boo, brave as he was, began to quiver, and as she strained to hear what he was hearing, she had to suppress a shiver. The sound, faint as it was, told of something terrible ahead.

They walked forward, Boo with the delicate, trippy gait of a creature half afraid to see what was there, yet unable to prevent itself looking; the equine equivalent of a nightdress-clad woman in a horror movie.

They stood in the gateway and stared at the scene in front of them. A huge HGV lorry was parked in the centre of the yard, its brightly lit rear revealed to them, its unexpected reds too garish in the dark. A woman in a quilted jacket hovered at the edge of the ramp, her hands raised to her face, while inside two men struggled to hold on to a horse who appeared strangely buckled, its rear end forced down, its front not visible. A partition appeared to have partly collapsed across it, and the two men, shouting and gesturing to each other, were trying to untangle it.

Blood was everywhere. It coated the floor, had splashed up on the metallic sides of the trailer; it carried towards Sarah in a fine mist so that she tasted a faint hint of iron on her lips. Boo snorted and backed away in fear.

'I can't stop it. I need another bandage, Bob.' One of the men was kneeling on the horse's neck, injecting it with something. He tossed the syringe aside. His arms were scarlet, his face smeared with red. The horse's legs thrashed convulsively, and the heavier man near the back cursed as a hoof connected with his knee.

'The vet's coming,' the woman shouted, 'but it'll take him a few minutes. He's up at Jake's.' She climbed into the lorry, attempted to brace the partition away from the horse.

'We don't have a few minutes.'

'Can I do anything?'

The woman turned, took in Boo, Sarah's riding hat – short-hand symbols that said she might be of some use. She jerked her head towards a stable. 'Bung him in there, sweetheart and help me lift this.'

'She's not insured, Jackie,' the older man grunted, as he wrestled with a bolt in the floor.

'We're not going to get this off him otherwise,' the man at the back said, in a thick Irish accent. 'Jesus, old fella, how the hell did you get yourself in this mess?' His head disappeared behind the partition. 'This sedative's making no damn difference at all. Have you got another syringe, Jackie?'

Sarah shoved Boo into the stable and ran back to the lorry.

'There's a cabinet in the office there,' the woman barked at her. 'It's open. Find a bottle marked – Ah, hell, what is it? – Romifidine and a syringe and bring them out, would you?'

She flew, energised by the terrible atmosphere, the desperate banging and crashing that was still coming from the lorry. She scrabbled in the cabinet until she located a small clear bottle and a plastic-wrapped needle. As she got back, the woman's hand was already thrust out for them.

'Ah, Jesus, Jackie, I think he's snapped it.' She heard the despairing voice in the lorry. Blood was dripping down the rubber mats and on to the cobbled yard. She watched it spread in oily ovals around each stone.

'Give him the sedative anyway. It's not going to make any difference to him if he has, and if he's borderline it might just keep him still long enough. Where's the bloody vet?'

'Here.' Jackie gestured to Sarah. 'Try and hold that up.'

Sarah climbed up on to the back and grabbed the bottom of the partition, which was badly buckled. Her hands slid along its base, already slick with blood. She stared out at the yard, trying not to look at the horse alongside her.

Jackie was ripping at the needle's plastic covering with her teeth. She unscrewed the bottle top, thrust the point into the neck and pulled the plunger, then handed it further back inside the lorry. Sarah jumped as a rear leg kicked towards her.

'You okay there, sweetheart?'

She nodded mutely. The two men were soaked in blood; a sickly slick swam around the horse's rear, its movement leisurely, ominous, almost pulsing. Sarah saw that her jeans, her jacket, were already smeared with it.

'Easy, fella, easy there now.' The Irishman was soothing the horse. 'There. His eyes are closing, Jackie. I think that one's done it. But I can't get to the leg until we've got the partition out.'

Sarah's back hurt, but she couldn't tell them. She glanced up as headlights swung into the yard, blinding her, then heard a car door slam, wet footsteps. A red-headed man was running up the ramp, his case already open. 'Ah, hell, this doesn't look too pretty.'

'We think he may have done his leg, Tim.'

'That's an awful lot of blood. How long's he been bleeding like this?'

'Minutes. I've tourniqueted the off fore, but it took a hell of a crack when he went down.'

The horse's legs were still now, save for the odd feeble kick. Sarah watched the vet crouch, his back to her, and begin his examination. His actions were obscured from view by the Irishman, and the part of the partition that had not yet collapsed.

'I couldn't tell you how he did it. He panicked when we unloaded the yearling, went up and somehow got his front leg over the top. When he pulled backwards he dragged the whole lot down on himself. It happened so fast, I can't believe it.'

'Never ceases to amaze me the trouble horses can bring on themselves. Come on, let's get this partition out so I can take a better look at him. You girls take the back end, and we'll pull him towards us and free the front.'

Sarah braced herself, sweating now, conscious of the curly-haired woman beside her who was puce with effort. Her jacket smelt of blood and cigarette smoke. Finally the huge central partition was released. They angled it, removing it carefully from the lorry, carried it down the ramp and stood it against the side.

Jackie wiped her hands on the front of her jeans, apparently heedless of the marks she left there. 'You all right?'

Sarah nodded. Her own jeans were dark red.

'Come away,' the woman said. 'Nothing you can do now. We'll go into the office. I'll put some tea on. You want a cup?'

The thought of hot tea was so tempting that Sarah was rendered briefly speechless. She followed Jackie into the little office and sat where she was told. The grey plastic chair was streaked immediately with the blood from her clothes.

'Rotten ruddy business,' Jackie was saying, as she filled the kettle. 'We only lose a couple a year, but it gets me every time. It's not Thom's fault. He's one of the careful ones.' She glanced behind her. 'Sugar? It's good for shock.'

'Yes, please.' She was shaking. She had caught a glimpse of the horse when the partition had gone: he had looked like Boo.

'I'll give you two. I'm having two. Bloody horse.'

A large whiteboard hung on one wall with some fourteen horses' names entered on it. Documentation, Defra guidelines and a list of emergency numbers were pinned beside its. Various hauliers had struck cards to the wall, beside the odd Christmas card and photographs of unnamed horses. Sarah recognised Jackie beside one.

'Here.'

She accepted the tea, grateful for the warmth of the hot mug in her chilled hands.

'I'll wait until they come out before I do theirs. If he's saved, they'll be a while yet.'

'Do you think he'll live?'

Jackie shook her head. 'I doubt it. Never seen a horse get itself in such a tangle. He must have bashed his leg hard to buckle the partition like that. And those thoroughbreds have such weedy legs . . .' She sat down heavily behind the desk, and glanced up at the clock. Then she looked at Sarah, as if seeing her for the first time. 'You're late to be riding. Not from round here, are you?'

'I – I was told to come to you. I need a stable for the night.'

Jackie scrutinised her. 'You off somewhere?'

Sarah took a sip of her tea. She nodded. If these last months had taught her anything it was to say as little as possible.

'You look very young.'

Sarah met her eye. 'Everyone says that.' She forced a smile.

Jackie opened a big book in front of her. 'Well, we can certainly do you a stable. Looks like we'll have one spare, after all. What's your horse's name?'

'Baucher,' Sarah said.

'Passport?'

Sarah reached into her rucksack and handed it over. 'All his vaccinations are up to date,' she said.

Jackie flicked through it, scribbled a number and handed it back to her. 'We're twenty-five a night, hay and food inclusive. Hard food is extra. You tell me what he needs and I'll sort it out.'

'Could we stay a couple of days? I need to sort out the next part of my journey.'

Jackie fiddled with her ballpoint pen. 'Stay as long as you like, sweetheart, long as you're paying. Just leave me a number where you can be contacted.'

'Can't I stay here?'

'Not unless you fancy a bed of straw.' Jackie sighed. 'Aren't you booked in anywhere?'

'I thought this place was for people too.'

'We don't do humans, sweetheart. It's not worth the hassle. The drivers tend to sleep in their lorries, and the others stay in one of the B-and-Bs. But I can give you a number if you like. Here.' She pointed at a list on the wall. 'The Crown can usually do you at short notice. Forty pound a night with an en-suite. Kath'll look after you. She's quiet this time of year. I'll give her a ring.'

'Is it far?'

'About four miles up the road.'

Sarah's shoulders slumped. She was silent for a few minutes while she forgot to get her voice under control. 'I rode here,' she said finally, her voice muffled by her collar. 'I haven't got any way of getting there.' She was so tired. She couldn't go any further. She would beg this woman to let her sleep on the office floor.

A muffled shot rang out.

They looked up. Jackie pulled a packet of cigarettes from a drawer in front of her, removed one with a flick of her wrist and tamped it on the desk. She waited a moment before she spoke again. 'Did you just say you rode here? From where?'

Sarah's pulse was still reverberating with that shot. 'It's . . . complicated.'

Jackie lit the cigarette, leant back in her seat and took a deep drag. 'You in trouble?' Her voice had hardened.

Sarah was familiar with that tone. It was the sound of someone assuming the worst of you. 'No.'

'That horse yours?'

'You saw his passport.'

The woman was staring at her.

'My name's on it. Look, he knows me. I'll make him call to me if it helps. I've had him since he was four.'

The vet was emerging from the lorry, his case closed.

'We've got a spare room at the back. Twenty-five quid and I'll throw in a bit of dinner, seeing as you got stuck in with us. I've promised Thom I'll sort him out tonight so another at the table won't make much difference. But,' she leant forwards, 'I'm keeping you off the books. There's something not quite right here, I'll put you up, but I don't want to get involved.'

They were interrupted as the door opened. The two men walked in, filling the little room. The Irishman shook his head.

'Ah, shame,' Jackie muttered. 'Here, sit down, Thom, I'll do you a tea. And you, Bob. Sit next to . . .'

'Sarah,' she said. She kept her hands around her mug, fearful that if she said or did too much she might lose the chance to stay.

'Fracture in front and a severed artery. Poor boy had no chance.' The Irishman's face was bleached with shock, smears of red on his skin where he must have touched it without realising. 'Tim never even had time to sign his papers. He's got a mare foaling. One in, one out, eh?'

'Ah, sod the tea.' Jackie slammed the lid down on the kettle. 'This calls for a drop of the medicinal.' She reached for the other drawer of her desk and pulled out a bottle of amber liquid. 'Not you, though, Sarah.' Her eyes flashed a warning.

She had guessed her age, Sarah thought. She wouldn't be implicated in more than she had to be.

Sarah kept her head down. 'I prefer tea,' she said.

Twenty

'Never deal with him when you are in a fit of passion. Anger, impatience, fear . . . virtually any human emotion undermines effective communication with a horse.'

Xenophon, *On Horsemanship*

Despite the rain, she was already outside the office, awkward in her smart suit and heels, pacing the pavement with small, impatient steps. As soon as she saw his car, she ran to it, briefcase and handbag thrust under her arm. He felt relieved: there was still some part of Natasha that he understood. He smiled as he leant over to open the passenger door, and she climbed in, disregarding the horns sounding from the traffic behind them. 'I thought you—'

'Don't say anything,' she interrupted, jaw set, hair slick with rain. 'And as soon as we've found her you and I don't have to deal with each other again. Okay?'

Mac's smile died on his lips. He had been about to pull into the stream of traffic, but he paused. 'Thanks, Mac, for swinging all the way across town to pick me up.'

'You want me to thank you? Okay. Thanks, Mac. Can't tell you how much I've been looking forward to this little outing. Is that better?' Her face was flushed with anger, dots of colour on her cheeks.

'You don't have to come, you know. You made that quite clear.'

'She's my responsibility, too. You made *that* quite clear.'

Mac's patience was already at a low ebb. 'You know what? This is hard enough as it is without dealing with your crap. If you want to come with me, fine, but if you're going to be like this, I'll drop you at the house now. We'll go in separate cars.'

'Dealing with my crap? Have you any idea what I've had to drop to come and look for her? Or what this has just done to my reputation?'

'Nice to see you again.' Natasha jumped as Cowboy John thrust his head through the gap between the front seats. 'Just thought I'd remind you folks that you have an audience.' He resumed lighting a cigarette.

She turned to Mac, open-mouthed.

'He knows about horses,' he explained, 'and he's known Sarah since she was a kid.'

When Natasha said nothing, he added, 'You going to sort the horse out once we find them, Tash?'

She rummaged in her handbag. 'So, where is she? Have you heard anything? I've got to be back at work as soon as possible.'

'Yeah,' Mac muttered, at last swinging the car out into the traffic. 'Because you're the only one with a real job, after all.'

'I'm in the middle of a big case, Mac.'

'Yeah. You said.'

She swivelled in her seat to face him. 'Meaning?'

'Meaning all you've done is go on about how difficult this is for you. How this is disrupting your life. How *I* have disrupted your life.'

'That's not fair.'

'But it's accurate. Have you considered the possibility that any of this might be down to you?'

Cowboy John sat back and tilted his hat over his face. 'Oh, Lordy.'

'*Me?*'

The traffic was terrible. Mac stuck his right arm out of the window, forcing his way into another, equally sluggish queue. 'Yes. You,' he said. Perhaps it was because he felt as if he had been driving in circles all day. Perhaps it was fear of where the girl was. Perhaps it was just the sight of Natasha, prim in her neat suit, forever treating him as the enemy, the guilty party, a convenient whipping boy. 'You were the one who walked out, Natasha. You were the one who signed up to look after her, then decided it was all too difficult.' He sensed the outrage in her silence, but he didn't care. 'You think you're the only one who's been inconvenienced here? I've had to cancel jobs, and John here has better things to do.'

He wrenched the wheel and whizzed up the inside lane. The car felt as if it was shrinking around him. 'Maybe if you'd stuck around, put Sarah before your own hurt pride, we wouldn't be in this mess.'

'You're blaming *me* for this?'

'I'm just saying you played a part.'

She was shouting at him now: 'Well, who brought his girl-friend home and paraded her around in front of Sarah in her underwear?'

'I didn't parade her around!'

'She had almost nothing on. And I walk into my house – our house – and there's this bloody prepubescent glamour model smirking at me in her knickers!'

'I like the sound of your house,' said John.

'You think that was nice for Sarah to see? When we'd been playing happy families around her?'

'Oh, don't pretend *that* had anything to do with Sarah going.'

'Well, it hardly made for a harmonious atmosphere, did it?'

'I said I was sorry.' Mac thumped the steering-wheel. 'I

told you it wouldn't happen again. But, come on, it's not as if you didn't have your boyfriend in our house, right? In my bedroom.'

'It's not *your* bedroom.'

'What was our bedroom.'

'Better and better,' said John, dragging on his cigarette.

'He didn't stay *once* while you were living there. So don't you—'

'Only because you had somewhere else to go.'

'Oh.' She sat back in her seat, arms folded. 'I wondered how long it would be before you brought that up.'

'Brought what up?'

'My second home. I was warned about this.' She shook her head. 'I should have listened.'

He glanced at her. 'What the hell is that supposed to mean?'

'That you'd use it against me when it came to negotiating a settlement.'

'Oh, for Chrissake, you're being ridiculous. You think I give a stuff about your rented bloody cottage? I couldn't care if you had the bloody *QE2* to spend your weekends on.'

'I hate to interrupt here.' John leant forward again, letting out a long plume of smoke. 'And, believe me, I could listen to you two for *hours*. But ain't we kind of losin' the thread?'

Mac's heart thumped uncomfortably against his ribs.

She sat as far away from him as she could reasonably get in the front of the small, slightly overloaded car – as if he was contaminated, as if she would rather be anywhere else in the world.

'Can you lovely people call a truce?' John asked. 'Just till we find her? That would be . . . nice.'

They sat in silence as Mac drove east across the city. He had clamped his jaw shut.

'Fine by me.' Her voice was small. She reached for the battered *A–Z*. 'Where are we headed, anyway?'

'She's going to love this.' John chuckled.

Mac kept his gaze firmly to the front. 'France,' he said, chucking her passport into her lap. 'She's headed for France.'

It took the entire clogged length of the Blackwall Tunnel to explain what had happened at the hospital. She had questioned them several times as to whether they had heard him correctly, whether the old man was even in his right mind, until Cowboy John had become irritable. 'He's sick, but he's just as sharp as you, lady,' he grumbled. He did not like Natasha, Mac could tell. He eyed her, as he did the hissing geese in his yard, with beady suspicion.

'Even if you heard right, I find it very hard to believe that even Sarah thinks she has a realistic chance of riding all the way to . . . Where is it?'

'Look at the map.' Mac gestured with a finger, eyes fixed on the road. 'Halfway down France.'

Natasha squinted. 'But she won't get there, will she?'

'She ain't goin' to make it past the coast. 'Less that horse can swim the Channel.'

'John and I think she won't even get to Dover.'

They emerged into the darkening evening sky, and Mac's heart sank when he saw that the traffic was just as dense and slow on the other side. He indicated right, pulling on to the dual-carriageway. 'He says the horse will need resting long before then.'

Natasha coughed pointedly, then rolled down her window. She sniffed, then swivelled in her seat. There was an ominous silence. 'Is that what I think it is?' she said.

'How do I know?' said John. 'I can't see in yo' head.'

'Is it . . . weed?'

He took the roll-up from between his lips and examined it carefully. 'I sure hope so, price I paid for it.'

'You can't smoke that in this car. Mac, tell him.'

'Well, I sure can't step outside, lady, can I?'

Natasha's head sank briefly into her hands. Mac caught John's eye in the mirror, the briefest glint of amused recognition.

Natasha raised her head. She took a deep breath. 'You know, Mr Cowboy, or whatever your name is, I'd really appreciate it if you didn't smoke drugs in the car. At least while we're stuck in traffic.' She was edging down in her seat, an eye on the cars to each side of them.

'It stops me gettin' car sick. And, 'sides, you guys fightin' makes me stressed. And that ain't good for us old folk. You see what it did to the Captain back there.'

Natasha swallowed. She looked like someone heading fast towards the end of a short touchpaper. 'Let me get this straight. If we don't let you smoke illegal substances in Mac's car, you're likely to throw up or die of stress.'

'That's about it.'

Mac watched her struggle to control her breathing. It appeared to take a while. For the first time in days he wanted to smile.

There had been a time, according to Cowboy John, when London's rush-hour lasted just that: one hour. Now the traffic began to slow, the queues lengthening, just after school pick-up and rarely eased for four hours. They could not, he remarked, with the detachment of a casual observer – or perhaps of someone who had just smoked the best part of a quarter-ounce of dope – have picked a worse time to set off. Oh, and if it was all the same to them, he needed to pee. Again.

Just to add to the tension, it had begun to rain heavily. Mac's car now sat in a long queue on the A2, the stream of red brake lights like the tail of some great red dragon intermittently visible between the squeaking trajectory of his windscreen wipers.

Natasha had been silent for the last half an hour, sending messages on her phone, flicking through paperwork and making notes. She had a hushed and heated exchange with someone about her court case, and a whispered conversation with someone he suspected was Conor. When she slammed the phone shut he felt slyly gratified. He fiddled with the radio for the fifteenth time, trying to find the latest traffic report.

'I don't know why you keep doing that,' she snapped. 'It's obvious we're stuck in traffic.'

Mac let it slide. He could see that her communications had wound her up. To explain that he was listening for news of horse-related accidents would not improve matters.

'My feeling is she's got to be out of London by now,' he said, tapping his fingers on the steering-wheel. 'I say we come off the A2 at the next junction, maybe follow a B road. She would probably have cut off a long time before this. If we're lucky, we might even overtake her.'

He stuck a hand out of the window at someone who allowed him into the adjoining queue of traffic. 'I suggest we go as far as we think she could go and if we haven't found her by eight o'clock we ring the police.'

In the back seat, all that was visible of John was his hat. It nodded. 'Sounds like a plan,' the hat said. 'Though I still ain't too happy about the police.'

'Because you'd have to throw your stash out of the window?'

'Sweetheart, you goin' to be prisin' that stash from my cold dead hands.'

'We can arrange that too,' she said sweetly.

Mac glanced at her. 'I've been thinking about something else. If we cancel your credit card, she won't have any money. She'll have to turn round and come back.'

Natasha considered this. 'But if we leave her with no money, she'll be at greater risk.'

Cowboy John's voice cut in: 'I don't think havin' no money's goin' to stop her. She's pretty determined.'

'It depends how much she's taken out already,' said Mac, 'but if she's allowed to keep on using it, there's no telling where she could go. We're almost facilitating her running away.'

'You absolutely sure she's taken your card?' John said. 'I tell you, I've known that girl a long time and she ain't the type to steal.'

Mac waited for Natasha to speak up, perhaps to mention fish-fingers in a supermarket, money missing from their home. But she sat across from him, apparently deep in thought. 'Tash?'

'If she keeps using it,' she said, thinking aloud, 'it'll tell us where she's been. It has a facility you can ring up to find out the details of your last transaction.' She turned to him, and for once she didn't look as if she was accusing him of something. 'Often within a couple of hours of it taking place. It's our best chance of tailing her without the police getting involved. And if she's booked into a hotel, well, great. We could go straight there.' She allowed herself a small smile. 'It's possible we might even find her tonight.'

Cowboy John let out a long puff of smoke. 'She ain't as silly as she looks, your missus.'

'I'm not his missus,' Natasha said briskly, and dialled again. 'Open your window, Cowboy. This car stinks.'

'Dartford,' she said triumphantly, fifteen minutes later. 'She withdrew a hundred pounds at Dartford some time before midday. We're on the right track.'

It had looked so simple on the road map, Natasha thought, running her finger along the little red line. The A2 followed in a fairly straight route through Sittingbourne, Gillingham, and on to Canterbury. But as the car moved along it in the

dark, the queues moving and stalling, rain and the steam of
three people's breath steadily obscuring the windows, there
was no sign that a girl and her horse had ever existed, let
alone come this way.

Natasha sat in silence. The further they travelled from
London, the greater the weight of the solid mass that settled
in her stomach. Every mile they passed she found herself
understanding a little better the magnitude of the task before
them. Sarah could be anywhere within a fifty-mile radius.
She could have gone east from Dartford. She might have
anticipated that any search party would head for Dover and
decided to travel to one of the minor ports. Worse, they might
have got it wrong, and she might not be making for France
at all.

By the time they reached Canterbury, Natasha became
convinced that they had gone too far. She would never have
reached this point, she told the men. Look at the weather.
Her eyes strained, making out imaginary figures in the dim
light, distracted by people, odd cars, under the streetlamps.
'I think we should turn back,' she said.

But Mac insisted Sarah would have come on this route,
and if she wasn't there, it meant they should keep going. 'She
left town at seven o'clock this morning,' he pointed out.
'She could have got a hell of a way by now.' He was hunched
over the wheel, his eyes scanning the dark horizons.

John seemed uncertain. The horse was strong and would
do whatever the girl asked of him . . .

'What?' Natasha turned to him. 'What were you going to
say?'

It was dark inside the car now, and John's face was hidden.
'I was going to say, provided they haven't had an accident.'

By seven o'clock the traffic had thinned a little, the signs
for Dover more frequent. They stopped four times, when
John announced, yet again, that he needed to relieve himself,

or when hotels and B-and-B's were signposted close by. But
when Natasha asked inside if a girl and a horse had checked
in, the receptionists without exception, looked at her, as if
she was insane. She couldn't blame them: it sounded mad
even to her.

Each time she returned to the car she asked the two men
again whether they were sure the grandfather had said she
would go to France, until Mac told her to stop treating them
like imbeciles. And, all the while, Ben's text messages loyally
informed her of the partner meeting that was taking place
without her.

Linda says not to worry

he finished, a sure sign, Natasha thought, that she should.

Some time in that last half an hour they had lost confidence. Mac kept up a running mathematical equation, trying
to calculate how far a girl and a horse travelling at a nominal
fifteen miles an hour might get, given that they were in adverse
weather conditions and without food. 'I think she'll stay somewhere outside Canterbury,' he concluded. 'Or maybe we
should head back to Sittingbourne.'

'They gonna be awful wet,' John said mournfully, wiping
his window with his sleeve.

'I think we should stop somewhere, ring all the hotels and
ask if they've seen her,' Natasha said. 'But I'm going to need
someone else's phone. Mine's running low.'

Mac reached into his pocket and handed his to her. Taking
it, she found herself thinking about the last year of their
marriage, during which his phone, as hers, had been
concealed, its flirtatious messages incriminatory, or a symptom
of what was falling apart. 'Thanks,' she said. She didn't want
to use it, after all. She didn't want to risk seeing messages
from that woman, missed calls that spoke of things he might
rather be doing.

'I have to pee,' said John, again.

'Well, we're going to need fuel,' Mac said. 'I vote we head
to Dover. If that's where she's headed, it doesn't matter if
we've passed her.'

'But if she's stopped at Canterbury, she won't make Dover
till tomorrow.'

'Well, I don't know what else to suggest,' Mac said. 'We
can't see a thing. We could drive around in the dark all night
achieving nothing. Let's head to Dover and then do as you
suggested, Tash, set up somewhere with a landline. We can
ring around and get ourselves something to eat while we're
at it. We're all exhausted.'

'And then what?' Natasha placed Mac's phone carefully
on the dashboard.

'Well . . . pray we can find out where she's staying from
your credit card, I guess. After that I have no bloody idea.'

The hotel was one of an anonymous mid-range multi-national
chain, two squat maroon-brick blocks linked by a glass
walkway. Natasha stood in the oversized reception area,
crumpled and sweaty in her suit, suddenly desperate to sit
still, to eat and drink something. Mac, in front of her, was
chatting to the receptionist, who smiled at him, a distinctly
non-corporate sort of a smile. Natasha noted it grimly and
turned away. Cowboy John was in an easy chair by the wall,
legs splayed, head hanging low between his bony shoulders.
Natasha registered the slight distance guests enforced around
him as they passed and felt briefly awkward for him. Then,
as he lifted his head and winked lasciviously at a young
woman, she realised her sympathy was probably wasted.

'Okay,' said Mac, shoving his wallet back in his pocket.
'We've got one double and one twin.'

'But surely we need three rooms.'

'That's all they've got left. If you want to try somewhere

down the road then go for it, but I'm shattered. This'll do me fine.'

Which room will you be sleeping in? she wanted to ask. But his face was etched with strain, and instead she followed him mutely towards the lifts.

It was John who settled the matter. 'I'm goin' to have a bath and somethin' to eat,' he said, taking a key from Mac as the doors opened at the second floor. 'You guys call me when you know what we're doin' next.' He strolled out into the corridor and then she and Mac were alone, suddenly self-conscious, in the lift.

The room, as with every hotel room Natasha thought she had ever slept in, was at the far end of the building. They walked down the carpeted corridor in silence. When they reached the door, she was about to speak but Mac handed her the key. 'You hit the phones. I'm going down to the ferry terminal to make sure she's not there.'

'Aren't you going to eat?'

'I'll get something while I'm out.'

She watched his back disappear down the corridor, the unexpected stoop to his shoulders, and grasped the full weight of the responsibility he felt for Sarah.

The image of his despair propelled her into the room where she sat for a moment, trying not to think of what was happening to her career in her absence, the ex-husband walking through the rainy streets of Dover, the awful, shaming lack of the things she should have felt in place of this resentment. Natasha Macauley did what she had always done when real life became too difficult: she put the kettle on, grabbed a notebook and pen, and set to work on the hotel phone.

It was almost half past ten when Mac returned. She had borrowed a telephone directory from Reception, had called not just all the hotels in the Dover area but all the hotels and

B-and-Bs within ten miles. Nobody had heard of Sarah Lachapelle or seen a girl with a horse. She had wondered whether to call Mac, but it was pointless. He would have rung if he'd heard anything, just as she would.

Cowboy John had called from his room half an hour previously, and announced that if nothing else was going on he'd get a few hours' shut-eye. She had told him to go ahead praying he wouldn't set his room alight. Stiff-necked and exhausted, she ordered food from Room Service and a bottle of wine, then walked the length of the room. She was stretching her arms above her head when she heard the knock.

Mac stood in the corridor. He said nothing as he walked past her and sat heavily on one of the twin beds. He let himself fall backwards, one arm shielding his eyes against the light of the room.

'Nothing,' he said. 'It's like they've vanished into thin air.'

Natasha poured him a glass of wine and held it out. He raised himself wearily and took it from her. His chin was grey with stubble and he still carried the tang of cold salt air on his clothes. 'I've been all over Dover. I've even walked the beaches in case she was down there.'

'Did you go to the ferry offices?'

'I asked the guys who load the vehicles. I figured they'd see if anyone came by. They told me that all animals were transported there on lorries. She can't get further than here, Tash. It's not possible.'

They sat in silence, drinking their wine.

'What if she's gone to another port? I assumed Dover . . . but what if it was Harwich? Or Sittingbourne?'

'She was going in the wrong direction for Harwich.'

'We're out of our depth,' he said. 'I think we should call the police.'

'You're underestimating her. She planned this, Mac. She's got my credit card. She'll be safe somewhere.'

'But you've rung all the hotels.'

She shrugged. 'Then perhaps she didn't get this far. I can't ring all the hotels in the south of England. Hell – maybe she's staying on a farm. Or at a riding stables. Perhaps she has a friend near here. There are a million places she could be.'

'Which is why we should call the police.'

Natasha sat at the end of the other bed and let out a growl of frustration. 'Oh, Jesus, Sarah. What the hell do you think you're playing at?' The words were out of her mouth before she realised she had said them aloud.

'I don't think she's playing, Tash.'

'You think she stole my card by accident?'

'I think she was desperate.'

'For what? We gave her everything she asked for. We took care of her horse. I was about to take her shopping to buy her grandfather whatever she wanted for him.' She shook her head. 'No,' she said. Fear and exhaustion made her severe. 'I think it was just all too much like hard work. She didn't like our rules and routines. She didn't like the fact that she couldn't go and see her horse when she wanted to. We were making her go to school, Mac, not allowing her to come and go as she pleased. Forcing order on to chaos. This is her way of repaying us.'

'Repaying us?'

'You're assuming she thinks like us. That she *is* like us. But you have to admit she's been a closed book from the start. We don't have the faintest ideas of who Sarah Lachapelle really is.' She looked up to see Mac staring at her.

'What?' she said, when it became unnerving.

'Jesus. You've become hard.'

It was like a blow.

'I've become hard,' she repeated slowly. A lump rose in her throat, and she forced it away. *Why do you think that is?* she wanted to say to him. *Who do you think made me this way?*

'Okay, Mac. Why do you always assume that Sarah's the victim in all this?'

'Because she's fourteen? Because she's got nobody?'

An image of Ali Ahmadi rose in front of her. 'That doesn't make her an angel. She's stolen from us, taken my card, hidden things from us. And now she's run away.'

'You've always seen the worst in her.'

'No, I just see her without your rose-tinted spectacles.'

'So why are you here? Why bother trying to find her?'

'Seeing her as she is doesn't stop me being concerned for her welfare.'

'Is this really about her welfare? Or is this just a matter of you not wanting to be seen to fail?'

'What the hell is that supposed to mean?'

'Doesn't look too good for you, does it? The legal champion of lost children unable to look after the one girl she took on. I think that's why you don't want us to call the police.'

'How dare you?' She fought the urge to hurl the wine in his face. 'I see these kids every day. I see them helpless and pathetic on the benches, then have to listen to them cheerfully swearing at me forty minutes later when I've got them off or found them somewhere else to live. I know that half the time they're going straight off to nick another car, or shoplift another bin-bag of clothes. I know these kids. I've been played by them. They're not stupid and they're not always helpless.'

She took off her shoes, hurling them on to the carpet. 'In some ways Sarah is a decent kid, but she's no better and no worse than any of them. And that I can see that doesn't make me a bad person, no matter what you might want to think of me.'

She went into the bathroom, slammed the door, and sat on the toilet lid. She held up her hands in front of her, saw that they were trembling, then flung a bathmat and two towels at the door in an impotent expression of fury.

There was no sound from the bedroom.

She sat there as the minutes ticked by, waiting to hear Mac get up and leave the room. He wouldn't want to stay with her any more than she wanted to be with him. She'd tell him it would be better if he shared Cowboy John's room.

But the worst of it was that there was truth in what he had said. She didn't want the police involved. She didn't want to have to explain the circumstances under which she had taken Sarah in, her utter failure to look after her or even ensure her basic safety. If they could just find her, Sarah could go quietly to someone more capable.

She let out a long, shuddering breath. Oh, it was easy for Mac to be outraged, to be the good cop yet again. Easy to be the nice one when it never came at any personal cost to him. It had been the story of their marriage. Natasha dropped her head into her hands, breathed in the smell of cheap bathroom cleaner and waited for her head to clear. She didn't want him to see how much he had got to her. She didn't want him to see anything of her at all.

When she emerged, her expression composed, her mind humming with rehearsed argument, it was to a silent room. Mac was asleep on the bed, his arm still half covering his face. She walked silently to the other single bed and stared at him, this man this almost-ex-husband, crushed by his proximity and by his dislike of her.

She found she couldn't stop looking at him, and realised now little she had seen of him over the past two months. Her eyes were drawn to his arms, his chest under the faded T-shirt. How many times had she wriggled into that tight embrace? And how many times, she reminded herself, had she turned her back on it, eyes screwed tight shut against silent tears? How could he despise her so much after all the love he had shown her?

Natasha poured the rest of the wine into her glass and

downed it in one long, resentful swallow. Then, almost reluctantly, she reached for the folded bedspread at the end of
Mac's bed and pulled it over him, up to his chest.

She turned off the light. She did not approach her own
bed, but sat by the window, gazing out at the windswept car
park, the distant inky blackness of the sea, still, against hope,
half expecting to see the shadowy figures of a girl and a horse
make their way down the darkened street.

When she woke, her neck stiff, her limbs folded uncomfortably into the chair, the room was illuminated by the watery
blue light of daybreak and Mac was gone.

Twenty-one

> *'If you would have a horse learn to perform his duty, your*
> *best plan will be, whenever he does as you wish, to show him*
> *some kindness in return.'*

Xenophon, *On Horsemanship*

Sarah was just finishing the last of Jackie's stables and jumped
at the sound of Thom's voice.

'I didn't mean to scare you,' he said, from the other side
of the stable door.

'I – I just didn't hear you.' She spoke into her scarf, her
hot breath bouncing back on her skin.

'I came to ask did you want some breakfast? Jackie's making.
She's pleased as punch that you've done all the horses for her.'

Sarah squinted into the low sun. 'I was up early. And she
washed my jeans and stuff . . .'

'Ah, manners *and* a work ethic. Your parents did something right.' He grinned. He had spent the previous hour
washing out the big lorry. She had been dimly aware of the
high-pressure hose behind the stables, water spattering off
metallic surfaces, sporadic scrubbing, his determinedly upbeat
whistling. The previous evening over dinner he had been
downbeat, still shaken by the death of the horse. He had
picked at his food, resisting Jackie's best efforts to cheer him
up. Sarah had been equally quiet, exhausted to the point of
near-catatonia by the day's events. She had eaten her meal

in near silence, then, as her eyes blurred with exhaustion, escaped gratefully to the spare room. Clearly Jackie and her husband liked an excuse to entertain: even as she drifted into sleep she could hear them laughing and talking.

She had woken shortly after six thirty, briefly bewildered by her surroundings. Then, almost reflexively as her memory returned, she had leapt from her bed, still in her T-shirt, and run from the house to find Boo.

When he thrust his head over the stable door and whickered, her breath returned. She let herself into the stable, shivering in the morning air. He stood quietly in his borrowed rug, showing little sign of the journey he had endured the previous day. She had checked his legs, lifted his feet, then, reassured, pressed her face to his neck before returning to the house where, unable to sleep, she had dressed and cleaned his stable.

Mucking out the others had not been an act of charity, despite what Thom seemed to believe: in the absence of a clear plan, she needed to do everything possible to secure accommodation for another night. There was a system of lairage she had known nothing about: ponies in transit during a family emigration; racehorses and eventers, whose value sat firmly in five or six figures, on their way to new homes. All, like her, awaited a new life they could not yet know. The horses of lesser value, the broken-down and infirm, those bound for the continent in cattle trucks, had no such rest. They would stay on board until they were unloaded into the slaughterhouse.

'Yesterday . . . was tough for you to see. I hope it didn't give you nightmares.' Thom had eyes that were either used to smiling or had spent too much time squinting into the sun. You would have known he was Irish even before he spoke.

She leant on her fork, picturing the stricken horse. 'Do you think he suffered much?'

'No. They go into shock. Like humans. And then the vet put him out pretty swiftly.'

'Are you sad?'

He shrugged, seeming surprised. 'Oh . . . no. He wasn't mine. I don't own the horses. I just shift 'em around.'

'Will his owner be sad?'

'Don't take this to heart, kiddo, but probably not. He was just a failed point-to-pointer with dodgy legs. The owner sold him in a job lot to a French dealer. To be honest, when I rang this morning, he was more concerned about the insurance claim.'

Sarah dislodged some dried mud from the stable floor with the toe of her boot. 'What was his name?'

'The horse? Oh, Lord, now you're asking . . .' He looked up towards the sky. It was then that Sarah felt free to look at him properly; she noticed, with a kind of appalled thrill, that his left hand wasn't real but made from a kind of flesh-coloured rubber.

'Diablo,' he said, suddenly looking at her. She flushed, embarrassed to have been caught staring. 'No, Diablo Blue. That's the boy. Right. Shall I tell Jackie you'll be in soon? I've got to shoot into Dover to get the partition fixed.'

She thought about it. Perhaps it was because he had been so much more shaken than Jackie and her husband the previous evening, or the way he stroked the horses' noses as he passed each stable, hardly aware that he was doing it. Perhaps it was that hand. But something about Thom told her he was not a threat.

'Can I get a lift with you?' she said, putting on her coat. 'I need to get to a cashpoint.'

In theory Thom Kenneally lived in Ireland, but he spent a good part of each week moving horses between England, Ireland and France. He had once been a jockey, he told her, until he'd lost part of his arm in a riding accident. Since then he'd struggled to settle in a job until he started transporting.

Not everyone could do it, he said. A lot of horses were reluctant to load, and it was not enough to have patience and a calm manner to get them on and off safely; you had to be able to read them, to see even before they set foot on the ramp whether they were going to pull backwards, kick or rear when they reached the top, sometimes even before they knew it themselves. He transported old ponies, experienced even-ters, occasionally fine-limbed racehorses, whose combined value caused him to drive with a thin sheen of cold sweat. Until the previous evening, he had only ever had one fatality in six years. But, no, it wouldn't put him off.

'The job suits me,' he said. They had left the partition with a welder, who had promised to have it back by midday. Thom would leave with his remaining cargo after lunch. 'I like the horses. Besides, my girlfriend's the independent sort. Needs her own space.'

'Does she like horses?'

He grinned. 'Not much. I think she knew it was this or me moving to some racing yard somewhere. At least now she doesn't have to deal with the animals morning, noon and night.'

'I'd love that,' said Sarah, and blushed.

'There's your cashpoint.'

He slowed the lorry, and pulled up outside a convenience store. Sarah climbed down from the cab and ran across the road. She pulled the card out of her pocket, fed it into the machine and typed in the number, glancing behind her to see if he was watching, then held her breath.

She had half expected a shrill refusal, perhaps even, in her worst nightmares, an alarm. But the machine was still aston-ishingly obliging. She withdrew another hundred pounds and thrust it deep into her pocket, apologising silently to Papa, Mac and Natasha as she did so. It was as she was about to run back across the road that she noticed the phone-box, an old-fashioned sort, red, with a glass-paned door. Thom appeared to be reading the newspaper so she nipped inside it, wrinkling her nose at the predictable reek of urine. It accepted the credit card, and she dialled the number.

The phone rang steadily at a distance. Finally, when she was about to give up, she heard a click. 'Stroke Ward.'

'Can I speak to Mr Lachapelle?' She had to shout over the noise of a passing lorry.

'Who?'

'Mr Lachapelle.' She held a hand over her other ear. 'It's Sarah, his granddaughter. Can you put me on to him? He's in Room Four.'

There was a brief pause.

'Hold on.'

Sarah stood in the little cubicle, gazing absently at the busy road. Thom, in the cab, saw where she was and nodded, as if to say she could take her time.

'Hello?' A different voice now.

'Oh. I want to speak to Mr Lachapelle. It's Sarah.'

'Hello, Sarah. It's Sister Dawson here. I'll just take the phone in. I have to tell you, though, he's had a bit of a setback. If it's noisy at your end, you might not be able to hear him too well.'

'Is he okay?'

There was the faintest hesitation, enough for Sarah's heart to sink.

'What time are you coming in? I can arrange for someone to talk to you and your foster-family.'

'I can't,' she said. 'I can't get to you today.'

'Okay. Well, he's doing . . . okay. But his speech isn't so good at the moment. You'll have to speak up to make yourself clear. It's quite a bad line. I'll put you on to him.'

The sound of feet, a squeaking door. A muffled voice: 'Mr

Lachapelle, it's your granddaughter. I'm just going to put the phone to your ear. All right?'

Sarah held her breath. 'Papa?'

Nothing.

'Papa?'

A long silence. Perhaps a sound. It was hard to tell over the noise of the traffic. She clamped her hand over her other ear. The nurse cut back in. 'Sarah, he *can* hear you. It would be best if you just talked to him for now. Don't expect too much in response.'

Sarah swallowed. 'Papa?' she said again. 'It's Sarah. I . . . I can't come in today.'

A noise, then muffled encouragement from the nurse: 'He can hear you, Sarah.'

'Papa, I'm in Dover. I had to take Boo. Things got difficult for us. But I'm ringing to tell you . . .' Her voice was breaking. She screwed her eyes shut, willing herself to keep it together, not to let him hear how she was feeling in her voice. 'We're going to Saumur, me and Boo. I couldn't tell you until we were away.'

She waited, trying to hear something, trying to gauge his reaction. The answering silence was painfully oppressive. She read a million things into it and, as it lengthened, felt her determination ebb.

'I'm sorry, Papa,' she yelled into the receiver, 'but I wouldn't have done this if I didn't have to. You know that. You do know that.' She had begun to cry, great salty tears plopping on to the concrete slab at her feet. 'It was the only way to keep him safe. For me to be safe. Please don't be angry,' she whispered, knowing he would not hear.

Still he said nothing.

Sarah wept silently until the nurse came back on the line.

'Did you say everything you wanted to say?' she asked brightly.

Sarah wiped her nose on her sleeve. She could see him so clearly, lying there, his face a mask of anxiety, of barely compressed fury. Even confined to his bed all those miles away she could feel the chill of his disapproval. How could he understand?

'Sarah? Are you still there?'

She sniffed. 'Yes,' she said, her voice artificially high. 'Yes, I couldn't hear you. There was a lorry going past. I'm in a phone-box.'

'Well, I don't know what you said but he wants me to say . . .'

Sarah's eyes shut tight against the brimming tears.

'He says, "Good."'

A brief pause. 'What?'

'Yes. That's definitely it. He says, "Good." He's nodding at me. All right? We'll see you soon.'

When she climbed back into the lorry, she turned towards the passenger window to hide her reddened eyes. She sat, letting her hair fall across her face, waiting for the sound of the key in the ignition.

Good. Papa's silent word kept ringing in her ears.

Thom didn't start the engine. When, eventually, she looked at him, he was watching her steadily. 'Okay, kiddo. You want to tell me what's up?'

He wasn't buying the sponsored ride. Her voice steady now, she had told him the story, the one she had rehearsed in her head for much of the morning, eyes clear, expression neutral.

'To France,' he repeated. 'You're doing a sponsored ride to France. To raise money for stroke victims. And you don't have any papers.'

'I thought I'd get them in Dover. I was going to ask you how.'

They were seated in a roadside café. He had bought her a muffin with her cup of tea and it sat on the plate in front of her, damp and solid in its plastic wrapper.

'And you're travelling by yourself.'

'I'm very independent.'

'Evidently.'

'So can you help me?'

He leant back in his seat, studied her for a minute. Then he smiled. 'Well, I'll tell you what, Sarah. I'll sponsor you. Give me your sponsorship sheets.'

Her eyes widened briefly, and she glanced away, but he had seen it.

'I think . . . I've left them in my bag.'

'Well, there's a thing.'

'But will you show me how to get the right papers for Boo to travel?'

He made as if to speak, then stopped himself. Instead he stared out of the window to where the cars, burdened under heavily laden roof-racks, headed in a line towards the ferry terminal. She fiddled with the wrapper of the damp muffin. There was no sell-by date on it. It might have been three years old for all she knew.

'I have a stepdaughter who's a little like you,' he said quietly. 'When she was around your age she used to get herself into all sorts of trouble, mostly because she kept everything bottled up and thought she could sort it out her way. Eventually – and I mean eventually –' he smiled wryly, locked in some private memory '– we were able to persuade her that nothing is so bad that you can't tell someone. You know that? Nothing.'

But he was wrong, Sarah knew. It was telling the truth that had got her into this mess to begin with. If she hadn't told Natasha the truth about Papa that first evening . . .

'Sarah, are you in some kind of trouble?'

She had perfected an expression of almost total blankness.

She turned it on him now, feeling oddly, as she did, that she should apologise for it. This is nothing personal, she wanted to tell him, but don't you see? You could be like the rest of them. You mean well, but you don't understand the damage you do.

'I told you,' she said evenly. 'I'm on a sponsored ride.'

His lips pursed, not so much an unfriendly expression as a mildly resigned one. He took a sip of his coffee. 'Jackie nearly didn't let you stay last night, you know. She's got a nose for trouble.'

'I paid her what she asked.'

'So you did.'

'I'm no different from anyone else.'

'Sure. Just your average teenage girl with no transport who's trying to get a horse across the water.'

'I told you. I can pay you too, if that's what you want.'

'I'm sure you can.'

'Well, then.'

She waited for him to look up from his coffee. He seemed to find it fascinating.

'You want to give me that credit card?'

'What?'

'The card you used to get the money out.'

'I'll pay you cash.' She felt her stomach tighten.

'I'd rather take a credit card, if I'm going to help you. Not a big deal, is it?' His eyes met hers. 'Unless, of course, your name isn't the name on the card . . .'

Sarah pushed away the plate and rose from her seat. 'You know what? I just needed a lift. I don't need you on my case just for a lift to the cashpoint. And I don't need you hassling me, okay? If you're not going to help me, just leave me alone.' With that, she was out of the door, striding across the car park to the main road.

'Hey,' he called, behind her. '*Hey*.'

When she didn't turn around, he yelled, 'You won't get papers without a vet. It'll take days, weeks even. And you need to be eighteen to sign them. I'm pretty sure you're not eighteen, Sarah. And I'm not sure how long Jackie's going to feel comfortable having you around, no matter how many stables you muck out. You need to think again.'

She stopped.

'I think, kiddo, you might want to think about going home.' His expression was kind. 'You and your horse.'

'But I *can't*. I just can't.' To her horror, tears had welled in her eyes and she blinked them away furiously. 'I haven't done anything wrong, okay? I'm not a bad person. But I can't go back.'

Thom kept staring at her. She dropped her eyes, trying to evade his gaze. It was as if he could see everything, her dishonesty, her vulnerability, not in the way Maltese Sal had, as if he was stripping away every bit of her that was worth something, but with a kind of sympathy. It was *worse*.

'Look, I really need to get there.' The cars whipped past them on the fast road. She thought, briefly, how unfair it was that these metallic horses should be allowed to cross so easily. 'I can't tell you anything else. But I have to get to France.'

She had left her jacket in the lorry. She stood in the cold car park, the sea wind whipping the hair around her ears, and folded her arms. Thom stared at her for a while longer, then turned away. She wondered if he was going to go back to his lorry, but he took a few steps, then stopped. Finally he turned back to her. 'So . . . if I don't help you, what will you do?'

'I'll find someone who will,' she said defiantly. 'I know I can get someone to help me.'

'That's what I'm worried about,' he muttered resignedly. He paused, considering. 'Okay,' he said. 'I might be able to get you to France. Yes,' as she tried to interrupt, 'you and your horse. But I need you to talk. That's the deal, Sarah. I'm not helping you until you tell me what's going on.'

'Diablo Blue' was reluctant to walk up the ramp. He snorted, planted both front feet at its base, eyes flashing white. His arched, muscular neck tensed, and his ears flicked back and forth, his legs tripping awkwardly at the unfamiliar feel of the protective padded bandages Thom had wrapped around his legs.

Thom was unfazed: he stood quietly beside him, talking to him gently when the horse refused to move, relaxing the tension on the long rope in the moments when the animal briefly stopped pulling backwards. He had asked Sarah to put on the bridle and then, as she watched, fed the long rope up through the bit, over the top of his head, by his ears, then down through the other side of the bit. 'When he pulls back, he feels pressure,' he explained. 'It's, like, consequences for bad behaviour, but it's kinder than some of the other devices the transporters use. Hey, it's okay. Don't look so worried. We'll take our time.'

'Jackie said she'd be back by one thirty.'

'Ah, we'll be gone long before then.' Thom sat on the ramp, a hand reaching up to stroke the horse's nose, his manner that of someone who had all the time in the world.

Sarah did not share his ease. Jackie would ask questions, demand explanations. Worse, she might convince Thom that he was making a mistake. 'She's only going to the feed merchants. Look, why don't I have a go?'

'No,' said Thom. 'You're too tense. In fact, you standing there isn't helping. Go and sit in the cab.'

'I don't—'

'Sit in the cab. It'll be quicker that way.'

His tone did not brook discussion. The horses already loaded in the lorry whickered anxiously, one pulling at a wisp of hay, then pushing its chestnut head over the partition to see what was happening outside. Sarah glanced back anxiously at the big bay horse on the end of Thom's rope, then did as she was told.

She climbed into the passenger seat, then reached into her pocket, feeling for the credit card. 'How much are you willing to pay for your passage?' Thom had said, and she had stepped back from him, fearful that she had read him wrongly. 'Let's go back in the café for a minute.'

She had despised him then, seeing in him just another conman, another hustler, until he had taken the phone from his jacket. They had sat at the same table. Her muffin was still there in its plastic wrapper.

'Clive? It's Thom Kenneally. About those horses.'

She had sat silently across from him at the Formica table as he explained to this unknown man – whom he knew well enough to ask after his children – that there was a problem with his lorry. 'I got to tell you, mate, I may have a few problems with the old insurance. The welders say there was a bolt gone in the partition, nothin' I could have seen but a bit of a loophole for them. You know what I'm saying? And if that's so, it's going to bugger your chance of getting any money, and my insurance'll go through the roof. Yes . . . Yes, it is, isn't it? Now. This Diablo Blue of yours, I see from the papers he wasn't in the Desert Orchid league, you know what I'm saying?' He laughed. 'He did, did he? Yes, I thought he wasn't the best sort. I was wondering if you could do me a little favour. Let me sort you out with a bit of cash compensation and keep it out of the books. Would that be of any use to you now? Less hassle all round?'

He chatted on for another five minutes, assuring the unseen Clive of the quality of the repairs, that, yes, he'd be delighted to take the two horses on Friday. He hoped they'd worked together long enough, etc., etc. When he finally rang off, it took the determined smile a few seconds to fade from his lips. He placed his phone back in his jacket. 'Okay, kiddo. You owe Mr Clive there three hundred and fifty smackers for his dead horse. If we head back to the cashpoint, you think that card will take the strain?'

'I don't understand . . .'

'That's the price of your horse's new papers,' he said. 'God help me for getting involved, but that's the price of your ticket.'

It had taken another ten drawn-out minutes, during which she chewed her remaining two nails down to the quick, before a dull thud of hooves and a thump told her the ramp had finally gone up. Then there was the sound of bolts being drawn, safety catches slid into place. The driver's door opened, letting in a gulp of cold air, and Thom climbed into the cab. 'Not so bad, was he, all things considered? The other two are great travellers. They'll help him.' He grinned. 'You can breathe now.'

He started the engine. The lorry vibrated, its huge engine growling into life. Sarah reached for her seatbelt.

'Did you leave Jackie the note?' He adjusted his mirror.

'And the cash. I told her I'd changed route and was going to Deal instead.'

'That's the girl. Ah, come on kiddo. Don't look so tense. We've air-ride suspension on here – super smooth for the horses. They get a better ride than we do. I bet you he'll be eating from his haynet before we've hit the end of the lane.'

She couldn't tell him that it wasn't Diablo Blue's demeanour that frightened her. It was the thought of Customs officials looking too hard at his description. It was the thought of someone who knew about horses working out that Diablo Blue had grown a whole two inches in the three weeks since his travelling papers had been issued.

'You sure about this?' Thom asked. 'It's not too late to go back, you know. I'm sure if I spoke to your foster-family we could work something out.'

Good, Papa had said. *Good*. The nurse had been certain of it. 'I just want to go. Now,' she added.

She glanced into the side mirror. Behind the stables, out of her view, the horse that was now Baucher lay under a tarpaulin, waiting for the local abattoir to take him away. The passports and travelling papers sat in a battered folder on the dashboard in front of her.

'Okay.' Thom swung the huge wheel round, and the lorry headed for the main road. 'It's the great big *bateau* for you, me and Mr Diablo Blue, then.'

Twenty-two

'A high-mettled horse must be kept from dashing on at full speed, and utterly prevented from racing with another; for as a rule, the most ambitious horses are the highest mettled.'

Xenophon, *On Horsemanship*

Cowboy John sat down with his fourth plate of egg, bacon and fried bread and rubbed his hands. 'Not bad,' he said, tucking his napkin into his collar. 'Not bad at all for motorway food.'

Mac had another swig of his coffee. 'I don't know how anyone could eat four breakfasts,' he said, eyeing the depleted breakfast buffet.

'I paid for it,' John said. 'Might as well get my money's worth.'

Actually, *I* paid for it, Mac observed silently. But it was a relief to spend time with someone cheerful so he said nothing. Around them the breakfast room of the Tempest International hummed with travellers; salesmen locked into telephone conversations, stressed mothers shepherding small children around a cereal-splattered table as fathers disappeared behind newspapers. Occasionally a moon-faced Eastern European girl would approach and offer to top up their coffee, where-upon John would announce, Why, yes! Thank you!

He appeared rejuvenated this morning, his smile a little readier under the battered brown hat, his collar and cuffs neatly pressed. Mac, whose clothes always tended to look as if he had spent several days in them, felt perversely dishevelled in his company. He had risen before dawn and, unable to sleep and in the absence of anything more useful to do, had again walked the deserted seafront, watching the early-morning ferries come and go in the encroaching light, listening to the forlorn cries of the gulls wheeling overhead, and wondering, with a sick dread, where in the world Sarah might be.

He had returned shortly after eight o'clock, let himself into the room and found Natasha not on the chair by the window, as she had been when he'd left, but curled up on the other single bed. The room was still, with only the dull murmur of voices down the corridor breaking the silence. Her knees were drawn up to her chin, a curiously childlike position, her hair half covered her face, and she was frowning, even in sleep. On the desk, even at this hour, her phone flashed with silenced messages. He considered checking them, in case Sarah had decided to call, but the thought of her waking and finding him violating her privacy stopped him. Instead he showered, did his best to freshen up with the lather-free hotel soap, then made his way downstairs to breakfast, where Cowboy John had apparently been availing himself of the facilities for some time.

'So what's the plan today, chief?' John wiped up a pool of egg with the corner of fried bread.

'I haven't a clue.'

'Well . . . I been thinking and I'd lay money on its she's round here somewhere. That girl ain't never been nowhere, not as long as I've know her. She can't swim the darn horse to France. So, the way I see it, she'll either find somewhere to leave him and go to France on foot, in which case someone could hang out by the ticket office, or she'll work out pretty quickly that she's stuck, and stay around here while she thinks up what to do next.'

'I can't imagine her leaving the horse.' Mac thought back to their abbreviated stay in Kent.

John grinned. 'My thoughts precisely, my man. So she's gotta get here and stay here likely as not. So let's not call the cops just yet. All we gotta do is make sure we got all the bases covered. Ring round the stables, ask hotels to check for any kids signing in using Natasha's credit card.'

Mac sank back in his chair. 'You make it sound simple.'

'Best plans usually are, and unless you got an alternative . . .'

Natasha appeared at the table. Her hair was damp and she seemed wary, as if she might be criticised for being the last up.

'Here.' Mac pulled out a chair. 'You want some coffee?'

'I didn't mean to sleep late. You should have woken me.'

'I thought you could do with the rest.' He saw the faintest flash of something pass across her face, saw her try to hide it. How easily an innocent remark could be misconstrued when every conversation was loaded with history.

'Your phone,' she said, handing it to him. 'You left it in your room. Your girlfriend's been calling.'

'Probably about a job I'd lined up for this morning . . .' he began, but she had already left the table for the buffet.

John leant forward. 'I been thinking something else.'

Mac was barely listening. She was standing by the bread basket, shaking her head as she spoke rapidly into her mobile.

'We may be worrying too much.'

Mac turned back to the table.

'Her old man. He trained that horse pretty good, better than any horse I've ever seen, and I been around horses a long time.'

'So?'

'She's safe with him.'

'Safe with who?' Natasha sat down, a piece of toast clenched between her teeth.

'The horse. John thinks she's safe with him.'

Natasha put the toast on her plate. 'So it's like Champion the Wonder Horse? It'll fight off attacking snakes? Warn of approaching Injuns?'

Cowboy John tipped his hat back and glared at her. He turned pointedly towards Mac. 'I mean she can outrun things, situations she don't like. And a lot of people are intimidated by horses. They're goin' to leave her alone, people who might otherwise feel quite happy approachin' a little girl out by herself.' He swigged his coffee. 'In my eyes she's a damn sight safer on that horse than she would be without him.'

Natasha drank some juice. 'Or she could be thrown from it. Or fall under it. Or be attacked by someone who wants to steal it.'

John eyed her warily. 'Boy, you're a cheerful soul. I can see why you're a lawyer.'

The young waitress was lingering by their table. Mac smiled and held up his mug. As she walked away, he caught Natasha's eye on him. It was not a friendly look.

'I think Mac would rather I'd been a waitress.'

'What the hell's that supposed to mean?'

'It means,' she directed her comments to John, 'that he was one of those men who used to say how much he liked smart women. Until "smart" came to mean "complicated" and "wised-up", at which point he decided he liked twenty-two-year-old waitresses and models instead.' She flushed.

'Yo' sayin' there's somethin' wrong with that?' John chuckled.

Mac took refuge in his coffee. 'Perhaps I just found it easier to be around people who weren't angry with me all the time.'

That had got her. He saw her colour, and felt curiously ashamed.

John rose stiffly from the table. 'Well, you two lovebirds

sure have reminded me why I stayed single. If you want to sort out a plan of action I'm goin' to brush my teeth. I'll be down and ready in five.'

They watched him saunter across the restaurant. Natasha chewed her toast. 'I'm sorry,' she said, into her plate. 'I shouldn't have—'

'Tash?'

She looked up at him.

'Can we call a truce? Just till we find her? I find this all . . . a bit exhausting.'

There was just the faintest flash of anger. He could see it, an unspoken 'Exhausting? You think this is my fault?'

'You're right,' she said. 'Like I said, I'm sorry.'

Across the dining room John had doffed his hat at the waitress. Mac watched his courtly bow. 'Okay. What's the plan? Because I haven't got one.'

'She can't get far,' Natasha said. 'I vote we give her till . . . four o'clock? If we haven't found her by then, okay, we call the cops.'

Natasha and Cowboy John sat on a bench outside the ticket office, their heads tucked low into their jackets in an attempt to shield themselves from the wind as the gulls shrieked above them. They had rung around most of the south of England that morning, from the two hotel rooms, and then, fidgety with cabin fever and anxiety, had come to meet Mac outdoors. Time had crept by, every hour with no sighting of Sarah adding to a growing unease. They sat outside the bleak Portakabin, watching the steady stream of foot passengers disembark from coaches, coming to buy tickets or simply to use the lavatories. Periodically, Ben would call up with some query, often from Richard, and she would shout the answer, her voice lifting against the sea breeze. Periodically Cowboy John stood, walked up and down the exposed stretch of tarmac and smoked impassively, occasionally lifting a slender hand to pin down his hat.

'I don't like this,' he said, gazing out towards the sea. 'This ain't Sarah.'

She barely heard him. She was thinking about what Linda had said when she'd asked if Conor had stuck up for her at the previous night's partners' meeting. 'He did try,' she had said, in a voice that suggested he hadn't tried very hard. 'Funnily enough, it was Harrington who really stuck up for you. In a conference call. I . . . um . . . happened to be listening in. He said your strategy had been . . . innovative, that going when you did would make no difference to the case.' She had seemed surprised that Natasha wasn't more pleased by this news.

The morning in court had gone well. Richard had quizzed the family doctor, and Harrington had quizzed the forensic accountant, skewering Mr Persey's claims of financial loss. He had been so shaken, Ben said, that Harrington claimed afterwards he would be surprised if they couldn't reach some kind of deal the following day. Natasha told him that was great, trying to ignore the envy and loss it invoked in her.

Mac was coming towards them now, clapping his hands, the hair at the front of his head blown upright by the wind. Watching him made her conscious of her creased suit, the slightly stale scent of her blouse. Her feet ached from walking around the town in her court shoes. She would have to buy herself a change of clothes if they didn't find Sarah soon.

'No sign?'

Natasha shook her head. 'Nobody remembers seeing a horse. But they said it would have been different staff in the ticket office last night. And they wouldn't let us see the passenger lists – data-protection laws.'

Mac swore softly under his breath. 'Nothing from the credit-card company?'

'That doesn't mean anything. Sometimes it takes a few hours for it to be processed.'

They were running out of ideas. And in the absence of any firm plan, the urgency of the previous day had slowly seeped away, to be replaced by a strange melancholy.

The day dragged on. They split, and took it in turns to drive or walk around Dover, or stay in the hotel room and ring their way through the telephone directory. A sweetshop owner on Castle Street swore she had seen a girl on a horse the previous evening but could offer no more information. Mac, increasingly frustrated, stopped people on the street, shop-owners, ferry-workers. Cowboy John retreated to his hotel room, rang the hotels they had rung the previous evening, just in case, and occasionally fell asleep. Natasha fielded more calls from work, explained that, no, she was not going to be back by tonight after all, and walked the damp streets of Dover, fighting an encroaching sense of despair.

They agreed to meet at six in a pub on the sea-front. Natasha had wanted to eat in the hotel, but John had said if he spent one more minute in that sanitised hell-hole he'd go stir crazy. The pub, untouched by the vagaries of fashion, was steeped in the odour of beer and old cigarettes. On sitting down he seemed to relax. 'Now this is more like it,' he kept saying, patting the battered velour seats as if he'd found a home from home.

Natasha waited until the men went to the bar before she dialled the number. She sat down, pressing her other hand to her ear to drown the noise of the television that blared sports results above her.

It took him eight rings to answer. She wondered whether he had seen who was calling and been unable to decide whether or not to pick up.

'Conor?'

'Yup.'

'I just wondered how you were.'

'Have you found her?'

'No.'

'Where are you?'

'Dover. She's definitely come this way but we can't locate her.' She wished, almost as soon as she had said it, that she had omitted 'we'.

'Right.'

There was a lengthy silence. Natasha glanced behind her at Mac chatting to the barmaid, perhaps explaining what he and John were doing there. She saw the girl raise her eyebrows and shake her head. She had witnessed this response so many times over the past twenty-four hours that she didn't need to hear the words.

'Conor?'

'Yup.'

'I just wondered . . .' She ran her fingers through her hair. 'I wanted to make sure we were okay. I hated leaving things like that.'

A short delay before he replied. 'You wanted to make sure we were okay?'

'I'm sorry I had to go off like that, but you must understand that I couldn't just leave it all to Mac.'

She heard, over the sound of the television, his breathing. 'You just don't get it, Hotshot, do you?'

'I explained to you about the job. I hear Harrington was great in court today. Me not being there—'

'No. You don't get it.' His voice was softer now.

'Get what?'

'Not once, Natasha, did you ask. Not once, when you were about to throw up your whole life for this thing did you think to ask me to help you.'

'What?'

'You didn't even consider asking me, did you? What does that say about us?'

Mac was laughing with the girl now.

'I didn't think you'd—' she said. 'Given what you—'

'No. You didn't think to ask. I don't know what's going on with you and Mac, but I don't want to be involved with someone who can't even be honest about her own feelings.'

'That's not fair. I—'

But he had already rung off.

Sarah was waving a piece of bread in the air, oblivious to the fact that her high English voice was attracting the attention of French diners at the surrounding tables. 'They're like this kind of brotherhood, you know. They have black caps and black uniforms . . .'

'Ah. I knew it would be about fashion,' Thom teased.

Sarah ignored him. '. . . and they can get their horses to do absolutely anything. They'll jump a chair about a foot wide. You know how hard it is to jump a chair?'

'I can imagine.'

'Papa always said that when he came to Le Cadre Noir it was the first time in his life he had felt understood. Like there were just a few other people in the world who spoke his language and all of them lived in that one place.'

'I know that feeling.'

'But they worked so hard. He would start riding at six in the morning, and sometimes go on all day, working on different horses, different movements. Some were at the *basse école* stage – that's more basic – and some at *haute école*. The horses all specialise in different movements. He had this favourite horse that specialised in *capriole*. You know what that is?'

'No.'

She blew out her cheeks. 'It's one of the most difficult things you can ask a horse to do. It comes from a battle manoeuvre and dates back thousands of years. The horse leaps up, using its back legs, and then when it's, like, suspended in mid-air, it kicks out behind. I used to think about what it would be like to be on a battlefield and you go to stab someone and then this horse is up and – yah!' She motioned the kicking out of his back hooves.

'Pretty scary.'

'Well, it must have worked or they wouldn't have kept doing it for so long.'

She had insisted on paying. He hadn't felt entirely comfortable about his supper being financed by a stolen credit card, but she had assured him she would pay back every penny when Papa was better, and the thing about Sarah was that you couldn't help but believe her.

When they had arrived in France and made their way down the *autoroute* she had become more and more animated, so that it was hard to reconcile the chatty, confident girl with the silent, wary child of the previous evening.

'Papa's friend John always jokes that what we do are circus tricks, but there are no tricks. You can only understand it when you see it. The horses do it because they love to. It's about training them to want to do it. That way when they perform there's no strain, no tension. And for that reason they're brought on really slowly, bit by bit, so that they understand how to do their job without resisting.' She took a mouthful of chocolate mousse. 'Is that how they train them in racing?'

Thom nearly choked on his coffee. 'No. Not really. No.'

The door to the service-station café opened and closed, allowing in another French family. They watched, eating, as the mother spoke to the two children, pointing out the things they were allowed to have from the buffet.

'So how long have you and your granddaddy been on your own?'

'Four years.'

'You never stayed in touch with your mum?'

'She died before Nana.'

'I'm sorry.'

'I'm not. I don't mean to sound horrible but . . . she was the kind of person who causes problems. I was really young when she left me. I miss my nana, though.' Sarah tucked her feet under her and broke off a piece of chocolate.

'Me, my nana and papa were really happy. People don't believe me when I say I don't miss my mum, but I never did. Not one day. Everything from that time, when I was with her, feels bad. I don't remember much, but I remember being scared. When my grandparents took me I never once felt scared. One day,' she said, gesturing at the French country-side, 'I'm going to bring Papa back here. We were meant to visit in November, you see. He really wanted to. But then he had his stroke and everything got . . .' She was silenced, then appeared to compose herself. 'When he hears I'm there, I think it will help him. When he's fit he can come over. He'll be happy.'

'You're pretty sure you can make all this happen.'

'My grandfather was one of the best riders in France. He could make a horse float in the air, do things it didn't know were possible.' She put the chocolate into her mouth. 'All I'm trying to do is ride a few miles.'

Tom looked at her, this child, her stowaway horse. She made it sound like perfect sense.

Natasha flipped her phone shut and swore. It was dark and the three of them were driving aimlessly around Dover, having just returned from a cashpoint situated in a sleepy, industrial area of the town, full of car workshops and nondescript low office blocks. This, according to the credit-card company, was the last place that money had been withdrawn. To be so close, and yet to have no sign of her, was steadily ratcheting up the tension in the little car. No one mentioned the earlier promise to call the police: they *knew* she must be close by. That little piece of plastic proved it. But why would a girl on a horse end up in a place like this?

Natasha turned in her seat to face Cowboy John. 'Tell me something, John. How did Sarah's grandfather end up living where he did? It wasn't . . . Well, it's not the nicest place, is it?'

'You think he set out to live somewhere like that? You think that was what he wanted from his life?'

Mac shrugged. 'We don't know anything about him other than that he seems to have raised a child who can defy gravity.'

John settled back in his seat with an almost palpable air of contentment. 'Okay. I'll tell you about Henri. He came from a pretty rough and ready background. Farming people, some-where in the south. There were problems with his dad, and when Henri was young he got out fast as he could and joined the military.'

She had guessed John was the kind of man who liked to tell a story and was happy to listen: it stopped her thinking. And Mac wouldn't mind: he loved hearing about people's lives; it came from years of indulging his photographic subjects.

'From there he ended up on horseback, mounted cavalry or some such, and in the 1950s he worked his way up until he was accepted by Le Cadre Noir, when they were building up again after the war.' He eyed the two people in front of him. 'That ain't no small achievement, you know. They're like, the top percentage of the whole country. It's an élite academy. Man, he loved that place. When he used to talk about it he'd stand a little straighter – you know what I'm saying?'

'Then how the hell did he end up living at Sandown?'

'Women.' John scowled at Natasha, as if she should somehow bear shared responsibility. 'He fell in love.'

Le Cadre Noir had been on one of its first international tours in 1960 when Henri Lachapelle had noticed the small, dark-haired woman at the front of the audience. She was there for each of the three performances. The great joke was she didn't really like horses; she had come with a friend, but had been transfixed by the young man in the stiff black collar who had made riding a horse look magical.

He had come out to see her after a performance one evening and, as he had described it to John years afterwards, it was as if everything in his life up to that point had been a rehearsal.

'I don't think he'd had too much in the way of love, and it hit him real hard,' John said, lighting another cigarette. 'They had three more evenings together, and then they wrote and visited for the best part of six months, getting together when they could. Problem was,' he said, 'being apart from her made him cranky. You know what young lovers are like, and Henri was never one to do things by halves. He started off not paying attention, then his performances suffered. He began to question things they were telling him in the school. In the end they told him it was their way or the highway and, in a fit of temper, he went. Got to England, married his girl and . . .'

'Lived happily ever after,' Natasha concluded, thinking back to that photograph. The woman who was well loved.

John's glare was withering. 'Are you kidding me?' he said. 'Who the hell gets to live happily ever after?'

Twenty-three

*'A disobedient horse is not only useless, but he often plays the
part of a very traitor.'*

Xenophon, *On Horsemanship*

Henri Lachapelle realised almost within the first year that he
had made a terrible mistake. It wasn't Florence's fault: she
loved him, kept herself pretty and tried to be a good wife. It
wasn't her fault that her anxiety about his happiness made
him feel little more than guilt or that this frequently mani-
fested itself in a kind of irritation.

He had asked Florence to marry him the evening of Le
Carrousel, breathless, bloodied and still covered with sand.
The audience in the seats around her had stood and cheered.
They had walked the streets of Saumur for hours, negotiating the drunks and the motorbikes, planning their future,
cementing their passion, giddy with dreams. The next morning
he had not appeared for early training but had packed his
few possessions in his kit-bag, and asked to see Le Grand
Dieu. He had informed him that he wished to be released
from his position.

Le Grand Dieu had peered at Henri's black eye, his
swollen cheek. He put his pen on his desk. There was a
lengthy silence.

'You know why we take the hind shoes off our horses,
Lachapelle?' he asked.

Henri blinked painfully. 'So they cannot hurt other horses?'

'And so that when they are learning to find their feet, when they flail and thrash and kick out, as they inevitably will, they do not accidentally hurt themselves.' He placed his hands on the table. 'Henri, if you do this, you will hurt yourself more deeply than you can know.'

'With respect, sir, I don't believe I can be happy here.'

'Happiness? You think that me cutting you loose will give you happiness?'

'Yes, sir.'

'There is no happiness in this world other than what is achieved by love of one's work. This is your world, Henri. A fool could see it. You cannot cut a man out of his world and expect him to be happy.'

'With respect, sir, I have made up my mind. I would like to be released.'

It had felt good to be so determined, to see his future so clearly. The only moment he had come close to changing his mind was when he walked down the covered yard to see Gerontius for the last time. The great horse whinnied as he approached, nudged his pockets, then rested his head on Henri's shoulder as Henri tickled his nose. Henri blinked back tears. He had never had to let go of anyone he loved before; until Florence he had never loved anyone. Just this magnificent, gentle horse.

He closed his eyes, breathing in the familiar scent of the animal's warm skin, feeling the velvet softness of his nostrils, the immutable sense of grace that came from being in his presence. And then, gritting his teeth and hoisting his bag over his shoulder, Henri Lachapelle turned and walked towards the gates of L'École du Cavalerie.

The first months in England had been tolerable, their trials masked by the quiet satisfaction he felt as a newly married man. Florence glowed under his attention; a million times a day he saw in her little things that enabled him to justify his decision. Her family, while obviously a little wary of the young Frenchman who had whisked their daughter off her feet, were polite. Not as antagonistic as his own father would have been, no matter whom he had brought home. Cleverly, Florence had asked him to wear his uniform when he first met them; the war still fresh in their memories, her parents' generation found it hard to see anything but good in a man in uniform. 'You're not thinking of settling in France, though?' her father had confirmed, several times. 'Florence is a family girl. She wouldn't do well so far from home.'

'My home is here,' Henri said, believing it. And Florence, seated beside him, had flushed with pleasure.

He had taken lodgings and, a matter of weeks after he arrived in England, they had married in Marylebone Register Office, so swiftly that for several months afterwards the neighbours cast suspicious looks at Florence's waistline whenever they passed. He set out to find work, travelled across London and to the suburbs, trying for employment as a riding instructor, but riding for pleasure was still very much the preserve of the wealthy, and on the few occasions he was taken on trial, his poor grasp of the language, impenetrable accent and formal opinions on riding won him few admirers. In turn, he found the English attitude to horses incomprehensible, their ill-thought out approach to equestrianism, based on the hunting field, sloppy, inexact and, worse, unsympathetic. They seemed to care more about dominating the horse than working with it or encouraging it to show itself off to its full advantage.

He found England a disappointment. The food was worse than he had received in the cavalry. The people seemed happy to eat everything from tins; there were few markets at which you could buy cheap, fresh food, the bread was spongy and tasteless, the meat ground to a brown gruel and re-formed into dishes with peculiar names: faggots, rissoles, shepherd's pie. On a few occasions he brought home fresh food and prepared it himself: tomato salad, fish enlivened with the few dried herbs he could find. But Florence's parents would widen their eyes over the dinner-table, as if he had done something subversive. 'Bit sharp for me,' her mother would remark, 'but thank you, Henry. Very kind of you to try.'

'Not my cup of tea, I'm afraid,' her father would say, pushing his plate to the centre of the tablecloth.

He felt stifled by the forbidding grey skyline, and would return to the narrow house in Clerkenwell to reveal that he had been 'let go' again, often without being paid what he was owed. It was impossible to argue in a language he did not yet understand. Family meals were tense. Florence's father, Martin, would ask over tea whether he had found another job yet, and when the answer was no, whether he might think about improving his English a little so that he could get a 'proper' one. One that apparently involved sitting behind a desk.

Florence would clasp his hand under the table. 'Henri is so very talented, Dad,' she would say. 'I know someone will find a role for him soon.' He became grateful that the language barrier precluded all but the most cursory conversations.

At night he dreamt of Gerontius. He rode out into the place du Chardonnet, seated in a slow, rocking canter, urging his brave old horse to switch his leading leg here, to flick his feet out in *passage* there. He danced, pirouetted, rose up on his back in a perfect *levade*, and saw the world laid out beneath him. And then, inevitably, he woke in the cramped bedroom of Florence's childhood, with its drab brown furniture, view of the high street, and his wife, her hair in rollers, snoring gently beside him.

A year on, he could no longer disguise the magnitude of

his error. The English were worse than Parisians, suspicious when he opened his mouth, the older men muttering disparaging comments about the war that they thought he could not understand. Those who surrounded him had no appetite for learning or for bettering themselves. They seemed to care only about earning money that they would drink on a Friday night with a kind of grim determination. Or they would stay locked in their houses, even when the weather was beautiful, curtains drawn, hypnotised by their new television sets.

Florence detected his unhappiness and tried to compensate, loving him more, praising him, assuring him that things would improve. He saw only the desperation in her eyes, felt her adoration morph into clinginess, and would announce that the following week he would leave to find work again, even when he knew there was no work to be had. Her attempts to disguise her disappointment merely fuelled his guilt and resentment.

It was April – almost fifteen months after he had arrived – when he plucked up the courage to write to Varjus. He was not a great communicator, and kept the letter brief:

My dear friend,
Would they take me back? It is too hard to live only with
gravity.

He handed it over at the post office feeling terrible guilt but also hope. Florence would understand. She could not want a husband who earned nothing, who could not provide her with a home. She would adapt to France eventually. And if not – here he would feel shame lodging deep within him – would it be so bad if he never returned? Surely she could not be happy as things were. Surely she understood that no man could continue to be so distant from the thing he loved.

He held the knowledge of that letter winging its way across the continent throughout another interminable supper. It was chicken. Mrs Jacobs had cooked it to a leathery texture and dressed it with some kind of cheese sauce. A small mound of unrecognisable vegetables sat beside it, diced into submission.

Henri sat in silence, forking pieces diligently into his mouth as Mr Jacobs muttered darkly about 'that Russian bloke' going into space. He seemed to take Mr Gagarin's exploration as a personal affront. 'I don't see what they're doing, sending men up into the sky,' he observed, for the third time. 'It's against all the laws of nature.'

Mr Jacobs was not a man, Henri had worked out very quickly, who liked change, and was pretty sure now that his daughter marrying a Frenchman fell into the 'unwelcome' category.

'I think it's exciting,' Florence ventured.

Henri was surprised: she rarely expressed an opinion that might contradict her father's view.

'It's romantic,' she added, cutting a piece of chicken neatly. 'I like the thought that someone's up there, amid all the twinkly stars, looking back at us.' She smiled at him, a secret smile. Her mother, he realised, was smiling at both of them.

'Florence has something to tell you, Henry,' she said, catching his confusion.

Florence wiped her mouth and put her napkin on her lap. She blushed a little.

'What?' he said.

'I was going to keep it secret a bit longer, but I couldn't. I told Mother. We're going to have to set another place at our table.'

'Why?' said Mr Jacobs, tearing his attention from his newspaper. 'Who's coming?'

Florence and her mother burst out laughing. 'No one's coming, Father. I'm – I'm in the family way . . .' She took Henri's hand over the tablecloth. 'We're going to have a baby.'

Well, they certainly did things differently in France, Mrs Jacobs remarked later to her husband, long after the younger couple had retreated to their room. For all the talk of Frenchmen being so sophisticated, she didn't think she'd ever seen a man so shocked in all her life.

Henri was leaving the flat when he met the postman on the landing. Varjus, true to his nature, had written back within a week. He ripped open the envelope and read the hastily written words, his face impassive.

Le Grand Dieu is a good man, an understanding man. I think if you approached him with humility, he might allow you this one mistake. Most of all, he knows you are a horseman! I look forward to your return, my friend.

'Good news, mate?' The postman thrust a folded magazine into number forty-seven's letterbox.

Henri screwed the note into a ball and thrust it deep into his pocket. 'I'm sorry. I don't speak English,' he said.

'Two paths', the Grand Dieu had said. Why had he not warned him how quickly they would turn into one?

He opened the front door to let himself into the narrow hallway. The smell of overcooked cabbage pervaded the air and he closed his eyes briefly in silent dread of whatever food was coming that evening. Then a sound made him stop. In the living room, on the other side of the anaglypta wallpaper, he could hear noisy sobs.

The kitchen door opened and Florence appeared. She navigated herself along the passageway and reached up to kiss him.

'What is this?' he said, hoping she would not detect the alcohol on his breath.

'I've told them that after the baby is born we're going to

France,' she said. Her voice was calm, her hands neatly folded in front of her. At the word 'France' another round of noisy sobs ensued.

Henri looked at his wife, confused.

She took his hands. 'I've been thinking about it for ages. You've given me everything – *everything*,' she glanced down at her belly, 'but I know you're not happy here, Henri. And it's too hard on you to expect you to be, with people having such closed minds, and the horse thing being so different over here and all. So, I've told Mother and Father that once we've recovered from the birth, you'll provide for me there. As you can probably tell, Mother hasn't taken it too well.'

She searched his face. 'Will Le Cadre Noir take you back, darling? I'm sure once I've got the hang of it I could keep a little house for you nearby. I'll learn French. Bring up the baby there. What do you think?'

Perhaps disconcerted by his lack of a response, she began to play with her cuff. 'I wanted to say we'd go now. But I wasn't sure about going through the birth not knowing how to speak to the doctors . . . and Mother would be beside herself if she wasn't with me. But I've told them we'll go after the baby comes. I hope I did the right thing . . . Henri?'

This brave, beautiful Englishwoman. Henri was moved beyond words. He didn't deserve her. She had no idea how close he had come . . . He stepped forwards and buried his face in her hair. 'Thank you,' he whispered. 'You don't know what this means. I will make sure we have a better future . . . for us and our baby.'

'I know you will,' she said softly. 'I want you to fly again, Henri.'

He heard the baby crying even before he reached the little house, a thin wail echoing over the quiet street. Even before he opened the door to their room he knew what he would find.

She was bent over the crib, uttering soothing noises, her hand fluttering vainly over the child. At Henri's approach, she turned. She was pale and her eyes spoke of long anxious hours.

'How long has she been crying?'

'Not long. Really.' She straightened up, stepping aside. 'Just since Mother went out.'

'Then why . . . ?'

'You know I'm afraid to carry her when you're not here. My hands aren't working again. I dropped a cup this afternoon and—'

He gritted his teeth. '*Chérie*, there is nothing wrong with your hands. The doctor said so. You just need confidence.'

He plucked Simone from her cot, deftly holding the tiny child close to his chest, and she quieted immediately. Her little mouth opened and closed near his shirt, seeking milk. Florence sat on the chair in the corner, holding out her arms to receive her, closing them around her daughter only when she was sure she had been safely delivered into her embrace.

While she fed the baby, Henri removed his boots, placing them neatly by the door. He took off his jacket and put the kettle on the stove. He had finally found a job on the railways. It was not so bad. Nothing was so bad, now that he knew it would be temporary. Neither of them spoke, the silence of the room broken only by the baby's greedy sucking and an occasional car passing outside.

'Have you been out today?'

'I meant to . . . but I told you, I was afraid to carry her.'

'Your parents bought us a pram. You could have put her in it.'

'I'm sorry.'

'Don't say sorry.'

'But I am . . . Henri . . .'

You don't have to be. If you would just be less compli-cated about everything. If you would be less anxious about the child, drop these ridiculous complaints about hands that supposedly won't work any more, the imagined dizziness.

'Nerves', the doctor had called it when, a matter of weeks after Simone was born, Florence had begun to complain that her body wasn't working as it should. Sometimes it was like this with new mothers, he had confided to Henri and her mother, as they stood in the narrow corridor after he had examined her. They saw terrors, dangers that weren't there. They might even hallucinate.

'At least she's bonded with the child,' he observed. 'She and Baby should stay with Granny for a while. Just until she has become a little more . . . comfortable with motherhood.' What could Henri have said? He had nodded his acquies-cence, marvelling that they could not see how every atom of him was straining towards the Channel.

Florence was crying again. He watched her try to wipe the tell-tale teardrops off Simone's cotton gown, her head bowed, and felt a suffocating weight drape itself over him. *How much longer?* he wanted to yell at her. He thought of Gerontius, perhaps even now waiting for him, his head bowed over the stable door.

'I'm sorry. I know you thought France would be the answer for us,' she said quietly.

And there it was. The thing that had hung, unspoken, between them for weeks. She could not cope alone, and he could not risk anything happening to the child. He could not return to Le Cadre Noir *and* be there to support her. He had no family he could place her with, no money to pay for nurse.

They would have to remain here, in reach of her parents.

He stood, walked over to her chair. 'I will write to Monsieur Varjus,' he said.

She glanced up. 'You mean . . .'

'We will stay in England a little longer.' He shrugged, his teeth gritted. 'It's fine. Really.'

Someone else would be riding his horse.

The baby's fingers opened and closed on her exposed skin, demanding, rhapsodic. 'Perhaps when I'm feeling a bit better . . .' Florence said quietly.

And next year, there would be new horsemen, écuyers, *waiting to take his place.*

When she placed her arm around his neck, sobbing her thanks into his aching shoulders, he realised with shame that he felt nothing but despair. His second thought was worse: how could a woman who was unable to use her hands hold on to him so tightly?

'It was about a year after that that I met him. He was working on the track above my yard. First time he'd seen horses since leaving his country, ones that weren't pulling a cart, anyhow.' Cowboy John tilted back his hat. 'I looked up one afternoon and saw him staring at my old mare as if she was a mirage. We were both new to the area then, both outsiders. I waved him down, and he ate his sandwiches outside that stable there, one hand rubbing my old mare's nose the whole time.

'A lot of people found him a little stiff but I liked him. We rubbed along fine. For years we'd sit there in my office, drinking tea, talking about the little farm he'd have in France one day, the riding school he was gonna set up once he'd made some money.'

'Is that what Florence wanted?' Natasha asked. She had been so lost in the story that she realised she had forgotten briefly why they were all in the car in the first place.

'Oh, Florence would have gone along with pretty much

anything that man asked her. I think she felt real guilty about what she'd saddled him with. She knew, like he did, that she wouldn't be able to cope in France, what with the illness. She spent most of her energy trying to make it up to him.'

'I don't understand. Illness?'

John looked at them, frowning. 'You two didn't know?'

'Know what?'

'Sarah didn't tell you? Her nan had – oh, whaddaya call it? – multiple sclerosis. She was in a wheelchair for years. Sarah was helping her grandpa look after the old lady almost from the time she could walk.'

They had given up on Dover and decided to head down the coast road towards Deal. Mac drove in the dark, calling out hotel names, just in case it was one that Natasha hadn't yet rung. Or hadn't rung twice. Natasha was still talking to John, her imagination captured by Henri Lachapelle's travails.

'The way Sarah talks about her grandparents, they sounded so close.'

John snorted. 'Sure they were close, but that man's whole life is one of regrets.'

'You mean Sarah's mother?'

'Oh, man, Simone was a mess. She was fiery, argumentative – the opposite of him. Everything he kept in, she let out. Florence couldn't manage her, didn't have the strength, and he tried to keep her on a tight rein, like he does Sarah. He was an old-fashioned disciplinarian, a little too much so for some tastes. He didn't like her mixing with the local boys, staying out late. The situation with Florence probably made him more protective than he would have been. But Simone wasn't having it. Oooh, no. She fought him every inch. The more he pulled her one way, she pulled straight back the other.'

He lit another cigarette. 'The sad bit is, he knows now he

handled her all wrong. He should have eased up. They were actually more alike than they knew. But it's hard, you know? When you think you're losing something, you don't always behave in the smartest way.'

Natasha glanced at Mac; he was engrossed in John's story.

'By the time he worked out what he was doing wrong, she was way down the road on the drugs and he couldn't get her back. Then there were about four, five years when she ran off to Paris and they never heard from her at all. 'Cept when she needed more money, of course. Damn near broke their hearts. I know he blames himself.'

'And then ten, eleven years ago, Simone turns up on their doorstep one day with this little child, sayin' she can't cope. She'd had a baby in France. Never said nothing to them. They got the shock of their lives.

'And she says she's goin' to sort herself out back here and starts leavin' the child with them. Each time it's for a bit longer and a bit longer, and then she doesn't turn up when she's meant to turn up, and in the end they apply for custody and get it. Simone never even turned up for the hearin'. He was mad at first – he was super-protective of Florence, of the extra burden it put on her to have to take care of a little one – but to tell you the truth, they was real happy to have Sarah around.'

He grinned. 'The day they got custody it was like the two of them got a whole new lease on life. The old man was thinkin' about horses again – and they were happy. Happiest I'd ever seen them together, anyhow. It was a blow when they heard Simone had died, but I guess it was a kind of relief too. He'd gone out looking for her for years, giving her money, sorting out the messes she'd gotten herself into, trying to get her straight – not that Sarah knows about any of that, you understand. He wanted to protect the little girl from it . . . some of what he knew . . .' John shuddered. 'No girl needs to know that about her mother . . .

'Anyhow, Florence passed away around – what? – four years past. After her funeral they got an offer from the council, some kind of financial incentive to give up their ground-floor place, they needed it for other disabled people. Well, he took the money, moved them to that flat in Sandown, and spent the money on Baucher, that Rolls-Royce of a horse of theirs. And from then on he began to seem like himself again. Everything was about getting Sarah into a better place.'

'He wanted Sarah to be like him,' she mused.

Cowboy John shook his head. 'You know what, Miss Lawyer Lady? He wanted the exact opposite. Oh, you can think what you like about her, but Sarah,' he said, his rheumy eyes looking into the distance, 'is the one thing that man ever felt he got right.'

The girl had fallen asleep. Thom drove on through the night, occasionally glancing at her, curled up on the front seat, her head resting against the window. And then, almost reflexively, at the CCTV monitor that showed her horse, partitioned between the other two, standing vigilantly as if he wouldn't allow himself to relax but was bracing himself for the next stage of his journey.

He had not told Kate what he was doing – he knew what she'd say. She'd tell him he was insane, accuse him of being irresponsible, of endangering the child's life. He knew that if his step-daughter, Sabine, had run off like that, hitched a ride with a stranger to another country, they would have been out of their minds with fear and worry.

But how could he explain he'd had to let the girl go? Even, hearing her chatter away these last hours, that he envied her a little. How many people got the chance to chase a dream? How many people even knew what they wanted? When she talked about her journey, about her love for the horse, the uncomplicated life she pictured for herself, her grandfather, he saw how easy it was to get hemmed in, buried in routine and mundane concerns.

None of it stopped him worrying, though, or thinking several times that he should stop the truck on the side of the road and call the police. He glanced up again at the CCTV. The horse lifted its head a little and, for a moment, gazed directly at the camera.

'Look after her, old fella,' said Thom, quietly. 'God knows, she's going to need all the help she can get.'

At a quarter past eight, they stopped at a fast-food restaurant to use the lavatory. John asked for a large, black coffee with two sugars – although Natasha pointed out that he'd be using the loo even more frequently – and strode off to the payphone to call the hospital. Routine, he announced cheerfully. He liked to call or pop in each day. The old man would want to know what was happening.

'What are you going to tell him?' she said.

'The truth. That we know she's close by, we just ain't worked out exactly where. He's a cussed old man, though. He's probably been telling her where to go so's we won't find her.' This thought made him laugh, and she watched him chuckle all the way to the phone.

She went to the table and put the plastic tray in front of Mac, trying not to notice that he flipped his mobile phone shut, as if he'd been checking a text message.

'If I say dark horse, are you going to hit me over the head?' he asked.

'She never said.'

'We never asked.'

'But she never said anything. I've talked to her about her grandparents, and all she ever said was that they were happy.'

'Perhaps,' said Mac, stirring creamer into his coffee, 'that was the only thing she considered important.'

She held up the black coffee as John returned, but he shook his head, his face sombre. 'Guys, I'm gonna have to split. Henri ain't too clever. If Sarah ain't around . . . Well, someone should be with him.'

'How bad is he?'

'They just asked me to come by. Well, they asked for Sarah, but I said that wasn't possible right now.' He was shuffling for change in his pockets, checking what he had with him. He looked tired suddenly, and a little frail.

Natasha stood up, reaching into her bag, the coffee forgotten. 'We'll take you to the station. Here.' She handed him some cash. 'Take that for the train.'

'I don't need your money, lady,' John said irritably.

'It's not for you, it's for him. So he doesn't have to be on his own. Oh, for goodness' sake, just get a cab from the station,' she said. 'You've earned it.'

He looked down at the notes she was holding out and, for the first time, the knowing, mocking expression was missing from his weathered face. He took them and tipped his hat to her. 'Well, thank you,' he said. 'I'll ring you when I know how he is.'

They were in the car before she realised that the sudden absence of his mordant humour had disconcerted her more than almost anything that had happened so far.

It was as they reached the station car park that her telephone rang. Natasha flipped it open. 'Yes, it is,' she said, glancing at John, who was letting himself out of the car. 'Sorry – can you repeat that?' The line was poor and she flapped a hand at Mac to turn off the engine. 'Are you sure? . . . Thank you very much for letting me know . . . Yes, I'll be in touch.'

'Everything okay?' John was holding open the rear door.

He was plainly eager to leave, but something in her face must have halted him.

She shut the phone.

'What?' said Mac. 'Don't just sit—'

'That was the credit-card company. You're not going to believe this,' she said. 'She's in France.'

Twenty-four

Sarah had been dreaming of horses, blood and motorways. She woke to a blast of cold air and saw Thom peering through the driver's door. She pushed herself upright. The clock on the dashboard told her it was a quarter to eight.

'Morning.' He was dressed and clean-shaven, as if he'd already been up for some time.

'Where are we?'

The atmosphere was curiously bright, as if the whole world was a few shades lighter than it had been in England. A short distance away she could see an immaculate stableyard, honey-coloured with a low, red-tiled roof, flanked by a dense, flat-surfaced hedge. Great tubs of carefully trimmed yew stood at the gates, and a man was mucking out a stable, swinging forkfuls of dirty straw into a wheelbarrow with cheerful ease.

'Just outside Blois,' he said. 'You've had a good night's sleep.'

'Where's Boo?' That same, reflexive panic.

'You mean Mr Diablo? In the yard.' He jerked his thumb towards the stables. 'We got here late last night but you were sparko and I didn't think it was fair to turf you both out late

at night. He's in the third stable along from the left. He's
fine. He was a little frothed up when we got here, but he's
good as gold.'

She blinked, just able to see Boo's nose reaching for a
haynet.

'You can have that night on me. But I need to be headed
back for Calais, Miss Sarah, so I'm afraid this is where you
and I must part.'

Sarah tried to collect her thoughts, as Thom helped her
tack up, and handed her two croissants, which he'd begged
from the owner of the lairage. He opened out a small map
on which he had marked her best route.

'It's sixty, seventy miles from here, headed south-west,' he
said, pointing her along a red road. 'I'd drive you if I could,
but I can't lose another four hours. It's beautiful riding
weather, though, and these roads are pretty quiet. I can't see
that you'll have too much trouble. Just take your time,
yes?'

She was close, she realised, with a sudden thrill. She could
see the name on the map. Compared to the size of France,
they were a matter of centimetres away.

'There's another lairage just here.' He had circled a village
with a ballpoint. 'Here's the phone number, just in case. Now,
I've rung ahead and they'll be expecting you. You should be
able to get a meal there tonight, but I'd try to grab something beforehand, just in case. And don't forget they're
expecting a horse by the name of . . .'

'Diablo Blue,' she said.

'Now, will you be okay?' He was serious, his face shadowed
with misgivings.

'Fine,' she said. She was pretty sure she would be. She'd
made it across the sea, hadn't she? She was travelling with
the finest horse in France and Papa's blessing.

'Here's my number. Will you do me a favour and ring me

if you get into trouble? Hell, ring me when you get where you're headed.' He placed the folded map in her hand. 'Just ring me. I'd be glad to know you're okay.'

She nodded, shoving the piece of paper deep in her pocket.

'And don't talk to anyone. Especially not anyone like me. Just – just keep your head down and keep going till you get there.'

She nodded again, a small smile this time.

'You have the euros we changed up?' She reached into her rucksack, feeling for the envelope.

Thom sighed. 'God help me. You're the strangest hitch-hiker I've ever met. But good luck to you and that big old horse of yours.' He hesitated, as if still unsure that he was doing the right thing.

'I'll be fine, Thom,' she insisted. She felt a pang to be leaving; she had felt safe with him. Nothing could happen to her or Boo in his care. She felt brief, unexpected envy of his step-daughter, whose troubles he had insisted on making his own, and added, after a moment, 'Thanks, though.'

'Bah,' Thom said. He stepped forward, holding out his good hand. She took it, feeling a little self-conscious. They both grinned, as if the thought had occurred to them both.

'It's been a pleasure travelling with you, young Sarah.' He waited for her to mount, then walked back towards his lorry. 'And your old man sounds like a fine fellow,' he yelled, turning back suddenly. 'When he finds out you got there, I'll bet you he's as pleased as Punch.'

The fields in France were wider than those *en route* to Dover, flat, sprawling expanses with no boundaries in sight. The earth, however, looked as it had in England: a rich, claggy brown, not yet drilled but turned in rough clods that resem-bled choppy seas. Boo, refreshed, strode out happily on the grass verges, his ears pricked forward, clearly glad to be on solid ground. His breeding meant that his winter coat was barely thicker than his summer one. Thom must have brushed him down while she was sleeping because he was spotless. They moved through a country that was alien, yet not so: the land of Papa's stories, a language she had heard from her youngest days. Seeing it on billboards, on road signs, she felt a little as if the country was speaking to her. As if it expected her to understand.

She passed through small villages, the streets quiet, civilised, the rows of small houses uniform, in grey stone, but for the odd carefully tended window-box or brightly painted shutters. A man walked past carrying two baguettes and a newspaper tucked under his arm. He nodded at her, as if a girl on a horse was nothing unusual. '*Bonjour*,' he said.

'*Bonjour*,' she replied, feeling faint joy as she spoke. It was the first French word she had uttered since she had been there. She stopped at an animal trough in the square, from which Boo took great draughts of water, his ears sliding back and forth comically as he gulped. She dismounted and rested there for half an hour, splashing her face with the cold water, eating her croissants and allowing a mother to approach with two solemn-faced small children so that they could pet him. The woman remarked that Boo was handsome, and Sarah replied, in French, that the Selle Français breed was known for it. She had grown up listening to Papa speak it, but hearing it from her own voice made her feel awkward.

'Ah,' the woman said, '*comme le Cadre Noir*.' To hear the name mentioned with familiarity was like a spur. She had spoken of it as others might mention the local sports centre, or Sarah's estate at home.

She remounted and they continued towards a signpost that pointed her to Tours. She left the other side of the village, past a windmill and over a bridge, and within minutes, was in open countryside again. She passed under motorways, through a vast field of whirring turbines, hearing the *thump, thump, thump* of their vast, elegant rotation like a heartbeat within her. Sarah, her spirits lightening with each mile, began to sing, a children's song she remembered Papa singing to her as a child. She pushed her scarf down from her face, feeling a growing excitement: '*Ah ah, Monsieur Chocolat! Oh, oh, Monsieur Cacao . . .*' Her voice rang out over the empty, frost-tipped fields. Boo champed at the bit and tossed his head, asking to go faster, and, impatient to arrive, conscious that she was only a matter of hours from her destination, she squeezed him on, the cold air tightening her skin, her body feeding off his energy. Her senses felt sharper, as if she was absorbing this new landscape through every cell. It was just her and her horse, unobserved, free; she felt this freedom like any other horse-borne traveller over a thousand years.

I'm in France, Papa, she told him silently, and it's beautiful. She pictured the old man in the bed, dreaming of the very roads she was travelling now, thinking with satisfaction of what she was about to do. And perhaps hearing his voice, his instruction, she straightened a little, corrected the precise angle of her lower legs, shortened her reins and began to canter, Boo's feet placing themselves rhythmically, elegantly along the grass verge in a manner that, had he seen them, might indeed have made the old man dip his head approvingly.

Even as a child she had hated lengthy car journeys. She never remembered the cheerful campsites, the caravans by the sea, the fairgrounds and ice-creams or overjoyed relatives that her siblings later recounted. When asked to recall her childhood journeys Natasha remembered only the endless motorways, the miles between exits punctuated by cries of 'Are we nearly there?', her parents bickering in the front seats, the surrep-

titious kicks and pinches from her sisters, squashed each side
of her in the back. She remembered the faint smell of vomit
when someone, inevitably, became car sick.

She was almost thirty years older now, but the dread had
never been supplanted by the supposed joy of the open road,
the excitement of getting to a new destination. While Mac,
during the holidays of their marriage, had loved road trips,
stopping where the whim took them, driving all night if he
had thought it would be fun, she had wished secretly for an
itinerary. The uncertainty of not having a meal and a pre-
booked bed to count on disconcerted her; and her suburban
outlook, as Mac seemed to see it, made her feel both inadequate and guilty for spoiling his fun. In the last couple of
years they had settled – to the satisfaction of neither – on
package holidays. She would sit by the pool, reading, trying
to disguise the work papers she had smuggled with her, while
he paced around the hotel complex, like someone trying to
remember where he had left something, and ended up
drinking with his new friends at the bar.

Natasha's credit card had been used, the previous evening,
at a French motorway service station. The difficulty, the
credit-card operator had advised, was that the transaction
had come up simply as 'La Bonne Route, Paris', a description that encompassed seven such places across northern
France.

'Well, I think we should head for the horse place,' Mac had
said on the ferry the previous night. They had managed to
get the car on to a late-evening crossing. She sat in near-
silence, staring out of the glazed window at the dark, churning
waters below, and tried to reconcile what she had heard from
the credit-card company with what she had believed possible.
How could Sarah have crossed the Channel with a horse?
How had she managed to get to France? None of it made
any sense.

'What if it's not her?' she said.

Mac handed her a bottle of water. He rested his feet on the seat beside her and she moved an inch away from them.

'What do you mean?' He took off the top and drank. 'God, I'm thirsty.' He hadn't shaved, and his chin bore a layer of stubble.

'What if she sold the card, or it was stolen from her? What if we're following the wrong person?'

'It's possible, but it'd be a hell of a coincidence for someone else to want to get to France. And, besides, we don't have any other leads, do we?'

Natasha pointed at the map on the table between them. 'Look at the distances here, Mac. John said a horse could travel thirty or forty miles a day at a push. It would have been tough enough for her to make it to Dover in that time. How could she have got across the Channel with a horse and then have ridden halfway down France? And, look, Saumur's more than three hundred miles from Calais. She hasn't a hope of getting that far.'

'So what are you saying?'

She leant back in her seat. 'We should turn round.' Her voice was uncertain. 'Or maybe call the police.'

Mac shook his head. 'Look, we're committed to a course of action now. I think we should head for Saumur.'

'But what if we're wrong?'

'And what if we're not? It makes sense that she'd go there. Her grandfather thinks that's where she's going. Your credit-card says so too.'

Natasha glanced out of the window. 'I think . . . I think we've got this wrong. We should have called the police yesterday morning. You're right – I didn't want to get them involved because I didn't want all of this out in the open. I admit it. But it's gone beyond that now, Mac. We're supposedly responsible for a fourteen-year-old girl who's lost, possibly in a strange country. I say when we get off the ferry we call the police. It's the responsible thing to do.'

'No,' he said, adamant. 'The moment we call the police, she loses the horse. She loses everything. No. She's only lost in that we don't know where she is. *She* may know exactly where she's going. I'm prepared to trust her to be okay.'

'That's not your decision to make.'

'I know. But I'll take responsibility if it goes wrong.'

'I'm her foster-carer too.'

When Mac's gaze was so direct, it still left her a little flustered. 'You know what? If you'd really wanted to call the police, you would have done it yesterday. You know very well, Tash, that neither of us wants the police involved, even if our reasons are very different.'

He had never been so decisive about anything when they were married.

'Anyway, we're here now. We've got an idea where she's headed. I say we drive to the horse place and wait for her there.'

Hurt made Natasha's voice harder than she had intended. 'And if you're wrong, if she's not safe, if she turns out not to be where we think, you'll be happy to live with that, will you?'

Since then they had barely spoken. Mac drove the car off the ferry at Calais, and on through the night. He didn't take the *autoroute*, but the smaller roads, roads on which a horse might travel, peering into the dark as he drove.

She dozed, and woke to the sound of his voice. He was speaking into his phone, low and insistent. 'It's not that,' he said, and, some time later, 'No, no, sweetheart. I don't think that's a good idea. I know. I know.' Natasha, uncomfortably awake, kept her face turned away, her eyes shut, her breathing determinedly regular, until he rang off. She left it another ten minutes before she yawned ostentatiously. At that point he suggested they pull into a rest stop and grab forty winks. It was after one in the morning, and there was little chance of them finding a hotel. 'We won't sleep long,' he said. 'A couple of hours at most. Then we'll drive on.'

After the silent tension of the past hour, Natasha was glad to accept. They pulled off the empty road into the car park of a service station, which was partially lit by a solitary sodium light. There were no other cars, and on the other side of a low, straggly hedge, the flat fields of the Somme were mournful in the dark, imbued with the weight of their history. The engine ticked its way to silence.

They sat awkwardly beside each other, a surreal parody, she thought, of some date, the prelude to a first kiss.

Mac, perhaps sensing this too, was distant and polite. He offered her the back seat and, with an equally polite thank-you, she had climbed into it, rolled her coat into a pillow and laid her head on it, conscious that in the morning her suit would be even more crumpled than it already was.

'You want to borrow my jacket? I'm not cold.'

'No, thank you.'

He fell asleep, as he had when they were married, like someone stepping off the edge of a cliff. With his seat tilted back, she could see his profile in the half-light, relaxed, his arm tilted across his forehead, and could hear the faint, regular sound of his breathing.

Natasha did not sleep. She lay in a strange car in a foreign country, her mind racing like the speeding traffic in the distance, thinking about her lost career, a man in London who didn't love her any more, a girl who was out there at that moment, somewhere under the same sky, a web of un-happiness and loneliness, with herself at the centre. She grew chilled, and, regretting Mac's jacket, remembered a boy she had once represented who had slept, for months, in a car park. She had won him the case, had been utterly determined to do so, but she couldn't recall having wondered what it must have been like for him.

All the while, through the elongated hours, the man with whom she had once hoped to spend her life, the man she had pledged to love, the man with whom, in a parallel universe, she should have been wrapped in a marital bed, listening to their children sleep, shifted and murmured in the front seat, a million miles away. Perhaps wishing, in dreams, for a distant long-legged lover. Natasha lay in the dark and grasped, to her surprise, that divorce was not a finite pain after all.

'Linda. Natasha.'

'How's it going? Have you sorted out your . . . family problems?'

They knew. Conor would have told them everything. Natasha regarded her creased skirt, her now-laddered stockings, painfully visible in the harsh light of morning. 'No. Not yet.'

'Where are you? When are you back?'

They had slept for hours, waking shortly after dawn. Mac had reached through the front seats and shaken her shoulder. When she had opened her eyes, confused and disoriented, it had been several seconds before she remembered where she was. A silent, bleary couple of hours' driving later, they had stopped at a service station to freshen up.

'I'm . . . not sure. It's taking longer than we thought. Can I speak to Ben?'

'He's out. With Richard.'

'Richard? Why is he out with Richard?'

'Did nobody ring you?'

'No – why?'

'It's the Perseys. They've settled. Their side approached us this morning and put a new offer on the table. More than she'd expected. And she's agreed timetabled access. God only knows if she'll stick with it, Richard says, but for now they're in agreement.'

'Thank God.'

'He's out celebrating with her now. He took Michael Harrington and Ben with him. They're going to the Wolseley for a champagne breakfast. She's a different woman already. I've told Ben to watch himself – she's been eyeing him like a hungry lion eyes a passing wildebeest.'

Richard hadn't bothered to call. Her fleeting gratitude that the case had been settled satisfactorily evaporated, tempered by the knowledge that she would receive no credit for it. In Richard's eyes she was no longer part of it.

She knew, in that moment, that she would not be made partner. Not this year. Not, perhaps, for many years. 'Lin?' she said. 'Is . . .' She sighed. 'Oh, never mind.'

A dull ache penetrated her temple. She stood in the car park of a French service station, in two-day-old clothes, rubbing it while she surveyed the vehicles that passed in a blur. How had she ended up here? Why had she not done what she advised every trainee to do and kept her client at arm's length? How could she not have guessed that the chaos of these children's lives was, in fact, infectious?

'So, how are you doing?'

'I'm fine,' she lied.

'No one here knows quite what to make of this,' Linda said carefully. 'You've held your cards close to your chest.'

'And now I'm paying for it, right?'

'There's a view that you could probably have handled things better.'

Natasha closed her eyes. 'I've got to go, Lin,' she said. 'I'll ring later.'

Mac was walking back across the car park. This was purgatory, she thought, her career ruined, her private life in tatters, she and her ex-husband destined to be stuck in a small car

for the rest of their lives, bickering as they tried to justify the
bad decisions they had made.

'Oh! Natasha! I nearly forgot to tell you. We had a visitor
here first thing. You'll never guess who.'

He had stopped to say something to two older women who
had just climbed out of a car. Whatever he said made them
laugh, and she could see the broad smile he had not bestowed
on her since long before he had moved out. Something in
her constricted.

'Mm?'

'Ali Ahmadi.'

Natasha tore her eyes from him. 'What did you just say?'

'Hah! I knew that would get you. Ali Ahmadi.'

'But that's not possible! He's on remand. Why has he been
let out before the case goes to trial?'

Linda laughed. 'That kid we read about was a *different* Ali
Ahmadi. Did you know Ahmadi is one of the most common
names in Iran? Apparently he's basically your Iranian John
Smith. Anyhow, the one you represented came in to tell you
he's got a place at sixth-form college and starts in September.
Sweet kid. He brought you a bunch of flowers. I've put them
in your office.'

Natasha sat down on a low wall, the phone pressed to her
ear. 'But . . .'

'I know. We should have checked. Who'd have thought
there'd be two of them? Nice, though, isn't it? Restores your
faith in human nature. I could never quite see him as the
violent type. Oh, and I gave him back that little horse pendant
we meant to send him. I hope you didn't mind. He was happy
to take it.'

'But – but he lied about the distance he'd travelled. He still
caused me to misrepresent his case.'

'That's exactly what I said to Ben. As the interpreter was
in we got the file out and asked her to have another look at

the translation notes. And she came across something interesting.'

Natasha didn't speak.

'Ali Ahmadi indeed said he'd travelled nine hundred miles in thirteen days, but not that he *walked* it. That was what we – the interpreter too – all assumed. Before he left, Ben asked him – oh, you wouldn't believe how well his English has come on! Unbelievable! Anyway, Ben asked him how he'd got so far. He explained that he'd walked some of the way, got a lift on a truck for some, and then he held up that little horse. Some of it he'd ridden. Mule or something. But that's the thing – he never lied to you.'

Natasha lost the thread of whatever else Linda was trying to tell her, where she had put the flowers, when she would call again. She lowered her exhausted head onto her hands and thought about a boy who had held her hands in a heart-felt gesture of thanks, a boy who had travelled nine hundred miles in thirteen days. A boy who had only ever told the truth.

When she looked up Mac was standing a few feet away, two polystyrene cups in his hands. He glanced away abruptly, as if he might have been staring at her for some time. She shut her phone.

'Okay,' she said, taking her coffee from him. 'You win. Head for Saumur.'

She had taken a wrong turning. She stared again at the little map, already worn soft from repeated foldings, which didn't seem to explain why the route that should have taken her past Tours and a few miles to the lairage Thom had booked had somehow led her into a never-ending industrial estate. For some miles she had been travelling roughly alongside a railway line, but as Thom's map didn't show the railway she had little idea if she was heading the right way or not. She had trusted her gut, trusted that at any moment now there would be a sign for Tours, or some other landmark. But it hadn't come, the verdant landscape slowly morphing instead into something reminiscent of the edge of London, a concrete expanse with vast, empty sheds, car parks, huge posters for Monoprix or Super-U, whose corners flapped desolately from their hoardings. Periodically a train would pass in a roar, causing Boo to flinch, and then there was silence, broken occasionally by a passing car.

The sun had begun to dip in the sky, the temperature dropping, and she was losing confidence as to whether she had correctly judged the direction in which she was moving. She halted, stared again at the map, then at the sky, trying to work out if she was still going south-west or in fact south-east. Clouds had gathered over the sun, making it harder to read the shadows. She was hungry, and regretted not having stopped at one of the friendly-looking markets she had passed through. She had been so impatient to keep moving. And so sure that by now she would have reached the stables.

The scenery had become bleaker, the buildings blank-eyed, apparently unoccupied for some time. She appeared to be heading into a sidings: the track had split and become more tracks, each with lines of stationary carriages, shuttered and graffitoed, a web of pylons and cables above her. Uneasy, Sarah decided to go back the way she had come. She gave a long, weary sigh and began to turn Boo.

'Que fais-tu ici?'

She spun round in the saddle to see five bikes, scramblers and mopeds, two with a passenger riding pillion. A couple wore helmets, the rest bareheaded. Smoking, hard-eyed. She knew these young men as she had known the boys on her estate.

'Eh? Que fais-tu ici?'

She didn't want to speak. She knew her accent would mark

her out as English. She turned away from them and walked on, steering Boo to the left. Something told her she couldn't ride through them. She would hope they lost interest and went away.

'*Tu as perdu les vaches, cowboy.*'

Her legs closed involuntarily around Boo's sides. A well-trained horse will detect even the faintest tension in its rider, and this movement, with the slightest increase in pressure on the reins, caught Boo's attention.

'*Hé!*'

One roared past. She could hear the others behind her, catcalling, talking to each other. Her face impassive, she rode on, realising she had no way of knowing if she was walking into a dead end. The industrial estate was enormous, comprising warehouse-size buildings and deserted car parks. Graffiti scrawled in red and black on the walls told of the lack of activity, perhaps of hope.

'*Hé! J'ai parlé à toi!*'

She heard a motorbike being revved up, and her heart thumped.

'*Eh! J'ai parlé à toi! Putain!*'

'*Allez-vous en,*' she said, trying to sound more confident than she felt. *Go away.*

They began to laugh. '*Allez-vous en!*' one catcalled, mimicking her voice.

Dark was encroaching now, Sarah began to trot. She sat very upright and heard the motorbikes skidding and revving behind her. There were more lights up ahead. If she could get back on to a main road they would have to leave her alone.

'*Putain! Pourquoi tu te prends?*'

One of the bikes had come up next to her, then dropped back. She felt her horse tense, his ears flicking, waiting for a signal not yet given. She rested her hand on his neck, gleaning comfort from him, trying to keep from him her rising panic. They'll go in a moment, she told him silently. They'll get bored and leave us alone. But the bike skidded in front of her. Boo stopped abruptly, his haunches dropping, his head shooting up into the air. Two more bikes swung round so that three were now facing her. Her scarf was up around her face, her hat jammed over her eyes.

Someone threw a cigarette on to the ground. She sat very still, one hand unconsciously stroking Boo's shoulder.

'*Putain! Tu ne sais pas qu'il est impoli d'ignorer quelqu'un?*' The youth had a north African appearance. He cocked his head at her.

'*Je . . . je dois aller au Tours,*' she said, trying to stop her voice quavering.

'*Tu veux aller au Tours . . .*' The laughter was unpleasant.

'*Je te prendrai au Tours. Montes à bord.*' He patted his seat, and they all laughed.

'*Il y a quoi dans ce sac?*'

She glanced from one to another. '*Rien,*' she said. *They were after her bag.*

'*Il est trop plein pour rien.*' One of the boys, pale-skinned, his shaven head tucked under a baseball cap, had climbed off his motorbike. She tried to keep her breathing steady. They're just like the boys at home, she told herself, showing off to each other. You just have to show them you're not afraid.

The boy walked slowly towards her. He was wearing a dirty khaki jacket, a packet of cigarettes in the top pocket. He stopped a few feet away, eyed her, and then, without warning, leapt forward, yelling, 'Rah!'

Boo snorted and jumped backwards. The boys laughed. 'Easy,' she murmured, closing her legs around him again. 'Easy.' The boy with the hat took a drag on his cigarette, and moved forward again. They wouldn't stop now, she guessed. They had scented some new game, some fresh torture. Discreetly she scanned the distance, trying to establish the best route past them, the way out. They would know this area, would have spent hours doing what they were doing now, revving bikes around it, killing time, looking for weak spots to plunder and destroy out of frustration and boredom.

'Rah!' This time, she was ready for him, and Boo flinched, but did not jump. She had him firmly between leg and hand now, telling him silently not to move, refusing him the chance to feel fear. He was uncertain, though. She could see his eye glancing back, his arched neck tensing, could feel his mouth at the end of the rein, playing anxiously with his bit. And as the bikes revved again, she knew what she had to do.

'*S'il vous plaît,*' she said, '*laissez-moi la paix.*'

'*Renvois-moi et je te laisserai la paix.*' He gestured towards her rucksack.

'*Hé! Putain! Renvois-le, ou j'en fais du pâté pour chien!*' The north African boy had said something about horsemeat, and the word was all the spur she needed. Sarah gathered Boo up, her legs quietly signalling her instruction. He refused to hear her for a few seconds, still transfixed by anxiety, then training took over, and he began to trot obediently on the spot, his legs lifting carefully, rhythmically, two at a time in an exaggerated version of *piaffe*.

'*Regardez! Un cheval dansant!*' The boys began to catcall, the bikes revving, drawing closer, closer, briefly distracted by what she was doing. Sarah bit down on her fear and tried to block out the noise, concentrating, building Boo's momentum, building a secret core of energy at his centre. His head dropped to his chest, his legs lifting higher. She felt his anxiety, her heart constricting at his trust in her, that he was prepared to do what she asked of him, despite his fear. She heard one of the boys yelling something else at her, but the noise was lost in the pounding of blood in her ears.

'*Alors, comme ça on se fait valser, hein?*' The boy on his feet had moved closer. His smile was hard, mocking. He reminded her of Maltese Sal. She used her right leg to move Boo discreetly away from him. Boo, now bouncing into *terre à terre*, fired by her growing impulsion, was also absorbing the tension in the atmosphere and it was all she could do to restrain him. An energy was building among the boys; dangerous, tensile. She could taste their hunger for trouble, for chaos. She could almost hear their thoughts, as they calculated the possibilities. *Please*, she told Boo. *Just once. You have to do this for me.*

'*Faites-la descendre!*' one of the boys yelled, gesturing to the others to get her off Boo. She felt a hand reach for her leg. It was all the prompt she needed. Her heels clamped to Boo's sides, her seat telling him to rise, rise, and then she yelled, 'Hup!' and he was leaping into the air, towering above them as, with a seismic bounce, his rear legs kicked out horizontally behind him. *Capriole!* The world stopped, stood still, and for a second, she saw what men in battle must have seen two thousand years ago – their opponents' faces filled with terror as the great beasts rose, defying gravity, into the air, their legs, their very selves transformed into airborne weapons.

Beneath her there was a shout of fear, of outrage. Two bikes fell over and the boy on his feet collapsed on to his rear. As Boo's front hooves hit the ground, she threw herself forward, her heels digging into his sides. 'Go!' she yelled. 'Go!' And the great horse leapt past the motorbikes, skidded around the corner, and flew down the asphalted road, back the way they had come.

In a darkened hospital room several hundred miles away, Henri Lachapelle, his head tilted to one side where it had been propped by the evening-shift nurses, woke and let his gaze settle on the blurred image of the horse beside him, waiting for it to clarify, solidify. It had somehow drawn closer while he slept, and now looked back at him, its iridescent eye gazing into his own with a kind of gentle reassurance, its patience apparently limitless. Henri's own eyes, dry and sore, closed and opened several times amid a creeping confusion. Then: *Gerontius,* he exclaimed, with gratitude. The horse blinked slowly, its nose dipping, as if in acknowledgement, and he tried to remember how they had ended up here. Little was clear now; it had become easier to allow himself to be carried by these new tides, to accept without fighting the ministrations, the faces of strangers.

He could feel the stiff leather of the boots around his calves, the soft black serge of his collar on his neck, hear the distant laughter of his fellow *écuyers* as they prepared themselves somewhere in the distance. The smell of woodsmoke, caramelised sugar and warm leather seeped into his nostrils, the soft breezes of the Loire valley meeting his skin. And then he was astride, riding out through the red curtain, his gloved hands light on the leather reins, his eyes fixed calmly between the cocked ears of his horse. He felt Gerontius's long, strong legs move beneath him, those distinctive, elegant paces, as familiar to him as his own stride, and a deep joy, a kind of euphoria, crept through him. Gerontius wouldn't let him down; this time he would prove himself. This time he would be *a man on wings.*

Because this time something was different: he barely needed to convey his request to the horse. There was a telepathy between them, an understanding that no Grand Dieu had thought to reveal to him. Before his spurs had whispered against the horse's sides, before he shifted his weight, or uttered a word, Gerontius had anticipated him. This noble creature, Henri thought, in amazement. How could I have abandoned him for so long?

The horse arched his neck, gathered himself in the centre of the arena, his silken coat gleaming under the arc lights, his hooves lifting beneath him, the two of them at the centre of a vortex of expectation – and then, with a *whoosh*, he was on his hind legs, an impossible height, not teetering or struggling, his proud head fixed and steady, looking out at the audience as if it were his right that they should glory in his achievement. And Henri was there, tilted behind him, legs braced, back perfectly straight, a gasp of exultation escaping him as he understood that this was it; they were airborne, and he need never come down.

And it was then that he saw her: the girl in the yellow dress, standing in her seat before him, her slim hands raised above her head. She was clapping, her eyes filled with tears of pride, a smile breaking across her face.

Florence! he cried. *Florence!* The applause that burst forth from the arena filled his ears, his heart, deafening him, the lights exploding in front of him – *Florence* – so that it became everything, bearing him ever higher, drowning out the distant shrill ringing of the machines, the urgent voices, the sudden bursting open of the ward door.

Mac was knocking at the door of her room. 'Are you ready? Madame said dinner at eight, remember.' Natasha had put on the badly cut trousers and the thin red cotton shirt that had been the only items she could find to fit at the local hypermarket, and said, wearily, 'Give me five minutes. I'll meet you down there.'

She heard his footsteps echoing along the corridor, bouncing off the wood panelling, and scrabbled in her bag for mascara, something that would enliven her pale, exhausted face.

They had arrived in the town shortly after five. Their first stop had been the École Nationale d'Équitation, the home of Le Cadre Noir, but the gates had been closed. A voice had come over the intercom, apparently irritated by Mac's insistent buzzing, to reveal that it was not open to the public until two weeks after Christmas. And, no, to Mac's next question, no English girl had arrived with a horse. Neither Mac nor Natasha's French was particularly good, but fluency had not been necessary to detect the tone of sardonic disbelief in the man's voice.

'She would never have beaten us here anyway,' Natasha pointed out. 'We're best finding a base and taking it from there.' She had checked the credit-card company again, but there had been no new activity. Sarah had taken no money since the previous evening. Natasha didn't know whether she found this reassuring or worrying.

The Château de Verrières was in the centre of the medieval town; it backed on to the École de Cavalerie. The château itself was vast, ornate, a thing of beauty; the kind of place they had stayed during the early days of their relationship when they had been trying to prove something to each other, when Mac had used aftershave and complimented her on whatever she had chosen to wear. When she had found something funny or endearing in behaviour that, within two years, she would be complaining about.

'I guess we may just as well stay in a nice place as a chain,' Mac said. He was trying to be cheerful, but she knew that since they had hit French soil his own fears had escalated, as had hers. They had been careful with each other, these last hours. It was as if the situation had grown so large, so weighty, that it left no room for other feelings. Perhaps it was that neither of them was as confident now as they had been of the outcome.

She arrived downstairs to find Mac seated in front of a boisterous log fire, explaining the situation to the château's owner. The Frenchwoman heard the story out with polite incredulity. 'You think the child has ridden here from Calais?' she repeated.

'We know she's headed for Le Cadre Noir,' Mac explained. 'We just need a way to speak to someone there – to find out if she has come.'

'Monsieur, if a fourteen-year-old English child had turned up here unaccompanied on a horse, the whole of Saumur would know. Are you sure she can come this far?'

'We know she withdrew money outside Paris yesterday evening.'

'But it is over five hundred kilometres . . .'

'It's possible,' said Natasha, firmly, thinking of Ali Ahmadi. 'We know it's possible.' She and Mac exchanged a glance.

'Nobody will be there now,' the woman said. 'If you like I can call the gendarmes and ask if such a thing has been reported.'

'That would be very helpful,' Mac said. 'Thank you. We'll take all the help we can get.' Then, as the chatelaine disappeared to check their food:

'You okay?'

'Fine.' She stared out of the window, willing the child to emerge from behind the trees at the far end of the bay hedge. She had begun to see Sarah everywhere; behind parked cars, fleetingly at the end of narrow lanes. *She will be here.* But when she recalled Ali Ahmadi, she did not think of his triumph of will, of a bunch of flowers awaiting her in her office, but of her own failures. She felt, with a sick dread, that she had made a colossal error.

Face to face with Mac over dinner, in such a romantic setting, she found she was not hungry and drank instead. Three, four glasses slipped down without her noticing. By tacit agreement, they decided not to talk about Sarah, but she couldn't think of anything to say and didn't know where to look. Facing Mac, her eyes rested on his hands, his skin, his ruffled brown hair. Unusually, he didn't speak much either, just wolfed his dinner and, periodically, made little sounds of approval.

'Delicious, isn't it?' he said, before he saw that she was barely pushing hers around her plate.

'Lovely,' she said. He seemed wary, as if he wasn't sure what to say next, and his awkwardness fed her own, so that when he refused dessert, saying he was going to take a long bath, they deflated a little with relief.

'I might walk around the grounds,' she said.

'You sure? It's pretty cold out there.'

'I need some air.' She tried to smile, but failed.

The cold air knocked the breath from Natasha's lungs, and she pulled her coat tightly round herself. It carried the faint tang of woodsmoke. To her right, she could make out the huge classical façade of the academy and, a short distance away, the wide, honeyed-stone streets of Saumur.

She walked towards a horse-chestnut tree and, on reaching it, stopped to peer up through the elegant branches at the sky, a vast, inky expanse unpolluted by urban glow, glittering with a million tiny pinpricks of light. She no longer thought of her job, her lost case, her ruined relationship. She dared not think of Sarah, and where she might be. She thought instead of Ahmadi, who had not lied to her. She felt ashamed of how quickly, how easily her opinion of him had been corrupted.

She was not sure how long she had been out there when she heard footsteps on the gravel path. It was Mac, and her heart lurched.

'What is it? Is it the police?' she said, when she realised he was holding a phone. 'Did they find her?'

His hair was dry – he couldn't have had a bath. 'That was Cowboy John.' His face was grave. 'It's the old man, Sarah's grandfather. He died this evening.'

She couldn't speak. She waited for him to be Mac, to laugh and apologise, tell her it had been a sick joke, but he did none of these. 'Jesus, Tash,' he said, finally, 'what the hell do we do now?'

She could hear the gentle creaking of the plane tree's branches in the breeze and felt, with exquisite clarity, the cold on her face. 'We find her,' she said, her voice odd and reedy is her ears. 'We have to find her. I don't see what else we—'

Something was rising in her chest, a horrible unfamiliar choking sensation that briefly filled her with panic. She brushed past him and walked briskly, then ran towards the house. She went through the elegant, cavernous hallway, up the mahogany stairs to her room. The tears came even before she had lain on the vast bed, face down, her arms over her head. She let the heavy coverlet absorb them, not sure why she was crying: for the girl, alone in a strange country, whose last link to her beloved family had been severed, the orphaned boy whose life she had misjudged, or even the catastrophic mess she had made of her own. Now, freed perhaps by alcohol, the strangeness of her surroundings, the wrong country, the dislocation of the past two days, Natasha's sobs racked her frame, seeming to haul their way up from her very depths. She cried silently, not knowing how she would ever stop.

She could hear the bikes behind her. She was galloping flat out now, breathing in short bursts, gripped by fear. Boo ran, his neck ramrod-straight, his hooves sending up sparks beneath her in the darkening light. She wrenched his head to the right, flying towards what looked like a road, heard tyres squeal behind her, another threatening cry of '*Putain!*' and found she was in a supermarket car park

She galloped across the parking spaces, dimly aware of shocked couples pushing trolleys, a driver, halted in mid-reverse. The motorbikes had spread out now; she could see them from the corners of her eyes. She tried to pull Boo back

– if she headed close to the supermarket there would be too many people for the boys to do anything to her – but his neck was rigid; impervious. Boo, terrified, was lost in a world of his own.

She leant back, the road markings blurring beneath him. 'Boo! Whoa!' she cried, but realised, with terror, that she was not going to be able to stop. Briefly recognising that she should just stay on, she jumped a small rail, a pot-hole, flew past an empty car park and saw she had reached the edge of the estate, that the black nothing beyond the low wall was empty countryside. She stood in her stirrups, hauling at one rein, an old trick that should have swung him into a tight circle, killing his speed.

But she had not understood how close the wall was, how impossible the angle she had created for him. She, like the horse, had not seen the drop on the other side of the wall, so that when he took off, still blind with fear, it was only as his front feet soared into mid-air that both horse and rider saw his mistake.

The sounds of the bikes disappeared. Sarah flew into the dark sky, dimly aware of a scream that might have been her own. And then Boo stumbled, his head disappearing beneath her, and Sarah was falling. She saw a brief flash of illuminated road surface, heard a terrible crunch, and everything went black.

When there was no response to his discreet knock, Mac turned the door knob, afraid that it might prompt some new antagonism between them. But he couldn't return to his room: she had looked so lost, her face blanched in the moonlight, the habitual self-possession dissipated.

'Tash?' he ventured softly. He said it again, then slowly opened the door.

She was on the canopied bed, her arms crossed over her

head. He thought, for a moment, that she might be asleep. And then, as he was about to close the door quietly, he saw the movement of her shoulders, caught the smothered hint of a sob. He stood very still. Natasha had not cried in front of him for years. For a long time after he had finally left, fifteen months ago, he had recalled her expression in the hallway, her jaw tense, her face utterly composed, as she stood in her work suit and watched him haul his belongings to the car.

But that had been an age ago.

Mac walked tentatively across the wooden floor. She flinched when he placed a hand on her shoulder. 'Tash?'

She lay there, unresponsive. He wasn't sure whether she was unable to answer, or simply waiting for him to go away.

'What is it?' he said. 'What's wrong?'

When she lifted her face from the covers, it was pale and blotchy with tears. What remained of her mascara had run down her cheeks, and he fought the urge to wipe it away.

'What if we don't find her?' Her eyes glittered.

The evident depth of her pain was shocking, and made her strange to him. He couldn't take his eyes off her. 'We'll find her.' It was all he could say. 'I don't understand, Tash—'

She raised herself to a sitting position, drew her knees up under her chin and buried her face in them. It took two attempts before he could make out what she was saying.

'He trusted us.'

He sat on the bed beside her. 'Yes, but . . .'

'You were right. It's all my fault.'

'No . . . no . . .' he murmured. 'It was a stupid thing to say and I shouldn't have said it. It's not your fault.'

'It is,' she insisted, her voice distorted by tears. 'I let him down. I let her down. I never looked after her like I should. But it was too . . .'

'You did fine. Like you said, you did your best. We both did our best. We weren't to know this would happen.'

He was astonished that something he had said could provoke such a reaction in her. Natasha had long seemed impervious to anything he did. 'Hey, come on, it was just words . . . I was angry . . .'

'No. You were right. I shouldn't have walked out. If I'd stayed . . . perhaps made her open up to me a bit more . . . But I couldn't be around you. I couldn't be around *her*.'

He could see her thin arms in the red shirt, smeared with the inky marks of her tears. He wanted to reach out a hand to her, but he was afraid that if he did she might close herself off again. 'You couldn't be around Sarah?' His voice was quiet, careful.

Her face was still now, the sobs subsided. 'She showed me I would never have been any good at it. Having Sarah there made me see . . . that perhaps there was a reason I never had children.' She swallowed hard. 'And what's happened to her since shows me I was right.' Her voice broke, and she was sobbing again, shaking, her body suddenly diminished.

Mac was stunned by her sudden grief for their lost babies. 'No, Tash,' he said quietly, reaching for her hand now. Her fingers were wet with tears. 'No . . . No, Tash. That's not it . . . Come on . . .' he protested, his own voice catching on the words. He pulled her close to him, put his arms around her, rocking her, hardly knowing what he was doing. 'Oh, Christ. No . . . you would have been a great mother, I know you would.'

He rested his face on the top of her head, breathing in the familiar smell of her hair, and realised that the tear sliding down his cheek was his own. And he felt his wife's arms creep around him so that she clung to him, a silent message that perhaps he had been needed, wanted, that he had had something to offer her, after all. They sat in the dark, holding each other, grieving, too late, for the children they had lost, the life together they had relinquished. 'Tash . . .' he murmured. 'Tash . . .'

Her sobs quieted, and in their place, unspoken, a question filled the air around them, became written in their skin where it touched. He lifted her face in his hands, her bruised eyelids, her damp skin, trying to read her, and saw something in it that made thought disappear.

Mac lowered his face to Natasha's and, with a low murmur, kissed her bottom lip, his hands tracing the planes of her face, strange yet familiar. For a moment, he felt her hesitate, and some distant part of him stalled too – *What is this? Do we stop?* – but then her slim fingers were clamped around his own, delicate animal sounds escaping her as her lips sought his.

And Mac was pressing her down, a sigh of relief and desire escaping him. He kissed her neck, her hair, fumbled with the buttons of her crumpled blouse, smelt the musk of her skin and became clumsy with desire. He felt her legs hook around his back, and observed, with some distant, still-thinking part of him, that she had never been like this. Not for years. That this Natasha was someone new, and his feelings about this were more complicated than he could begin to deal with.

He opened his eyes and looked down at her in the faint light from the window, the smeared mascara, the unwashed hair, the faint pulse in her arched, pale throat, and the tenderness he had felt was smothered by something dark and male. It answered something in him that he had not been able to acknowledge to her in the days of their marriage. This was not a matter of retreading old ground. This was not someone he even recognised.

'I want you.' He heard her voice in his ear as if it were a

surprise to her, husky with something of her own, something greedy and desperate. 'I want you,' she said again, and Mac, pulling his shirt over his head, understood that although it had not actually been a question there was only one possible answer.

Twenty-five

'The rider himself is in extreme danger if anything happens
to his horse.'

Xenophon, *On Horsemanship*

A white bird was circling above her; it moved in huge, lazy circles, emitting a droning hum that grew louder and then, when the noise became unbearable, receded. Sarah blinked, unable to distinguish it clearly against the bright light behind it, pleading with it silently to quieten.

She lay very still as the noise grew in volume, and this time the ground vibrated beneath her so that she frowned, conscious of the pain in her head, in her right shoulder. Please, she willed it, no more. It's too loud. Her eyes screwed shut against it, this brutal invasion of her senses. Finally, as it became unbearable, the noise stopped. She felt a vague gratitude, before it was interrupted by a different kind of noise. A door slamming. An exclamation.

Ow, she thought. *My shoulder.* Then: *I'm so cold. I can't feel my feet.* The light was dimmed and she opened her eyes a fraction to see a dark shape looming above her.

'*Ça va?*'

Panic took hold even before her conscious self had understood why. Something was wrong, very wrong. She blinked, the pain forgotten as she made out the shape of a man staring down at her. She discovered she was lying in a drainage ditch.

She clawed herself upright, scrambling backwards until she met a concrete post.

Men. Motorbikes. Terror.

The farmer stood a few yards from her, his face concerned, his huge yellow agricultural machine a short distance away, its door hanging open where he must have jumped down.

'*Que faire?*' he said.

Sarah's eyes refused to focus. She glanced around, beginning to make out the expanse of ploughed field, the distant sheds of the industrial estate. The industrial estate. A leap into the dark.

'My horse,' she said, jumping to her feet and letting out an involuntary yelp of pain. 'Where is my horse?'

The farmer was backing away, gesturing at her to stay where she was. '*Je telephonerai aux gendarmes,*' he said. '*D'accord?*'

She was already stumbling forwards, along the road, trying to clear her head, her vision. 'Boo!' she shouted. 'Boo!'

She didn't see the farmer's suspicion as his thick, square fingers hesitated on the buttons of his mobile phone. If she had, she might have read it. Drugs? it said. Madness? There was mud all down one side of her, a bruise on her face; some kind of trouble?

'*Tu as besoin d'aide?*' he said, cautiously.

She did not hear him.

'Boo!' she shouted, clambering on to a concrete post, wincing as she tried to keep her balance. Her body ached; her vision refused to clear. But even she could see that the fields were empty, except for a few distant crows, the steam of her breath. Her voice simply disappeared into the still morning air.

She turned back to the man. '*Un cheval?*' she pleaded. '*Un cheval brun? Un Selle Français?*' She was trembling; a mixture of cold and fear. This couldn't be happening. Not now, not after all this. Fear gripped her hard, shaking her awake, incapacitating her with the enormity of what had happened. It was too big a thing, too terrible a prospect. He could not have gone. Of course he could not have gone.

The farmer was standing by the door of his machine now. '*Tu as besoin de mon aide?*' he said again, less keen somehow this time, as if hopeful that this foreigner would announce that, no, she was fine.

In fact Sarah, already limping down the road, not sure where she was going to look first, was too busy shouting her horse's name to hear him. The sheer blinding shock of Boo having gone overrode the pain she could feel in her shoulder, the repetitive hammering in her head.

She had walked almost the whole length of the ploughed field before she realised that her horse was not the only thing that was missing.

Almost thirty miles away, Natasha also woke to an unexpected sense of absence. Even before she worked out that the sound she had heard was Mac disappearing into the bathroom, she had been aware of the loss of his body beside hers. She still felt the weight of his arm across her, the solid length of his leg pressed into the back of hers, his breath warm on her neck. Without him she was untethered, as if she was floating loose in space instead of tucked cosily into a vast double bed. *Mac*.

She heard him lift the loo seat and allowed herself a small smile at this indication of domesticity. She burrowed deeper under the covers, lost in the fug that told of hours of pleasure, of desire met and reciprocated. She thought of him, of his lips on her, his hands, his weight, the intensity in the way his eyes had examined her, as if all the previous year had not been washed away but made irrelevant by the strength of their feelings. She thought of her own actions, her lack of inhibition, the desire, this thing, that had sprung so unexpectedly, as if it were quite separate from who she had thought she was. It was as if their past arguments, their cruelties, the things that had kept them from being themselves with each other, had heightened everything. She had surprised him, she knew, and she had surprised herself. How long had it been since she had felt like the better version of herself in his eyes?

She slid over to his side of the bed, breathing in the still warm imprint of his skin. She heard the lavatory flush, the sound of running water as he washed his hands. Would it be wrong to wrap herself around him again before they got up and restarted the search? Would it be wrong to use his lips, his hands, his skin, to fortify herself against the day ahead? What would it feel like to bathe in that huge, claw-footed bath, to reclaim that strong body as hers, inch by soapy inch? I love him, she thought, and the knowledge came as a relief, as if to admit it meant she could stop struggling.

She sighed with contentment. Then, prosaically, she rubbed her eyes, conscious of the mascara smears of the previous evening, tried to smooth her hair, which was matted at the back of her head. Her body glowed, prickled with anticipation and she urged him silently to hurry. She wanted him against her, around her, inside her. She felt a hunger for his physical self that she had thought did not exist in her any longer. She never felt like this with Conor. She had felt physical desire, yes, but it had been like quenching an appetite they both acknowledged, rather than this giddy, visceral feeling of being one half of a whole, of feeling even a temporary absence like an amputation.

It was at that point that she heard the voice. At first she had thought it was someone out in the corridor, but as she lay, straining to hear, she realised Mac was talking. She climbed out of bed, wrapping the bedspread around her, padded barefoot to the bathroom door, hesitated for a moment, then rested her ear against the old oak panel.

'Sweetheart, let's talk about this later. You – you're impossible.' He was laughing. 'No, I don't . . . Maria, I'm not going to have this discussion now. I told you, I'm still looking. Yes, I'll see you on the fifteenth . . . Me too.' He laughed again. 'I've got to go now, Maria. I'll speak to you when I'm home.'

For years afterwards, Natasha would struggle to disassociate a smell of beeswax from a premonition of disaster. She backed away from the door, the smile gone, the glow transformed as if by alchemy into ice in her blood. She had just made it to the bed when he emerged from the bathroom. She slowed her breathing, rubbed her face, unsure how to appear to him.

'You're awake,' he observed. She could feel his eyes on her. His voice was roughened by lack of sleep.

'What's the time?' she asked.

'A quarter past eight.'

Her heart was beating uncomfortably inside her chest. 'We'd better get going,' she said, casting around on the floor for her clothes. She didn't look at him.

'You want to get up?' He sounded surprised.

'I think it would be a good idea. We have to speak to the police, remember. Madame . . . was going to ring them for us.' She could see her knickers under the great walnut chest of drawers. She flushed at the thought of how they had ended up there.

'Tash?'

'What?' She pulled them on, her back to him, the bedspread hiding her naked body from him.

'Are you okay?'

'I'm fine.' She wrestled the knickers over her hips and turned to him. She kept her gaze bright, neutral. Behind it she wished him a slow, painful death. 'Why? Shouldn't I be?' He was trying to read her mood. He smiled, shrugged, a little uncertain.

'I just think we should get on,' she continued. 'Remember what we're doing here.' And before he could say anything, she had grabbed her things and was headed for the bathroom.

The gendarme had spoken to the administrative staff at Le Cadre Noir before he had come to the château.

'There have been no reports of such a girl here,' he said, as they sat in the drawing room over coffee provided by Madame, who had retired to a discreet distance, 'but they have assured me they will certainly let you know should she arrive. Will you be staying on?'

Natasha and Mac glanced at each other.

'I guess so,' said Mac. 'This is the only place Sarah's likely to come to. We'll stay until she gets here.'

Their story had prompted the same response in the policeman as it had in Madame: faint disbelief, the query hanging in the air as to how would-be parents could tolerate the idea of a child travelling so far alone. 'May I ask why you think she would head for Le Cadre Noir? You are aware that it is an élite academy?'

'Her grandfather. He was a member, or whatever you call it, a long time ago. It was he who seemed to believe that she would come here.'

The inspector seemed satisfied with that response. He scribbled a few more notes in his pad.

'And she has been using my credit card. We know that it has been used *en route* in France,' Natasha added. 'All the indications are that she is headed this way.'

The policeman's expression revealed nothing. 'We will place the gendarmes within a fifty-mile radius on alert. If anyone sees her, we will let you know.' He shrugged. 'It will not be easy, though, to distinguish one young woman on a horse around here – you must understand that in a place like Saumur we are surrounded by people on horseback.'

'We do understand,' said Natasha.

After the policeman had left, they were silent. Natasha gazed around the room at the heavy drapes, the stuffed birds in glass cases.

'We could drive around,' he said. 'I guess it's better than sitting here all day. Madame said she would ring if anything happened.' He made as if to touch her arm, but Natasha moved away, busying herself with her bag.

'I don't suppose it makes sense for both of us to travel,' she said. She wanted to punch him when he wore his vaguely hurt expression. 'I'll have a walk around the academy. You go. We'll keep in touch.'

'That's ridiculous. Why would we split now? Natasha, we'll go together.'

There was a brief pause. She gathered up her things, refusing to look at him. 'Okay,' she said finally, and left the room.

There were hoofprints at the far end of the ploughed field. She had tried to run across it, spying them, but a thick collar of mud, sticky and heavy, had attached itself to her boots, making all but the slowest movement impossible. Finally, she had reached the end, but after a few muddy clods on the tarmac, Boo's trail had disappeared.

She walked for another hour, zig-zagging across the fields, wandering into copses, her voice hoarse from shouting, until she found herself in the next village. By then she was shaking, her body chilled and empty. Her shoulder ached, her stomach was gripped by hunger pangs. Cars sped past her, not noticing or not caring, occasionally sounding a horn if she ventured too close to the road.

It was as she reached the village that she saw the little row of shops. The scent of bread from the *boulangerie* was rich and comforting, completely out of reach. She thrust a chilled hand into her pocket, and came up with three coins. Euros. She couldn't remember why they might be there: Thom had put her money in an envelope into her missing rucksack. Change. From some brief transaction the previous day. She stared at the coins, at the *boulangerie*, and then at the telephone box in the square opposite. Everything was gone: her passport, Boo's papers, her money, Natasha's credit card.

There was only one person who might be able to help her. She reached into her inside pocket for the photograph of Papa; it was crumpled, and she tried to straighten it with her thumbs.

She walked stiffly across the square, went into the *bar tabac*, and asked for a telephone. '*Tu as tombé?*' the woman behind the bar said sympathetically.

Sarah nodded, suddenly aware of her clothes, the mud. '*Pardonnez moi*,' she said, checking that she had not left a trail of footprints.

The woman was staring at her face, frowning in concern. '*Alors, assaies-toi, chérie. Tu voudrais une boisson?*'

Sarah shook her head. 'English,' she said, her voice barely rising above a whisper. 'I need to call home.'

The woman eyed the three coins in Sarah's hand. She reached out a hand and touched the side of her face. '*Mais tu as mal à la tête, eh? Gérard!*'

A few seconds later a moustachioed man appeared behind the bar, clutching two bottles of a cherry-coloured syrup, which he placed on the bar. The woman muttered to him, gesturing towards Sarah.

'Telephone,' he said. She rose, made for the public phone, but he shook his finger. '*Non, non, non. Pas là. Ici.*' She hesitated, unsure it this was safe, but decided she had little choice. He lifted the bar and shepherded her through to a dark hallway. A telephone stood on a small chest of drawers. '*Pour télé-phoner*,' he said. When she held out her coins, he shook his head. '*Ce n'est pas nécessaire.*'

Sarah tried to remember the code for England. Then she dialled.

'Stroke Ward.'

The sound of an English voice had an unexpected effect: it made her suddenly homesick. 'It's Sarah Lachapelle,' she said, her voice tight. 'I need to speak to my grandfather.'

There was a silence. 'Can you hold on a moment, Sarah?'

She heard murmuring, the kind that takes place when someone puts a hand over the receiver, and glanced anxiously at the clock, not wanting to cost the French couple too much money. She could see the woman through the doorway, serving someone coffee, talking animatedly. They were probably discussing her, the English girl who had fallen from her horse.

'Sarah?'

'John?' She was thrown by his voice, having expected a nurse.

'Where are you, girl?'

Sarah froze. She didn't know what to tell him. Would Papa think it was okay to tell John where she was? Or would he want her to keep going? Telling the truth had had a habit of backfiring.

'I need to speak to Papa,' she said. 'Can you put him on, please?'

'Sarah, you need to tell me where you are. We got people looking for you.'

'No,' she said firmly. 'I don't want to talk to you. I want to talk to Papa.'

'Sarah . . .'

'It's important, John. Really important. Please do this for me. Please don't make it difficult . . .' She was close to tears.

'I can't, sweetheart.'

'You can. I spoke to him the day before yesterday. If you put the phone to his ear he can still hear what I—'

'Sarah, girl, yo' grandpa's gone.'

She stared at the wall. Someone had turned on a television in the bar, and she could hear the distant roar and excited commentary of a football match. 'Gone where?'

A long pause. 'Sarah, baby, he's gone.'

A new cold crept over her, flooding her from the ground up.

She shook her head.

'No,' she said.

'Baby, you need to come home now. It's time to come back.'

'You're lying,' she said. Her teeth were chattering.

'Sweetheart. I'm so sorry.'

She slammed down the phone. Her whole body was shaking, and she wanted to sit down. She sank, very quietly, to the linoleum floor and sat there, while the room travelled gently around her.

'*Alors!*' She was not sure how many minutes had passed, but she was dimly aware of the woman shouting for her husband, and two pairs of hands hauling her to her feet. She was walked through to the main bar, sat gently on one of the red leatherette banquettes, and then the woman was placing a steaming mug of hot chocolate in front of her and unwrapping cubes of sugar, which she stirred into it.

'*Regardez!*' another customer was saying. '*Elle est si pâle!*'

Someone else muttered something about shock. She heard them as if from a distance. She was aware of more faces, sympathetic smiles. Someone removed her riding hat and she was ashamed of her dirty hair, the mud under her fingernails. There was nothing left. Papa was gone. Boo was gone.

The woman was rubbing her hand now, encouraging her to drink the hot chocolate. She sipped politely, wondering if she might throw it up.

'*Tu as perdu ton cheval?*' someone was saying, and her brain felt so strange that it took her several attempts to nod.

'*De quelle couleur est il?*'

'*Brun,*' she said dully. She felt weightless, heard everything at a remove. She wondered, briefly, if they stopped holding her hands, whether she might float up into the atmosphere and disappear. Why wouldn't she? There was no one left to anchor her to the earth, no one who cared about her. There was nothing to go on to, nothing to return to. Boo was probably lying dead in a ditch like the one she had been found in. The boys might have chased him for miles. He would be stolen, crashed into, absorbed into this vast country and never seen again. And Papa . . . Papa had died while she had been gone. She would never see his hands again, never see his strong old back grooming, dipping and brushing, his jaw set with the effort. They would never sit in front of the television, commenting on the news. Nothing made sense.

She had a sudden vision of herself, a small dot, completely alone in the universe. There was no place for her now, no person, no home of her own. That sudden knowledge was so enormous she thought she might faint. Then she realised that the people were staring at her and wished they would go away. She thought, abruptly, that she might lie down on the banquette and sleep for a hundred years.

There were murmurings of concern. She felt her eyelids droop, and then the woman was pushing the mug to her lips again.

'*C'est le secousse,*' someone said, and actually lifted her eyelids to check.

'I'm fine,' she said, wondering how you could say something so patently true yet untrue at the same time.

'Mademoiselle.' A thin man with a cigarette was standing in front of her. '*Le cheval est brun?*'

Sarah looked up at him.

'*Il est de quelle taille? Comme ça?*' He held his hand high, close to his shoulder.

Suddenly she could focus. She nodded.

'Come, come,' he said. 'Please come.' She felt the woman's supporting arm under her own and was suddenly grateful for it. Her legs no longer seemed to belong to her. They felt weak, like pipe-cleaners that might bend under the least pressure. She blinked, the glare of the morning light too bright after the gloom of the bar. And then the woman was climbing into the back seat of a car with her, the thin man getting into the front. They could be taking me anywhere, Sarah thought absently. She was doing everything Papa had told her not to. Somehow she couldn't work up the energy to care. *Because Papa is gone.* She rolled the words around in her mind, but nothing happened. I cannot feel anything, she thought.

A mile or two on they were pulling into a farmyard, down a driveway littered with rusting farm machinery; huge towers of baled straw shrink-wrapped in shining black plastic. A goose hissed angrily as they got out, and the thin man shooed him away.

Then, turning the corner of a huge shed, she saw him: he was standing in a cow byre, his saddle and bridle placed neatly at the far end of the gate. 'Boo?' she said disbelievingly, the pain in her shoulder forgotten.

'*Il est le vôtre?*' the man said.

Boo whickered, as if to answer conclusively.

'*Le fermier l'a trouvé ce matin, en haut par le verger. En tremblant comme une feuille, il a dit.*'

She barely heard him. She wrenched herself from their grasp and propelled herself towards him. She clambered over the gate and half fell into the shed, her arms around his neck, her tear-stained face pressed against his skin.

Who would have thought a girl could cry so much for a horse? they said, in the *bar tabac*, some time later, long after

Sarah had been sent on her way with another hot chocolate and half a baguette inside her. She had cried solidly for thirty minutes, while she bandaged the horse's poor bloodied knees, while she stroked him and cooed to him, and refused to leave his side. It wasn't quite normal to see a girl so emotional about an animal.

'Ah. You know these girls,' the woman from the bar said, running a duster over the bottles. 'Passionate about animals at that age. I was the same.' She paused and nodded at her husband, who had been distracted briefly from his newspaper. 'Still am, of course,' she added, with a snort, and, to the laughter of the customers, made her way back into the kitchen.

Mac waited for Natasha to climb into the car before he fired the ignition. She had barely spoken to him all morning. Every time he attempted to say something, to make some reference to what had happened, she would adopt what he thought of as her marital face, showing pent-up disapproval and unspoken recrimination. It was hard to work out how to respond to it: she had wanted him last night – it wasn't as if he had forced himself on her. Why the hell was she treating him like this?

Mac knew he had done the right thing, but it was hard to reconcile the needy, passionate creature of last night with the cold, shuttered woman beside him. He had woken wrapped around her, his lips pressed in sleep to the nape of her neck, and his first thought had been a kind of excitement. There were possibilities: something had cracked open between them, revealed itself. Perhaps, he had thought, it was not too late. It wasn't just the sex, although that had frankly astonished him. It was as if she had peeled away a layer of herself, allowed only him to see something she had closed off for so long. Afterwards, she had cried again, through release this time, and holding her, whispering to her, he had felt that she had granted him something. It had seemed astonishing to him that they could have wasted so much time apart.

I want you.

So, how to explain this morning? Mac knew he loved this mercurial, complicated wife, but he didn't know if he had the energy to keep breaking down the barriers she seemed so determined to erect between them. You're right, he told her silently. Men do get fed up with 'difficult' women, and this is why: you take a glorious situation and create something toxic within it.

'Did you hear me on the phone this morning?' he asked suddenly.

She'd never been any good at lying. Her cheeks flushed. 'No,' she said.

'We're not together, me and Maria, if that's what this is about. We're friends. We were meant to be doing a job together today. I had to cancel.'

She waved a hand. 'Look. Here we are.'

'She has a new boyfriend,' he said, but she was already out of the car.

They had pulled up at the École National d'Équitation, and now Mac followed her to the offices where a young woman, her hair tied back in a ponytail, her glowing skin telling of a life spent outside, shook their hands. She apologised for the misunderstanding of the previous day: they had not understood the situation, she explained, or their connection to Le Cadre Noir.

Mac took a moment, while Natasha was explaining, to study some of the photographs, sepia-tinted, of horses frozen in mid-air at impossible angles, men in peaked caps and braided uniforms perched on them calmly as if there was nothing odd in riding an animal that was standing on two legs at an angle of forty-five degrees. Further up, there was a black roll of

honour; all the *écuyers* of Le Cadre Noir since the 1800s, their
names, just one or two a year, outlined in gilt. One jumped
out at him: Lachapelle, 1956–60. He thought of the old man,
who had probably never known that his time here had been
commemorated, that he had been honoured in this way, and
was sad that someone whose life could have been spent in
the pursuit of beauty, of excellence, should pass his last years
where he had. He understood a little better now the old man's
fervent desire, his fierce instruction of Sarah. What could you
want for your children other than excellence and beauty? Or
satisfaction in the art of pursuing it?

'Here,' he said, pulling out a folder of photographs. 'This
is Sarah and her horse. You can see her face a bit better in
this one.'

The woman examined them, nodded. 'She rides very well.'
It was hard to see whether she was humouring them.

'Her grandfather's name is Lachapelle. That's him.' He
pointed at the roll.

'Is he with you? We have many reunions. We have a publi-
cation, *Les Amis du Cadre N—*'

'He died last night,' Natasha said.

'Is this why she has run away?'

'No,' Natasha said, glancing at Mac. 'We think she doesn't
know yet.'

The woman handed Mac the photographs. 'I'm sorry we
cannot be of more help, but if we hear anything, Madame,
Monsieur, we will of course let you know. Would you like to
look around while you are here?'

A young man was appointed to give them a tour, and they
walked out into the *Carrière Honneur*, a vast outdoor sand
school where a man in a black cap was riding a sprightly
chestnut, watched by a dozen horses from an immaculate
row of stables. He cantered one way, then another, his mount
snorting with the effort.

As they walked, the young man began to explain: this was where the show horses were kept, that way were the dressage horses, over here were the show-jumpers. There were some three hundred altogether. It was a world of order, of high standards met and maintained. Mac felt curiously reassured that a place like this still existed.

'Why are we sightseeing?' Natasha would grumble occasionally, as they walked on through an avenue of trees to the next stable block, the next sand arena, a world devoted to a pursuit neither of them understood. But he knew she felt as he did: what else could they do? At least here they had a greater understanding of what Sarah was aiming for. Several hundred miles from home, it was, paradoxically, the closest they had come to her.

Natasha flipped open her phone. 'I'll try the credit-card company again,' she said. 'It's been a couple of hours.'

'You are on holiday here?' their guide said, in heavily accented English, as Natasha strode away.

'Not quite,' Mac replied.

'Photographer,' the young man said, pointing at Mac's bag.

'Yes. But I'm not here for work.'

'You should photograph Le Carrousel. This is the show that marks the end of the student year. All the *écuyers* perform.'

'Excuse me a moment.' His phone was ringing.

'What is it?' Natasha said, breaking off from her call.

He turned away from her, running his hand over his head as he listened. 'Oh, Christ,' he said, closing his phone.

'She knows,' Natasha guessed. 'She knows he's dead.'

Mac nodded.

Her hand flew to her mouth. 'Then she knows she's got nothing left.'

Mac wondered if the colour had drained from his face as well as hers. They stared at each other, oblivious to the horses, the beauty of the setting. 'Put a block on the card, Tash,' he said finally. 'If she's decided she's not coming here after all, we have to stop her going anywhere else.'

'But then she'll be at greater risk. We've got to make sure she has enough money to eat, to sleep under cover. It's freezing at nights.'

'But we could chase her around France for weeks. There are a million places where you could park a horse. We've got to stop this.'

'I know that, but cutting her off from her only source of support isn't the way.'

'If we'd cut off that financial support in England she wouldn't have made it half so far.' It sounded like he was blaming her. He couldn't help it.

'She'd have found another way.'

'But we've been looking for two days and two bloody nights and we still have no idea where she—'

'Monsieur?' The young guide was pressing his walkie-talkie to his ear. 'Monsieur? Madame? *Attendez, s'il vous plaît.*' He spoke in rapid French. Then: 'There is an English girl here. A girl with a horse. Mademoiselle Fournier says you should come with me.'

It was not how she had imagined it, her triumphant arrival. For the first two days of her journey she had pictured it repeatedly, the elation as she reached the place that would surely feel like a second home to her. It was her destiny. It was in her bones, as her grandfather had said.

But for the last five miles Sarah had held the words to her as a crutch, the thing she required to keep moving. She had plodded through Saumur, oblivious to the elegant wide streets, the honeyed buildings, the timeless beauty of the river front. Boo, exhausted, drew curious looks with his bandaged knees, passers-by occasionally tutting with disapproval, as if she should not be riding an injured animal. She knew she looked barely less odd, with her bruised face and muddy clothes. Twelve kilometres, eight kilometres, four kilometres . . . She had urged him to keep moving, had bitten down hard to stop herself crying at the pain in her shoulder, the headache that wouldn't go away.

She had almost let out a sob when she saw the signs for the École de Cavalerie, then recognised on a residential street the Georgian façade of the horseshoe-shaped building. But there were no horses: the men who walked its courtyards wore no black but the camouflage of modern warfare. 'Le Cadre Noir?' she had asked one, as he crossed the place du Chardonnet.

'*Non!*' He had looked at her as if she was mad. '*Le Cadre Noir n'a pas été ici depuis 1984. C'est à St Hilaire de Fontaine.*' He pointed towards a roundabout. '*C'est pas loin d'ici . . . cinq kilometres?*' She had thought, briefly, that she could not go on. But she had braced herself and followed the soldier's instructions around several roundabouts, through a small town and then, so far away now that she feared she was lost again, up a long, verdant path, flanked by fields of horses.

And suddenly there it was, larger than she had thought, more modern in aspect. This was not the elegant antiquity of Papa's pictures, a courtyard full of uniformed people. There were security gates, six Olympic-size arenas, restaurants, car parks, a tourist shop. She rode through the open gates, few people paying her attention, her eyes almost closing with exhaustion, until she saw the sign, 'Grand Manège des Écuyers', that told her her journey was at an end.

She walked Boo around the covered arena, past the front entrance, where the next performances were listed with ticket prices, along its length and round to the rear, where sawdust hoofprints and a concrete path from the stables told of an equine route in. From the other side of the huge wooden doors, she could hear a man's voice. She straightened a little, took a deep breath, then leant across, wincing, and banged, several times on the door. There was a brief silence inside, broken by someone instructing, '*Hup!*' Sarah took a breath and banged again, her fist insistent on the wooden panels.

She heard a bolt slide away from her and the door opened to reveal a cavernous interior: a modern cathedral floored with sand. Around its edges stood a number of horses, all mounted, their riders in the distinctive black and gold uniform she knew from her childhood, as if engaged in some kind of dress rehearsal. The air was hushed, reverential, each man focused on the movements of his glossy, muscled horse.

The man who had opened the door stared at her, then castigated her in French, flapping his arms. She was so tired she could barely make out what he was saying, but she cut across him: 'I need to speak to the Grand Dieu,' she said, her voice cracking with tiredness. '*Je dois parler au Grand Dieu.*'

There was a brief, stunned silence, and she took advantage of the man's momentary inaction to ride past him. Boo pricked his ears.

'*Non! Non!*' A man with a walkie-talkie was hurrying after her.

'*Que faire?*' An old man in a peaked cap came towards them from the other end of the school. His face was scored with lines, his eyes hooded. His black uniform was immaculate, starched, as if it might be holding up the body within.

'*Désolé, Monsieur.*' The younger man had taken hold of Sarah's reins and was pulling Boo round towards the exit. '*Je ne sais pas ce que—*'

'*Non!*' Sarah pushed Boo forwards, swatting at the man's hand. 'Let go of him. I need to speak to Le Grand Dieu.'

The man strode up to her. He looked at Boo's bandaged knees, then at Sarah. '*Je suis le Grand Dieu.*'

She sat a little more upright.

'*Mademoiselle,*' he said, his voice low and grave, '*vous ne pouvez pas entrer ici. C'est Le Cadre Noir. C'est pas pour—*'

'I have to ride for you,' she interrupted. '*Je – je dois monter mon cheval pour vous.*' She was aware that the other riders were gradually stopping what they were doing, that she had become the focus of attention. 'I can't go back. You have to let me ride.'

He was lifting a hand to motion her out. 'Mademoiselle, I am sorry, this is not a place for you. You and your horse are in no condition . . .'

She could see another man on a walkie-talkie now, perhaps summoning security. Panicking, she fumbled in her jacket and pulled out the photograph of Papa. '*Monsieur! Regardez! C'est Henri Lachapelle.* You know him. He was here.' She held it in front of him, her arm straight, hand trembling. 'You know him.'

He stopped, took it from her. The other man was talking urgently now, gesturing towards her. 'Henri Lachapelle?' he said, observing it closely.

'*Mon grandpère.*' A lump had risen in her throat. 'Please. Please. He told me to come. Please let me ride for you.'

The old man glanced behind him at the other horsemen, then at the photograph again. While he was staring at it, the other man walked briskly back across the arena, holding his walkie-talkie. He murmured something in the old man's ear, and nodded towards his handset.

Both men looked up at her.

The old man's eyes were assessing her. 'You have . . . you have ridden here from England?' he said slowly.

She nodded, hardly daring breathe.

He shook his head a little, as if finding it hard to comprehend. 'Henri Lachapelle,' he murmured. And then he strode slowly away from her, his gleaming black boots sending up clouds of sand. Sarah sat very still on her horse, unsure what to do. Was this his way of telling her to go? She watched the man with the walkie-talkie follow him. Then she saw that they were gesturing to the other riders to move back, instructing them to line up at the sides of the school.

The Grand Dieu stood at the end of the vast arena. He gazed at her for a long time, and then he nodded. '*Commence.*'

There had been some confusion over where the girl had gone: their guide had initially misheard, taking them to one of the outdoor arenas, before an urgent exchange had them reversing in their tracks. Natasha hurried after Mac, her feet blistered in her court shoes, trying not to let euphoria take over. 'It might not be her,' she had told him, trying to keep the excitement from her face.

He had raised an eyebrow. 'How many other English girls on horses do you think they see around here?'

Their guide gestured to them. They had hurried through courtyards, through long stableyards, where horses stood eating peacefully in stalls, out into the brisk winter air until, outside a tall white building, Natasha recognised the ponytailed woman who had met them.

'*Ici, Madame,*' she said, beckoning. 'She is in the Grand Manège des Écuyers. Our presentation arena.' As Natasha passed her, the girl had smiled, her eyes wide. 'She has come all the way from England? Alone? *C'est incroyable,* eh?'

'Yes,' said Natasha. 'It is.'

They were back in the front foyer beneath the photographs, the gilded roll of members past. Another door opened, and she saw that Mac, in front of her, had stopped in his tracks. No one spoke. The building was vast, a monument to the art of horsemanship, the echoing space inside dotted with black-clad men on horses. It was like walking into an old master, she thought. They could have stepped back five hundred years. The man with the walkie-talkie murmured something to the girl, who gestured to them to follow her to the audience seating below.

She felt Mac's hand tugging at her sleeve. 'Tash, look,' he said quietly.

Natasha followed his line of vision, walking down the steps after him until they reached the side of the arena.

Sarah was riding very slowly towards the centre. Her horse, the boisterous, glossy animal that had been in such rude health in Kent, was scratched and muddy. Two makeshift bandages sat bulkily on his knees and there were burrs in his tail. His eyes were hollow with exhaustion. But it was Sarah she saw: the child was so pale that she seemed ghostly, ethereal. A huge bruise had half closed one eye; her back and right leg bore a continent of mud. She looked too small for the great horse, her thin hands red with cold. To all this she seemed oblivious: she was lost entirely in what she was doing.

A short distance away an old man stood unnaturally upright in his black coat and breeches. He was watching Sarah, as she asked Boo to trot, to canter, created small, elegant circles around the men who stood on their own horses, watching impassively. Natasha found she could not take her eyes off her. Sarah looked like someone else, frail and older than her years. The horse slowed to a trot, then moved diagonally across the vast space, his hooves flicking forward in a balletic movement as if each step was suspended briefly by air alone. And then, straightening, almost impossibly, he slowed until he was doing it without moving forward.

Sarah's face was a mask of concentration, the strain revealing itself in the shadows around her eyes, the tense set of her jaw. Natasha watched the minuscule movements of her heels, the tiny messages she sent through the reins. She could see the horse listening, accepting, obeying even through its fatigue, and understood that while she knew nothing about horses, what she was watching was beautiful, something that could only be achieved through years of relentless discipline and endless work. She glanced at Mac, beside her, and knew that he could see it too. He was leaning forward, his eyes locked on the girl as if willing her to succeed.

The horse's legs moved up and down, a rhythmic dance, his great head lowering in obedience to the task. Only the flecks of spittle that sprayed from his mouth betrayed the effort this movement cost him. And then he was travelling around, dancing a circle around his own hindquarters, a controlled, flowing manoeuvre that made Natasha want to applaud for the elegance, the unlikeliness of it. Sarah murmured something to Boo under her breath, a small hand reaching out to thank him; a tiny gesture that brought tears to Natasha's eyes. Then, as the horse rose suddenly on to his hind legs, teetering, absorbed in the effort of combating gravity, she was crying, tears streaming down her cheeks as she watched the lost child and the broken horse giving their all. She felt, she realised, proprietorial.

She felt Mac's hand surround hers and squeezed it, grateful for its warmth, its strength, afraid suddenly that it might let hers go. And then Sarah was cantering around the edge of the vast arena, a beautiful, slow, controlled pace, almost too slow for movement, her body as motionless as if she had been carved. And as Natasha glanced at the old man, she saw that the others, on the horses, had removed their hats, were sliding them down their chests in a formal gesture, and one by one were striking off in the same direction, following her, their heads dipped, as if in salute to what they had seen.

Mac dropped her hand and reached for his camera, firing off shots. Scrabbling for a tissue, Natasha realised she was glad. What Sarah had done was magnificent. She should have someone to record it for her.

The horse slowed to a trot, then to a walk. The men replaced their hats, glancing at each other, as if even they were surprised by what they had found themselves doing. As the girl walked up the centre of the arena, facing the old man, they peeled off to the sides to watch. Sarah, grey now with the effort of what she had achieved, stopped her horse squarely in front of him, all four feet lined up neatly beneath him, his shoulders now slick with the sweat of effort and exhaustion.

'She's done it,' Mac was murmuring. 'Sarah, you beauty, you've only done it.'

The girl, breathing hard, dropped her head, saluting the old man, a warrior, returning from battle. The old man removed his own hat, nodding in reply. Natasha could see, even from where she was sitting, how intently the girl was watching him, how every atom of her strained to hear his judgement. She discovered she was holding her breath and reached again for Mac's hand.

The Grand Dieu stepped forward. He looked at Sarah, as if he was trying to see something in her that he had not already seen. His face was sombre, his eyes kind.

'*Non*,' he said. 'I am sorry, young lady, but *non*.' He reached out a hand and stroked her horse's neck.

Sarah's eyes widened as if she couldn't quite believe what she was hearing. She clutched Boo's mane, then glanced to the spectator area, perhaps seeing Natasha and Mac for the first time. Then, with an almost imperceptible breath, she slid off her horse in a dead faint.

Twenty-six

*'Excess of grief for the dead is madness; for it is an injury to
the living, and the dead know it not.'*

Xenophon, *On Horsemanship*

She was silent for the short journey back to the château,
accepting without protest Natasha's hand around hers,
perhaps there for reassurance, perhaps from fear that she
might disappear. They didn't push her to speak; it was understood that this was not the time for questions.

When they reached the château, Natasha took Sarah
upstairs to her room, undressed her as if she was a much
younger child, and laid her on the big bed. As she brought
the covers over the thin shoulders the girl closed her eyes
and slept. Natasha sat beside her, one hand resting on the
arc of her sleeping body, as if that small human contact might
offer comfort. She was not sure she had ever seen anyone
look so pale, so hollowed-out. Now that she allowed herself
to consider the scale of what Sarah had been through she
was profoundly shaken.

For a few moments after the Grand Dieu had given his
verdict, chaos had broken loose. As Sarah had hit the sand
she and Mac had run, in tandem, into the arena, Mac scooping
up the seemingly lifeless body as the Grand Dieu caught hold
of the horse. Dimly aware of the shouted exclamations,
Mademoiselle Fournier's hands flying to her face as Mac

passed through, Natasha remembered being surprised by how effortlessly he had lifted Sarah, as if she weighed nothing, and how moved she had been by the protective way in which he held her close to him. Some minutes later, as Sarah gradually came round in an office close by, they had placed themselves on each side of her, Natasha cradling her head. The epic nature of her journey had briefly separated her from them, making her someone to whom neither of them knew how to respond.

And then Sarah had looked up at Mac, uncomprehending, and closed her eyes again, as if what she saw was too much to cope with.

'It's all right, Sarah,' Natasha found herself saying, stroking her sweaty, matted hair. 'You're not alone. You're not alone now.' But the girl hadn't seemed to hear her.

The resident doctor, summoned from the other end of the École Nationale, had diagnosed a fractured collar-bone and severe bruising, but recommended that what the child needed more than anything was rest. Tea was brought. Orangina. Biscuits. Sarah was urged to eat, drink, and obliged half-heartedly. Voices spoke urgently in French. Natasha barely heard them. She held the girl, who seemed unable to support herself, trying to will strength and courage into her. Trying to apologise for all the ways in which she had failed her.

C'est incroyable. The tale had spread swiftly across the École Nationale, and groups of people emerged, some in jodhpurs and peaked caps, to glimpse the young English girl who had ridden halfway across France.

C'est incroyable. Natasha heard it whispered as Mac carried Sarah to the car. She observed, as if from a distance, that the glances that followed them were a little less admiring. As if Sarah's triumph could only have been achieved by some deficiency on her and Mac's part. She felt no resentment at this; in her view they were probably right.

Boo was taken to the veterinary centre to have his injuries dressed and would spend the night in the stables. It was, the Grand Dieu remarked, the least they could do for such an animal. Mac said afterwards that he had stood in front of the stable for some time, gazing over the door as Boo, fed, watered and bandaged, lowered himself on to the thick straw and rolled, with a low groan of pleasure, in the deep, golden bedding.

'*Alors,*' the old man had said, not looking at Mac. 'Every time I think I know everything about horses, there is something more to surprise me.'

'I feel the same way about humans,' Mac said.

The Grand Dieu placed a hand on his shoulder. 'We will talk tomorrow,' he said. 'Come to me at ten. She deserves an explanation.'

And now, finally, Sarah slept, Natasha watching her as if the price of keeping her close was eternal vigilance. Late afternoon stretched into evening, the skies darkening to black. Natasha had eaten a bar of chocolate, drunk a bottle of water from the minibar and read a few pages of a book that had been left by a previous guest. Sarah did not stir. Periodically, alarmed by the girl's stillness, she would creep over and check that she was breathing, then head back to her chair.

When she emerged into the corridor, some time after eight, Mac was waiting for her. He looked as if he had been there for some time. New lines were scored into his face, she noted, the strain of the last few days revealing itself. She closed the door quietly behind her. He got to his feet. 'She's fine,' she said, 'but she's out cold. Do you want to see—'

He shook his head. Then he let out a long breath, attempting to smile. 'We found her,' he said.

'Yes.' She wondered why neither of them seemed to feel the elation they might have expected.

'I keep thinking—' He broke off. 'The way she looked . . . what could have happened . . .'

'I know.'

They stood there, not moving. The corridor was steeped in the smell of old polish; the ancient rugs muffled sound. She couldn't take her eyes off him.

He took a step closer and nodded to his room. 'You want to crash in mine?' he said. 'I mean, if she's in your bed, you'll have nowhere . . .'

There would always be another Maria.

When she spoke, her voice was neutral, businesslike. 'I – I don't think she should be left alone,' she said. 'I'll sleep in the chair in there. I wouldn't feel—'

'You're probably right.'

'I think so.'

'I'll be next door if you need me.' He tried to smile, his face sad and too knowledgeable, as if Sarah's return had allowed him, too, to consider how close they had come to triumph and disaster. And, just for a moment, she couldn't help herself: her fingers touched the new lines under his eyes. 'You need to rest too,' she said softly.

The way he looked at her then made her see that she was lost. All that vulnerability, that love . . . a steel door sliding back to reveal something she had thought long disappeared.

And then it was gone. He was staring at his feet. Fiddling in his pockets. 'I'm fine,' he said, not meeting her eye. 'You two sleep well. Call for me in the morning.'

Sarah slept so deeply that when she awoke it took several minutes to work out where she was. She raised her head from the pillow, her eyes gritty, and saw out of the long window the distant leaves of a horse-chestnut tree. A car passed, and the sound hauled her into wakefulness.

She pushed herself upright, conscious of the stale smell of her skin, her grubby clothes. It was then that she spotted

Natasha. She was curled up in an armchair, a blanket pulled up to her chin, her bare feet just visible.

Sarah vaguely remembered the feel of her hands stroking her hair, the surprising timbre of fear and relief in her voice when she'd said her name. And then she thought back to the arena, the sorrowful look in the Grand Dieu's eyes when he had said *non*.

Something painful lodged in her chest. She lay back on the soft white pillows and stared up at the high, high ceiling, the only visible barrier between her and a huge, empty world.

Non, he had said.

Non.

'If she doesn't want to talk, I don't think we should push her.' Natasha was standing in the great hallway while Mac settled the bill.

She gazed down the steps to where Sarah waited in the back of the car, her temple resting against the rear window. She appeared to be staring at nothing.

'It's not just that she doesn't want to talk about her grandfather, Mac. She doesn't seem to want to talk at all.'

The police had found her passport, with the empty wallet and a few belongings, on the road to Blois. Even the handing over of the precious dog-eared paperback of Xenophon did not stir her from inertia.

Mac took back his credit card, and thanked Madame, who had insisted on making up a small package of food for the girl. Everyone urged Sarah to eat, Natasha thought, as if food could fill the huge holes that had swallowed her life.

'She's exhausted,' he said. 'She's been driven by this idea for the last however long it was, perhaps a lot longer than we know about, and she's just been told it's not going to happen. Her grandfather died. She's ridden five hundred miles or more. She's shocked, tired and disappointed. And she's a teenager. I think it's in the handbook that they're meant to spend vast swathes of time not talking to you.'

Natasha wrapped her arms around herself. 'I suppose you're right.'

The sun emerged sporadically, as if it was playing cat and mouse with the loaded grey clouds, but none of them noticed that the short drive from the château to Le Cadre Noir was picturesque. The gateman had obviously been warned to expect them; Natasha saw him peer curiously at the back seat as they passed through.

Mademoiselle Fournier was waiting for them outside the main stables. She greeted them both with kisses, as if what they had been through had made them familiar to each other, then held Sarah's shoulders, beaming. 'How are you feeling today, Sarah?' she said. 'I am sure you needed to sleep.'

'Fine,' she muttered.

'You want to see your horse while we are waiting for Monsieur Varjus? Baucher has had a very comfortable night. He must be strong, we think. He is just over here . . .'

She had begun to lead them towards the show block when Sarah cut in: 'No,' she said.

There was a brief, awkward silence.

'I don't want to. Not now.'

Mac's apology was audible in his voice. 'I suspect Sarah is probably waiting to speak to the Grand Dieu.'

Mademoiselle Fournier's smile did not falter. 'Of course. I should have thought. If you would follow me?'

The office was lined with photographs, certificates and medals. Natasha watched as Mac examined each image closely.

Monsieur Varjus entered, as if he had just come from some other, more important task. He brought with him another man, whom he introduced as Monsieur Guinot, something to do with the course administration. Sarah sat between her and Mac. She seemed, Natasha observed, to have shrunk in on herself, as if she had decided to take up less space in the world. Natasha's hand edged towards her, but travelled no further. Since waking that morning, Sarah had reinstated the wall around her. The vulnerability of yesterday had dissolved.

The Grand Dieu was wearing his black uniform, his boots polished to a deep gloss, a flattening of his hair telling of previous hours on horseback. He sat at his desk, and considered Sarah for a moment, as if surprised again that a child of such a size could be responsible for what he had witnessed the day before. He explained in heavily accented English that Le Cadre Noir accepted no more than five new members each year, usually only one or two. There was an exam, overseen by some of the most senior horsemen in the country, for which the minimum age was eighteen. To join, she would not only need to succeed in all these but would have to be a French national.

'You'll have that, Sarah, if you were born in France,' Natasha observed.

Sarah said nothing.

'All this aside, Mademoiselle, I would like to say that what you did was magnificent. You and your horse. "A good horse makes short miles." You know who said this? Your George Eliot.' The old man leant over the desk. 'If you can fulfil the requirements of our system there is no reason why, within a few years, you and your horse should not return here. You have both ability and courage. To achieve what you have achieved at your age is . . .' he shook his head '. . . something I am still having difficulty in accepting.'

He looked down at his hands. 'I would also like to tell you that your grandfather was a fine horseman. I was always very sorry that he left. I believe he should have been a *maître écuyer*. He would be very proud of what you have achieved.'

'But you're not going to take me.'

'Mademoiselle, I cannot possibly take a fourteen-year-old girl here. You must understand this.'

Sarah looked away, biting her lip.

Mac spoke: 'Sarah, you heard what Monsieur Le Grand Dieu said. He thinks you're very talented. Perhaps we can work out how best you two can keep training and maybe some day you'll be back here. Tash and I want to help you.'

Sarah was staring at her stark white plimsolls, bought with a change of clothes by Mac that morning. There was a lengthy silence.

Outside, Natasha could hear hooves on concrete, a distant whinny. *Sarah, please say something.*

Sarah looked up at the Grand Dieu. 'Will you take my horse?' she said.

'Pardon?' The old man blinked.

'Will you take my horse? Baucher?'

Natasha glanced at Mac, her own confusion reflected on his face. 'Sarah, you don't want to give away Boo.'

'I'm not talking to you,' she said firmly. 'I'm talking to him. Do you want him?'

The old man's eyes flickered towards Natasha's. 'I don't know if now is the time to—'

'Do you think he's talented? *Est-ce que vous pensez il est bon?*'

'*Mais oui. Il a courage aussi, c'est bien.*'

'Then I give him to you. I don't want him any more.'

The room fell silent. The man from the administrative section muttered something in the Grand Dieu's ear.

Natasha leant towards them. 'Gentlemen, I think Sarah is very tired still – I don't think she—'

'Stop telling me what I mean!' Her voice filled the little room. 'I'm telling you, I don't want him any more. Monsieur can have him. Will you take him?' Her voice was insistent, imperious.

The Grand Dieu looked carefully at Sarah, as if assessing how serious she was. He frowned. 'This is what you genuinely want? To give him to Le Cadre Noir?'

'Yes.'

'Then, yes, I will gratefully accept, Mademoiselle. It is obvious he is a very gifted horse.'

Something in Sarah seemed to relax. She had clenched her jaw so tightly that Natasha could see the outline of a muscle in her cheek. Sarah straightened her shoulders and turned to he. 'Right. Can we go now?'

It was as if they were all paralysed. Mac's jaw hung open. Natasha had begun to feel ill. 'Sarah . . . this is a huge decision. You love that horse. Even I know that. Please take some time to think about it. You've been through an awful—'

'No. I don't need any time. I just want someone, for once, to listen. Boo is staying here. Now, if we're going back, I want to go now. *Now*,' she said, when nobody moved. 'Or I'll go by myself.'

It was all the prompt they needed. They rose as one, Mac shooting a bemused look at the old man as he followed Sarah into the sunshine.

'Madame,' Le Grand Dieu said, when they were out of Sarah's earshot. He took her hand in both his own. 'If she wants to visit him, or even if she changes her mind, it's fine. She is young. A lot has happened . . .'

'Thank you,' Natasha said. She would have said more, but something had lodged at the back of her throat.

He glanced out of the window to where Sarah stood in the sunshine, her arms crossed, kicking at a stone. 'She is just like her grandfather,' he said.

The rain began to full in unremitting sheets shortly after they left Saumur, the stormclouds colluding in a forbidding block across the horizon, then scudding towards them. They drove in silence, Mac's car forging through plumes of surface water, his attention on the road.

Natasha almost envied him: the silence within the little car had become oppressive, the time to be alone with her thoughts unwelcome. Occasionally she would glance up at the mirror on her visor, seeing the reflection of the thin figure on the back seat gazing out at the passing scenery. Sarah's face was impassive, but the air of misery that hung about her was so overwhelming that it had permeated the whole car. Twice, Natasha had tried to tell Sarah that it was not too late, they could return for the horse, but the first time Sarah had ignored her, and the second she had put her hands over her ears. Natasha was so disturbed by this that her voice had faltered to nothing.

Give her time, she kept telling herself. Put yourself in her shoes. She has lost her grandfather, her home. But she couldn't make sense of it: why would a girl who had fought so hard to keep her horse, the one thing she had left in all the world, her link with the past and perhaps her future, let it go so casually?

She thought back to the last moments of their visit to Le Cadre Noir. The Grand Dieu had accompanied them to the stables. 'I would like you to see your horse before you leave, Sarah,' he said, 'to ensure you find his condition satisfactory.'

Natasha had guessed his motive: he believed that seeing Boo would change her mind, would force her to contemplate the true ramifications of what she had decided.

But she had walked almost reluctantly towards the stable and stood a few feet back, too far away to see properly over the high door. 'Please,' he urged. 'See how much better he looks this morning. See what our vet has done to his injuries.'

Go on, Sarah, Natasha had urged silently. Wake up. See what you are about to do. She no longer minded the prospect of being responsible for Boo. At that point she would have done anything, anything, to alleviate the girl's suffering. But Sarah glanced only briefly at the vet's handiwork. Even when the horse had stuck his head over the door and made a proprietorial sound of greeting, one that had seemed to emanate from deep within his belly, she had not moved towards him. Her shoulders stiffened, her hands pushed a little deeper into her pockets, and then, with the slightest of nods towards the Grand Dieu, she had turned and walked towards the car, as the horse, ears pricked, looked after her.

It was not only Sarah and her losses that preoccupied Natasha. As the rain beat down, obscuring the brake lights of the vehicles ahead and camouflaging the road, she had found herself watching Mac's hands as they drove closer to Calais. When they left this car in England it would all be over for her too. There would be a negotiated agreement over who occupied the house for its final weeks, some financial discussions, and then he would be gone to his new home, and she would be alone, picking up the pieces of what remained of her life. She had nothing. She had lost her treasured home, jeopardised her career, ruined a potential relationship. She had lost the man she loved. It was a terrible thing to discover you no longer wanted the life that stretched ahead of you.

She closed her eyes. When she opened them, gazing out at the town below the motorway, she caught a glimpse of a girl riding a bicycle, stooped, moving through the empty street with a steady grace that belied the weather. She recalled suddenly the train journey, months before, when she had seen a girl astride a rearing horse in a London back-street. It hadn't been the unlikeliness that had cemented the image in her mind but the calm, the sense of girl and animal working in harmony. Even in a split second she had recognised that.

And then a voice popped into her head: the strained, high-pitched tones of Constance Devlin, her witness: *It will be surprisingly easy for Lucy to head down the wrong path. All you have to do is stop listening.*

'Mac, stop the car,' she said suddenly.

'What?' said Mac.

'Stop the car.' She knew only that she could not allow this journey to continue. Mac pulled up and, as he looked on, confused, she found herself clambering out, opening the rear door. 'Come on,' she said to Sarah. 'You and I need to talk.'

The girl shrank away from her as if she was mad.

'No,' Natasha said, not even sure where the words were coming from. 'We're not going any further, Sarah, until you and I talk. Come on. With me.'

She took her hand, then pulled her out of the car and through the rain until they reached the awning of a café opposite. She heard Mac's protest, and her own determination as she told him to leave them alone.

'Right.' Natasha pulled out a chair and sat down. There were no other customers; she wasn't even sure the place was open. Now that she had Sarah here she had no clear idea of what she wanted to say. She just knew she couldn't go on in that car, surrounded by the waves of pain, of silent suffering, without doing *something*.

Sarah flung her a look of deep distrust and sat down beside her.

'Okay, Sarah. I'm a lawyer. I spend my life trying to anticipate the games people play, trying to out-think them. I'm a pretty smart judge of character. I can usually work out what makes people tick, but I'm struggling here.'

Sarah stared at the table.

'I cannot work out why a girl who would lie, steal and cheat to keep a horse, a girl who only had one aim in life, which revolved around that horse, would throw it all away.'

Sarah said nothing. She turned away, her hands resting on her knees.

'Is this some kind of temper tantrum? Are you thinking that if you throw it all up in the air someone will step in and change the rules for you? Because if it's that, I can tell you they're not going to change anything. Those men work according to principles set down three hundred years ago. They won't shift them for you.'

'I never asked them to shift anything,' she snapped.

'Okay, then. You don't think they're telling the truth when they say you'll be good enough one day? I don't know, perhaps you can't be bothered to try?'

She didn't reply.

'Is it about your grandpa? Are you afraid you can't look after the horse without his help? Because we can help you there, Sarah. I know you and I haven't got off to the best start but that – that was because we weren't honest with each other. I think we can improve that.'

Natasha waited. She was aware that she had sounded as if she was talking to a client. But she couldn't help it. That's my voice, she said silently. That's the best I can do.

But Sarah just sat there. 'Can we go home now?' she said.

Natasha screwed her eyes shut. 'What? That's it? You're not going to say anything?'

'I just want to go.'

Natasha felt the swell of a familiar anger. Why do you have to make this so difficult, Sarah? she wanted to yell. Why are you so determined to hurt yourself? But instead she took deep breath, and said calmly, 'No. We can't do that.'

'What?'

'I know when someone's lying, and I know you're lying to me. So, no, I'm not going to take you anywhere until you tell me what's going on.'

'You want the truth.'

'Yes.'

'*You* want to talk about the truth.' She laughed bitterly.

'Yes.'

'Because you *always* tell the truth.' Her tone was mocking now.

'What do you mean by that?'

'Uh . . . like you're still in love with Mac, but you don't tell him?' She nodded towards the car where Mac, just visible through the rain-washed window, was poring over a road map. 'It's so obvious it's pathetic. Even in the car you don't know what to do with yourself around him. I see you sneaking little looks at him. The way you accidentally brush into each other the whole time. But you won't tell him.'

Natasha swallowed. 'It's complicated.'

'Yes, it's complicated. Everything's complicated. Because you know like I do—' There was a break in her voice. 'You know like I do that sometimes telling the truth makes things worse, not better.'

Natasha stared across the road at Mac. 'You're right,' she said finally. 'Okay? You're right. But whatever I feel about Mac, I can live with it. When I look at you, Sarah, I see someone who is throwing away a lifeline. I see someone who is creating more pain.' She leant forward. 'Why, Sarah? Why would you do this to yourself?'

'Because I had to.'

'No, you didn't. That man thought you might be good enough in a few years if you—'

'In a few years.'

'Yes, in a few years. I know it seems like a long time when you're young, but that time will fly.'

'Why can't you just leave it? Why can't you trust me to make the right decision?'

'Because it isn't the right decision. You're destroying your future.'

'You don't understand.'

'I understand that you don't have to cut everyone out of your life just because you're hurting.'

'You *don't* understand.'

'Oh, believe me, I do.'

'I had to let him go.'

'No, I'm telling you you didn't. Christ! What was the thing your grandfather wanted more than anything for you? What would he say if he knew what you'd done?'

Sarah's face whipped round. Her expression was ferocious. She was shouting now: 'He'd understand!'

'I'm not sure he—'

'I *had* to let him go. It was the only way I could protect him!'

There was a sudden silence. Natasha sat very still. 'Protect him?'

The girl swallowed. It was then that Natasha saw it: a glistening at the corner of Sarah's eyes, a tremor in her whitened knuckles. When she spoke again, her voice was soft. 'Sarah, what happened?'

Suddenly, abruptly, she began to cry, a terrible, grief-stricken sound. She cried as Natasha had cried thirty-six hours earlier, gulping sobs of utter loss and desolation. Natasha hesitated for just a moment, then pulled the girl to her, holding her tightly, murmuring words of comfort. 'It's okay, Sarah,' she said. 'It's okay.' But as the sobs slowly subsided into hiccups and Sarah began to whisper a halting tale of loneliness, of secrets, debt, fear and a dark path so nearly taken, Natasha's own eyes filled with tears.

Through the blur of the windscreen, Mac watched Natasha holding Sarah so tightly that there was a kind of fierceness in it. She was talking now, nodding, and whatever she was saying, the girl was in agreement. He didn't know what to do; it had seemed clear that Natasha had some plan in mind. He didn't want to interrupt if she was managing to elicit some explanation for the past three days.

So he sat in the car, watching, waiting, hoping she had

some way of making this thing better. Because he was pretty sure he didn't.

A woman arrived at the table, the owner probably. Natasha was ordering something, and as he watched, she turned to him. Their eyes locked, hers suddenly bright, and then she was beckoning him to join them.

He climbed out of the car, locked it behind him, and went to where they were sitting under the awning. They were both smiling, shy smiles, as if they were embarrassed to be caught so close to each other. His wife, his almost ex-wife, he thought, with an ache, looked beautiful. Triumphant, almost.

'Mac,' she said, 'there's been a change of plan.'

He glanced at Sarah, who had begun to pick at the basket of bread in front of her. 'Would this change of plan involve a horse?' he said, scraping back a chair.

'It certainly would.'

Mac sat down. Behind them, the skies were clearing. 'Thank God for that.'

All the way back to England, Natasha sat with Sarah in the rear of the car, their voices a low murmur, occasionally lifting to include Mac in the conversation. They would not return to Saumur today; Sarah knew a man, she told them, the one man she would trust to bring Boo back for her. They had rung Le Cadre Noir who, to Sarah's visible relief, seemed to have been expecting their call. The horse was fine. He would be safe there until someone came to collect him. No, Natasha said, she didn't think Sarah would return in person – 'I'm afraid we have a funeral to arrange,' she said softly.

Occasionally Mac would glance back at the two heads, organising, talking, seemingly now in perfect communion. Sarah would stay with Natasha. They were considering all options: boarding-schools – Natasha rang her sister who said she had heard there was one that took horses – or livery yards far from that part of London. There would be no more problems with Sal, Natasha told her. Without Sarah's signature on the terms and conditions, his claim on the horse was worthless, and she would send a legal letter telling him as much and warning him to keep away. And Boo would be safe. They would find a different kind of life for him. Somewhere he could run in green fields.

Natasha, Mac thought, was doing what she did best: organising. Occasionally, when Henri Lachapelle was mentioned, Sarah's face crumpled a little and Natasha's hand reached out to squeeze hers, or just to pat a shoulder. Little acts of kindness to tell her, again and again, that she was not alone.

Mac saw all this in the rear-view mirror, his gratitude tempered by the odd sensation of exclusion. He knew Natasha was not deliberately leaving him out, that whatever had occurred between the two of them he would keep Sarah in his life too. Perhaps this was Natasha's gentle way of telling him that their night together had been a mistake, that away from the intense atmosphere of the search she was seeking to return to a more stable existence with Conor. What had this been, after all? Some kind of swansong? Closure? He dared not ask. He told himself that sometimes actions spoke louder than words, and by that account what she was saying was pretty clear.

When they reached Calais, Sarah finally telephoned the man she had said could transport her horse back to England. She took Natasha's phone and walked away across the tarmac for some time, as if she needed this conversation to be private. Mac was struck by how relaxed she seemed about the prospect of leaving Boo in another country, until he thought about it: there was no place – other than with her – that she would rather have him.

'You're very quiet,' Natasha remarked, as Sarah talked some distance away, walking between the cars queuing for the ferry, her left hand pressed to her ear.

'I guess there's nothing I need to say,' he said. 'You two

seem to have it all figured out.' She shot him a strange look then, perhaps catching the edge to his voice.

'Here,' said Sarah, returning, before either of them could say anything else. 'Thom wants to talk to you.' She stood close to Natasha as she took the phone, as if the distance between them had been bridged.

He watched Natasha talking, his thoughts now so dense and complicated that he couldn't listen properly to what she was saying. Something had changed in her, her face softening, lightening. She had been denied motherhood, but it was as if she had found a new purpose. He turned away, conscious suddenly that he couldn't hide how he felt.

'No, that's really not . . . Are you sure?' she said, and then, after a pause, 'Yes. Yes, I know.'

He turned back her as she ended the call. She was looking at Sarah. 'He won't accept any money,' she said. 'He won't hear of it. He said he's headed that way in the middle of the week and he'll bring Boo back then.'

Sarah's smile was brief and surprising, as if she was as taken aback as Natasha by this act of generosity.

'But there's a catch,' Natasha added. 'He said that in return you have to invite him to your first performance.'

The beauty of young people, Mac thought afterwards, was that hope could still be restored. Sometimes it took only a few words of faith to reilluminate a spark of confidence that the future could be something wonderful, instead of a relentless series of obstacles and disappointments.

'Sound like a fair deal,' Natasha said.

Sarah, nodded.

If only, Mac thought, as he headed towards the car, the same was true of adults.

Natasha fiddled with the key in the lock, and opened the front door on to a dark hallway, flicking on the lights. It was shortly after one in the morning, and Sarah, bleary with sleep, walked in and up the stairs on automatic pilot, as if she was at home. Natasha followed her, straightened her bed, handed her a fresh towel, and finally, when she was sure that the girl would sleep, came slowly down the stairs.

It was the first time in forty-eight hours that she had felt confident Sarah would not disappear again. Something had changed; there had been a seismic shift in the ground between them. She realised that, despite the responsibility she had just taken on, despite knowing that she was effectively signing herself up to several years of financial commitment and an emotional roller-coaster, she felt – at some deep level – a kind of excitement she had not felt in years.

Mac was on the sofa in the living room, his long legs stretched out, feet on the linen-covered footstool, car keys still in his hand. His eyes were closed, and she allowed herself a lingering glance at him, taking in the rumpled clothes, the indisputably male presence. She forced herself to turn away. It was a kind of masochism to keep looking.

He yawned, pushed himself upright, and Natasha busied herself, afraid he would feel her scrutiny. The floor, she noticed, was carpeted with photographs, row upon row of ten-by-twelve prints, lined up on the polished wood floor where he must have left them days ago, the morning he had discovered Sarah gone. It was as she let her gaze run over the series of black-and-white images, the horses in mid-movement, the glowing tones of Cowboy John's shrewd old face, the images that heralded Mac's renewed appetite for what he did best, that her eyes fell on one in particular.

The woman was on the telephone. She was smiling, oblivious to the camera's attentions, surrounded by the bare branches of a garden, the light low and gentle behind her. She was also beautiful: the winter sun reflected on her skin, her eyes were softened with an unknown pleasure. The camera's gaze was not a cool reflection of some shuttered image: it was intimate, a secret collusion with its subject.

She stared at it for several seconds before she realised the woman was herself. It looked like some idealised version of her, a person she had ceased to know, a person she had believed long buried in the acrimony of the divorce. She felt something in her tighten and break. 'When did you take this?'

He opened his eyes. 'A few weeks ago. In Kent.'

She couldn't tear herself away from it. 'Mac?' she said. 'Is this how you see me?'

Eventually she dared to look at him. The man before her had new lines of sadness on his face; his skin was grey with tiredness, his lips pursed as if prematurely accepting disappointment. He nodded.

Her heart had begun to thump. She thought of Henri, of Florence, of Sarah, bravely blurting out the truth into a rainy unknown. 'Mac,' she said, her eyes still on the photograph, 'I have to tell you something. I have to tell you even if it turns out to be the stupidest, most humiliating thing I ever did.' She took a deep breath. 'I love you. I always have loved you, and even if it's too late for us I need you to know that I'm sorry. I need you to know that letting you go will always be the greatest mistake of my life.'

Her voice had begun to quaver, breathlessness hijacking it. She held the picture between trembling hands. 'So now you know. And if you don't love me, it's okay. Because I've told the truth. I'll know I did everything I could, and if you don't love me, there's absolutely nothing that would have changed that.' She finished in a rush.

'Actually, it's not okay,' she added. 'In fact, it'll probably kill me a little bit. But I still had to tell you.'

His usual relaxed charm had deserted him. 'What about Conor?' he said, almost snappy.

'It's over. It was never . . .'

'Fuck,' he said. Then he stood up. 'Fuck.'

'Why are you—?' She stood up, shocked by his outburst, the uncharacteristic cursing. 'What do you—'

'Tash,' he said, striding across his photographs, which skidded across the polished floor. He was inches from her. She held her breath. He was so close she could feel the warmth of his skin. *Don't say no*, she willed him. *Don't make some terrible joke, and find a diplomatic reason to leave. I can't do this a second time.*

'Tash.' He took her face in his hands. His voice was low, broken. 'Wife.'

'Do you mean—'

'Don't shut me out again.' His words were almost angry. 'Don't shut me out.' She had begun to apologise, but the words were lost in their kisses, their tears. He picked her up and she wrapped herself around him, her legs, her skin against his skin, her face buried in his neck.

'It'll be a long way back,' she said, much later, when they walked up the stairs to their bedroom. She was holding two of his fingers. 'Do you really think we can . . .'

'One step at a time, Tash.' He lifted his head towards the sleeping girl above them. 'But at least we know it's possible.'

Epilogue

'A horse is a thing of beauty . . . None will tire of looking at
him as long as he displays himself in his splendour.'

Xenophon, *On Horsemanship*

The journey from the house that Mac had built to the little
side-street behind Gray's Inn Road took forty-five minutes in
the daytime, half an hour on top of that if attempted in rush-
hour. Natasha glanced at the clock, calculating that she had
only minutes to finish her paperwork before she had to leave.

'Going to beat the traffic?' Linda came in with a pile of
legal-aid papers that needed signing.

'Probably not,' Natasha said. 'Not on a Friday.'

'Well, have a good one anyway. And don't forget we've got
that new chap in at nine on Monday. The immigration
specialist.'

Natasha had stood up and was gathering things into her
bag. 'I haven't forgotten. Don't you stay too late, will you?'

'I'll be a while longer. I want to sort out the filing. That
temp last week completely mucked up my system.'

Macauley and Partners had suffered a difficult birth, but
almost eighteen months on, Natasha was beginning to feel
that her choice to set up on her own had been right. There
had been little point in remaining at Davison Briscoe; it wasn't
just that Conor had taken her news so badly – he had perhaps
believed she and Mac to be together long before they had

reunited – but the scars of the Persey case were visible in the way Richard had no longer treated her as a partner-in-waiting. In fact, from the day she returned, he had barely seemed to see her as a worthy addition to the firm at all. When she had discovered he was inviting Ben out to lunch more often than he was speaking to her, she had known it was time to move.

Thank God for Linda. Having her trusted assistant jump ship with her to run the office had kept her afloat, not just professionally but emotionally. She suspected Davison Briscoe had missed Linda Blyth-Smith almost more than they had missed her.

'Have a good weekend, Lin.' She threw her coat over her arm, ready to run down the stairs.

'You too. Hope it all goes well.'

Gray's Inn Road was already thickening with traffic, the queues snaking all the way to the West End. It was a couple of minutes before she spotted him, pulling in on the other side of the road. She glanced to each side of her, then ran across between the slowly moving vehicles, her bundle of papers clasped to her chest.

'Dead on time,' said Mac, as she leant across to kiss him. 'How about that for service?'

'You're a marvel.' She dumped her papers in the footwell. 'And you,' she said, peering past him at the baby beaming at her from his car seat, 'have wiped banana all over your dad's jacket.'

'You're kidding,' said Mac, glancing behind him. 'How could you, mate?'

'She's going to be so proud of us.' Natasha chuckled, did up her seat-belt and gazed around her at the mobile dustbin that was Mac's car.

It had become a running joke, Mac and Natasha's appearance at such events. They inevitably arrived in Mac's increasingly battered car, with epaulettes of baby sick or smelling slightly of whatever nappy had exploded on the way. Surrounded by the gleaming four-wheel-drives and vast Mercedes of the other parents, they had found they came over like mischievous schoolchildren. The day they had brought Cowboy John with them to visit (no dope, they had made him promise, no, not even a little bit), Mac had taken particular delight in introducing him to the headmaster's wife as 'Sarah's previous teacher'.

'You teach a lot of circus skills here?' Cowboy John had enquired innocently. And then, when the woman had looked blankly at him, 'Lady, are you ever in the market for a few trays of real good avocados?'

John lived an hour's drive from Sarah's school, in a weatherboarded white cottage with his two elderly horses in a nearby field, and continued to sell produce of uncertain origin to passers-by. On Sarah's return, he had apologised to her, uncharacteristically awkward, saying he had let her down. He'd let the Captain down. He still couldn't work out what the Sam Hill Sal had been playing at; John had paid off the Captain's debt and Sal had known it. Sarah had glanced at Natasha. 'I should have talked to you,' she said quietly. 'I should have told someone.' By tacit agreement they had never mentioned Sparepenny Lane stables again.

'So what's this we're going to again?' Mac asked. The traffic flowed gently across the Westway, feeding the London traffic out into the green of the suburbs and on.

'It's an . . .' Natasha rummaged for the letter '. . . end of year celebration for gifted and talented pupils. We get to listen to some kids playing instruments, a poetry reading—' here Mac groaned '—and Sarah's singing. Not really,' she said, as his head turned. 'Sarah . . .'

'. . . is doing what Sarah does. She won't notice what we look like,' Mac said, pulling out into the queue of cars. 'Soon as she's anywhere near Boo, that girl's head is somewhere in the clouds.'

Everyone knew the refrain of working mothers about the impossibility of balancing childcare with work, Natasha thought, as they made their way slowly across the city. But it was impossible to take in the sheer brain-frazzling relentlessness of the juggling act until it happened to you. In her own case, she had acquired two children and a horse within nine months. The great irony was that, after all those years of being told to reduce her stress levels, drink less, think positive thoughts and have carefully timed sex, she had conceived during the most fraught, drunken three days of her life.

But that, they agreed, when they lay on each side of him, gazing at his fat limbs, his cheeks, his Mac-like thatch of hair, was the beauty of it. He had come because he was meant to.

The Kent house had long gone, replaced by a new rented cottage, the London house taken off the market. Mac, Natasha and the baby spent weekdays there while Sarah was at a select boarding-school just beyond the north-western tip of the M25, one of the few schools in the country that didn't just accept horses but could offer tuition at the level Sarah needed. The cost was crippling, even with her scholarship. 'But, hey,' Mac would say, when the termly request for funds arrived, and they would deflate a little over the kitchen table, 'no one ever said families came cheap.'

They didn't begrudge the money. There, Sarah had flourished, unremarkable among other teenagers whose families were absent for a variety of reasons. And although she would never be particularly academic, she had worked hard, made friends and, most importantly, acquired a faint sheen of happiness.

At weekends, when they drove up to their rented house four miles from the school, and she stayed with them, her conversations were dominated not just by Boo's behaviour in the arena, his many achievements or minor disappointments, but increasingly by the activities of her friends. She would never be the most gregarious of girls, but she had brought a couple to meet them. Nice teenagers, polite, focused, already looking towards their lives beyond school.

Equally, she would never be the most open or affectionate of people: there was a natural diffidence, a wall that rose swiftly if she felt unhappy or insecure. But, comfortable with them in the little house, she would chat away about David and Helen and Sophie, and so-and-so's horse that wouldn't box when they went to the event at Evesham, and Natasha and Mac would exchange a silent look of satisfaction across the kitchen table. They had come a long way. Each of them.

The school playing-fields were packed with cars, their gleaming paintwork creating a glossy patchwork across one side of the cricket pitch. Parents were making their way across the grass, the women in high heels laughing, clinging to their husbands as they sank into the ground. Sarah had seen them even before the steward had motioned Mac's car into a space. She was running over, her immaculate jodhpurs and white shirt gleaming. 'You made it,' she said, as Natasha climbed out, feeling her skirt stick to the back of her legs.

'Wouldn't miss it,' said Mac, kissing her cheek. 'How are you, sweetheart?'

But Sarah was already wrenching open the car's rear door. 'Hello, Henry, my little soldier! Look at you!' She wrestled with his seat-belt, and then she had him, held in front of her, grinning as he reached for her hair. 'He's grown again!'

'You'll get banana all over that shirt. Hello, love.' Natasha kissed her, noting that the baby was not the only one to have grown. Each week when they saw her, Sarah was morphing subtly into womanhood. There was little of the skinny child they had first known. She was taller than Natasha, as solid and glossy as her horse. 'Are you all prepared, then?'

'Yup. Boo's going beautifully. Ooh, I missed you. Yes, I did. Yes, I did.' Sarah was hugging Henry, prompting the same delighted response she always elicited from him.

Henry had cemented their new family, Natasha thought, as she often did. When they had revealed Natasha's pregnancy to Sarah, several weeks after they had recovered from the shock, the social workers had expressed concern that she might feel pushed out, that it might heighten her sense of instability. But Natasha and Mac had suspected the opposite, and they had been right. It had been so much easier when there was a little person she could love unconditionally.

They began to walk to the arena where the seats were already filling. A boy in uniform handed them a programme of the evening's events. Sarah's interpretation of Le Carrousel got top billing, Natasha noticed, with pride.

'Do you want me to babysit this weekend?' Sarah was saying, deftly untangling Henry's fingers from her hair. 'I don't mind. I haven't planned anything.'

'I thought you had a party.' Natasha was searching in her bag for a wet-wipe. The tell-tale smears of banana were already marching across Sarah's white-clad shoulder. 'Weren't you going somewhere with those girls from the sixth form?'

It was the smallest glance, but Mac caught it. 'Uh-oh. What's this about?'

'What? Can't I just offer to babysit?'

Mac's tone was mock-stern. 'What are you after, young lady?'

'I've saved you really good seats. Look, I didn't get one for Henry, but I thought you'd have him on your lap. You'll be able to see everything here.'

Mac paused. 'Come on, you. What is it?' He'd always been better than Natasha at reading her.

She tried to look embarrassed, but she was beaming. 'I've been accepted for the course.'

'What course?'

'At Saumur. The summer training course. Six weeks under Monsieur Varjus. I got a letter this morning.'

'Sarah, that's wonderful.' Natasha hugged her. 'What an achievement. You didn't think you had a chance.'

'The teachers here sent a CD of us and wrote in support. Monsieur Varjus said in his letter he could see definite signs of progress. He actually wrote to me himself.'

'Well, that's wonderful.'

'I know.' She hesitated. 'But it's really expensive.' She whispered the sum.

Mac whistled. 'That's a hell of a lot of babysitting.'

'But I've got to go. If I do well at this, it'll stand me in good stead when I make my application. Please! I'll do anything.'

Natasha pictured the estate car she and Mac had inspected in the showroom the previous week, and watched it disappear. 'We'll find it. Don't worry. There might be some of your Papa's money left . . .'

'Really? *Really?*' Someone was calling her, their voice lifting over the crowd. She glanced behind her, and then at her watch, swearing softly under her breath.

'You'd better go.'

The orchestra was tuning up. Sarah thrust Henry at Natasha, gasped an apology and ran towards the stables. 'Thank you!' she yelled, waving over the heads of the spectators. 'Thank you so much! I'll pay you back some day. Really!'

Natasha held her son close to her, watching her go. 'You already did,' she said quietly.

Sarah adjusted her girth and straightened, running her hand lightly over the neat plaits she had spent all morning sewing into Boo's mane. From this space, behind the hastily erected screens, she could see the crowd settling, could just make out Natasha handing Henry to Mac, then delving into her bag. A camera. She saw Mac take it from her, shaking his head fondly.

She loved Mac's photographs: her room here was plastered with them. After Papa died, Mac had collected all the old photographs they'd found in the flat in Sandown, pictures of her and Nana, old sepia-tinted images of Papa on Gerontius, and he had copied them, doing something clever digitally so that the images were clearer, larger, Papa's face more visible. The day of the funeral, he and Natasha had framed a few, placing them in her room so that she had found them when they'd returned to the house. 'We know we're not your original family,' they had told her that night, 'but we'd like to be your second one.'

She had never asked why they had named the baby Henry, but she guessed she knew. He knitted the two sides of her life together. Sometimes she even thought she saw a bit of Papa in him. Even if that didn't make sense. She still saw Papa everywhere – in the things Boo was taught to do; she heard his voice in her head whenever she rode. *Watch me now, Papa,* she would tell him silently.

The evening air was thick with the scent of newly mown grass, a faint hint of strawberries from the tea tent that had been set up behind the arena. There was a brief hush, then the orchestra began to play, the violin music to which they had spent weeks practising. She saw Boo's ears prick as he recognised the sound, felt his weight shift beneath her as he readied himself for the task ahead.

Tonight they would probably share a takeaway in the little cottage on the other side of the village. Mac would tease her about boys, and Natasha would ask if she'd help to bathe Henry. She always said it as if Sarah would be doing her a huge favour, even though they both knew she loved it. In two months she would be in France.

She had a sudden sense of being . . . if not where she was meant to be then somewhere she belonged. It was as much as anyone could ask for.

She glanced at Mr Warburton, her riding instructor, who was muttering beats under his breath as he held Boo's rein.

'You ready?' he said, looking up. 'Remember what I told you. Calm, forward, straight and light.'

Sarah sat up a little straighter, closed her legs around her horse and rode out.

Acknowledgements

This book would not have been possible without the technical help and support of a number of people. I would like particularly to thank solicitor John Bolch. Any legal mistakes are completely my own, or tweaked to adjust the needs of the plot.

I am also grateful to Yolaine and Thierry Auger of Château de Verrières in Saumur, photographers Mark Molloy and Andrew Buurman, Sheila Crowley of Curtis Brown, Carolyn Mays, Auriol Bishop, Eleni Fostiropoulos and Lucy Hale of Hachette UK, Linda Shaughnessy and Rob Kraitt of APWatt.

Thanks also to Annabel Robinson of FMCM, Hazel Orme, and Francesca Best. Cathy Runciman for French translation, wine pouring and endless friendship, and Hannah Mays, Chris Luckley and Sonya Penney for a definite education during the first trip to Le Cadre Noir.

Further thanks to Drew Hazell, Cathy Scotland and Jeannie Brice, as well as Barbara Ralph.

To the various members of Writersblock; you know who you are.

Thanks also to Simon and Charlotte Kelvin, whose generous donation to charity means they will be popping up in some form in a future novel.

To my family, Lizzie and Brian Sanders and Jim Moyes, and most of all to Charles, Saskia, Harry and Lockie. Horse riding is research. Honest.

*　　*　　*

In 2007 I read a piece in *Philadelphia Weekly* magazine by journalist Steve Volk about a 14 year old girl called Mecca Harris. She spent all her time outside school hours at an urban stables in Philadelphia, taught a love of horses, and skill at riding, by the Philadelphia Black Cowboys, an institution that offers children in the city's toughest neighbourhoods a chance, through horses, to seek a different way of life.

She had a natural ability, and determination, and was chosen to play polo against Yale, with the all-black Work to Ride team. In autumn 2003 she received application forms from a prestigious Polo school in California, but she never got as far as filling them out.

On October 15 2003 Mecca Harris, her mother and her mother's boyfriend were found murdered in their home, victims of an alleged drug killing.

This story stuck in my mind not because of the compelling pictures of Mecca, a skinny little jockey, her braids visible under her riding hat. But because, while my life was never underprivileged as hers was, I could have been that girl. My teenage years were spent at urban stables dotted around London backstreets; my arenas the local parks. Horses kept me out of trouble (although my parents may disagree) and gave me a passion that has lasted thirty years.

I now live on a farm. I get to keep a horse in green fields, instead of under a railway arch. Mecca Harris should have had her green fields. This book is dedicated to her, and children like her, for whom horses can be a way out.

Read on for an extract of Jojo Moyes's engaging and
beautifully evocative new novel

THE LAST LETTER FROM YOUR LOVER

Have you ever received a letter that spoke to your heart?

My dearest and only love . . .

*You are the single greatest thing that has happened to
me in my life . . .*

*Please don't love him. I can't sleep, tormented by knowing
that he is lying next to you, haunted by the possibility of
seeing you with him . . .*

*A bold decision is the only way forward. I'll be at Platform 4,
Paddington at 7.15 on Monday evening and there is nothing
in the world that would make me happier than if you found
the courage to come with me . . .*

Know that you hold my heart, my hopes, in your hands.
Your,
B.

Or does your love life read more like this:

Got to go out to a dinner, gorgeous. Sorry – behind already. Later X

**Romantic and poignant, Jojo Moyes's sweeping tale of
passion, adultery and heartbreak is also a quiet lament
for the lost art of the love letter.**

Coming out in hardback in July 2010

HODDER &
STOUGHTON

*Happy birthday! Enclosed is your birthday present, which
I hope you like . . .*

*I am thinking of you especially today . . . because
I have decided that although I love you I am not in love
with you. I don't feel that you are God's One for me.
Anyway, I really hope that you like your present and that
you have a fantastic birthday.*

Female to Male, via letter

Prologue

Ellie Haworth spies her friends through the throng and weaves her way through the bar. She drops her bag at her feet and places her phone on the table in front of them. They are already well lubricated – it's in the tenor of their voices, the extravagant arm movements and loud laughter, the empty bottles between them.

'Late.' Nicky holds up her watch, wagging a finger at her. 'Don't tell us. "I had a story I had to finish."'

'Interview with wronged MP's wife. Sorry. It was for tomorrow's edition,' she says, sliding into the empty seat and pouring herself a glass from the dregs of a bottle. She pushes her phone across the table. 'Okay. Tonight's annoying word for discussion: "later".'

'Later?'

'As a sign-off. Does that mean tomorrow or later today? Or is it just some horrible teenage affectation that actually means nothing at all?'

Nicky peers at the glowing screen, 'It's "later" plus an X. That's like "goodnight". I'd say tomorrow.'

'Definitely tomorrow,' says Corinne. '"Later" is always tomorrow.' She pauses. 'Or it could even mean the day after.'

'It's very casual.'

'Casual?'

'As in something you might say to the postman.'

'You'd send a kiss to your postman?'

Nicky grins. 'I might. He's gorgeous.'

Corinne studies the message. 'I don't think that's fair. It could just mean he was in a hurry to do something else.'

'Yeah. Like his wife.'

Ellie shoots a warning look at Douglas.

'What?' he says. 'I'm just saying, don't you think you're past the point where you should be deciphering text-speak?'

Ellie gulps her wine, then leans forward over the table. 'Okay. I need another drink if I'm about to get the lecture.'

'If you're intimate enough with someone to have sex in their office, I think you should be able to ask them to clarify when you might be meeting them for coffee.'

'What does the rest of the message say? And please tell me it's nothing about sex in his office.'

Ellie peers at her phone, scrolling down the messages. '"Tricky calling from home. Dublin next week but not sure yet what plans are. Later x."'

'He's keeping his options open,' Douglas says.

'Unless he's . . . you know . . . not sure what his plans are.'

'Then he would have said, "Will call from Dublin." Or even "I'll fly you out to Dublin."'

'Is he taking his wife?'

'He never does. It's a work trip.'

'Perhaps he's taking someone else,' Douglas murmurs, into his beer.

Nicky shakes her head meditatively. 'God, wasn't life easier when they had to ring you and speak to you? Then you could at least gauge rejection from the sound of their voice.'

'Yes.' Corinne snorts. 'And you could sit at home by the phone for hours waiting for them to call.'

'Oh, the nights I spent –'

'– Checking the dial tone was working –'

'– and then slamming down the phone just in case that had been the exact minute they rang.'

Ellie hears them laugh, acknowledging the truth in their humour, some small part of her still waiting to see the little screen illuminate suddenly with a call. A call that, given the hour and that things are 'tricky at home', isn't going to happen.

* * *

Douglas walks her home. He is the only one of the four of them living with a partner, but Lena, his girlfriend, is big in technology PR and often at her office until ten or eleven at night. Lena doesn't mind him coming out with his old friends – she has accompanied him a few times but it's hard for her to penetrate the wall of old jokes and knowing references that come with a decade and a half of friendship; most of the time she lets him come alone.

'So, what's going on with you, big boy?' Ellie nudges him as they skirt a shopping trolley that someone has left on the pavement. 'You didn't say anything about yourself back there. Unless I missed it all.'

'Not much,' he says, and hesitates. He shoves his hands into his pockets. 'Actually, that's not quite true. Um . . . Lena wants to have a baby.'

Ellie looks up at him. 'Wow.'

'And I do too,' he adds hastily. 'We've been talking about it for ages, but we've decided now that there's never going to be a right time so we might as well get on with it.'

'You old romantic.'

'I'm . . . I dunno . . . quite happy about it, really. Lena's going to keep her job, and I'll look after the baby at home. You know, provided everything happens as it should and . . .'

Ellie tries to keep her voice neutral. 'And that's what you want?'

'Yeah. I don't like my job anyway. Haven't done for years. She earns a fortune. I think it'll be quite nice pottering round with a kid all day.'

'Parenthood's a bit more than pottering round—' she begins.

'I know that. Mind out . . . on the pavement.' Gently he steers her round the mess. 'But I'm ready for it. I don't need to be out every night in the pub. I want the next stage. That's not to say I don't like coming out with you guys, but sometimes I do wonder whether we shouldn't all be . . . you know . . . growing up a bit.'

'Oh, no!' Ellie clasps his arm. 'You've crossed over to the dark side.'

'Well, I don't feel the same way about my job as you do. For you it's everything, right?'

'Almost everything,' she concedes.

They walk on in silence for a couple of streets, listening to the distant sirens, the slammed car doors and muffled arguments of the city. Ellie loves this part of the evening, buoyed by friendship, temporarily free of the uncertainties that surround the rest of her life. She's had a good night at the pub, is headed home to her cosy flat. She's healthy. She has a credit card with plenty of unused capacity, plans for the weekend, and she's the only one of her friends not yet to have found a single grey hair. Life is good.

'Do you ever think about her?' Douglas asks.

'Who?'

'John's wife. Do you think she knows?'

The mention of her dissipates Ellie's happiness. 'I don't know.' And when Douglas says nothing, she adds, 'I'm sure I would, if I were her. He says she's more interested in the children than him. Sometimes I tell myself there might even be some little part of her that's glad she's not having to worry about him. You know, about keeping him happy.'

'Now *that* is wishful thinking.'

'Maybe. But if I'm really honest, the answer's no. I don't think about her and I don't feel guilty. Because I don't think it wouldn't have happened if they'd been happy or . . . you know . . . connected.'

'You women have such a misguided view of men.'

'You think he's happy with her?' She studies his face.

'I have no idea if he is or not. I just don't think he needs to be unhappy with his wife to be sleeping with you.'

The mood has shifted slightly, and perhaps in recognition of this, she lets go of his arm, adjusting her scarf around her neck. 'You think I'm a bad person. Or he's a bad person.'

It's out there. The fact that it has come from Douglas, the least judgemental of her friends, stings.

'I don't think anyone's a bad person. I just think of Lena, and what it would mean for her to carry my child, and the idea of dicking around on her just because she chose to give my baby the attention I felt was mine . . .'

'So you *do* think he's a bad person.'

Douglas shakes his head. 'I just . . .' He stops, looks up into the night sky before framing his answer. 'I think you should be careful, Ellie. All this trying to decipher what he means, what he wants, it's just bullshit. You're wasting your time. In my book things are generally pretty simple. Someone likes you, you like them, you hook up, and that's pretty much it.'

'Nice universe you live in, Doug. Shame it doesn't resemble the real one.'

'Okay, let's change the subject. Bad one to bring up on a few drinks.'

'No.' Her voice sharpens. '*In vino veritas* and all that. It's fine. At least I know how you feel. I'll be fine from here. Say hi to Lena for me.' She runs the last two streets to her house, not turning back to view the old friend behind her.

The *Nation* is being packed up, box by box, for transfer to its new glass-fronted home on a gleaming, reclaimed quay to the east of the city. The office, week by week, has been thinning: where once there were towers of press releases, files and archived cuttings, now empty desks, unexpected shiny lengths of laminated surface, are exposed to the harsh glare of the strip lighting. Souvenirs of past stories have been unearthed, like prizes from an archaeologist's dig, flags from royal jubilees, dented metal helmets from distant wars and framed certificates for long-forgotten awards. Banks of cables lie exposed, carpet tiles have been dislodged and great holes opened in the ceilings, prompting histrionic visits from health and safety experts and endless visitors with clipboards. Advertising, Classified and Sport have already moved to Compass Quay. The Saturday magazine, Business and Personal Finance are preparing to transfer in the next weeks. Features, Ellie's department, will follow along with News, moving in a carefully choreographed sleight-of-hand so that while Saturday's newspaper will emanate from the old Turner Street offices, Monday's will spring, as if by magic, from the new address.

The building, home to the newspaper for almost a hundred

years, is no longer fit-for-purpose, in that unlovely phrase. According to the management it does not reflect the dynamic, streamlined nature of modern newsgathering. It has too many places to hide, the hacks observe bad-temperedly, as they are prised from their positions, like limpets clinging stubbornly to a holed hull.

'We should celebrate it,' says Melissa, head of Features, from the editor's almost-cleared office. She's wearing a wine-coloured silk dress. On Ellie, this would have looked like her grandmother's nightie; on Melissa it looks like what it is – defiantly high fashion.

'The move?' Ellie's glancing at her mobile phone, set to silent, beside her. Around her, the other Feature writers are silent, notepads on knees.

'Yes. I was talking to one of the librarians the other evening. He says there are lots of old files that haven't been looked at in years. I want something on the women's pages from fifty years ago. How attitudes have changed, fashions, women's preoccupations. Case studies, side by side, then and now.' Melissa opens a file and pulls out several photocopied A3 sheets. She speaks with the easy confidence of someone accustomed to being listened to. 'For instance, from our problem pages: "*What on earth can I do to get my wife to dress more smartly and to make herself more attractive? My income is £1500 a year, and I am beginning to make my way in a sales organisation. I am very often getting invitations from customers, but in recent weeks I have had to dodge them because my wife, frankly, looks a mess.*"'

There is a low chuckle around the room.

'"*I have tried to put it to her in a gentle way, and she says that she doesn't care about fashions or jewellery or makeup. Frankly she doesn't look like the wife of a successful man, which is what I want her to be.*"'

John had once told Ellie that, after the children, his wife had lost interest in her appearance. He had changed the subject almost as soon as he had introduced it, and never referred to it again, as if he felt what he had said was even more of a betrayal than sleeping with another woman. Ellie had resented that hint of gentlemanly loyalty even while a bit of her admired him for it.

But it had stuck in her imagination. She had pictured his wife: slatternly in a stained nightdress, clutching a baby and haranguing him for some supposed deficit. She wanted to tell him she would never be like that with him.

'One could put the questions to a modern agony aunt.' Rupert, the Saturday editor, leans forward to peer at the other photocopied pages.

'I'm not sure you'd need to. Listen to the response: "*It may never have occurred to your wife that she is meant to be part of your shop window. She may, in so far as she thinks about these things at all, tell herself that she's married, secure, happy, so why should she bother?*"'

'Ah,' says Rupert. '"The deep, deep peace of the double bed".'

'"*I have seen this happen remarkably quickly to girls who fall in love just as much as to women who potter about in the cosy wrap of an old marriage. One moment they're smart as new paint, battling heroically with their waistlines, seams straight, anxiously dabbed with perfume. Some man says, 'I love you,' and the next moment that shining girl is, as near as makes no difference, a slut. A happy slut.*"'

The room fills briefly with polite, appreciative laughter.

'What's your choice, girls? Battle heroically with your waistline, or become a happy slut?'

'I think I saw a film of that name not long ago,' says Rupert. His smile fades when he realises the laughter has died.

'There's a lot we can do with this stuff.' Melissa gestures towards the folder. 'Ellie, can you dig around a bit this afternoon? See what else you might find. We're looking at forty, fifty years ago. A hundred will be too alienating. The editor's keen for us to high-light the move in a way that will bring readers along with us.'

'You want me to go through the archive?'

'Is that a problem?'

Not if you like sitting in dark cellars full of mildewing paper policed by dysfunctional men with Stalinist mindsets, who apparently haven't seen daylight for thirty years. 'Not at all,' she says brightly. 'I'm sure I'll find something.'

'Get a couple of workies to help you, if you like. I've heard there's a couple lurking in the fashion cupboard.'

Ellie doesn't register the malevolent satisfaction crossing her editor's features at the thought of sending the latest batch of Anna

Wintour wannabes deep into the bowels of the newspaper. She's busy thinking, *Bugger. No mobile reception underground.*

'By the way, Ellie, where were you this morning?'

'What?'

'This morning. I wanted you to rewrite that piece about children and bereavement. Yes? Nobody seemed to know where you were.'

'I was out doing an interview.'

'Who with?'

A body-language expert, Ellie thought, would have identified correctly that Melissa's blank smile was more of a snarl.

'Lawyer. Whistleblower. I was hoping to work something up on sexism in chambers.' It's out almost before she knows what she's saying.

'Sexism in the City. Hardly sounds groundbreaking. Make sure you're at your desk at the right time tomorrow. Speculative interviews in your own time. Yes?'

'Right.'

'Good. I want a double-page spread for the first Compass Quay edition. Something along the lines of *plus ça change.*' She is scribbling in her leather-backed notebook. 'Preoccupations, ads, problems . . . Bring me a few pages later this afternoon and we'll see what you've got.'

'Will do.' Ellie's smile is the brightest and most workmanlike in the whole room as she follows the others out of the office.

Spent today in modern day equivalent of purgatory, she types, pausing to take a sip of her wine. *Newspaper archive office. You want to be grateful you only make stuff up.*

He has messaged her from his hotmail account. He calls himself Penpusher; a joke between the two of them. She curls her feet under her on the chair and waits, willing the machine to signal his response.

You're a terrible heathen. I love archives, the screen responds. *Remind me to take you to the British Newspaper Library for our next hot date.*

She grins. *You know how to show a girl a good time.*

I do my best.

The only human librarian has given me a great wedge of loose papers. Not the most exciting bedtime reading.

Afraid this sounds sarcastic, she follows it with a smiley face, then curses as she remembers he once wrote an essay for the *Literary Review* on how the smiley face represented all that was wrong with modern communication.

That was an ironic smiley face, she adds, and stuffs her fist into her mouth.

Hold on. Phone. The screen stills.

Phone. His wife? He was in a hotel room in Dublin. It overlooked the water, he had told her. *You would love it.* What was she meant to say to that? *Then bring me next time?* Too demanding. *I'm sure I would?* Sounded almost sarcastic. *Yes*, she had replied, finally, and let out a long, unheard sigh.

It's all her own fault, her friends tell her. Unusually for her, she can't disagree.

She had met him at a book festival in Suffolk, sent to interview this thriller writer who had made a fortune after he had given up on more literary offerings. His name is John Armour, his hero, Dan Hobson, an almost cartoonish amalgam of old-fashioned masculine traits. She had interviewed him over lunch, expecting a rather chippy defence of the genre, perhaps a few moans about the publishing industry – she always found writers rather wearying to interview. She had expected someone paunchy, middle-aged, puddingy after years of being desk-bound. But the tall, tanned man who rose to shake her hand had been lean and freckly, resembling a weathered South African farmer. He was funny, charming, self-deprecating and attentive. He had turned the interview on her, asking her questions about herself, then told her his theories on the origin of language and how he believed communication was morphing into something dangerously flaccid and ugly.

When the coffee arrived, she realised she hadn't put pen to notepad for almost forty minutes.

'Don't you love the sound of them, though?' she said, as they left the restaurant and headed back towards the literary festival. It was late in the year and the winter sun had dipped below the low buildings of the quietening high street. She had drunk too much, had reached the point at which her mouth would race off defiantly before she had worked out what she should say. She hadn't wanted to leave the restaurant.

'Which ones?'

'Spanish. Mostly Italian. I'm sure it's why I love Italian opera, and I can't stand the German ones. All those hard, guttural noises.' He had considered this, and his silence unnerved her. She began to stutter: 'I know it's terribly unfashionable, but I love Puccini. I love that high emotion. I love the curling *r*, the staccato of the words . . .' She tailed away as she heard how ridiculously pretentious she sounded.

He paused in a doorway, gazed briefly up the road behind them, then turned back to her. 'I don't like opera.' He had stared at her directly as he said it. As if it were a challenge. She felt something give, deep in the pit of her stomach. Oh, God, she thought.

'Ellie,' he said, after they had stood there for almost a minute. It was the first time he had called her by name. 'Ellie, I have to pick up something from my hotel before I go back to the festival. Would you like to come with me?'

Even before he shut the bedroom door behind them, they were on each other, bodies pressed together, mouths devouring, locked together as their hands performed the urgent, frantic choreography of undressing.

Afterwards she would look back on her behaviour and marvel as if at some kind of aberration seen from afar. In the hundreds of times she had replayed it, she had rubbed away the significance, the overwhelming emotion, and was left only with details. Her underwear, everyday, inappropriate, flung across a trouser press; the way they had giggled insanely on the floor afterwards underneath the multipatterned synthetic hotel quilt; how he had cheerfully, and with inappropriate charm, handed back his key to the receptionist later that afternoon.

He had called two days later, as the euphoric shock of that day was seguing into something more disappointing.

'You know I'm married,' he said. 'You read my cuttings.'

I've googled every last reference to you, she told him silently.

'I've never been . . . unfaithful before. I still can't quite articulate what happened.'

'I blame the quiche,' she quipped, wincing.

'You do something to me, Ellie Haworth. I haven't written a word in forty-eight hours.' He paused. 'You make me forget what I want to say.'

Then I'm doomed, she thought, because as soon as she had felt his weight against her, his mouth on hers, she had known – despite everything she had ever said to her friends about married men, everything she had ever believed – that she required only the faintest acknowledgement from him of what had happened for her to be lost.

A year on, she still hadn't begun to look for a way out.

He comes back online almost forty-five minutes later. In this time she has left her computer, fixed herself another drink, wandered the flat aimlessly, peering at her skin in a bathroom mirror, then gathering up stray socks and hurling them into the laundry basket. She hears the *ping* of a message and hurls herself into her chair.

Sorry. Didn't mean to be so long. Hope to speak tomorrow.

No mobile-phone calls, he had said. Mobile bills were itemised.

Are you in hotel now? she types rapidly. *I could call you in your room.* The spoken word was a luxury, a rare opportunity. God, but she just needed to hear his voice.

Got to go out to a dinner, gorgeous. Sorry – behind already. Later X

And he is gone.

She stares at the empty screen. He will be striding off through the hotel foyer now, charming the reception staff, climbing into whatever car the festival has organised for him. Tonight he will give a clever off-the-cuff speech over dinner and then be his usual amused, slightly wistful self to those lucky enough to sit at his table. He will be out there, living his life to the full, when she seems to have put hers perennially on hold.

What the hell was she doing?

'What the hell am I doing?' she says aloud, hitting the off button. She shouts her frustration at the bedroom ceiling, flops down on her vast, empty bed. She can't call her friends: they've endured these conversations too many times, and she can guess what their response will be – what it can *only* be. What Doug had said to her was painful. But she would say exactly the same to any of them.

She sits on the sofa, flicks on the television. Finally, glancing at the pile of papers at her side, she hauls them on to her lap, cursing Melissa. A miscellaneous pile, the librarian had said, cuttings that bore no date and had no obvious category – 'I haven't got time to go through them all. We're turning up so many piles like this.' He was the only librarian under fifty down there. She wondered, fleetingly, why she'd never noticed him before.

'See if there's anything that's of use to you.' He had leant forward conspiratorially. 'Throw away whatever you don't want but don't say anything to the boss. We're at the stage now when we can't afford to go through every last bit of paper.'

It soon becomes apparent why: a few theatre reviews, a passenger list for a cruise ship, some menus from celebratory newspaper dinners. She flicks through them, glancing up occasionally at the television. There's not much here that'll excite Melissa.

Now she's leafing through a battered file of what looks like medical records. All lung disease, she notes absently. Something to do with mining. She's about to tip the whole lot into the bin when a pale blue corner catches her eye. She tugs at it with an index finger and thumb and pulls out a hand-addressed envelope. It's been opened, and the letter inside is dated 4 October 1960.

My dearest and only love,
I meant what I said. I have come to the conclusion that the only way forward is for one of us to take a bold decision.
I am not as strong as you. When I first met you, I thought you were a fragile little thing, someone I had to protect. Now I realise I had us all wrong. You are the strong one, the one who

can endure living with the possibility of a love like this, and the fact that we will never be allowed it.

I ask you not to judge me for my weakness. The only way I can endure is to be in a place I will never see you, never be haunted by the possibility of seeing you with him. I need to be somewhere where sheer necessity forces you from my thoughts minute by minute, hour by hour. That cannot happen here.

I am going to take the job. I'll be at Platform 4, Paddington, at 7.15 on Friday evening, and there is nothing in the world that would make me happier than if you found the courage to come with me.

If you don't come, I'll know that whatever we might feel for each other, it isn't quite enough. I won't blame you, my darling. I know the past weeks have put an intolerable strain on you, and I feel the weight of that keenly. I hate the thought that I could cause you any unhappiness.

I'll be waiting on the platform from a quarter to seven. Know that you hold my heart, my hopes, in your hands.

Your

B

Ellie reads it a second time, and finds her eyes welling inexplicably with tears. She can't take her eyes off the large, looped handwriting; the immediacy of the words springs out to her more than forty years after they were hidden. She turns it over, checks the envelope for clues. It's addressed to PO Box 13, London. It could be a man or a woman. What did you do, PO Box 13? she asks silently.

Then she gets up, replaces the letter carefully in the envelope and walks over to her computer. She opens the mail file and presses 'refresh'. Nothing since the message she had received at seven forty-five.

Got to go to a dinner, gorgeous. Sorry – behind already. Later X

NIGHT MUSIC

Jojo Moyes

Isabel Delancey has always taken her gilded life for granted. But when her husband dies suddenly, leaving her with a mountain of debt, she and her two children are forced to abandon their home and move to a crumbling pile in the country.

With the house falling down around their ears, and the last of her savings fast disappearing, Isabel turns to her neighbours, not knowing that her mere presence there has stirred up long-standing obsessions.

As she fights to make her house a home, passions and lives collide. Isabel will discover an instinct for survival she never knew she had – and that a heart can play a new song . . .

Out now

HODDER